08-ANP-065

D0020267

Praise for the no
#1 *New York Times* best
Debbie Maco

"Macomber never disappoints. Tears and laughter abound in this story of loss and healing that will wrap you up and pull you in; readers will finish it in one sitting."
  —*Library Journal* (starred review) on *Cottage by the Sea*

"Macomber's patented recipe of idyllic small-town life with a touch of romance is sure to result in a summer best-seller."
    —*Booklist* on *Cottage by the Sea*

"Macomber's writing and storytelling deliver what she's famous for—a smooth, satisfying tale with characters her fans will cheer for and an arc that is cozy, heartwarming and ends with the expected happily-ever-after."
    —*Kirkus* on *Starting Now*

"No one tugs at readers' heartstrings quite as effectively as Macomber."
    —*Chicago Tribune*

"The reigning queen of women's fiction."
    —*Sacramento Bee*

"It's impossible not to cheer for Macomber's characters…. When it comes to creating a special place and memorable, honorable characters, nobody does it better than Macomber."
    —*BookPage*

"You can always trust Macomber…to tug at your heart strings and keep you turning pages."
    —*AARP*

DEBBIE MACOMBER

Seaside Springtime

Previously published as
For All My Tomorrows and *Yours and Mine*

mira

If you purchased this book without a cover you should be aware
that this book is stolen property. It was reported as "unsold and
destroyed" to the publisher, and neither the author nor the
publisher has received any payment for this "stripped book."

mira™

Recycling programs
for this product may
not exist in your area.

ISBN-13: 978-0-7783-3178-0

Seaside Springtime
Copyright © 2021 by Harlequin Books S.A.

For All My Tomorrows
First published in 1989. This edition published in 2021.
Copyright © 1989 by Debbie Macomber

Yours and Mine
First published in 1989. This edition published in 2021.
Copyright © 1989 by Debbie Macomber

Home for the Holidays
Copyright © 2021 by Brenda Novak, Inc.

All rights reserved. No part of this book may be used or reproduced in
any manner whatsoever without written permission except in the case of
brief quotations embodied in critical articles and reviews.

This is a work of fiction. Names, characters, places and incidents are either the
product of the author's imagination or are used fictitiously. Any resemblance to
actual persons, living or dead, businesses, companies, events or locales is entirely
coincidental.

This edition published by arrangement with Harlequin Books S.A.

For questions and comments about the quality of this book, please contact us at
CustomerService@Harlequin.com.

Mira
22 Adelaide St. West, 40th Floor
Toronto, Ontario M5H 4E3, Canada
www.Harlequin.com

Printed in Lithuania

MIX
Paper from
responsible sources
FSC® C021394

Also available from Debbie Macomber and MIRA

Blossom Street

The Shop on Blossom Street
A Good Yarn
Susannah's Garden
Back on Blossom Street
Twenty Wishes
Summer on Blossom Street
Hannah's List
"The Twenty-First Wish"
   (in *The Knitting Diaries*)
A Turn in the Road

Cedar Cove

16 Lighthouse Road
204 Rosewood Lane
311 Pelican Court
44 Cranberry Point
50 Harbor Street
6 Rainier Drive
74 Seaside Avenue
8 Sandpiper Way
92 Pacific Boulevard
1022 Evergreen Place
Christmas in Cedar Cove
   (*5-B Poppy Lane* and
   A Cedar Cove Christmas)
1105 Yakima Street
1225 Christmas Tree Lane

The Dakota Series

Dakota Born
Dakota Home
Always Dakota
Buffalo Valley

The Manning Family

The Manning Sisters
   (*The Cowboy's Lady* and
   The Sheriff Takes a Wife)

The Manning Brides
   (*Marriage of Inconvenience* and
   Stand-In Wife)
The Manning Grooms
   (*Bride on the Loose* and
   Same Time, Next Year)

Christmas Books

A Gift to Last
On a Snowy Night
Home for the Holidays
Glad Tidings
Christmas Wishes
Small Town Christmas
When Christmas Comes
   (now retitled *Trading Christmas*)
There's Something About Christmas
Christmas Letters
The Perfect Christmas
Choir of Angels
   (*Shirley, Goodness and Mercy,*
   Those Christmas Angels and
   Where Angels Go)
Call Me Mrs. Miracle

Heart of Texas

Texas Skies
   (*Lonesome Cowboy* and
   Texas Two-Step)
Texas Nights
   (*Caroline's Child* and
   Dr. Texas)
Texas Home
   (*Nell's Cowboy* and
   Lone Star Baby)
Promise, Texas
Return to Promise

CONTENTS

FOR ALL MY TOMORROWS

Debbie Macomber

Prologue

The mournful sound of taps cut through the coarse gray afternoon. Lynn Danfort stood tall and proud before her husband's casket, refusing to release the emotion that clawed at her chest. Her two children were gathered close at her sides, as though she could hold on to them tightly enough to protect them from the reality of this day.

Seattle's police chief, Daniel Carmichael, assisted by Ryder Matthews, neatly folded the American flag that rested atop the polished casket and calmly presented it to Lynn. She tried to thank the police chief, but realized she couldn't speak. Even nodding was more of an effort than she could make.

When they'd finished, Pastor Teed spoke a few solemn words, and then slowly, in coordinated movements, Gary Danfort was lowered to his final resting place.

Lynn repressed a shudder as the first shovelful of dirt slammed against his casket. The sound reverberated in her ears, magnified a hundred times until she yearned to cover her head and scream out for them to stop. This was her husband...the father of her children...her best friend...and

Gary Danfort deserved so much more than a cold blanket of Washington mud.

Shot in the line of duty. Pronounced dead at the scene. At first Lynn had refused to believe her husband was gone.

The thick dirt fell again, and Lynn believed.

The tightening in her chest worked its way up the constricting muscles of her throat and escaped on a sob as the shovel was handed in turn to the men and women who had so proudly served with Gary. The trembling increased as each dull thump echoed like a somber edict in her tortured mind.

Hope was gone.

Dreams destroyed.

Death the victor.

Tears welled like hot liquid in the corners of her eyes, her first for that day. She'd wanted to be strong—it was what Gary would have wanted—but now she let them fall. The moisture seared crooked paths down her ashen cheeks.

A voice violated her pain. "It's time to go."

"No."

"This way, Mrs. Danfort."

Again she shook her head. "Please. Not yet."

Her strength was depleted, and for the first time since she'd learned of Gary's death, she needed someone—someone she loved, someone who had loved Gary. She looked around for Ryder. Her friend. Gary's partner. Godfather to their children.

Her gaze scanned the crowd until she found him, standing in front of Chief Carmichael.

A protest swelled in her throat as she watched him pull his badge from his wallet and place it in the police chief's palm.

Ryder turned to her then, his pain and grief as strong as her own. She could see that Chief Carmichael was trying to reason with him, but Ryder wasn't listening. His gaze reached over the crowd of mourners until it found Lynn. Their eyes met and locked.

Lynn pleaded with him not to leave her.

His gaze told her he must. Regret clouded the harsh features as his eyes shifted to Michelle and Jason, her children.

Then, silently, Ryder Matthews turned and walked away.

One

"Lynn, there's a call for you on line one."

"Thanks." She reached for her phone and pressed it against her shoulder, securing it with her ear. "Slender, Too, this is Lynn speaking."

"Mom?"

Lynn released a silent groan and rolled her eyes toward the ceiling. It wasn't even noon and this was the fifth phone call she'd received from the kids. "What is it, Michelle?"

"Jason ate the entire box of Cap'n Crunch cereal. I thought you'd want to know so you could take appropriate action."

"I didn't take it all." Jason's eight-year-old voice echoed from the upstairs extension. "Michelle ate some, too."

"I didn't."

"Did, too."

"Didn't."

"Michelle! Jason! I've got a business to run!"

"But he did, Mom, I swear it. I found the empty box stuffed in the bottom of the garbage. And we all know who put it there, so don't try to lie your way out of this one, Jason Danfort. And, Mom, while I've got you on the phone, I think you should have a serious discussion with Jason about his Super Heroes Club."

Lynn closed her eyes and prayed for patience. "Michelle, this conversation will have to wait until I'm through here. Where's Janice?"

It was the third week of June. School had been out for a grand total of five days, and already Michelle and Jason were at each other's throats. The high-school girl, whom Lynn was paying top dollar to look after the kids, had revealed all the maturity of an eleven-year-old, which was Michelle's age. One child responsible for two more. This wasn't working, and Lynn's options were limited.

"Janice is checking the garbage to see what else Jason's hiding in there."

"Mom, you can't expect me to live like this," her son interjected. "A man is a man. And a man's got to do what a man's got to do."

"Right," Lynn responded without thinking.

"You're agreeing with him?" Michelle's shrill voice echoed her outrage. "Mom, your son is stealing food and you seem to think it's perfectly all right."

"I'm going out on a mission," Jason cried in self-defense. "I could be gone three or four hours doing surveillance. I'll need nourishment, but if you're so concerned about your stupid cereal, I'll put it back."

"Can you put a hold on this war until I get home?" Lynn demanded of the two.

Silence.

Lynn mentally calculated a list of effective threats that had worked in the past. Regrettably her mind came up blank. She was a strong, effective businesswoman, but when it came to her children she was at a loss as to how to deal with them—especially in matters such as stolen Cap'n Crunch cereal.

"Lynn." Sharon Fremont, her assistant, stuck her head around the door. "Your aerobics class is ready and waiting."

"Listen, kids, I've got to go. *Please* don't fight and don't call me at work unless it's an emergency."

"But, Mom…"

"Mom!"

"I can't talk now—I've got a class waiting." Lynn checked her watch. "I'll be home by four. Now be good!"

"All right," Michelle muttered. "But I don't like it."

"Me, either. If I'm not home when you get here," Jason whispered into the phone, "you know where to find me."

"You think you're so smart, Jason Danfort," Michelle whined, "but I know your hiding place—I have for weeks."

"No, you don't."

"Yes, I do."

"*Kids*, please!"

"Sorry, Mom."

"Yeah, sorry, Mom."

Lynn replaced the phone. Michelle and Jason claimed they were sorry. Somehow she doubted that.

The house was suspiciously quiet when Lynn let herself in at three-forty-five that same afternoon.

"Michelle?"

Silence.

"Jason?"

More silence.

"Janice?"

"Oh, hi, Mrs. Danfort."

The fifteen-year-old appeared as if by magic, and every aspect of her peaches-and-cream complexion spelled guilt. The teenager rubbed her palms back and forth and presented a forced smile.

"Where are Michelle and Jason?" Lynn asked, and slipped the sweatband off her forehead. She hadn't taken time to shower, preferring to hurry home dressed in her turquoise spandex leotards and top, in an effort to deter yet another world war.

"They're both gone," Janice announced, her eyes avoiding Lynn's. "That's all right, isn't it?"

"It's fine."

"Oh, good."

Lynn reached for the mail, shuffling through the pile of bills and setting them back down on the counter unopened.

"Jason's with his Super Hero friends, and Michelle's over at Stephie's."

"That's fine. I'll see you tomorrow morning then."

"Sure," Janice said and was through the door before Lynn could figure out why she wore the look of a cat burglar caught with a bagful of goodies.

Mulling it over, Lynn traipsed over to the fridge and took out a cold soda—her carbonated drink-for-the-day. This was a family rule—no one drank more than one can a day, otherwise her children would go through a 12-pack by noon.

She sat, plopped her feet on the chair across the table from her and took a sip, letting the cool liquid revive her.

"Mom," Michelle called, as she raced through the front door. She stopped abruptly when she found Lynn in the kitchen.

"Hi, sweetie," Lynn answered and smiled. "Did you ever solve the Cap'n Crunch caper?"

"Jason pulverized it into sand and poured the entire bag into his canteen." She raised her eyes toward the ceiling in mute testimony to what she thought about her brother's odd ways. "You've got to do something about him, Mother. That cereal was half mine, too, you know."

"I know… I'll talk to him."

"You say that, and then nothing ever happens. He should be punished. That boy has no sense, and you're not helping. He honestly thinks he's the Incredible Hulk. Any other mother would put a stop to it."

"Michelle, please, I'm doing the best I can. Wait until you're a mother…there are just some things you have to make judgment calls on." Lynn couldn't believe she'd said that. It was like an echo from the past, when she'd battled with her younger brother and her mother had said those identical words to her.

"At least let me decide Jason's punishment," Michelle cried. "I know that boy better than anyone. Let me give him what he deserves."

"Michelle…"

"Mom." The screen door burst open and Jason roared into the kitchen, dressed like his hero, his shoulders arched forward as he knotted his fists and puffed out his chest to dispay his muscles. He let loose with a scream that threatened to crack the walls.

Michelle plugged her ears and cast her mother a look that spoke volumes.

"Jason, please," Lynn pleaded, placing her fingertips to her temple. "If you're going save the world do it outside."

"Okay," he answered with a grin, and cheerfully lowered his weapon.

Her son was dressed in his camouflage pants and a grimy green sweatshirt. His face was smeared with green coloring. His knees were caked with mud, and he looked as if he'd battled long and hard all afternoon.

"So how's the war going?"

"We won."

"Naturally," Michelle said in a know-it-all voice that

caused Jason to slowly turn in her direction, and gave her the evil eye.

"Not in the house," Lynn reminded him.

"Right," he answered slowly, baring his teeth at his sister.

Michelle placed her hand over her flat chest. "I'm shaking in my boots with pure terror at the thought of you coming to get me."

Jason's eyes narrowed into menacing slits. "You better do something about her, Mom, or she's going to suffer a slow, painful death."

"Jason, I don't like you talking like that."

"Answer me this," he cried with indignation. "Does Edward Norton have to put up with a big sister like this one?"

"You're not Edward Norton."

"Not yet," he said forcefully. "But someday I'm going to be."

Lynn prayed this was a stage her son was going through because, like Michelle, she'd about had it with Jason's antics.

"When are we leaving for the picnic?" Michelle asked, glancing toward the bulletin board.

"Picnic?" Lynn echoed. "What picnic?"

"The one Dad's ol' police buddies invited us to—the one with the notice on the bulletin board."

Lynn dropped her feet and whirled around to check her calendar. "Is today the twentieth?"

Both Michelle and Jason nodded.

"Oh, great," Lynn muttered. "I'm supposed to bring potato salad."

"Do what you always do," Jason suggested. "Buy it at the deli. Why should today be any different?"

Lynn reached for her drink and hurried toward the stairs, taking them two at a time. She stripped off her top and reached blindly toward the shower dial when she noted the bathroom counter. Something stopped her, but she didn't know what. Something wasn't quite right.

In a flash, she recognized what was different. Reaching for a towel to cover her torso, she stormed out of the bedroom. "Michelle. Jason. Front and center—pronto."

Both kids came racing into her bedroom.

"All right," she said, her voice wobbling, "which one of you got into my makeup?" Her gaze narrowed, and what she saw on her son's face answered her own question. "Jason… that's my green eye shadow all over your face! My *expensive* green eye shadow."

"Mom, your shower's running," Jason said, pointing in that direction. "You're wasting precious liquid, and you always say how we should conserve water. Remember the drought a couple of years ago—you wouldn't want to start another one, would you?"

"He used my eye shadow," Lynn announced to her daughter, while she returned to the bathroom to turn off the shower. The day had started off badly. First Michelle and Jason had found every excuse known to mankind to call her at the office, and now this!

"If you look real close, you'll note the black under his eyes looks a lot like *your* eye liner, too," Michelle said once Lynn reentered the room.

"My eyeliner, too?"

A look of betrayal crossed Jason's young features. "Okay, Michelle, you asked for this. I wasn't going to tell, but now you're forcing my hand."

Michelle stiffened. "You wouldn't dare," she whispered.

Jason squared his shoulders. "Michelle and Janice were in your room this morning, Mom. I felt it was my duty to find out what they were doing—"

"Jason…" Michelle's frail voice rose an octave, pleading.

"They were trying on your bras. The real fancy lace ones."

"Oh, my goodness." Lynn sank onto the foot of her bed. Nothing was sacred anymore. Not her makeup. Not her underwear. Nothing. And worse, she was paying a teenage neighbor girl to snoop through her drawers.

"Mom," Michelle moaned. "I need a real bra…you haven't seemed to notice, but I'm filling out my training one." She paused and turned to face her traitor brother. "Get out of here, Jason. This is woman talk."

"Trust me, Mom, she doesn't need anything. She's as flat as—"

"Jason!" Lynn and Michelle cried simultaneously.

He jerked up both hands. "All right, all right. I'm out of here. I felt you needed to know the truth… I was only doing my duty as your son and as Michelle's brother."

Lynn's fingers were trembling as she ran them through her thick brown hair. She reached behind her head and released the clip that held her hair neatly in place.

"You and Janice aren't allowed in my bedroom, young lady," she said. "You know that."

Michelle buried her chin in her shoulder blade, looking miserable.

"I can't have you sorting through my things while I'm at work."

"I know… I'm sorry," Michelle murmured, still not looking at her mother. "We didn't mean to try them on, but they looked so pretty and Janice said you'd never know, and I didn't think it would hurt until Jason—"

"This just isn't working," Lynn whispered. "You and Jason are constantly bickering. Janice is fifteen, going on ten. I can't stop running my business just because you kids are out of school. It may be summer, but we still have to eat!"

"It won't happen again," Michelle promised. "I'm really sorry."

"I know, honey." But that didn't change things. Janice was too immature to be watching Michelle and Jason, and the children were too young to stay on their own.

Michelle straightened her shoulders. "What are you going to do to Jason for getting into your makeup? I know I shouldn't have tried on your bras, but Jason shouldn't have gotten into your things, either."

"I don't know yet," Lynn answered.

"Hey, are we going to the picnic or not?" Jason demanded from the other side of the bedroom door.

"He was listening," Michelle whispered with righteous indignation. "I bet you anything, he had his ear to the door and the minute we started talking about him, he broke in."

"We're going to be late for the picnic if you two don't stop this," Lynn commented, eager to change the subject.

She hated to think what Michelle and Jason would do once they learned she was putting them in a day-care center. They were going to hate it, but she didn't have a choice.

After what had happened today, her mind was made up.

Two

Toting the carton of potato salad in one hand, and with a blanket tucked under the other, Jason marched across the park lawn with crisp military precision. With his head held high and proud, he angled toward the assigned picnic area at Green Lake. Lynn and Michelle, holding the handles of the picnic basket between them, followed.

Lynn's smile was forced as she raised a hand to greet the men and women who had once worked with her husband. She remained good friends with several of the other wives on the force, although there were lots of new faces these days.

"I'm so pleased you could make it," Toni Morris called out, walking toward Lynn. "It's good to see you, stranger!"

Lynn let go of the basket and hugged her friend, who was a former policewoman. She didn't see nearly enough of Toni these days and treasured the few times they could be together. "It's good to be here."

"How's everything?"

Lynn knew that pert and practical Toni would easily see through a false smile and a cheerful facade. This summer had gotten off to a rotten start, and she was troubled. With the other police wives, she could grin and nod and claim her life was a bed of rose petals and because they wanted to believe that, they wouldn't question her.

But not Toni, who had married an officer of the law herself and who was well aware of life on both sides of the coin.

"Life's so-so," Lynn answered honestly. Afternoons like this one made her feel she'd failed as a mother. Like so many other women, she wore two hats—one for work and another at home. Michelle and Jason came first in her life, but she *had* to earn a living. What Slender, Too, didn't drain from her energy tank, the kids did. She felt stretched to the limit, and there was only so much elastic in her.

Toni slipped her arm around Lynn's waist, glanced in Michelle's direction and pointed toward a picnic table with a red checked cloth spread across the top. "Michelle, go ahead and set your stuff next to mine. Kelly's getting her feet wet at the lake. Go on down and surprise her—she's dying to see you."

"Oh, good! Wait until she sees my hair, she's going to flip," Michelle announced, and raced like a speeding freight train, taking the basket with her.

"Okay," Toni murmured, looking thoughtful. "Tell me what's wrong?"

For lack of a more precise answer, Lynn shrugged. "Nothing's working out this summer the way I hoped it would. Michelle and Jason are constantly bickering. The babysitter is snooping through my drawers. Jason's into this Super Hero stage and is slowly driving me bananas. He doesn't seem to make the connection between what happened to Gary and the war games he plays with his friends."

"He doesn't," Toni assured her. "He's a perfectly normal eight-year-old, and this thing with the war games is just a stage he's going through. Both Michelle and Jason are perfectly normal kids."

"I don't know if they'll ever get used to me working. I swear they use every excuse in the book to phone me at work. Michelle wanted me to know Jason used the ink up in my felt-tip pen. And Jason was convinced Michelle hid his army canteen from him. And then there was a fiasco over the Cap'n Crunch cereal. Honestly, Toni, how can I be expected to supervise them and run a business, too?"

Toni's look was sympathetic.

"It's as if they feel the need to compete for my attention," Lynn added. "I don't know what to do anymore."

"Who's watching them this summer?"

"A neighbor girl, and I think that's a major part of the problem. Michelle's at that transitional age when she's too young to stay by herself and yet resentful of having someone look after her. I'd hoped to solve that by hiring a neighborhood girl, but it simply isn't working."

"Can you find someone else?"

Lynn shrugged again. "At this late date? I doubt it. And the programs at the 'Y' filled up so fast it made my head spin. Parents register months in advance for summer day care."

Toni studied her a moment longer. "It's more than problems with the kids and summer vacation, though, isn't it?"

Lynn had to stop and think about that. Toni was right—she usually was. For the past several months Lynn had been experiencing a restlessness that came from the deepest part of her inner self. She hadn't been sleeping well and often awoke feeling depressed and out of sorts, without understanding why.

"You're not taking care of yourself," Toni said, after a thoughtful moment.

Lynn blinked, not sure she understood her friend. She'd never been more physically fit—in fact she looked as good, if not better, than she had as a twenty-year-old bride. Her hair needed to be cut, but finding the time was the biggest hangup there.

"You can't always be the perfect mother *and* an astute businesswoman," Toni went on to say. "You need time to be you."

"Me?" Lynn repeated. She wasn't exactly sure who *she* was anymore. There'd been a time when her role in life had been clearly defined, but not anymore. Since Gary had died, she viewed herself as a quick-change artist who leaped through hoops—some small, others large—in an effort to make it to the end of the day or the end of the week. She felt as if she'd been cast adrift in a lifeboat and she was the only one strong enough to man the oars.

"Be good to yourself," Toni continued. "Splurge. Take a whole day and relax at the beach or shop to your heart's content."

"Good idea," Lynn whispered, feeling a nearly overwhelming urge to cry. "I'll do exactly that the next time I find the time."

"When did you last go out on a date?"

"I haven't in months, but don't try to convince me that's the problem," Lynn said, her voice sharp and strong. "It's a jungle out there, with lots of lions and tigers roaming about. After my last hot date with a forty-year-old mechanic who lives with his mother, I decided I'd let Mr. Right find me. I'm done with the dating scene. Finished. Kaput."

"The mechanic was a tiger?" Toni gave her a look that suggested therapy was sure to help.

Lynn sighed. "Not exactly. He was more of a warthog."

"And exactly what type of beast interests you? A cheetah? Gorilla?"

"Tarzan interests me," Lynn said, and laughed. Soon Toni's chuckles mingled with her own.

"Come on now, Lynn, you're not really serious about refusing to date anymore? You're too young to resign yourself to life alone."

"I'm not interested in remarrying—at least not for now." There'd been a time, albeit short, when Lynn had seriously considered re-marrying and making a new life for the kids and herself. She hadn't expected Prince Charming to come charging into her living room atop a white stallion, but she hadn't been prepared for all the court jesters, either. Soon after she'd reentered the dating world, she'd discovered how shockingly naive she was and exited with a speed that convinced her friends she hadn't tried nearly hard enough. Her friends, however, were married or involved in satisfying relationships. They weren't the ones forced to mingle with warthogs and court jesters.

"There's something you should know," Toni announced, tossing a glance over her shoulder.

"Don't tell me you've got someone here you want me to meet. Toni, please, don't do that to me."

"No, not that."

"What, then?"

"Someone's here all right, but I didn't bring him."

"Who?" Her friend had seldom looked more serious. Lynn had been aware the entire time they were talking how Toni had kept her on the outskirts of the group. Sensing that whatever her friend had to say was important, Lynn met her look, feeling Toni's anxiety.

"Ryder Matthews stopped by," Toni announced. "In fact, he's here now."

"Ryder," Lynn echoed, her voice little more than a hoarse whisper. Emotion circled her like smoke rising from a campfire, twirling around her, choking off a reply. Lynn wasn't exactly sure what she felt. Relief mostly, she decided, but that was quickly followed by resentment that flared, then vanished as fast as it came. Ryder had turned his back and walked away from her—literally and figuratively. A week after Gary's funeral a letter with a Boston postmark had arrived from Ryder. He'd told her he'd had to leave the force, and asked her forgiveness for leaving her and the kids when they needed him most. He promised her that if she were ever to need anything, all she had to do was let him know and he would be there. Lynn didn't doubt his word, but she never asked—and Ryder had never come. He promised to keep in touch, and true to his word, he'd faithfully remembered Michelle and Jason on their birthdays and Christmas, but he never directly wrote Lynn again.

And now Ryder was back. Ryder Matthews. She loved him like a brother, but she couldn't help resenting the way he'd abandoned her. She didn't want to have anything to do with him, but she'd needed him at one time and then had gone about proving exactly the opposite. Her thoughts were as knotted and twisted as pine wood.

"Are you going to be all right?" Toni asked.

"Sure. Why shouldn't I be?" But she wasn't. Lynn felt as though the world had been briefly knocked off its axis. She squared her shoulders and stiffened her spine, mentally and physically preparing for whatever was to follow. She'd waited a long time to talk to Ryder and now she hadn't a clue about what she would say.

"Apparently he just moved back to Seattle," Toni added.

Lynn nodded, not knowing how else to respond.

"He's an attorney now and recently joined some prestigious uptown law firm. He kept in touch with several of the guys, but his return surprised everyone."

Lynn knew that Ryder had been accepted into law school following graduation from college but had grown restless after the first year, eager to make a more concrete contribution to society. After he dropped out, he'd applied and was accepted into the police academy, where he'd met Gary.

"Well," Toni urged her. "Say something."

"What's there to say?"

"I don't know," Toni admitted. "But every time Joe's talked to him the last couple of years, all he does is ask about you and the kids."

"Wh-what did he want to know?"

"How you were. How the kids were doing. That sort of thing. He may have stayed away from you, but I know for a fact that you were never far from his thoughts."

"He could have asked me himself."

"Yes, he could have," Toni agreed. "I'm sure he's going to want to later. I just felt you should know he's here so it won't come as a shock."

"I appreciate that," Lynn said, although she wasn't sure there was anything to say to Ryder. There had been once, but not now.

Ryder Matthews spotted Jason first. Gary and Lynn's son had sprouted like a weed, and just catching a glimpse of the boy produced an involuntary smile. He looked like a miniature commando, with his face painted...was that green? He was dressed in fatigues with a green sweatband strapped across his forehead as though he planned to stalk through a jungle at any minute.

Ryder's gaze left the youth to scan the picnic area. He located Michelle next. The preteen was standing by the lake, talking to another girl. She'd changed, too. The girl-ish features had disappeared, and the promise of a special beauty shone from her sweet oval face. Her hair was shorter now, the pigtails and bright ribbons replaced with carefully styled curls. The eleven-year-old was several inches taller, too, as was Jason. Ryder smiled, pleased with the changes he noticed in them both.

A couple of minutes later, he allowed his gaze to search for Lynn. Gary's Lynn...*his* Lynn. When he found her, talk-ing to Toni Morris in the picnic area, a rush of air left his lungs as though someone had playfully punched him in the stomach. She was everything he remembered and more. Only heaven knew how he'd managed to stay away from her so long. He'd never forgotten her face, or the athletic grace with which she moved. The sunlight had always seemed to bounce off her hair, and the one way he could think to de-scribe the husky sound of her voice was smoky molasses. He recognized every line of her creamy smooth face, which was dominated by high cheekbones, a stubborn chin and that wide, soft mouth.

Lynn's hair was much longer now, the thick dark length woven in a single braid that gently fell against her back. She wore fashionable white shorts and a pink tank top that showed off her golden tan. She carried herself with such pride and grace that it humbled him just studying her. Ryder watched as she smiled and waved to another friend, while standing with Toni. She paused and glanced in his direc-tion. Although Ryder was fairly certain she hadn't seen him, he felt the physical impact of her smile halfway across the park. He'd always found Lynn attractive, had admired her from the first, but the years had matured her elegant beauty.

Just looking at her caused his heart to swell with pride. Everything he'd learned about her revealed an inner fortitude. She was strong, stronger than he'd realized. She'd walked through the valley in the shadow of grief and destruction and come out the other side, confident and strong.

Ryder loved her for it.

The need to talk to her burned in his chest. There was so much that had to be said, so much he needed to explain. It had taken him three long years to surface from the tragedy of Gary's death. Three years to come to grips with himself.

For the first year, he'd submerged himself in his classes, preferring to bury his head in books and study until all hours of the night. Anything but sleep, because sleep brought with it the nightmare he longed to forget. Law school had given him a purpose and an excuse. There wasn't time to think, and for the next twelve months school anesthetized him from painful memories he longed to forget.

The second year had been much the same, until the anniversary of Gary's death had arrived. He hadn't been able to sleep that night, playing back the details in his mind over and over again until his heart had started pounding so violently he could hardly breathe. He knew then that he would have to deal with the emotions surrounding his partner's death, or they would haunt him for the rest of his life unless he sought professional help. That second year had been the most draining; it had been the time he'd dealt with his feelings for Gary and, perhaps even more importantly, his feelings for Lynn.

It happened unexpectedly, when he was the least prepared to deal with it, following a conversation with Joe Morris, Toni's husband. Joe had told Ryder that Lynn had started to date a mutual friend, Alex Morrissey. At first, Ryder was pleased because he longed for Lynn to find a new life, but he wasn't thrilled with her choice of men. Lynn could do better than Alex. He was relieved when he called

Joe a few weeks later and found out that Lynn had stopped seeing Alex but had accepted a date with Burt, another mutual friend. But Ryder didn't like Burt any better—he was downright irritated about the whole matter. Burt would make a terrible stepfather and Alex wouldn't be much better. In fact, Ryder couldn't think of a single man worthy of Lynn and Michelle and Jason.

Then it came to him so sharply that he was left stunned by the shock. He was in love with Lynn and had been for years. When Gary was alive, the three of them had been inseparable—the very best of friends. He hadn't realized his feelings for her then, hadn't been honest enough with himself to have been able to face it.

It had been an old joke between them, the way Ryder had drifted in and out of relationships. Little wonder! Every woman he ever dated simply couldn't compare to Lynn. He may have been close to acknowledging what was happening, because he'd started thinking about returning to law school long before Gary's death. But after the tragedy, his love for Lynn had been so repressed it had taken two years for him to even recognize his feelings for her.

Knowing what he did, the third and final year of law school had been sheer hell. Ryder's greatest fear was that Lynn would find someone to love and remarry before he could get back to her.

Now he was back, ready to build bridges with the past, ready to start life again. Everything hinged on Lynn. Not a day went by that he didn't think about her and the children. Not a night passed that he didn't plan their reunion.

For the first time in years, Ryder felt a strong urge to reach for a cigarette. Years of habit directed his hand to his empty shirt pocket. A momentary sense of surprise was followed by a chagrined pat against his chest. He'd given up the habit before joining the force, and that had been a life-time ago. How odd that he would feel the need for a smoke now, after all these years.

"Toni," Lynn asked without looking up from the table where Michelle had set their picnic basket. "Have you seen Jason? He disappeared the minute we arrived." She sliced a pickle in half and added it to the pile on the plate. "Knowing him, he's probably doing surveillance, checking out the area for enemy agents." She paused and licked the juice from her fingertip, and reached for another dill pickle. It was then that she realized she was talking to thin air. Toni was standing across the picnic area from her.

"Has he found any yet?"

The strong male voice froze her fingers, and slowly Lynn raised her eyes to meet Ryder Matthews. "Found any?" she asked, hardly able to speak. Just seeing him again brought a throb of excitement.

"Enemy agents?" Ryder asked.

She shook her head. The weight of his gaze held her prisoner. Instinct told her to go back to the task at hand, act nonchalant, friendly. "Hello, Ryder," she managed finally when her heart had righted itself. "It's good to see you."

"Hello, Lynn." His voice was warm and husky. It felt like a warm blanket wrapped around her shoulders on a cold winter night.

"Toni mentioned that she saw you earlier," she said, taking pains to keep her voice even.

"I thought she might have." He stepped closer to the picnic table.

"Want a pickle?" It seemed crazy that she hadn't seen Ryder in three years and all she could think to do was offer him something to eat.

"No, thanks."

Her fingers trembled slightly and she slipped the knife through the cucumber and added the slices to the plate. "She also said she'd heard something about you passing the bar."

"She heard right."

"Then congratulations are in order." Once more she struggled to keep her voice and emotions on an even keel.

"Lynn..." He paused and rubbed the back of his neck as if weighing his words. "It's time we talked," he said slowly, thoughtfully.

The silence that followed screamed at her. She expelled her breath and dropped her hands to the table. "That isn't really necessary. I know why you're here."

Three

"You know why I'm here?" Ryder echoed, his frown darkening.

Lynn closed her eyes and nodded. She'd known almost immediately why Ryder had left her alone the day of the funeral. She also knew why he'd found it essential to resign from the police force. Seeing him confirmed it. Even the most casual study of his features revealed that the years had weighed heavily upon him. Although they were close to the same age, Ryder looked several years older. She'd forgotten how tall he was—well over six feet, with wide shoulders and a powerful torso. His hair was as dark as his eyes, and his features had a vividness that drew her gaze to his face as effectively as a puppet's string. A soft smile touched her mouth as she pictured him standing in front of the jury box delivering the final argument to an important case. She was pleased with the image that formed in her mind. Ryder would do well as an attorney, but then Ryder Matthews was the type of man who would succeed at whatever he set out to accomplish.

When Toni had announced Ryder was at the picnic, Lynn's feelings had been ambivalent. Her instinct had been to lash out at him, hurt him the same way he'd hurt her, but she realized now how senseless and immature such thoughts were. She couldn't do that. Ryder had suffered, too, perhaps even more than she had. He hadn't left her because he'd wanted to—he'd gone because the pain had been too overwhelming to allow him to stay. Law school had just been a convenient excuse.

"Probably more important," Lynn told him, smiling sadly, her heart aching for them both, "I know why you went away."

"Lynn, listen—"

"Please, this isn't necessary." Her long nails pressed against the underside of the picnic table as she leaned her weight against it. "You've blamed yourself, haven't you? All these years you've carried the guilt of what happened to Gary."

Ryder didn't answer her, but pain flashed in and out of his eyes like a flickering light until he regained control.

"Don't. Gary loved his job. It was his life—what he was meant to do. He knew the risks, accepted them, thrived on them. I knew them, too." She had to keep talking, had to say what needed to be said before she succumbed to the emotion welling inside her throat and choked off her voice. Ryder had lived with the regrets and the guilt long enough; it was time for her to release him so he could make peace with himself. It was the reason he'd come to her, and she could do nothing less for the man she'd once considered family.

Ryder looked away and then slowly shook his head. "I was the one who told him to walk around the back of that house. It was my decision, my choice, I—"

"You couldn't have known," she said, cutting him off. "No one could possibly have guessed. It wasn't your fault— it wasn't anyone's fault. It happened. I'm sorry, you're sorry.

The entire Seattle Police Department is sorry, but that isn't going to bring Gary back."

Time had done little to erase the memory of the tragic incident that had led up to her husband's death. Everything had been so routine, so mundane. Gary and Ryder had been called to investigate the report of a suspected prowler. The two men had arrived on the scene and split up. Ryder went to the left, Gary to the right. A crazed drug addict, desperate for another fix, had been waiting. He panicked when Gary stumbled upon him, and frantic, the addict had turned and quickly discharged his weapon. A wild shot had gone through Gary's head, killing him instantly.

"It should have been me." Ryder's words were harsh and ground out, each one a breathless rasp.

"No," she countered. "I can't blame you, and I know in my heart that if Gary were standing here right now, he wouldn't fault you, either."

"But—"

"How he loved working with you." Her voice cracked and she bit into her lower lip until she'd composed herself enough to continue. "The best years he had on the force were the ones spent as your partner. The two of you were more than fellow officers, you were friends. Good friends. Gary loved his job because you were such a big part of it."

Ryder lowered himself onto the bench beside the picnic table, leaned forward to brace his elbows against his knees and clasped his hands. "He trusted me, and I let him down."

"You trusted him, too. It wasn't you who fired that gun. It wasn't you who turned on him. Fate did, and it's time you accepted that. I have. There's no bitterness left in me. I couldn't go on—couldn't be a good mother, if my life were marked with resentments."

Ryder was silent for so long that Lynn wondered what he

was thinking. His brow was creased in a thick frown, his eyes dark and unreadable. He held himself so completely still that she feared he'd stopped breathing.

"We should have had this discussion long before now," he murmured.

"Yes, we should have," Lynn returned. "But you've corrected that. You're free now, Ryder, truly free. Nothing's going to hold you back any longer—your whole life is about to start again. It's your time to soar."

Slowly he rose to his feet, his frown intact. He studied her closely, as though he didn't know how to respond to her.

"I wish you the best, Ryder. You're going to do well as an attorney. I know it—I can feel it in my blood." She felt the urge to hug him but suppressed it. Instead she made busywork around the picnic table. "It really was good to see you again." She could feel the weight of his eyes on her, demanding that she look at him.

"I'm back now," he said. "I intend to stay."

"I…heard that. I'm happy for you and proud of everything you've managed to accomplish." She lifted the container of potato salad Jason had carried from the car and set it in the middle of the picnic table.

"I'd like to see you again."

Lynn fiddled with the paper napkins. "I suppose that will be inevitable. The precinct tries to include the children and me in their social functions. We attend when we can. I imagine you'll receive the same invitations."

"I didn't mean that way. I want to take you to dinner, spend time getting reacquainted…date."

Lynn's gaze, which she'd so carefully trained on the checkered tablecloth, shot upward. She was sure she'd heard him incorrectly. Was Ryder talking about a date? It would be like having dinner with her own brother. He couldn't have surprised her more had he suggested they climb a tree and pound their chests like apes. She opened her mouth, then closed it again when no fleeting words of wisdom surfaced to rescue her. In addition to everything else, Lynn was well aware of Ryder's dating habits. He never went out with any woman for long. It used to be a big joke between her and Gary how Ryder used to drift from one relationship to another. The longest she could ever remember him dating one woman was a couple of months.

"I'd like to gain back that closeness we once shared," he elaborated.

"We already know each other, in some ways probably better than we know ourselves."

"And there are ways we haven't even begun to explore."

Lynn watched as his gaze gently fell to her lips. They stood so close that she could see gold flecks in his dark irises. Doubt was there and mingled with another emotion she couldn't identify. The desire to ease his pain welled inside her. She longed to wrap her arms around him and absorb the hurt and let him soak up hers. Once more she resisted, attributing these strange feelings to the closeness they'd once shared.

"Well?" he asked, though not impatiently. "Can I pick you up tomorrow night for dinner?"

She shook her head. "I'm flattered, Ryder, but no."

"No?" he echoed, surprised.

"I could give you any number of reasons, but the truth of the matter is I simply don't have much time for a social life right now. I bought a business, and the kids keep me hopping, and frankly, I don't think it would be a good idea for us to form that kind of friendship—there are too many ghosts."

"Because of Gary?" he asked. "Or is it because I walked away from you?"

"Yes...no...oh, heavens, I don't know." She glanced at her watch and was shocked to see that her hand was trembling. "I have to round up the kids now, so if you'll excuse me."

His eyes narrowed, and Lynn could see that he was debating on whether or not he should argue with her. Apparently he'd decided against it, and Lynn was grateful. Instead he reached out and gently touched the side of her face. A warmth radiated from his light caress, and Lynn blinked, having difficulty sorting through the sensations that bolted through her. Her stomach muscles constricted, and her heart shot into her throat. A brother shouldn't make her feel this way. A lover maybe, but not a brother. Something was wrong with her, terribly wrong.

"I want you to think about it." He dropped his hand and removed a business card from his wallet. "Give me a call when you change your mind...or if you need anything. I'm here for you now."

Lynn picked up the card and read his name and phone number, searching the words as though they could reveal what was happening to her.

"I mean it, Lynn."

For the past year, Ryder had planned this first meeting with Lynn, going over and over it in his mind, practicing what he was going to say until he'd memorized each line, each bit of dialogue. Yet nothing had gone as he'd planned, nothing had happened the way he'd hoped. Lynn had assumed he'd been crippled by guilt and that was what had kept him away all these years. Until she started to speak, Ryder hadn't realized how many unresolved feelings he still harbored for his late partner.

Everything had been so clear in his own mind. He knew what he wanted and knew what he had to do in order to get it. It shouldn't come as any big surprise that it wasn't going to be easy to escape the ghosts from the past. But then, Ryder realized, obtaining anything of value rarely came without effort.

He was so deep in thought that he didn't notice the boy who stood in front of him until the lad spoke. The dark brown eyes studying Ryder were wide and serious.

"You're Uncle Ryder, aren't you?"

Ryder was astonished, Jason hardly seemed old enough to remember him.

"My mom has a picture of you and my dad on the fireplace," Jason explained, before Ryder could question him. "You send me something for my birthday every year and Christmas, too. You buy real good gifts. I wanted to send you a list last year, but Mom wouldn't let me."

Grinning, Ryder asked, "So you recognized me from my picture?"

Jason nodded. "Except you've got a different color of hair on the side of your head now."

Ryder smiled at that. "I'm getting old."

"You used to be my dad's best friend, didn't you?"

"We were partners."

"Mom told me that, too." Jason paused and removed a canteen from his belt loop. With a good deal of ceremony, the eight-year-old opened the lid and poured a granulated pink-and-wheat-colored substance into the palm of his hand. When he'd finished, he lifted the canteen to Ryder in silent invitation. Without knowing what it was that Jason was eating, Ryder held out his open palm. When Jason had finished, Ryder sampled the mixture and decided that whatever it was, it didn't taste bad.

"It's cereal," Jason explained. He was silent for a moment, frowned and then asked, "Do you have any older sisters?"

"One."

"Yeah, me, too. They can be a real pain, can't they?"

"At times." Ryder finished licking up the last of the crumbs, then brushed his hands free of the granules. "But trust me, Jason, girls have a way of improving with age."

"That's what my grandpa says, but personally I can't see it. The Incredible Hulk doesn't have anything to do with them, except to save their lives."

"Your dad saved mine once."

Jason's eyes brightened. "My dad saved your life? Really?"

Ryder nodded, regretting bringing up the subject of Gary, but it was too late now. "More than once actually."

"Can you tell me about my dad? Mom talks about him and you a lot—or at least she used to before she bought Slender, Too. She told me she doesn't want me to forget him, but to tell you the truth, I hardly remember anything about him, even when I try real hard. My mom talks to me about the mushy things he used to do, like getting her roses on their anniversary, but she never talks about the good stuff."

Now that he'd fallen into the trap there wasn't anything to do but continue. Jason was hungry for information about his father, and it would be unfair to cheat the boy. "Gary Danfort was a special kind of man."

"Tell me about how he saved your life."

"Sure," Ryder answered and chuckled, then he talked nonstop for thirty minutes, relaying story after story about his exploits with Gary Danfort. They both laughed a couple of times and Ryder was surprised by how good he felt. In fact, he'd never missed Gary more than he did that minute, talking to the other man's eight-year-old son. Ryder expected the kind of raw emotional pain that came when he thought of his former partner, but instead he experienced a cleansing of sorts that would have been difficult to put into words.

When he'd finished, Jason's wide brows knit together, forming a ledge over his deep brown eyes. He looked as if his eager mind had soaked in every word, like a dry sponge sipping up spilled water.

"Mom told me he was a hero," Jason commented, when Ryder had finished, "but I never knew exactly what he did."

"You're going to be just like him someday," Ryder told the youth, and was rewarded with the widest grin he'd ever seen.

"The man who killed my dad is in prison," Jason added, unexpectedly, "but Mom said I should try not to hate him because the only person that would end up hurting is me."

Ryder wished he could be as generous in spirit. "Your mother is a wise woman."

"She's hardly home anymore the way she used to be," Jason added, and released an elongated sigh. "She bought a business last year and it takes up all her time. She's only home afternoons and nights now, and when she is, she's pooped."

Ryder frowned. He remembered when he'd heard about Lynn buying the franchise, and thought it would be good for her. "What does she do there?" He assumed she'd taken over the management, but not an actual teaching position.

"She makes fat ladies skinny."

"I see." Once more Ryder was forced to swallow a chuckle. "And how does she manage that?"

Jason pointed a finger at the sky and vigorously shook it three times. "Exercise. Exercise. Exercise."

Unable to hold it inside any longer, Ryder laughed aloud.

"It's not really funny," Jason said. "These ladies are serious and so is Mom."

"It's not that, son."

Faintly, in the distance, Ryder heard Lynn calling Jason's name. The youngster perked up immediately. "I've got to go. I bet it's time to eat. Are you going to sit with us? Mom forgot all about the picnic until Michelle reminded her. We were supposed to bring potato salad, but Mom picked some up at the deli. It's not as good as what she usually makes, but it tastes okay. We brought along hot dogs and mustard and pickles my Grandma put up last summer and a bunch of other stuff, too. You don't have to worry about not bringing any food because we've got plenty. You can stay, can't you?"

Four

"I don't like this one bit," Jason muttered from the back eat of the five-year-old Honda Civic.

"To be honest, I'm not overly pleased myself," Lynn returned, tightening her grip on the steering wheel. Jason was so outraged at the prospect of spending his summer with a bunch of preschoolers that he'd refused to be in the front seat with her. But where her son chose to sit was the least of Lynn's worries.

"I'm too old to be in a day-care center."

"You're too young to stay by yourself."

"Then how come Michelle gets to stay with the Morrises?"

"We've been over this a hundred times, Jason. Michelle is staying with Mrs. Morris until I can find someplace permanent for her."

"What's the matter with Janice? She may be a little ditzy, but she was all right."

"How many times do I have to remind you that I can't trust the three of you alone together? You know why as well as I do."

"But, Mom, I can handle Janice."

"That's the problem!"

"Why can't I stay with Brad?"

"His mom works, too."

"But why can't I go where he goes?"

"I tried to get you into the day camp, but it's full. Your name's on a waiting list, and as soon as there's an opening you can switch over there."

"I can't believe you're doing this to me," Jason muttered disparagingly. He crossed his arms over his chest and sulked.

"Jason, I'm your mother. Trust me, I don't like it any better than you, but there doesn't seem to be any other solution. Maybe later in the summer a better idea will present itself, but for now, you're going to the Peter Pan Day-care Center."

"The Peter Pan Day-care Center?" Jason cried and bounced his head against the back of the seat. "I suppose you want me to call the teacher Tinker Bell."

"Don't be cute."

"If Dad were here, this wouldn't be happening."

Jason might as well have punched her in the stomach; his words had the same effect. The pain rippled out from her abdomen, each circle growing wider and more encompassing until the ache reached her heart and centered its strength there. Since Jason had met Ryder, he'd used every opportunity to bring up his father—and Ryder. But using Gary against her was unfair.

"Well your father *isn't* here," Lynn returned sternly, "and I've got to do what I think is best."

"Putting me in with a bunch of little kids is the best thing for me?" Jason cried, his voice filled with righteous indignation. "I'm not a baby anymore, Mom."

"Third grade isn't exactly high school."

"I can't believe my own mother is doing this to me," her

son grumbled, sounding as though she'd turned traitor on him and was selling him into a life of slavery.

"Will you stop laying on the guilt," Lynn cried. "I feel bad enough as it is."

"If you felt that bad, you'd find a place with a different name. I bet Edward Norton's mother would never have done anything like this to him."

"Jason!"

"Peter Pan, Mom?"

"Think positive...you could teach the other boys your Super Hero games."

"Right," he said, but his voice lacked any enthusiasm.

After Lynn had left a tight-mouthed Jason at the day-care center, she drove to her salon. This last week hadn't been her best. If matters had been shaky before the precinct picnic, they were worse now. One of her instructors had quit, leaving Lynn to fill in until a replacement could be hired and trained. The night before she hadn't gotten home until after six and both kids were tired, hungry and cranky—an unpleasant combination. If that wasn't bad enough, Jason had been bringing up Ryder's name every afternoon like clockwork until Lynn was thoroughly sick of hearing about the man. She had trouble enough dismissing Ryder from her mind without Jason constantly talking about him. He repeated word for word what Ryder had told him about his father and the reason Ryder couldn't stay and eat with them the day of the picnic.

Lynn was smart enough to realize that it wasn't Jason's chatter that disturbed her. It was the fact that her son mentioned Ryder's name in such a reverent whisper, as though he were speaking of the Incredible Hulk himself. Lynn's feelings toward Ryder were still so muddled and unclear, she wasn't sure she could identify them. Even if she could, there wasn't time to do anything about them. What had really confused her was his dinner invitation. It had been more than a surprise—it had been a shock. As much of a jolt as seeing him again had been. She felt girlish and immature and uncertain of everything. After Gary's death, she'd faltered for a while, and staggered under the weight of shock and grief. It had taken her a long while to root herself once more, and find purpose for her and the children. But those few minutes with Ryder had knocked her off balance more than anything else since Gary's funeral.

The only thing they had in common anymore was their love for Gary. Ryder may have suggested getting together for dinner, but Lynn was convinced it had been a token offer. He was probably as surprised at himself for even suggesting it. He hadn't contacted her since, and she was grateful.

By noon, the same day she'd dropped Jason off at Peter Pan's, Lynn was exhausted. She was working at her desk, nibbling her lunch, when her assistant stuck her head in the door.

"A Mr. Matthews is here to see you. Should I send him in?"

The pen Lynn was holding slipped from her fingers and rolled across the desktop. She caught it just before it fell off the edge and onto the floor.

"Mr. Matthews?"

"Yes," Gloria answered, and wiggled her eyebrows expressively. "He's cute, too. Real cute. He's got a voice so husky it could pull a sled."

"Ah…" Lynn tried to laugh at her employee's joke while glancing frantically around the room, seeking an excuse, any excuse, to send Ryder away. None presented itself. It was one thing to talk to Ryder at Green Lake where there were blue skies and lots of people. But it was another matter entirely to sit across her desk from him, when she was wearing pink leotards and a sleeveless top.

"Lynn, what about Mr. Matthews?"

"Sure, go ahead and send him in."

"A wise decision," Gloria whispered, and pushed open the door so Ryder could step inside.

He walked into her tiny office, and his presence seemed to stretch out and fill every corner and crevice in the room.

Lynn stood, her heart pounding as fast and hard as a piston in a clogged engine. "Hello, Ryder. What can I do for you?" She hoped her voice sounded more confident than she felt.

"Hello, Lynn. I've got the afternoon free and since I was in the neighborhood, I thought I'd stop and see if you could have lunch with me."

This second invitation surprised her as much as his first one had. She twisted around and pointed to her unopened yogurt and a rye crisp that was only half gone. "As you can see, I've already eaten."

"That doesn't look like much of a lunch to me."

"I wouldn't dare bring a hamburger in here," she said, forcing a smile. "I'd be mobbed."

Ryder chuckled and pulled out a chair.

Reluctantly, Lynn sat, too.

"I hadn't heard from you." He spoke first, looking strong and confident. His mouth twisted into a slow, sensual smile that told her he'd been waiting for her call.

A simple smile caused her stomach to knot.

"I was hoping you'd get in touch with me," he added.

Lynn blinked, wondering if she was missing something. "I was supposed to contact you?"

Ryder nodded. "You were going to consider going out to dinner with me."

Lynn's eyes widened involuntarily. "No, as I remember, I said I didn't have the time and that I felt it was better for us to leave matters between us the way they were."

"I asked you to dinner; I didn't suggest an affair."

Extending her lower lip, Lynn released a breath that was strong enough to ruffle her bangs. "Ryder...you've been gone three years. You were Gary's best friend; you were *my* friend, too, but my life is different now."

"So different you can't indulge in one evening's entertainment?"

"Yes... I mean, no." Even now Lynn wasn't exactly sure why she felt she had to refuse his offer. Something elemental, a protective device she'd acquired since becoming a widow, slid securely into place. "I can't," she answered after a brief hesitation, her voice strong and determined.

"Why not?"

"Ryder, this is crazy. I'm not anything like the women you used to date. I think of you as a friend and a brother... not that way."

"I see."

It was obvious from how he looked at her that he didn't. "But more importantly," she felt obliged to add, "you don't owe me this."

"*Owe* you this?" The smile vanished, replaced with a piercing dark gaze that would intimidate the strongest personality.

"It's been three years now, and you seem to feel—"

"You amaze me the way you assume you know what I'm thinking," he said and stood, bracing his hands against the edge of the desk. "This time you're wrong."

His face was only a few inches from hers, and, although she tried not to look at him, his gaze dragged hers back to his. She braced herself, for *what* she didn't know—a clash of wills, she supposed. Instead she found herself sinking into the control and power she found in his eyes. It was like innocently walking into quicksand. It demanded all her strength to pull herself free. She was so weak when she managed to look away that she was trembling.

"Will you or won't you go to lunch with me?" Ryder asked.

He could have been asking about the weather for the casual way in which he spoke, but Lynn noted his voice had acquired a different quality. And yet his words weren't heavy or deep or sharp. She blinked, not sure what was happening to her or if her mind was playing games with her. What she saw and heard in Ryder was *purpose*. He wanted something from her and he wasn't about to give up until he achieved it.

"I..."

"Lunch with an old friend isn't so much to ask."

Lynn braced herself and kept her tone as even as possible, belying the jittery, unstable feeling inside her. "Ryder... I have my own life now. I just don't have the time to dig up the past, and, unfortunately, all we have in common anymore is Gary."

He said nothing, and his silence was more profound than the most heated argument. Lynn knew Ryder, knew him well, or at least she had at one time. He was intelligent and perceptive, and she prayed he could make sense of her jumbled thoughts even if she couldn't.

"I'll give you more time—since you seem to need it," he said, after what felt like the longest moment of her life.

Lynn nodded, her throat dry.

With that, Ryder Matthews turned and walked out of her office, but Lynn had the feeling he was coming back. She frowned and absently reached for her yogurt.

* * *

"Michelle," Lynn called, standing in front of the stove. "Call Jason home for dinner, would you?"

"Where is he?"

"Brad's... I think." She turned off the burner and opened the cupboard to take down the dinner plates. As a peace offering to her disgruntled son, Lynn was fixing his favorite meal. Tacos, with homemade banana cream pie for dessert.

Michelle finished making the phone call. "Brad's mom says he isn't there."

Lynn paused, distinctly remembering Jason telling her he was going to play at Brad's house. "Try the Sawyers' place then." Jason was sure to be there.

Michelle reached for the phone and hung up a minute later. "He's not there, either."

"He isn't in the yard, is he?"

"No," Michelle was quick to confirm. "I already checked there. Personally I think he needs to be taught a lesson. We should just sit down and eat without him. He knew you were cooking dinner, and if he chooses to disappear, then let him go without."

"I planned tacos tonight just for him."

"All the better."

"Michelle, we're talking about an eight-year-old boy here."

"A *spoiled* eight-year-old boy."

Both Michelle and Jason were always so eager to see the other disciplined. Lynn prayed this was a stage her children were going through, because she found it downright irritating.

"Dinner's an effort to smooth his ruffled feathers for putting him in the day-care center. I don't want to use it against him."

"I'll see if he's at the Simons's," Michelle offered on the tail end of a frustrated sigh.

From the way her daughter walked toward the phone, Lynn could tell that her daughter heartily disapproved of her parenting techniques.

"While you're calling I'll check upstairs and see if he's there," she offered. It would be just like Jason to lie down and fall asleep while everyone was frantically searching for him.

The first thing Lynn noticed was that his bed was made and his room picked up. That in itself was a shock since she'd often claimed his room was a death trap and only the Hulk himself would be brave enough to venture inside.

The note propped against his pillow caught her eye and she walked over to it. The few words seemed to leap off the paper and cut off her oxygen supply. Lynn read them non-stop twice. Her knees went so weak she had to reach out and grip the headboard to keep from falling.

"Jason isn't at the Simons's, either," she told Michelle as calmly as possible, once she returned to the kitchen.

"I know," Michelle said, impatiently. "I just got off the phone with Scott's mother. If you aren't going to take dinner away from him, I sincerely hope you punish him for this. I'm hungry, you know."

Lynn pulled out a chair and sat down. Her mind was whirling and she felt sick to her stomach.

"Where could that little brat be?"

"I...don't know," Lynn said, and her voice came out sounding like a rusty door hinge.

Michelle swung around, her eyes curious. With a trembling hand, Lynn handed her Jason's note.

"He's run away?" Michelle cried and her voice cracked. "My baby brother has run away?"

Five

The first thing Lynn did was phone the police station. Certainly they could tell her what to do in instances such as this. Although Lieutenant Anderson, the officer who answered her frantic call, was reassuring, he told her that until Jason had been missing twenty-four hours, there wasn't anything the authorities could do.

"Did he actually claim he was running away?" The lieutenant asked sympathetically.

Lynn's fingers tightened around Jason's carefully lettered note. "Not exactly…he said that I wouldn't need to worry about him anymore and that he could take care of himself."

Lieutenant Anderson's hesitation told Lynn everything she wanted to know. "I'm sorry, Mrs. Danfort, but there isn't anything more I can do."

"But he's only eight years old." Her voice wobbled as she struggled to hold back the fear. Lynn's imagination was tormenting her every minute that Jason was missing. Surely the men who had worked with Gary would be willing to do something to help her. Anything.

"I'm sure your son will be back before nightfall," the officer offered.

Lynn wasn't nearly as convinced. "But anything could happen to Jason in twenty-four hours' time. He's upset and angry…he could get into a car with a stranger…isn't there someone you could phone?"

Again the man hesitated. "I'll give the officers on patrol a description and ask them to keep an eye out for him."

Lynn sighed, grateful for that much. She wasn't sure Lieutenant Anderson would have been willing to do even that if he hadn't known Gary. "Thank you. I want you to know how much I appreciate this."

"No problem, Mrs. Danfort, but when you find Jason, call me."

"Yes," Lynn promised. "Right away." Her fingers felt like blocks of ice when she replaced the receiver. The chill extended down her arm and stopped at her heart. Lieutenant Anderson sounded so confident, as though eight-year-old boys ran away from home every day of the week. His attitude gave her the impression that as soon as Jason got hungry he would have a change of heart and head home. Maybe so, but it was a dark, cruel world out there and the thought of her son facing it alone frightened Lynn beyond anything else.

"Well?" Michelle asked, studying her mother once she'd finished talking to the police. "Are they forming a search party?"

Lynn shook her head. "Not yet."

"You mean they aren't going to bring in bloodhounds?"

"No."

"Oh, I guess they're right. Searchlights and helicopters will work much better since it's getting so close to nighttime."

"There aren't going to be any searchlights, or any helicopters."

"Good grief," the preteen shouted, obviously growing more agitated by the minute. "Exactly *what* are the authorities planning to do to find my baby brother?"

Darn little, but Lynn couldn't tell her daughter that. "The lieutenant promised to give Jason's description to the officers who are patrolling our area."

"That's it? That's the extent of their plans!" Michelle wore a shocked look.

Worry was clawing away at Lynn's insides.

"Mom," Michelle cried, "what are you going to do?"

Lynn wasn't sure. "I…I don't know." The lump in her throat felt as large as a Texas grapefruit as she desperately tried to force her mind into some type of positive action.

"Shouldn't we call someone?" Michelle suggested, tears brightening her eyes. "I could kill him, I could just kill Jason for this."

"It's the Peter Pan Day-care Center," Lynn said in a strangled voice that was barely above a whisper. He'd hated the idea from the very first, but she'd been forced to enroll him in a center that wasn't geared to a boy his age. There hadn't been anyplace else with openings.

Michelle's gaze was incredulous. "He wouldn't go there!"

Lynn stared at her daughter, wondering at Michelle's farfetched reasoning. The day-care center would be the last place Jason would think to hide. "Of course he wouldn't… don't be silly." Lynn's sense of panic was growing stronger each minute. "What about his friends?"

"I've already called everyone in the neighborhood," Michelle reasoned, rubbing her palms together and pacing the kitchen like a caged beast.

"What about Danny Thompson?" Lynn whispered, remembering a boy from school whom Jason had been thick friends with several weeks before school had been dismissed earlier in the month.

Michelle gnawed on her lower lip. "Nope, the Thompsons are on vacation, remember?"

Lynn vaguely did. "Michelle, think," she pleaded. "Where would he go?"

The girl shook her head, then shrugged her shoulders. "I swear to you, Mom, if you don't spank him for this, I will."

"Let's worry about punishing him once we find him." Although the need to shake some sense into her son *did* carry a strong appeal, Lynn kept her thoughts to herself.

"Uncle Ryder," Michelle shouted as though she'd just invented pizza. "I bet you anything, Jason contacted Ryder. Don't you remember…every other word out of his mouth for the past week has been Ryder this and Ryder that. He's been talking about him every day since the picnic."

"But Jason doesn't have any way of contacting Ryder," Lynn countered. "He doesn't know his phone number."

"Who says?"

Now that she thought about it, maybe Ryder *had* given Jason his phone number, but Lynn was sure Jason would have mentioned it earlier if Ryder had. He would have repeated every conversation at length, Lynn was convinced of that. No, Jason didn't have any way of getting in touch with Ryder—at least that she knew about.

"Mom, call Uncle Ryder," Michelle pleaded.

"But—"

"Mom, please, he could be our only hope!"

Ryder picked up the TV controller and absently flipped stations. Television really didn't interest him. Neither did dinner. His meeting with Lynn at noon hadn't gone well and he blamed himself. Lynn wasn't the same woman he remembered—for that matter, he wasn't the same man either. She'd changed, matured, grown. In the past three years, she'd learned to deal effectively with the blows life had dealt her. She was competent and confident and stronger than he would ever have believed. That had pleased and surprised him. He'd been foolish to picture himself as a knight in shining armor, rushing to Seattle to rescue her from an unknown fate. Lynn didn't need anyone hurrying to her aid. She was doing just fine all on her own.

Another problem that Ryder had only now fully understood was that Lynn had always looked upon him as an endearing older brother. He knew she considered the thought of the two of them romantically involved as absurd. She seemed to find the thought of them kissing as downright incestuous. He supposed that was a natural response, after all, since they'd never viewed each other beyond good friends while Gary was alive.

Gary.

The role his former partner had played in his and Lynn's relationship presented an additional insight. Ryder had failed to realize that Gary had been the cohesive person in their friendship. Ryder had been Gary's partner and friend and Lynn had just been Gary's wife—at first. They'd eventually become fast friends as well, but Ryder was beginning to understand that, without Gary, that friendship had changed for Lynn. His three-year absence hadn't helped, either.

Ryder slouched back against the sofa and rubbed his hand across his face. He was expecting too much, too soon. All he had to do was give Lynn more time, and make himself available to her and the kids. He would invent excuses to drop by, win Lynn over little by little, until she was as comfortable with him as she had been in the old days. When the time was right he would hold and kiss her, Ryder mused. All he needed now was patience.

An idea started to form…a good one. A smile bounced from his eyes to his mouth, curving up the corners of his lips. Without realizing what he was doing, he stood and moved into the kitchen, unexpectedly ravenous. His hand was on the refrigerator when the telephone rang.

"Ryder," Lynn said, trying to control the anxiety in her voice. "I'm sorry to bother you…"

"Lynn, what is it?"

The alarm in Ryder's voice told her that no amount of fabricated poise was going to disguise the terror that had gripped her soul. She closed her eyes and slumped against the kitchen wall in an effort to compose herself before she started explaining Jason's note.

"Here," Michelle said, ripping the telephone out of her mother's hand. "Let me do the talking."

Lynn wasn't given an opportunity to protest.

"Uncle Ryder, this is Michelle," the youngster stated in a crisp, clear voice. "If you care anything at all about your godson then I suggest you get over here right away. Jason is missing and God only knows what's happened to him. He could be dead. Mother's in a panic, and frankly I'm upset myself." With that she replaced the receiver with a resounding force.

"Michelle," Lynn groaned. "That was a terrible thing to do to Ryder. He won't know what to think."

"What is there to think?" she demanded with irrefutable logic. "Jason's missing, we're worrying ourselves sick. Uncle Ryder is possibly the only man alive we know who can tell us what we should be doing to find that little monster."

"It still wasn't fair to frighten him like that," Lynn argued, reaching for the phone. She punched out his number a second time and let it ring ten times before she hung up.

"He isn't going to answer the stupid phone," Michelle stated the obvious. "Honestly, Mom, Ryder really cares about Jason and me."

That bit of dialogue threw Lynn for a spiraling loop.

"How do you know that? Good heavens, you haven't seen him in years. I'm surprised you even remember him."

"Sure I do. Ryder always sends us nice Christmas gifts and he makes sure we hear from him on our birthdays."

"He's your godfather."

"I know. But I remember him from before…" She paused and a soft smile produced a dimple in both cheeks. "He used to sit me in his lap and tell me that I was going to grow up to be a princess someday. And if I was lucky, and he used to tell me that he was certain that I was very lucky, then I was going to be as pretty as my mommy."

"He told you that?"

Michelle nodded. "He used to make me laugh by telling me silly jokes, too." She hesitated and grinned. "I remember once that he told me that you can lead a horse to water but you can't teach him to do a side stroke. I love Ryder. I'm glad he's back. It's almost like…" She paused and dropped her gaze, her expression sobering.

"Like what, honey?"

"Like the way things were before Dad died."

Michelle's words had a peculiar effect upon Lynn. She flinched as if stepping back to avoid an unexpected blow. Everything had been different since Gary's death. It was as if part of her had been waiting to wake up and discover the last three years had all been a nightmare. And yet so many positive things had happened in her life. She'd discovered herself, accepted her weaknesses, conquered numerous fears. On the negative side of Gary's death, she'd come to view the years she was married as idealistic, and that was a mistake. Her marriage hadn't been a stroll through Camelot, and it was wrong to compare every man she dated to Gary. Over the time he'd been gone, she'd found it increasingly difficult to imagine another man fitting into her and the children's lives. She wasn't a carefree adult any longer. The ability to flirt and play cute were long gone. But if she was different, and she was, then so were men. Lynn hadn't been kidding when she told Toni Morris that the dating world was a jungle.

"I think I hear Ryder now," Michelle announced and raced out of the kitchen toward the front door. "Don't worry, if anyone can find Jason, he can."

Michelle was gone even before Lynn could stop her. The fact was, Lynn had trouble slowing down her own pace. She reached the door just in time to watch Michelle hurl herself into Ryder's arms and burst into flamboyant tears.

Ryder looked shocked by the preteen's emotional outburst. His gaze flew across the yard to Lynn who was standing on the front porch. One of her hands was braced against the wide support beam and the other hung limply at her side. In another time and place she would have wanted him to hold and reassure her too...but not now. She had to be strong, had to believe Jason would be found no worse for wear and everything was going to be all right. God wouldn't be so cruel that he would take both her husband and her son from her.

Ryder gently patted Michelle's back, and the tender way in which he spoke to the girl brought involuntary tears into Lynn's eyes. She looked away rather than let him know she was so close to weeping herself.

With one arm wrapped around Michelle's waist, Ryder led her to the top of the porch where Lynn was waiting.

"I can't seem to make much sense out of Michelle's story," he told Lynn. "Perhaps you'd better tell me what's going on with Jason."

Lynn opened her mouth to do exactly that, but when she started to speak, her voice cracked. Tears burned for release, tears she could barely control.

"He... I'm afraid Jason's decided to run away," she said and handed him her son's farewell note.

Six

Ryder took the creased note Lynn handed him and read the few short lines. "What did he take with him?"

Lynn's eyes rounded at the unexpected question. "I... I didn't think to check."

"Uncle Ryder, the police aren't doing anything to find Jason," Michelle informed him between loud sniffles. "No bloodhounds. No helicopter. No searchlights. Nothing."

"He'll need to be missing twenty-four hours before they get involved."

"I talked to Lou Anderson," Lynn explained, leading Ryder into the house and up the stairs to Jason's bedroom. "He's a lieutenant now and he was kind enough to give a description of Jason to the patrol officers, but I don't know if that'll do much good."

"It's something." Ryder paused just inside the bedroom door, surveying the room. "Did he pack any clothes?"

Systematically Lynn opened and closed her son's drawers, one after the other, until she'd finished with the chest. She couldn't see that he'd taken anything with him.

"I can tell you right now, he didn't bother with clean underwear," Michelle said with smug look. "If he brought anything it'd be those silly army things he treasures so much. He lives in those disgusting things. Mom practically has to wrestle him to the ground to get him to take 'em off so she can wash them."

Ryder looked to Lynn, who nodded.

"Just a minute," Michelle cried, "I just thought of something." Following that announcement, she raced down the stairs.

"Are you all right?" Ryder asked Lynn in the same tender voice he'd used earlier with Michelle. She didn't know how to deal with this gentle, caring concern. Part of her wanted to lean on him and let him absorb some of this dreadful fear that attacked her common sense like fiery darts. Lou Anderson was probably right: Jason would be home as soon as he got hungry. But then there was the off chance that her son had stumbled into real trouble.

"I don't know what I feel," she answered and lifted her hand to brush aside a stray lock of hair. To add to her dismay, she noted that her fingers were trembling. "I blame myself for this, Ryder. This is the first summer I haven't been home with the kids and it's been a disaster from the start. I don't know how other single parents manage home and a job. There've been so many problems."

Ryder motioned for Lynn to sit on the edge of Jason's mattress and when she did, he sat beside her.

"I didn't have any choice," Lynn continued, staring straight ahead at the wall and the life-size poster of her son's idol, Edward Norton as the Incredible Hulk. "I had to enroll Jason in the Peter Pan Day-care Center. I couldn't leave Michelle and Jason by themselves."

"I take it Jason isn't overly fond of Peter Pan's?"

"He hates it." She pinched her lips together as she remembered the martyred look he'd given her when she'd gone to pick him up that afternoon. It was enough to melt the hardest heart. "He...he would hardly talk to me on the way home. He claimed they made him eat tapioca pudding with a bunch of four-year-olds...his pride was shattered."

Ryder placed his arm over Lynn's shoulder and caressed the length of her upper arm in slow, even strokes that gently soothed her. The weight of his body, so close to her own, felt incredibly strong and confident. Without realizing what she was doing, she relaxed and had to fight the urge to rest her head against his shoulder.

"I've tried so hard to be a good mother, Ryder. I knew he was going to hate it there. I was trying to make it up to him by cooking his favorite dinner. He loves tacos and banana cream pie... I should have known that wouldn't be enough to appease him."

"You *are* a good mother, Lynn, don't be so hard on yourself."

"It's not only Jason running away," she admitted with a wobbly sigh. "The way he idolizes Super Heroes concerns me. That boy lives in a dream world in which he's the hero. Toni Morris told me it's a stage all little boys go through, but I can't help worrying. I can't help thinking—"

A breathless Michelle hurled herself into the room, interrupting Lynn. "I should have known," she announced dramatically. "The Oreos and a bunch of other goodies are missing, including a brand-new box of Cap'n Crunch cereal."

"He wouldn't think to take a sweater, but food didn't escape his notice," Lynn pointed out to Ryder.

"That thief took off with my fruit nuggets," an outraged Michelle continued.

"Your what?" Ryder's brow puckered with the question, obviously not understanding the significance.

"Fruit nuggets," Michelle repeated and slapped her hands against her sides in outrage. "Mother kindly explain!"

"It's a dried, gooey form of cherries, grapes, strawberries and other fruit that look like gumdrops."

"Ah."

"They were mine. Mom bought them for me and Jason knew it. That boy isn't any better than a...a..." Apparently Michelle couldn't think of anything low enough to compare him to. With her hands braced against her hips, the girl looked as outraged as if Jason had walked away with the national treasury stuffed into his pockets. A public hanging would be too good for him.

Ryder stood. "I think I've gleaned enough to know where he might be."

Apparently Ryder knew something Lynn didn't.

"Where?" Michelle demanded, noticeably eager to get her hands on her brother and her fruit nuggets while there was still time.

"I imagine he's taken along his backpack and his sleeping bag as well."

Michelle tossed open the closet door and peered inside. "Yup, both are missing."

Lynn leaped up and looked for herself. Sure enough, both were conspicuously absent.

"We've already phoned everyone in the entire neighborhood," Michelle advised Ryder. "I can guarantee you he isn't with any friends who live around here."

"I didn't think he would be."

"You'll call?" Lynn leaned against the closet door, her eyes wide and appealing.

"Every half hour, in case that boy's got the sense he was born with and decides to come home on his own. Otherwise I'll keep looking until he's found." His low voice was filled with an unwavering determination.

That lent Lynn some badly needed confidence. For the first time since finding Jason's note, Lynn felt a glimmer of reassurance.

"Ryder." The sound of his name vibrated in the air. He stopped abruptly and turned to her. Lynn held out her hand and grasped his fingers, squeezing them as hard as she could. "Thank you," she said in a strangled whisper. "I... didn't know what to do or who to call."

He brushed his fingertips across her cheek in the briefest of touches. It was the touch of a man who would walk through hell to bring Jason back home. A shiver of awareness skidded down Lynn's spine and she managed a weak smile.

"Ryder will find him," Michelle murmured after he'd left. "I know he will."

"I do, too," Lynn answered.

The wooded area behind the local park was the logical place for Ryder to begin his search. From his experience earlier with his godson, Ryder remembered how much the boy loved exploring. He probably had a fort all prepared for this little exercise, and had thought most matters through before leaving home.

He quickly located several well-traveled paths that led deep into the thicket.

Within a matter of minutes, Ryder stumbled upon a fallen tree with a Star Wars sleeping bag securely tucked beneath a shelter that had been carefully dug out. A canteen rested beside that. Ryder checked the contents and when he discovered granulated cereal, he knew he'd found his prey.

All he had to do now was wait.

That didn't take long. About five minutes later, Jason came traipsing through the woods with a confidence his military hero would have envied. He stopped abruptly when he saw Ryder, his young face tightening.

"If you're here to take me home, I'm not going."

"Okay," Ryder agreed with an aloof shrug.

"You mean you aren't going to make me go back?"

Ryder shook his head. "Not unless that's what you want, and it's obvious to me that you don't." He straightened, stuck the tips of his fingers into his jeans pockets, and glanced around the campsite Jason had so carefully built. "Nice place you've got here."

Jason's eager grin revealed his pride. "Thanks. I'd offer you something to eat, but I don't know how long my food supply is going to last."

Once more Ryder shrugged and made a show of patting his stomach. "Don't worry about it, I'm saving my appetite for tacos and banana cream pie."

Jason's gaze shot up so fast it was a wonder he didn't dislocate his neck. "Tacos? Banana cream pie?"

"Smelled delicious, too."

Looking disconcerted, Jason swallowed and Ryder could have sworn the boy's mouth had started to water. In a gallant effort to disguise his distress, Jason walked over to the tree trunk and hopped onto the smooth bark. "I didn't want to have to run away like this, but Mom forced my hand."

"Peter Pan did it, right?"

"How'd you know?"

"Your mom told me."

"I suppose she sent you here."

"In a manner of speaking," Ryder answered smoothly. "She was pretty worried."

"I told her not to in my note," Jason fired back defen-

sively. "Gee whiz, you'd think I couldn't take care of myself or something. That's the whole problem, Ryder, Mom
treats me like I'm a little kid."

Ryder cast his eyes to the ground in order to hide his
smile before Jason saw it. To his way of thinking an eight-
year-old was a kid!

"I was planning to move back home as soon as school
started, and the way I figure it, that's only six weeks. I've
got to if I'm going to play with the Rockets."

"The Rockets?"

"My soccer team—we took first place last year. I made
more goals than anyone, but Mom says it's a team sport and
I can't take all the credit even though I worked the hardest
and scored the most."

Feigning a pose of nonchalance, Ryder leaned against
the fallen oak and crossed his arms and legs. "So Peter
Pan's is the pits?"

"You wouldn't believe how bad it is. Half the time I was
afraid some old lady was going to check me to see if I'd
wet my pants."

"That bad?"

"Worse. It's unfair because Michelle gets to go over to
her friend's house, but Mom sticks me in some kiddy fac-
tory." Jason drew a fruit nugget out of his pocket and popped
it into his mouth, aggressively chewing it. "Mom's real nice
and for a sister there are times when Michelle isn't half bad.
The problem, the way I see it, is that I'm surrounded by
women who can't understand a man like me."

"I've had the same trouble myself," Ryder confided.

His godson looked impressed. "I thought as much. You
were wearing a tortured look the day I saw you at the lake."

"A tortured look?"

"Yeah, that's what I heard Mom say on the phone once.

She was talking to Mrs. Morris about a man she'd gone out to dinner with and she said that and something else about him roaming the moors with Heathcliff...whatever that means."

Despite his effort not to, Ryder chuckled.

"Later, I asked Mom what she meant and she said that he frowned a lot. You were frowning, too."

Ryder supposed that he *had* been scowling that day. There'd been a good deal on his mind, not the least of which was finding a way to approach Lynn after three long years. He couldn't stroll up to a woman after that length of time and casually announce he was in love with her.

"I wanted to go to day camp with Brad—he's my best buddy—they do neat stuff like horseback riding and field trips, but Mom checked it out and they're already full up." He reached for another fruit nugget, paused and stared at it in the palm of his hand. "I don't suppose the banana cream pie was homemade?"

"It looked to me like it was."

Jason licked his lips. "I wonder if there were any left-overs?"

"Oh, I'm sure there are. No one felt much like eating. Your mother was too upset and Michelle was crying."

"Michelle cried because of *me*?" Jason looked astounded. "But I took her fruit nuggets. Oh, I get it," he said, nodding vigorously. "She didn't know it yet."

"She noticed that first thing; there was something about the Oreos and some Cap'n Crunch cereal missing, too, now that I think about it."

"I have to eat, you know. I left Michelle the shredded wheat."

Ryder examined the end of his fingernails, pausing to

clean beneath a couple before adding, "Don't worry, Michelle understands."

"Then why was she crying?"

"I don't completely understand it myself. She was sobbing so hard it was difficult to understand her, but from what I could gather, she was afraid something terrible could happen to you."

Jason lowered his gaze and rubbed his hands over the thigh of his army pants. "A drunk shouted at me, but I ran away from him…he didn't follow me, though, I made sure of that."

"I see."

Jason hesitated. "He might have seen which way I headed, though."

"That's a possibility," Ryder agreed.

Jason looked distinctly uncomfortable. "So you're sure Mom's all right."

"No, I can't say that she is. Your mother's a strong woman and it takes a lot to upset her, but you've managed to do that, son."

The boy's gaze plunged. "I suppose I should go home then…just so Mom won't worry."

"That sounds like a good idea to me. But before you do, I think we should have a talk—man to man."

Every minute that Ryder was gone felt like a lifetime to Lynn. She couldn't sit still, couldn't stay in one room, but paced between several. Not knowing what more she could do, she phoned everyone in the neighborhood and asked them to keep an eye out for Jason, although Michelle had already talked to all of Jason's friends. When she'd finished with that, she wandered back into her son's bedroom, but became so depressed and worried that she soon left.

Lynn was in the laundry room cleaning a cupboard when she heard Michelle's muffled cry. "Mom, Mom."

Dropping the rag, and rushing into the kitchen, Lynn discovered her daughter pointing to the inside of the junk drawer, tears raining down her face.

"What is it?"

"Jason left me a note," she sobbed. "He told me he was sorry for taking my fruit nuggets, but he needed them to live. He saved me all the grape ones…they're my favorite."

Lynn felt like bursting into tears herself.

"Ryder's going to find him."

Michelle had repeated those same words no less than fifteen times in the past hour. He hadn't phoned, which caused Lynn to be all the more nervous.

"I know." But the longer Ryder was gone, the less confident Lynn grew. Within an hour, she'd been reduced to cleaning cupboards.

Both Lynn and Michelle heard the car door slam from the driveway. Like a homing pigeon, Michelle flew to the living room window and pushed aside the drape.

"It's Jason and Ryder."

Lynn felt the weight of a hundred years lift from her shoulders. "Thank God," she whispered.

Seven

Jason walked into the house, his chin tucked so low against his shoulder that Lynn could see the crown of his head.

"Hello, Jason," she said, clenching her hands tightly together in front of her.

"Hi, Mom. Hi, Michelle."

Jason's voice was so low, Lynn had to strain to hear him speak.

Michelle sniffled loudly in a blatant effort to let her brother know how greatly he'd wronged her. She crossed her arms in an act of defiance, then whirled around, unwilling to face him or forgive him.

Ryder's hand rested on Jason's shoulder. "He was camping in the woods behind the park."

"The woods…behind the park," Lynn repeated, hardly able to believe what she was hearing. Even now the nightmares continued to ricochet off the edges of her mind. All the tragic could-have-beens pounded against her temple with agonizing force. If something had happened to Jason while he was hiding there, it could have been weeks before he was found.

"I believe Jason has something he'd like to say to you," Ryder continued.

The boy cleared his throat. "I'm real sorry for the worry I caused you, Mom."

Michelle whimpered softly.

"You, too, Michelle."

Somewhat appeased, the girl slowly turned to face her brother, apparently amenable now to entertain thoughts of mercy.

"I promise I won't run away or hide or do anything like this ever again, and if I do, you can burn my army clothes and tear up my poster of the Hulk." Having made such a gallant offer seemed to have drained Jason's energy bank. He paused, looked up at Ryder, who patted the boy's shoulder reassuringly and then continued. "I don't like that Peter Pan Day-care place, but I'm willing to stick it out until I go back to school. Next year we'll know to sign me up for day camp with Brad at the beginning of the summer so I can be with my best friend."

The knot in Lynn's throat felt as if it would choke her. The emotion that had blistered her soul demanded release. Heavy tears filled her eyes as she nodded, blurring her vision. Moisture ran down the side of her face and she held out her arms to her son.

Jason ran into them, his small body hurled against hers with enough force to knock her a step backward. He buried his face in her stomach and held on to her with such might that breathing was nearly impossible.

Michelle waited until Jason had finished hugging Lynn before she wrapped her arms around him in a rare display of affection. "You deserve the spanking of your life for this," she declared in high-pitched righteousness, "but

I'm so glad you're back, I'm willing to let bygones be bygones…this once."

Jason tossed her a grateful glance. "Here," he said, digging his hands into his pockets. "I still got some of your fruit nuggets left."

Michelle looked down at the gooey, melting fruit pieces in his palm that had bits of grass and dirt stuck to them, wrinkled her nose and shook her head. "You can go ahead and eat them."

Jason was noticeably surprised. "Gee, thanks." He stuffed the entire handful into his mouth and chewed until a multicolored line of juice crept out of the corner of his lip. He abruptly wiped it aside with the sleeve of his shirt.

Michelle cringed. "You are so disgusting."

"What'd I do?" He asked and smeared more of the sugary fruit juice across his cheek.

Rolling her eyes, Michelle pointed toward the kitchen. "Go wash your hands and face before you touch something."

The pair disappeared and Lynn was left standing alone with Ryder. "I don't know how I can ever thank you," she told him. "I was so close to falling to pieces. When I found Jason's note it was like acid had burned a hole straight through me. I…I can bear just about anything but losing either of my children." She wiped the moisture from her cheekbones and tried to smile, failing. "I don't know how you guessed where he was hiding, but I'll always be grateful."

"I was here for you this time," he whispered.

"Oh, Ryder, don't blame yourself for the past. Please."

"I'm not. I went away because I had to, but I'm here now and if you've got a problem, I want to be the first one you call."

Lynn wasn't sure she understood his reasoning. He'd

walked away from her when she'd needed him most and calmly strolled back into her life three years later, looking to rescue her. For the most part, Lynn didn't need anyone to save her, she'd managed nicely on her own. She was proud of her accomplishments, and rightly so. In the time since Gary's death, she'd come a long way with little more than occasional parental advice. If Ryder thought he could leap into her life, wearing a red cape and blue tights, then he was several years too late. She was about to explain that to him as subtly and gently as possible, when Jason stuck his head around the kitchen door.

"Can I have a taco and some pie?"

Between her relief that her son was all right and calling Lieutenant Anderson to tell him he'd been found, Lynn had completely forgotten dinner. "Ah...sure." She tossed a glance at Ryder. "Have you eaten?"

He grinned and shook his head.

"Then please join us. It's the least we can do to thank you."

Ryder followed her into the kitchen and while Lynn brought out the grated cheese, cubed tomatoes and picante sauce, Ryder helped Michelle and Jason set the table.

The easy friendship between Ryder and the kids amazed Lynn. It was as if he'd never been away. They joked and laughed together so naturally that she found it only a little short of amazing. Lynn didn't know of any male, other than the children's grandfather, that the kids seemed more at ease with.

With Jason safely home, the terrible tension had evaporated and dinner proved to be a fun, enjoyable meal. Lynn was convinced the reason Jason loved tacos so much was that he could make a mess without getting corrected for eating like a pig. Bits of fried hamburger, cheese and lettuce circled the area where he was eating. Blithely unaware, Jason downed three huge tacos and took seconds of pie.

"I'm a growing boy, you know," he told Lynn when he delivered his clean plate to the kitchen counter.

The phone rang and Michelle leaped upon it as if answering it before the second ring was a matter of life or death. "It's Marcy," she announced, pressing the receiver to her shoulder. "Can I go over to her house? She got a new pair of jeans she wants me to see."

Lynn twisted around to look at the wall clock. "All right, but be back by eight."

"Mom, that's only a half hour."

"It's eight or not at all."

"All right, all right."

Jason yawned, covering his mouth with his palm, and after clearing the table, plopped himself down in front of the television. The next time Lynn glanced in his direction, her son was sound asleep.

"How about some coffee?" she asked Ryder.

"That sounds good."

He quickly loaded the dinner dishes into the dishwasher while Lynn started the coffee.

Lynn carried two steaming mugs into the living room where Ryder was waiting. He was standing in front of the television where a framed photograph of Gary rested. He turned, looking almost guilty, when she entered the room. He walked over to her to take one mug from her hand.

Her gaze skimmed across the photo of her late husband and back to Ryder. From the disconcerted look he wore, she knew he didn't want to discuss Gary, and she decided not to press the issue.

Smiling, she motioned for him to sit. He sat in the recliner and she took a seat on the sofa, slipping off her sandals and curling her feet beneath her.

"Well, this has certainly been an eventful day," she said, heaving a giant sigh. Rarely had any day been fuller or more traumatic. She'd effectively dealt with all the problems at work and had come home and faced even bigger ones there.

Ryder took a sip of the hot coffee. "It's been a good day for me. I'd forgotten how much I love Seattle. It feels right to be back here."

"It's good to have you." Lynn didn't realize how much she meant that until the words had already slipped from her lips. Ryder had always been a special kind of friend. For years she and Gary and Ryder had been thicker than thieves. Ryder was the brother Gary never had, and they were the best of friends. So Lynn's relationship with Ryder had fallen neatly into place because of his close association with her husband.

"I'm glad to be back, too." The color of Ryder's eyes intensified as his gaze held hers.

He dragged his look away with a reluctance she could feel all the way from the other side of the room. The undercurrents between them were so powerful that Lynn feared if she waded into anything beyond polite conversation, she would be pulled under and drown.

"Seattle's changed, though," he commented in a voice that was slightly husky. "I hardly recognized the downtown area for all the new construction."

"I saw from your business card that your office is on University Street. How does it feel to be a white-collar worker?" Her gaze moved from Gary's photo to Ryder.

"I don't know if I'll ever get used to wearing a tie every day. I'm more comfortable in Levi's than in a suit, but I suppose that'll come in time."

Lynn smiled, and talked about the many changes happening in the Seattle area. She was pleased that some of the old camaraderie between her and Ryder had returned. When Gary and Ryder had been partners, the three of them had often sat and chatted over a pot of coffee or a pitcher of beer. They'd camped together, hiked together, taken trips to Reno together. They attended concerts, cheered on the Seattle Seahawks and taken skiing classes together. More often than not they'd been a threesome, but every now and again, Ryder would include his latest love interest. Gary and Lynn had delighted in baiting Ryder about how short his "interest span" was when it came to any one woman. He'd responded to their teasing with good-natured humor. He liked to joke, saying he was trying to find someone who was as good a sport as Lynn but was not having any luck.

The three of them were comfortable together—there wasn't any need for pretense. When Michelle was born, Ryder had been her first visitor, arriving at the hospital even before the birth. When Gary and Lynn had asked him to be their daughter's godfather, Ryder's eyes had shone with pride. He was as excited as Gary, carrying pictures of his goddaughter in his wallet and showing them to anyone who would stand still long enough to look. The case was the same with Jason. Ryder had been a natural with the kids, as good as Gary and just as patient and loving. Both Michelle and Jason had grown up with Ryder as a large part of their lives.

Then Gary had died and Ryder had abruptly moved away. Not only had Lynn lost her husband, but in one fell swoop, her two best friends as well.

Ryder must have read the confusion and doubt in her face because he started to frown. The television drew his gaze and his scowl deepened. He hesitated and then blurted out. "I had to leave in order to keep my sanity."

"Ryder, please, I understand. You don't need to explain."

"No, I don't think you do. Let me explain it one last time and then that'll be the end of it. My staying, continuing to be a part of your and the kids' lives would have been a constant reminder of Gary. Every time you looked at me, the memories would have been there slapping you in the face. You needed time to deal with your grief and I had to separate myself from you to get a grip on my own. Perhaps if I hadn't been with him that night…if the circumstances had been different, then the possibility of my remaining in Seattle would have been stronger. But I *was* there and it changed both our lives."

It was possible that Ryder was right, but Lynn didn't know anymore. She didn't want to think about the past and Ryder obviously found it equally painful.

"I'd been considering going back to law school even before…Gary died," Ryder confessed. "I think I may have even mentioned it at one point. I'd dropped out of graduate school in order to enter the academy because I wanted to make a more direct contribution to society. The idea of working with people, helping them, upholding law and order strongly appealed to me. At the time I couldn't see myself stuck away in some law office."

"You think you wasted your time on the force?" That would have surprised Lynn since she'd always assumed Ryder had loved his job as much as Gary had.

He shook his head. "I don't regret it at all. I saw where my effectiveness in a courtroom could be enhanced with my knowledge of police work. My parents had set aside a trust fund for me in case I *did* decide I wanted to go back to school. That had long been an option for me."

"And now you've achieved your goal," Lynn said and sipped her coffee. "I'm proud of you...you were always one to go after something when you wanted it. Gary was the same way. I think that's one reason you two were always such close friends—you were actually quite a bit alike."

"You share some of those character traits yourself."

He held himself rigid, refusing to relax. Their conversation was making him all the more uncomfortable, Lynn noted, and she knew all her talk about Gary was the cause.

"Tell me about Slender, Too."

She smiled at the question, knowing it was a blatant attempt to change the subject. She let him. "I've had the salon for about ten months. Buying that franchise was the scariest thing I've ever done, and I've managed to make a living with it, but it hasn't been easy."

"The kids seem to have adjusted to you working outside the home."

Lynn supposed they had, but the going hadn't been easy. Perhaps if she'd worked outside the home earlier in their lives Michelle and Jason might have adapted better. But they were accustomed to having her there when they needed her. The day-care problems this summer were a good example of how their lives had changed since she'd bought the business.

"If you run into any more problems, I want you to call me," he said, and straightened. He uncrossed his long legs and leaned forward, resting his elbows on his thighs.

"Ryder, I appreciate the offer, but there are few things I can't handle anymore."

"But there are some?"

She hesitated. After what had happened with Jason that evening, she didn't have a whole lot to brag about. "A few things every now and then."

"So call me and I'll do what I can to help straighten those things out."

"Ryder, honestly, you're beginning to sound like you want to be my fairy godfather."

He chuckled, but the sound quickly faded. "The last thing I want is for you to see me as an indulgent uncle."

His face and voice were fervent. It was the same expression he'd given her when they'd met at the precinct picnic, and she found it as disconcerting now as she had then.

Lynn was standing before she had a reason to be. Her mind searched for a logical excuse for why she'd found it necessary to bolt to her feet. The undercurrents tugging at her grew stronger. "Would you like some more coffee?" she asked, then her gaze rested on his still full mug.

"No, thanks."

Refilling her own mug justified the question, although hers was no closer to being empty than Ryder's, but she needed an excuse in order to escape.

Moving into the kitchen, she stood in front of the coffee-pot. Lynn heard Ryder walk over and stand behind her. The warmth and proximity of his body were a distraction she chose to ignore.

He rested his hands on her shoulders and stroked her arms in a reassuring motion. "The past few years have been hard on you, haven't they?"

Lynn's hands were shaking as she lifted the glass pot and refilled her mug. "I've managed." Dear sweet heaven, she mused, could that rickety, wobbly voice really be hers? Ryder may have said something more, Lynn didn't know. It took everything within her not to be conscious of the strength of his broad chest, which was pressing against her back. Perspiration beaded her upper lip and although she would have liked to blame it on the heat, the day had actually been cloudy with the temperature in the low seventies.

"Lynn, turn around."

Reluctantly she did what he asked, all the while conscious of how close they were.

With a deliberate action, Ryder removed the mug from her fingers and set it aside. Lynn felt as if she were in a daze, hypnotized and immobile. Anytime else, with anyone else, she would have demanded to know the other person's intentions. But not with Ryder.

She knew what he wanted.

That knowledge would have troubled her except that she was honest enough to admit she wanted it, too.

He placed his hands on her shoulders once more, and his touch so confused her senses that voicing her thoughts became impossible. He slowly glided his fingers over her face, down her cheek to her neck. He reached for the French braid, which fell down the middle of her back, and pulled the strands of hair free, easing his hands through it. His gentle stroke was that of a lover, appreciating a woman's beauty.

Lynn's breath jammed in her throat and her heart started beating like a rampaging herd of buffalo. She refused to look up at him, concentrating instead on the buttons of his shirt because it was safe to look there.

"Lynn."

The demand in his voice was unmistakable. She had to glance up, had to meet his eyes. When she did, she couldn't stop staring at him. They were so close she could see every line in his rugged features. His nostrils flared slightly and the action excited her more than his touch had. Sexual excitement and longing, which had been dormant for years, filled her. The feelings felt foreign and yet perfectly natural.

He lowered his lips to hers.

Slowly, moving as though directed by Ryder's thoughts, hypnotized by what she witnessed in his eyes, Lynn moved in his arms, going up on her tiptoes, raising one hand to clench his shoulder for support.

He brushed his mouth against hers, softly, tenderly, in a butterfly kiss that teased and tantalized her. Her lips trembled at the swell of pure sensation. A soft rasping breath escaped, but Lynn didn't know if it came from her or Ryder. Her eyes were closed, blocking out reality, excluding everything but this incredible whitecap of sensation that had lapped over her. She wanted to deny these sensations, but it was more than she was capable of doing in that moment— more than Ryder would allow.

Still trembling, Lynn repositioned her upper body, hoping to escape his arms. She soon realized her mistake as the softness of her breasts grazed the hard wall of his chest.

Ryder's breath caught. While once she'd sought to move away, now her arms slid around his neck.

He kissed her then, the way a starving man samples his first bite of food. His lips caressed, tasted and savored her mouth until they were both breathless. Gasping, Lynn met his ravishing hunger with her own powerful need. She was shaking so hard that if he were to release her, she was convinced she would collapse onto the floor.

Passion built between them until Lynn felt as though her entire body had been seared.

His mouth left hers to slide across her cheek to her ear. An involuntary moan escaped as he nibbled her lobe.

"How I've dreamed of holding you like this," he murmured, his voice husky and low. His breath felt warm and moist against her skin.

The front door slammed and the sound reverberated around the kitchen like a ricocheting bullet. Lynn broke away from Ryder so fast that she would have tumbled to the floor if he hadn't secured her shoulders. Once he was assured that she was stable, he released her, dropping his hands to his sides.

"I'm back," Michelle announced, racing into the kitchen with the fervor of a summer squall.

For some obscure reason, Lynn felt it essential to reach for her coffee. She took a sip and in the process nearly spilled the entire contents down her front.

Michelle stopped abruptly and looked from Ryder to her mother and then back to Ryder. "I'm not interrupting anything, am I?"

"No...of course not," Lynn said quickly. The words stumbled over her tongue like rocks crashing off the edge of a cliff and bouncing against the hillside on the long tumble downward.

"Your mother and I would like a few minutes alone," Ryder inserted, staring straight through Lynn.

"Oh, sure."

Michelle had turned and started to walk out of the room when Lynn cried. "No...don't go...it's not necessary." She knew she was contradicting Ryder, but now in the harsh light of reality, she felt ashamed by the way she'd succumbed to his kissing. She awkwardly struggled to rebraid her hair.

Michelle was noticeably confused. Her gaze jerked from her mother back to Ryder. "I wanted to show Marcy my magazine. We were going to go up to my room. That's all right, isn't it? She's asking her mom now if she can come over here."

It took Lynn a full minute to decide. With Michelle gone, she would have to face Ryder alone and she didn't know if she could bear to look him in the eye. She'd behaved like a love-starved creature, giving in to him in ways that made her blush all the way to the marrow of her bones. She'd clung to him, kissed him with an abandon that made her feel weak at the memory.

"Mom?"

"Ah…sure, that's fine."

Michelle gave her an odd look. "Are you all right?"

"Of course," she answered in a falsely cheerful voice.

"You look all pale, like you did when you came downstairs with Jason's note." The girl's gaze narrowed. "He hasn't run away again, has he? That little brat… I knew I was being too generous to forgive him so easily."

"He fell asleep in front of the television," Ryder answered for her. "I don't think you'll have any more problems with him running off."

"It's a good thing you talked to him, Ryder. Someone had to. Mom tries, but she's much too easy on that boy. Mothers tend to be too softhearted."

The doorbell chimed and Michelle brightened. "That's Marcy now."

She ran to answer the door, and rather than face Ryder, Lynn walked away from him and into the family room where Jason lay curled up on the sofa, sound asleep.

"Jason," she whispered, nudging him gently. "Wake up, honey."

"He's dog-tired," Ryder said when Jason grumbled and rolled over in an effort to ignore his mother's voice. "Let him sleep."

"I will once I get him upstairs," she said. Her heart began to pound against her ribs in slow, painful thuds. It took all the courage she could muster just to look in Ryder's direction.

"Here," Ryder said, stepping in front of her. With strength she could only envy, he lifted the sleeping boy into his arms and headed for the staircase.

Jason flung his arms out and lifted his head. He opened his eyes just enough to look up and assess what was happening.

"Your mother wants you upstairs," Ryder explained.

Jason nodded, then closed his eyes, content to let Ryder carry him. That in itself told Lynn how exhausted her son was. From what she'd learned over dinner, Jason had been planning his escape for several days. The boy probably hadn't had a decent sleep in two or three nights.

Lynn walked up the stairs behind the two; all the while her heart was hammering with trepidation. Once Jason was tucked into his bed, her excuses would have run out and she would be forced to face Ryder. It wasn't likely that she was going to be able to avoid him. She could try to lure Michelle and her friend into the kitchen, but Lynn wasn't likely to interest them in coming downstairs when there was a teen magazine clenched in their hot little hands.

Ryder set Jason on the edge of his mattress and peeled off the boy's shirt.

"He should probably take a bath."

"Ah, Mom," Jason grumbled, and yawned loud enough to wake people in three states. "I promise I'll take one in the morning." He made a gallant effort to keep his head up, but it lobbed to the side as if it had suddenly become too heavy for him to support.

"A bath in the morning," Lynn muttered under her breath. "Those are famous last words if I ever heard them."

Ryder shared a grin with her and the simple action went a long way toward easing some of the tension that was crippling her.

Next Ryder took off Jason's tennis shoes. A pile of dirt fell to the floor as the first sneaker was removed from the boy's foot.

"If Michelle were here, she'd be screaming, 'oh, yuck.'" Lynn joked in an effort to ease more of the tension.

Soon Jason was in his pajamas. He didn't hesitate in the least before climbing between the sheets. He curled up in a tight ball, wrapping his arms around his pillow as though it were a long lost friend and they'd just recently been re-united.

"He won't wake up till morning," Ryder said, and gently smoothed the hair at the top of her son's head.

"Do you want any more coffee?" Lynn asked, on her way out of the bedroom.

"No."

She was so grateful she actually sighed with relief. Maybe he would decide to go home and give her the space she needed to think. Her thoughts were like murky waters and had clouded her reasoning ability. Kissing Ryder had been curious enough, but to become a wanton in his arms was something else entirely.

He waited until they were back in the kitchen before he spoke. "I don't want coffee or dessert. You know what I want." His voice was so low and seductive that just the sound of it caused tiny goose bumps to break out over her arms.

"Ryder…" She meant to protest, to say something—anything that would put an end to this madness. But Ryder didn't give her the opportunity. Before she could object, he turned her into his arms. Any opposition she'd felt earlier disappeared, like snow melting under an August sun, the minute he reached for her.

Ryder's arms closed convulsively around her waist.

"Please…don't."

"I've waited too long to go back now."

Lynn didn't understand any of what was happening, but

when Ryder reached for her, she couldn't find it within herself to resist. His mouth swooped down on hers, his kiss possessive and hard, and yet incredibly soft.. Against every dictate of her will, Lynn lifted her arms to encircle his neck, and shamelessly gave herself over to his kiss.

Ryder groaned.

Lynn whimpered.

He kissed her again and again with a thoroughness that left her shivering, as if in a single minute he wanted to make up to her for all the years they'd been apart.

"No," she cried. "Please...no more." She twisted her face away from him and buried it in his shoulder.

"Lynn..."

"I...think you should go home now."

"Not until we've talked."

"But we're not talking now and I don't know what's happening between us. I need time to think. Please...just go. We'll talk, I promise, but later." Lynn had never felt more unsettled about anything in her life.

He hesitated. He gently stroked her hair as though he had to keep touching her. "It's too soon, isn't it?"

"Yes," she cried. She didn't know if that were true, but was willing to leap upon any excuse.

Slowly, as though it was causing him pain to do so, Ryder dropped his arms and stepped away from her.

A chill descended upon her as he moved away and she lifted her arms, cradling them around her waist.

"I'll be back, you know," he whispered. "And next time, I won't be willing to listen to any excuses."

Eight

"This is a rare treat," Toni Morris said when Lynn slid into the booth across from her in the seafood restaurant close to Lynn's salon. "It's been months since we last had lunch together."

Lynn's smile was noticeably absent as she picked up the menu and glanced over the day's specials. She decided quickly upon a Crab Louie and spent the next several moments adjusting the linen napkin on her lap.

"Well," Toni said, propping her elbows atop the table and lacing her fingers, "are you going to come right out and tell me why you arranged this meeting or are you going to keep me in suspense for half the meal?"

Lynn should have known Toni would see through this invite ruight away. "What makes you think there's something I want to talk about?"

Toni grinned, the simple action denting dimples in both cheeks. The thing Lynn found amazing about this former policewoman was her ability to be both tough and tender. She could look someone in the eye, cut them to the quick with her honesty and then heal them with a smile.

"You mean other than the fact you phoned me at ten-thirty last night suggesting we meet?"

Lynn's gaze darted past her friend. "It was a bit late, wasn't it?"

"Don't worry, you didn't get me out of bed."

The waitress came to take their order and Lynn was given a few minutes respite. She'd wanted to gradually introduce the subject of Ryder, but her friend wasn't going to allow that, which was probably best. Left to her own devices, Lynn was likely to avoid anything that had to do with the man until the last ten minutes of their lunch.

"Ryder came by last night," she said in as normal a tone as she could manage. "Actually I phoned him, desperate because Jason had run away and I thought he might have contacted Ryder."

"Jason did *what*?"

"You heard me…he hates Peter Pan's so much that he decided to live in the woods behind the park until soccer practice started the first week of September and then come home."

Momentarily speechless, Toni shook her head and reached for a breadstick. "That child amazes even me."

"Because I was desperate, I called Ryder and he found Jason for me."

"How?"

"Heaven only knows. I called him because…well because Jason mentioned Ryder's name every ten seconds after they met at the precinct picnic and I thought Ryder might know where Jason was hiding. Actually Michelle had insisted. By the time he arrived I was a candidate for the loony bin."

"I don't blame you. Good grief, Lynn, you should have let me know."

"There wasn't anything you could have done. I called

the station and talked to Lou Anderson. You know him, don't you?"

"Yes, yes, go on—how did Ryder know where to find Jason?"

"It was a matter of simple deduction. Unfortunately I was in too much of a panic to think straight. Ryder arrived, asked several pertinent questions and used simple logic. Once Ryder went looking for him, Jason was home within the hour."

"Thank God." Toni expelled a tight sigh. "That boy is something else."

"Tell me about it." Lynn lowered her gaze and nervously smoothed an already creaseless napkin. "Ryder stayed for dinner and later we talked and…" A lump of nervous anticipation blocked her throat. It was one thing to tell her friend that Ryder had kissed her and another to admit how strongly she'd reacted to it.

"And what? For heaven's sake, woman, spit it out."

Despite everything, Lynn laughed.

"You want me to help you out?" Toni joked. "Ryder came over, found Jason, stayed for dinner and the two of you talked. Okay, let's go from there. Knowing you both the way I do, I'd guess that Ryder kissed you and you went into a tizzy."

Lynn nearly swallowed her glass of ice tea whole because Toni was so close to the truth. "How'd you know?"

Toni waved a bread stick like a band leader wielding a baton. "Let's just say I'm not the only one able to deduce matters from the evidence presented me."

Shaken, Lynn stared at her friend, wondering how much more Toni had guessed. She looked amazingly pleased by what had happened, as though she'd orchestrated the entire event herself.

"But Ryder isn't the first man to kiss you in the past three years." Toni's curious smile deepened, causing the edges of her mouth to quiver slightly.

"No, he isn't," Lynn admitted, "but he's the first one who's made me feel again. He appears to want to make up to me for the years he was away, insisting I call him when I stumble into any roadblocks. He doesn't seem to understand that I've changed and when something bothersome crops up, I prefer to find my own solutions."

"He's changed, too, you know."

"But I fear his concern for me and the kids is motivated by guilt."

"The kiss, too?"

"I...I don't know," Lynn answered, wavering. "He came by the salon yesterday, wanting to take me to lunch. I turned him down."

"Why?"

"For the same reasons I didn't want to have dinner with him when he suggested it at the picnic."

"Which are?"

"Oh, Toni, stop. You know as well as I do that I just don't have time right now for a social life. Good grief, I probably shouldn't even be taking a whole hour for lunch today. This summer's been hectic at the salon, I can't seem to find good permanent help. The new girl phoned in and said she wouldn't be able to make her shift—she didn't even bother to give me an excuse. I think she'd rather be at the beach. I suspect the only reason she took the job in the first place was to tone up her muscles and get paid for it at the same time. It's been one problem after another for the past three weeks."

Toni's eyes grew serious. "Those are all excuses not to see Ryder and you know it."

"It isn't!"

"Ryder loves you..."

"We're friends—that's all. If he feels anything toward me it's rooted in his relationship with Gary. He helped me yesterday when Jason disappeared, like an older brother would help a younger sister."

"Is that the way he kissed you? Like a brother?"

Toni's words whooshed the argument out of Lynn like hot air from a balloon and with it went all pretense. "No, and that's what concerns me most."

"In other words, it felt good."

"*Too* good," she admitted in a tight whisper. "Much too good."

Their salads arrived and Lynn looked down at the lettuce covered with fresh crab meat and realized her appetite had vanished. She picked up her fork, but after a couple of moments, set it back down again. When she looked up, she noticed that Toni was watching her, her friend's eyes revealing her concern.

"It isn't the end of the world to like it when a man kisses you," Toni said with perfect logic. "If the truth be known, I've been worried about you lately. You've been so involved with Slender, Too, working far harder than you should have to, in addition to keeping up with the kids and the house. Something's going to have to give soon."

"Like my sanity?" Lynn tossed out the words jokingly, but actually she wasn't so far off base. It was the only rational way she could explain what had happened between her and Ryder. For the past year, she'd been dating occasionally, but no one had made her feel the way Ryder did. It had been months since a man had touched her. Months since she'd allowed her body to feel anything sexual. Just the memory of the way Ryder's hands had felt against her shoulders and back, the way he'd run his long, strong fingers through her hair, caused a rush of sensation shooting all the way down to her toes.

"Ryder cares about you and the kids," Toni said, still looking thoughtful and disturbed.

Lynn didn't want to hear that, not because she didn't believe it, but for the other reasons. "He thinks he can leap into my life after three years as if…as if nothing had ever happened."

"I don't think that's his intention."

"Well, I do!" Lynn flared. Toni chose to ignore her short temper, Lynn noted, and took a bite of her salad before answering. "Then what do you think?"

"I can only guess at what Ryder intends. If it bothers you so much, why don't you ask him?"

Toni's question hung between them like a tight rope walker, suspended in midair.

"But one word of warning, my friend," she added softly, "be prepared for the answer."

"What do you mean by that?"

"Just that I know you both. Ryder didn't come back here by accident—he planned it."

"Of course he did. He was accepted into a law firm in Seattle. He's familiar with the courts here and police procedure. It only makes sense that he'd want to set up practice in this area."

"Yes, it *does* make sense, but for other reasons, too."

"Right," Lynn answered defiantly. "He seems to think I need to be saved from myself and I find that both insulting and irritating. His whole attitude suggests I've bungled my family's lives for the past three years, and that everything's going to be better now that he's back. Well, I've got news for Ryder Matthews. *Big news.* I got along without him then and I can do it now."

Toni didn't say anything for several tortuous moments. "Don't you think you're confusing two separate issues?"

"No." Lynn answered without giving the question adequate thought. "He was a friend—a good one, and he feels a certain amount of guilt over Gary's death. If Ryder came back for any specific reason, it was to purge himself from that."

Toni arched her finely penciled brows. "I see. Then you have all the answers."

Not quite, but Lynn wasn't sure she was ready to admit as much. "I think I do."

"Then Ryder's task is going to be more difficult than he imagined."

"What do you mean?"

Toni glanced at her watch and sighed. "Listen, I'd like to stay and talk, but I promised to meet Joe. He wants to look at lawn mowers during his break." She offered Lynn a cocky smile and murmured, "From the sounds of it, you've got everything figured out, anyway."

"I...I don't know that I do." That was more difficult to admit than Lynn cared to think about. She knew Ryder, she knew herself, but they'd both changed.

"You'll figure everything out—just give yourself time." Toni set her napkin beside her plate and reached for the tab, studying it before retrieving her wallet. "I will make one suggestion, though."

"Sure."

"The next time Ryder stops by, ask him why he moved back to Seattle. You might be surprised by the answer." Following that, she scooted out of the seat and was gone.

By the time Lynn returned to the salon, she was more

confused than ever. She'd wanted to talk out her feelings to Toni, but something had gone awry. It took her a while to realize what. Secretly Lynn had wanted Toni to tell her that kissing Ryder was all wrong. She'd hoped her friend would explain that she and Ryder had marched neglectfully into an uncharted area in a relationship that was best left alone. Unfortunately, Toni hadn't. Instead her friend had thrown questions at her Lynn didn't want to answer.

Lynn was forced to acknowledge that whatever her relationship had been with Ryder before he moved to Boston, it had now been altered. That much had been obvious from the minute she saw him at the picnic. Only it had taken time for Lynn to recognize that. She and Ryder weren't going to slip back into those old familiar roles, although Lynn would have been content to do so.

With her not-so-subtle questions, Toni kept insisting Lynn own up to her own feelings, which at the moment were difficult to decipher. Okay, so Ryder's kiss had affected her. She would figure out why and that should be the end of it.

Sharon walked into the office almost as soon as Lynn arrived. "Carrie phoned after you left. She won't be able to come in today."

Lynn groaned inwardly. "Is she sick?"

"She claims she was up half the night with some flu bug."

Lynn slouched down into her chair and released a frustrated sigh. "Great."

"Do you want to toss a coin and see which one of us stays until eight?"

Lynn was touched by her assistant's generosity. "No, I'll do it."

"What about Michelle and Jason?"

Lynn shrugged, there wasn't anything else to do. "I'll

pick them up at four. They'll just have to stay here with me until closing time."

Sharon chuckled. "Jason's going to love that. Can't you just see him down here with his camouflage gear, waving at all these women in fancy tights?"

"I'll keep him busy drawing pictures in my office." That was optimistic thinking in action.

Sharon regarded her silently for a long moment. "You're sure? I can probably make arrangements with my sitter, if you want."

"No, I'll do it. Thanks anyway." It was her business and she was the one responsible. Besides, Sharon had stayed late one night this week already and Lynn couldn't ask that of her a second time.

"Okay, if you're sure." Sharon looked doubtful.

"I am. Were there any other calls?"

"Yeah, that guy with the husky voice phoned ten minutes after you left. He asked that you return his call and gave me the number. It's on your desk."

So Ryder had contacted her at lunchtime—somehow Lynn had expected he would.

"Anything else happen?"

"Not much. There were two or three more calls; I left the messages on your desk."

"Thanks, Sharon."

"No problem, it's what you pay me for."

Lynn sorted through the pink slips that were on top of her desk. She found it interesting that Sharon would specifically mention Ryder's call, but none of the others—except Carrie's.

From dealing with Ryder in the past, Lynn knew if she didn't return his call, he would keep trying until she answered. It was best to deal with him when she was the most prepared. Besides, she already knew what he wanted—he'd told her so himself when he'd left her the night before. He wanted to talk. Well, she didn't and she planned on telling him as much.

With resolve straightening her backbone, Lynn punched out his telephone number and waited. A secretary answered, her voice cool and efficient, conjuring up pictures of someone young and attractive. A pang of jealousy speared its way through Lynn. She found the emotion completely ridiculous. Ryder could be working with Miss Universe for all she cared.

"Ryder Matthews."

"Ryder, it's Lynn. I got the message that you called."

"Yes. I checked out a couple of day camps and found one in your area with an opening. Ever hear of Camp Puyallup?"

Lynn was so astonished it took her a full moment to find her breath. "Of course I have. It's the camp Jason wanted to attend, but they were full… I checked it out myself. Jason's friend Brad goes there."

"There's an opening now if Jason's interested."

"But…we're on their waiting list, we were told it wasn't likely that he'd get in this summer. How did you manage it?"

Ryder hesitated as if he didn't want to admit something. "I phoned first thing this morning and was able to pull a few strings."

Lynn didn't know whether she should be furious or overjoyed. She knew how *Jason* would react, however, Her son would be in seventh heaven at the thought of escaping Peter Pan's. Lynn supposed she should be grateful Ryder had intervened on her behalf, but she didn't like him stepping into her life and "pulling strings." She could find her own solutions. All right, this day-care problem with Jason had been a thorn in her side and her son's as well.

"Jason will be pleased." It took an incredible amount of discipline to tell Ryder that much, although she tried to let him know in the cool way in which she spoke that she didn't appreciate what he'd done.

The ensuing silence was loud enough to create a sonic boom.

"I didn't mean to offend you." It was apparent from the clipped way in which he released his words that Ryder was upset. "I was only trying to help, Lynn."

"I know." She closed her eyes and let out a ragged sigh. It would be ridiculous to punish Jason because of her foolish pride. He was miserable at the center where he attended now and Camp Puyallup would be perfect for him.

"The camp director wanted to meet Jason tonight. Could you stop by with him for a few minutes after work?"

Lynn felt like weeping. "I can't...not tonight." As it was, her schedule was going to be exceptionally tight. She would barely have time to pick up Jason and Michelle and be back at the salon in time to lead Carrie's four-thirty aerobics class.

"You can't take Jason! Why not?"

"I've got to work late. In fact, I was going to bring the kids down here with me."

"For how long?"

"Until closing."

"Which is?"

"Eight." It sounded like an eternity to Lynn. She could just see herself leading a dance aerobics class and trying to keep Jason out of mischief all at the same time. Tonight was going to be "one of those nights."

"Then I'll take Jason down myself," Ryder offered. "In fact, I'll pick up both kids; we'll make a night of it. I'll treat them to dinner and a movie afterward."

"Ryder, no. That isn't necessary."

"You'd rather have both kids down there with you? They'll be bored stiff."

Lynn didn't have any argument. Ryder was right. Given the choice between going to dinner and a movie with Ryder and staying holed up in her office, Lynn knew who the kids would want to spend the evening with. And she couldn't blame them.

"Well?"

"I...suppose that would be all right. I'll call Peter Pan's and tell them you'll be by to pick up Jason. Michelle's spending the day with Marcy...you met her last night."

"What time will you be home?"

"As soon after eight as I can manage."

Another silence followed, and Lynn was convinced Ryder was debating on whether to say something about the long hours she was putting in. She was grateful when he didn't.

"I'll have the kids home about that time."

"It's good of you to do this, Ryder. I appreciate it."

She could feel his smile all the way through the telephone line. "That wasn't so hard, was it?" he asked in a light teasing voice that was mellow enough to melt her insides.

It was apparent that he hadn't a clue as to how difficult it had been.

Ryder set down the phone and grinned lazily. He leaned back in his swivel chair and cupped his hands behind his head, satisfied by this unexpected turn of events. He was going to see Lynn again far sooner than he'd anticipated and that pleased him immeasurably.

Lynn had amazed him on two accounts. The first and foremost had been the way in which she'd responded to his kiss the night before. The plain and simple truth was that for the past six months, Ryder had been living on the edge. His biggest fear was that Lynn was going to meet another man and fall in love before he could get back to Seattle. He hadn't been eating properly—nor had he been sleeping well. There were so many hurdles to leap when it came to loving Lynn that fear had crowded his heart and his mind.

But holding and kissing her had sent him sailing over the first series of obstacles without a problem. She couldn't have responded to him the way she did without feeling something—and it wasn't anything remotely related to a brotherly affection. She'd wanted him. Ryder could feel it in his bones.

He hadn't been able to sleep for long hours afterward. Every time he closed his eyes, he imagined tasting her sweet mouth. If she'd wanted him to make love to her, and Ryder knew she did, it only touched the surface of the desire he'd experienced for her. By the time he arrived back at his apartment, his whole body had ached with need.

Months ago, when Ryder had first realized he was in love with Lynn, his first fleeting reaction was that it was wrong to feel the way he did. The best thing was for him to stay out of her life and let her find happiness elsewhere. It didn't take him much time to realize he couldn't allow that to happen. Like it or not Lynn was a part of him, and releasing her to love another man would be like chopping off his own arm. He could have managed it, but he would have gone through the remainder of his life aching his loss. Last night had confirmed that he'd made the right decision to woo Lynn. She was going to love him and the knowledge was enough to make him want to stand on top of his desk and shout for joy.

The second way in which Lynn had surprised him was how promptly she'd returned his phone call. It was almost as if she'd been eager to talk to him. Unfortunately, Ryder knew otherwise. He'd heard it in the sound of her voice, the minute he'd picked up the phone. She'd wanted to deal with his call and be done with it. Under different circumstances, Ryder would have been prepared for a two- or three-day wait before she contacted him. He didn't have time to delay and would have phoned her again until he reached her, but she'd surprised him first. Ryder didn't doubt that Lynn had been frustrated and confused over their encounter in her kitchen the night before. Talking to him would be the last thing she wanted to do, but she'd taken the initiative and he was proud of her.

Over the years, Ryder had learned to cherish his independence, and he could well appreciate Lynn's needs in that area. But darn it all, she couldn't manage everything on her own. It was time she set aside her pride and accept his willingness to lend her a helping hand.

She needed him just as much as he needed her.

Dropping his arms, Ryder briefly closed his eyes and let the tide of love for Lynn and the kids ebb over him. Things were going to work out just fine…just fine indeed.

Nine

Silence yawned through the living room when Lynn let herself into the house. Exhausted, she looped her purse on the doorknob to the entryway closet and walked directly into the kitchen. Usually she led two aerobics classes in a single workday, but on this one, she'd been forced to do four twenty-minute dance sessions. Every muscle in her weary body was loudly voicing its objection to the strenuous activity.

Lynn groaned when she stepped into the kitchen, rotating her neck to ease the stiffness there. The place was a disaster. As an experiment, Lynn had given Michelle a key to the house so her daughter could come and go as she pleased.

That was a mistake. From the looks of it, Michelle had decided to bake something. Now that she thought about it, she vaguely remembered Michelle phoning to ask permission to mix dough for chocolate-chip cookies. The entire conversation remained blurry in Lynn's mind, but from what she recalled, the actual baking part would take place at Marcy's house.

A fine dusting of flour littered the countertops like frost on a winter's morning. The sugar bowl was open and chocolate chips were scattered from one end of the kitchen to the other.

Lynn popped a chocolate morsel into her mouth and let it melt on her tongue. It tasted incredibly good. She was beyond hungry—she'd barely touched her crab salad at lunch and it was hours past dinnertime.

It was after she'd finished wiping down the counters that Lynn found her daughter's note, promising to clean up the kitchen once she got home. Tiny print at the bottom of the page informed Lynn that her daughter had hidden her share of the cookies from Jason, they were somewhere safe in the house and Michelle would get one for her when she was home from the movie.

Opening the freezer door, Lynn found a frozen entree, and after reading the cooking directions, set it inside the microwave.

Seven minutes sounded like an eternity as she plopped herself down in the living room, removed her shoes and stretched her feet on top of the ottoman. If she could only close her eyes for a moment and rest…for just a minute.

Indistinctly, as if it were coming from a great distance, she heard the timer on the microwave beep. She didn't have the energy to move.

"Mom."

Lynn bolted awake, her feet dropping to the floor with a thunderous thud.

"Mom, guess what?" Jason flew into the room at the speed of a charging elephant, carrying with him—of all things—a stuffed furry basketball. "Ryder took me over to Camp Puyallup and I met everyone and they said I could join their troop. Brad and me are going to be partners tomorrow. Isn't that the greatest thing since…since hand grenades?"

Lynn managed to smile through her brain fog. "That's... wonderful, Jason."

"It's more than great...it's hell good."

"Hell good?"

"That's what everyone says when something is stupendous," Michelle informed her mother.

"I see." Lynn rubbed a hand over her face to wipe the sleep out of her eyes, hoping the action would unclog her mind. When she looked up Ryder was standing there, staring down on her. He was impossibly handsome and when he grinned, deep grooves formed at the sides of his mouth. Lynn felt as if the sun had come out and bathed her in its warm light. His smile was designed to disarm her and, to her chagrin, he succeeded. She smiled back despite her best intentions to cool things between them. She hated to admit, even to herself, how powerless she felt when she was around Ryder. It frightened her, and oddly enough, excited her all at the same time.

"Hi," he said, in that low, husky voice of his. "You look exhausted."

Lynn met his gaze steadily, refusing to allow herself to be sucked into his male charm, and knowing it would do little good to resist. She felt like she was swimming upstream against a raging current, battling for every inch of progress.

"Ryder took us out for Chinese food," Jason announced, plopping himself down on the ottoman in front of his mother. "And then—"

"I want to tell," Michelle cried impatiently. "You already told her about dinner."

"But *I* won the basketball. I should be the one to tell her."

"There was a carnival with rides and everything in the parking lot at the Fred Meyer store," Michelle announced, spitting the words out so fast they fell on top of each other. She ignored her brother's dirty look and continued, "We stopped there and Ryder let us go on all the rides we wanted."

"I won this." Jason held out a furry orange ball, beaming proudly.

"With a little help from Ryder." Michelle's singsong voice prompted the truth.

"Okay, okay, Ryder got down most of the pins, but I knocked some over all by myself."

"Congratulations, son." Lynn couldn't remember the last time Jason had looked so happy. His eyes shone with it and, for the first time in recent memory, he wasn't wearing his army clothes. Lynn didn't know what Ryder had said or done to get him to change, but whatever it was had worked better than anything she'd been able to come up with. A twinge of resentment shot through her, which she stifled. Her thoughts were petty, and she was angry with herself for being so small-minded.

"I got a mirror with Beyonce's profile sketched on it," Michelle announced, smugly holding it up for her mother's inspection.

A flash of her own image reflected back at her and caused Lynn to cringe. She looked dreadful—

"Yeah, but you didn't win that." Jason chimed in, interrupting her thoughts. It seemed he wanted to be sure his mother was aware no skill had been involved in obtaining Michelle's mirror.

"Actually Ryder was kind enough to buy it for me," Michelle answered in a disdainfully prim voice meant to put her obnoxious brother firmly in place.

"I want to show Brad my basketball," Jason said, turning his back on his sister. "Can I go over there…it isn't even dark yet."

Oh, the joys of summer, Lynn mused. It was almost nine and almost as light as it had been at three that afternoon.

"Marcy loves Beyonce. I want to run over to her house, too, can I?"

Lynn took one look at her children's eager expressions and nodded. Both vanished, leaving Ryder and Lynn alone in their wake. To her dismay, her empty stomach growled and Lynn flattened her hand over her abdomen.

"When was the last time you ate anything?" Ryder asked. His eyes blazed at her as though she'd committed some hideous crime and he was about to arrest her.

Lynn regarded him with a trace of irritation. "Noon. Listen, Ryder, I appreciate you taking the kids for me tonight. It's obvious they had the time of their lives, but I'm a big girl, I can take care of myself. I've even managed to feed myself a time or two."

"Not while working twelve-hour shifts."

"How much time I put in with my own salon is none of your business."

A frown darkened his features and as if to completely discredit her, her stomach growled again, this time loud enough to stir the cat who was sleeping on the back of the sofa.

"Come on," he said, "let's get you some dinner before you pass out."

"I can take care of myself."

"Then do it!"

With quick, efficient movements, Lynn marched into the kitchen and pulled the TV dinner out of the microwave. Whirling around to face him, she yanked open the silverware drawer and jerked out a fork.

"You can't eat that garbage." Ryder contemptuously regarded her meal, wrinkling up his nose as if he found the very smell of it offensive.

"I most certainly *can* eat this...just watch me." Before he could argue with her, she stabbed her fork into watery mashed potatoes. They tasted like liquid paper and she nearly gagged, but she managed to swallow the bite and pretend it was nectar from the gods.

"Lynn, stop being so incredibly stubborn and throw that thing out before it makes you sick." He removed the plastic carton from her hands.

Lynn grabbed it back before he could place it in the garbage. "Stop telling me what to do."

"Okay, I apologize. Now throw that out and cook yourself something decent. You can't work that many hours and treat your body this way."

"Since when have you become an expert on *my* body?" she yelled, growing more furious by the minute.

"Since last night," he yelled back.

Their eyes met in a defiant clash of wills. His were dark and narrowed and hers wide and furious. From the way the grooves at the edges of his mouth whitened, Lynn knew he was having trouble keeping a rein on his temper. For some obscure reason, that bit of insight pleased Lynn. It pleased her so much she had to resist the urge to laugh. He was clearly determined to bend her will to his no matter what it cost. And she was equally determined not to. Most anyone else would have been intimidated by his fierce gaze, but she wasn't. She knew Ryder well—besides, the stakes were far too high.

When he turned away and started sorting through her refrigerator, Lynn laughed out loud. "Just exactly what do you think you're doing?"

He ignored her completely.

Lynn slapped her hands against her sides and groaned. "Good grief, Ryder, don't you see how ridiculous this is? The two of us aren't any better than Michelle and Jason."

He set several items on top of the counter, then started searching through her cupboards until he found a frying pan.

"You're wasting your time," she told him, as he peeled off slices of bacon and placed them in the skillet.

"No, I'm not."

Lynn found the entire episode highly amusing. "If you think I'm going to eat that, you're sadly mistaken."

He didn't rise to her bait.

As if to prove her point, she took another bite of the atrocious entree, choking down a rubbery piece of meat that was floating in something that resembled gravy.

The distinctive odor of frying bacon filled the kitchen, slowly waltzing around Lynn, wafting under her nose and causing her mouth to water. She downed another bite of mashed potatoes, nearly gulping in an effort to force the tasteless mass down her throat.

For all the attention Ryder was giving her, she might as well have been invisible.

"You're wasting your time, Ryder," she told him a second time, angry that he was ignoring her.

He cut a tomato into incredibly thin slices and stacked them in a neat pile. Next he buttered the bread, added just the right amount of salad dressing and then started building the sandwich with thick layers of bacon, lettuce and tomato.

"I'll end up giving that to the cat," she warned.

He folded the bread together, placed the BLT—Lynn's favorite kind of sandwich—on a plate and poured her a tall, cold glass of milk. Next he carried both the glass and the plate to the table and pulled out a chair for her, silently demanding that she sit down and eat.

"I told you it was a waste of time," she said, crossing her arms and purposely directing her nose in the opposite direction.

"Lynn," he coaxed softly, "come and eat."

"No." A lesser woman would have succumbed, but she was beyond reason. More than a silly sandwich was at stake; Ryder was challenging her pride.

Apparently he was prepared for her argument because he marched back to her. He settled his hands on her shoulders and tightened them just a little so she felt his fingers firmly against her flesh, but not painfully. She was conscious of an odd sensation that surged through her blood, an awareness, an exhilaration as if she'd been frozen for years and years and was only now beginning to melt.

"Sit down and eat."

She shook her head.

"My goodness, you're stubborn."

She gave him a saucy grin, hoping to mock him. She realized her mistake almost immediately—Ryder wasn't a man to be scorned. Harsh lines formed around his mouth and between his eyebrows and fire blazed from his eyes. Lynn had to do something and quick.

"Just who do you think you are?" she flared, attacking him, taking the offense rather than being forced into a defensive position. "You have no right—absolutely none—to tell me what to do."

Ryder's hold tightened on her shoulders and Lynn realized an instant later that she'd made her second tactical error. But this time she was too late to do anything about it.

"I'll tell you what gives me the right," he growled. "This." Before she knew what was happening, his mouth was on hers—his lips hard and compelling and so hot she felt singed all the way to her toes. He kissed her with a fierceness that claimed her breath. Her eyes were shut tightly and to her further humiliation, low growling sounds rose from the back of her throat that only seemed to encourage him. Lynn tried to resist—she honestly tried. Her mind scrambled with a hundred reasons why she should free herself, but it was useless. Beyond impossible. While her head was screaming at her to put an end to this madness, she slid her arms around his neck, clinging to him. She burrowed her fingers through the thick, dark hair at the back of his head, and her tongue darted in and out of his mouth in a game of cat and mouse.

Ryder slid his moist lips from hers to the scented hollow of her neck. Lynn drew in several deep, wobbly breaths in a reckless effort to regain her composure. She had melted so completely in Ryder's arms that he would have to peel her off.

"Lynn."

His harsh intake of breath gave her little satisfaction. He, too, had apparently been just as affected by their kissing.

"Yes?" Her own voice was low and gravelly.

"Why do you find it so necessary to argue with me?"

"I...I don't know."

"You're so hungry you're almost sick with it, and still you won't eat. Why?"

She shook her head, not bothering to mention that she'd cooked the frozen dinner and had every intention of suffering through that—would have, in fact, if he hadn't insisted on cooking her something else. But instead of arguing, she moved her head just a little and opened her mouth against his throat, kissing it. She felt his body tense and smiled, loving the exhilarating sensation of power the action provided her.

"I'm always cranky when I get overly hungry," she explained.

Ryder chuckled, but the sound of his amusement was tainted with chagrin. "Next time, I'll remember that."

Lynn wasn't sure she wanted him to, not when she enjoyed his methods of persuasion so much.

"Will you eat the sandwich now?"

Lynn didn't even have to think about it. "All right."

Ryder released her, and she meekly sat down at the table. She had just taken her first bite when Michelle and Marcy strolled into the kitchen.

"Hi Mom, hi, Ryder." She pulled out a chair, twisted it around and plopped herself down. "Have you told Mom about Wild Waves yet?" The question was directed to Ryder.

He frowned. "Not yet."

"What about Wild Waves?" Lynn inquired, almost afraid to ask. The water park was in the south end of Seattle and a popular recreation spot. Machine produced waves and huge slides attracted large crowds.

Michelle grinned from ear to ear in a smile that would dazzle the sun. "Ryder's taking the three of us to the park Saturday. We're going to take a whole day off and have fun like a real family, isn't that right?"

Lynn could feel the heat building up in her cheeks. Not only was Ryder dictating what she ate, but now he apparently meant to take control of her whole life.

"Michelle," Ryder said, glancing at the girl. "Maybe it would be best if you gave your mother and me some time alone."

Ten

Ryder waited until Michelle and her friend had vacated the kitchen. Lynn was irate. Her eyes flashed fire at him, but that was nothing new. She'd been in a foul mood from the moment he walked into the house with the kids. By heaven the woman could be stubborn—Ryder hadn't realized how obstinate until recently. Couldn't she see that he was only trying to help her? From the way she was acting, one would assume he'd committed some terrible crime against women's rights. From what the kids had told him, Lynn hadn't had a full day off in months, but apparently suggesting a fun outing was paramount to being a male chauvinist pig. Especially on the heels of their showdown over the sandwich.

All Ryder had wanted Lynn to do was take care of herself, and surely that wasn't so terrible. As for this Wild Waves thing, she needed a day to relax, but from the way her narrowed eyes were spitting fireballs at him, she fully intended to argue with him about this, too.

"What's this about taking Saturday off and going to Wild Waves?" Lynn demanded when he didn't immediately explain.

"I thought it might be a fun thing to do."

"I assumed you were working in a law office and understood minor things like making a living and responsibility? Obviously you think I'm independently wealthy."

"You know that's not true." He tried not to respond in like anger, but to remain coolheaded and reasonable. Apparently the food hadn't had enough time to defuse her bad mood.

"Then you assume that it's no problem for me to flutter in and out of the salon at will? Besides, the lawyers that *I* know work at least six-day weeks."

"My schedule isn't like that, and you know it." For now his workload was light. But it wouldn't always be that way. He wanted to take advantage of the summer months as best he could, using this time to court Lynn and spend time with Michelle and Jason.

"How could I possibly know anything about your schedule?" she demanded. "You show up at my place at noon, wanting to take me to lunch. Then the next thing I know, you're telling me you have Saturday free to laze away in some park." She finished the sandwich, stood and carried the empty plate to the sink, then turned to face him, her back braced against the kitchen counter. "Well, I can't take time off when I feel like it. Saturday isn't free for me and I have no intention of taking it off—I'm short-staffed as it is."

He shrugged, accepting her decision. There was little else he could do, although his disappointment was keen. "Then don't worry about it. I'll be happy to take the kids myself."

Her mouth was already open, the argument dying on her lips. "But—"

"Lynn, I thought Wild Waves was something you might enjoy as well."

"You should never have mentioned my coming in front of the kids. Now they're going to be disappointed."

He mulled that over, then nodded. "You're right." But Michelle and Jason had complained that all their mother ever did was work, suggesting a family outing had slipped out without him giving the matter the proper thought. A day completely free of worry and commitment sounded like just the thing for Lynn. Michelle and Jason both claimed she worked too hard, and Ryder was witness to the fact himself. She was driving herself toward a nervous breakdown, putting in ten-and twelve-hour days, skipping meals, and it didn't look as though she was sleeping well, either.

Ryder longed to wrap her in his arms and protect her. But holding Lynn when she was in this mood was like trying to kiss a porcupine. He could feel her bristle the minute Michelle had innocently mentioned the outing. Kissing her into submission wasn't going to work a second time. In fact, Ryder felt a bit guilty about having used that technique earlier, but she'd angered him so much that holding her had been his only weapon against her stubborn pride. For some obscure reason, he'd managed to convince himself he could control the passion between them. Wrong. The minute her sweet tongue had started teasing him, he'd been on the brink of lifting her into his arms and hauling her up those stairs. The only thing that had stopped him was the thought of Michelle and Jason bursting in on them. Thank heaven he had enough common sense to cut the kissing off when he did.

The time had come to wake up and smell the coffee. When it came to his feelings for Lynn, Ryder was playing with a lit stick of dynamite and the sooner he owned up to the fact, the better. Who did he think he was, anyway? Superman? He couldn't kiss her like that and not pay the consequences. Just the memory of the way her silky, soft body had moved against him was enough to make his mouth go dry. He'd waited all these months to claim her as his own, he could wait a little longer. When they *did* make love, and

Debbie Macomber

that was inevitable, the timing would be right, and not the result of some heated argument.

"Don't misunderstand me, I'd enjoy a day off," Lynn admitted with some reluctance, "but I just can't."

"I understand," Ryder returned, although he had trouble accepting it. He walked over to her side and placed his hands on her forearms. She stiffened, which frustrated him all the more. He dropped his arms, not wanting to force another confrontation. The day would come, he assured himself, when she would welcome his touch. For now, she was frightened and confused and in need of a good deal of patience.

"Hi Mom, hi Ryder." Jason stepped into the kitchen, set his basketball on the tabletop and leaned forward. "What's happening?"

"Nothing much," Lynn said and set her plate and glass in the dishwasher.

"You ask Mom about Wild Waves?" The question was directed to Ryder.

"She has to work, son."

Disappointment flashed from his eyes and the smile he'd been wearing folded over into a deeply set frown. "We can still go, can't we?"

"If it's all right with your mother."

"Of course it's all right," Lynn answered eagerly, as though to make up for the fact she wouldn't be with them.

Jason nodded, but none of the excitement returned. "We had a good time tonight. Ryder let me go on as many of the rides as I wanted and when that sissy Michelle was afraid to try the hammer, he went with me."

"A man's got to do what a man's got to do," Lynn joked and when she glanced in Ryder's direction, he grinned. "I'm pleased you had such a good time. I hope you remembered to properly thank Ryder."

"Of course I did." Jason pulled out a chair and folded his arms over the top of the stuffed basketball, his look thoughtful. "You took us to Wild Waves once, Mom, don't you remember? But that was when you were home. You used to do a lot of things with Michelle and me before you went to work with those fat ladies…but you don't do much of that anymore."

"I need to make a living, honey."

"I suppose," Jason returned with an elongated sigh. "But sometimes I think we were better off when we were poor."

"Jason," Lynn argued, staring at her son incredulously, as though she couldn't believe her own ears. "That's not true."

She cast Ryder a sideways glance as if she felt it was important for him to believe her. He smiled, telling her that he did.

"I'll be able to take you to Wild Waves another time."

"But when?" Jason cried. "You're always telling me about all the great things we're going to do some day and they never happen."

"Jason, you're being completely unreasonable. Why… look at what we've done this summer."

"What? What have we done this summer, Mom?"

It was apparent that Lynn was searching her memory and was surprised to discover she'd spent far less time with her children than she realized. Her expression became a study in parental guilt. Her energy level was frayed to the edges as it was, and although Ryder had intended to stay out of the discussion, he stepped to Lynn's side and slipped his arm around her shoulder, hoping to lend her his strength. She didn't appreciate the action and he dropped his arm almost immediately.

"The only place we've gone *all* summer is to the precinct picnic," Jason told her righteously.

"I think it's time for bed, Jason, don't you?" Ryder suggested. "You've got a big day at camp tomorrow."

His eyes widened and his grin blossomed, spreading from ear to ear. "Right. Do you want me to tell Marcy it's time to go home, Mom?"

Lynn shook her head. "I'll do that. Now up to bed, young man."

"Okay." He walked over and kissed her cheek, then looked at Ryder and rolled his eyes. "Women expect that kind of thing," he explained, as if it were important for Ryder to understand that he didn't take to kissing girls.

"I know."

With that, Jason traipsed up the stairs and into his room. Lynn stood with her arms folded, staring after her son as though she couldn't quite believe what had just transpired. "He always has an excuse for staying up late. I can't remember the last time he didn't argue with me over bedtime."

With Lynn so exhausted, Ryder realized it was time he left. He didn't want to go, but what he longed for wasn't important right now—Lynn's health was.

"It's time I thought about heading home." He was a bit disappointed when she didn't suggest he stay longer, and mildly annoyed when she didn't so much as walk him to the door. It was all too obvious that she was glad to be rid of him, and that dented his pride. He'd come a long way with Lynn in a short amount of time, but miles of uncharted road stretched before him. At least when he kissed her, he had her attention. That small piece of information helped ease his mind as he climbed inside his car and drove off.

The following afternoon, Lynn sat at her desk, expelled a deep breath and reached for the phone. She couldn't delay calling Ryder any longer. Her finger jabbed out the number of his office as if to punish the phone for making this conversation necessary. Silly as it sounded, Lynn preferred contacting him at Crestron and Powers. It was less personal than calling him at his apartment. She fingered his business card until the honey-voiced secretary came on the line and efficiently announced the name of the firm. Whoever she was, this woman with the peaches-and-cream voice, Lynn didn't like her.

"Could I have Ryder Matthews's office please?"

"May I ask who's calling?"

It was on the tip of Lynn's tongue to demand to know just how many women Ryder had phoning him, but she realized in the nick of time how ridiculous that would have sounded. That thought alone was enough to prove that she'd made the right decision—she *needed* a day off.

"Lynn Danfort," she answered after a moment. "If he's busy, he can return the call."

"I'll put you through," the woman purred, and Lynn resisted the urge to make a face.

"Lynn, this is a pleasant surprise." Ryder came on the line almost immediately. "What can I do for you?"

Lynn dragged herself away from her thoughts. "Ryder, hello." She felt so foolish now. "It's about Wild Waves on Saturday. I...I was wondering if it would be all right if I *did* decide to tag along." There—that hadn't been so bad. Ryder was a gracious man—he'd never given her reason to think otherwise.

"That would be great. I'd love to have you."

"I talked with my assistant, Sharon, and she said that she'd cover for me." Lynn wouldn't mention what else Sharon had said. The woman seemed to think Lynn was a first-class idiot to turn down an outing with Ryder Matthews. *Any* outing, even if it included Michelle and Jason. For her part, including the kids was the only way Lynn would agree

Debbie Macomber

to see Ryder. When it came to dealing with her late husband's best friend, she was more confused than ever. She'd thought to avoid him as much as possible. That had been her intention after he'd asked her out that first day at the precinct picnic and then later when he'd come to the salon. She'd refused him both times. But circumstances seemed to keep tossing them together.

Lynn would have liked to blame Ryder for everything that had happened, but she couldn't even salvage her pride with that. And when he'd kissed her, it had been like setting a match to a firecracker, her response was that explosive. Every time Ryder came close to her, Lynn had been left indelibly marked. In the beginning she'd tried to pass her reaction off to the fact she'd been without a man for a long time. She'd dated a bit in the past couple of years, but no one else had been able to elicit the feeling Ryder had— no one except Gary, and that frightened her.

"I'd thought we'd make a full day of it and leave about ten-thirty."

"That sounds fine to me." Sleeping in sounded glorious. "I'll pack us a picnic lunch."

"Bring lots of suntan lotion and plenty of towels."

"Right." Her enthusiasm level increased just talking about the outing. It'd been so long since she'd spent a carefree day lazing in the sun.

"I'm really looking forward to this, Ryder."

He sighed and a wealth of satisfaction hummed through the wire. "Good."

After a few words of farewell, Lynn replaced the telephone receiver, but her hand lingered on the headset. For some obscure reason she couldn't explain or understand, she had the feeling everything was going to change between her and Ryder because of this outing.

Eleven

"Mom, look!"

Lynn and about thirteen other women turned in the direction of the young voice, glancing toward the water where the youngsters were bobbing up and down on the swirling waves. It took Lynn a couple of seconds to realize the boy's voice hadn't belonged to Jason.

The minute the four of them had arrived at Wild Waves, Jason had hit the water like the marines attacking Normandy beach and had yet to come out almost two hours later. Every now and again, Lynn saw him sitting atop his brightly colored tube, riding the swelling waters as if he were master of the seas. To say he loved the waterworks park would be an understatement.

Michelle, on the other hand, had spent an hour fixing her hair before Ryder had arrived. When Lynn had been silly enough to mention that all that mousse would be wasted once she got wet, Michelle had given her a look that suggested Lynn was brain dead. Later Michelle explained that she was styling her hair in case she happened to run into someone she knew. This "someone" was obviously a boy.

"It couldn't be a more perfect day had we planned it,"

Lynn told Ryder, who was lying back on the blanket, his face turned to the sun, his eyes closed. He'd recently walked out of the pool and his lean muscular length glistened in the bright golden light.

"I *did* plan it," he joked. "I told the person in charge of weather that we needed sunshine today. One word from me and it was arranged."

"It seems I've underestimated your influence." Her voice was teasing, but she couldn't disguise her pleasure. Ryder had been right; she needed this, far more than she'd been willing to admit. "Do you have anything else arranged that I should know about?"

A slow, easy smile worked its way across his face. "As a matter of fact, I do, but I'm saving that for later." He opened his eyes and looked up at her, his grin devilish and filled with boyish charm. "I suggest you be prepared."

"For what?"

He giggled his eyebrows up and down several times.

Despite the effort not to, Lynn laughed. It felt so good to throw caution to the wind and leave her worries behind her at least for this one day. She hadn't so much as called Sharon to see how things were going at the salon. If there were problems, she didn't want to know about them. It was amazing how comfortable it felt to bury her head in the sand—or in this case, the water.

"Mom, I'm starved."

This time the voice was unmistakably Jason's. Lynn twisted around and found her son wading out of the deep blue water, his inner tube under one arm and a snorkel in the other.

Lynn straightened and reached for the picnic basket, and small cooler which were loaded with goodies. She brought out a turkey sandwich and a cold can of soda.

Jason fell to his knees and automatically reached for the soda. "Gee, this is fun. Did you see the wave I just took?"

"I...can't say that I did," Lynn admitted. She set out the potato chips and fresh fruit—seedless grapes were Jason's favorite, and she'd packed several large bunches.

"Where's Michelle?" Ryder asked, looking toward the slide area.

"The last time I saw her, she was talking to some guy," Jason told him in a disgruntled voice. "She's hardly been in the water all day. I asked her about it and she got all huffy and told me to get lost. Personally, I think she's afraid of getting her hair wet." He said this with a sigh and a meaningful shrug as if to suggest Lynn arrange intensive counseling for her oldest child. Between bites, Jason added. "I don't think I'll ever understand girls."

"I gave up trying years ago," Ryder admitted.

"Then why do we have anything to do with them?"

Her son was completely serious. "Jason! What a thing to ask."

"*You're* all right, Mom," he was quick to assure her. "It's all the others. Look at Michelle—here we are at the neatest water place in the whole world and she's afraid to go in past her knees because she's doesn't want to splash her hair. It's ridiculous, don't you think?"

"No," Lynn shot back. Michelle was at an age when maintaining her looks was important to her. That was all part of growing up. Within a few years, Jason was sure to experience the same level of conscientiousness. She was sure he wouldn't find it quite so silly then.

"If you'll notice, your mother hasn't spent much time in the water, either," Ryder pointed out. He sat up and shot Lynn a mischievous grin.

"You're worried about your hair, too?" Jason cried as though he couldn't believe his ears. "My own mother!"

"Not exactly."

"Then how come you've only been in the pool a little bit?"

It was more a matter of crowd control. When Lynn first arrived, she'd taken out an inflated raft and had been quickly overpowered by what seemed like several thousand kids, each one eager to ride the waves. All those thrashing bodies had gotten in her way. She simply needed more space.

"Mom?" Jason asked, a second time. "Explain yourself."

Lynn laughed. "There are too many kids out there."

"Too many kids," Jason repeated, stunned.

"I go in and cool off when I get too hot, but other than that I prefer to lie in the sun and perfect my tan."

It looked as though Jason was about to make another derogatory comment referring to her wanting a golden tan. To divert his attention, she took out a package of potato chips and handed them to him. Her tactic worked, and within a minute the boy was too busy wolfing down his lunch to care how much time she spent in the water. As soon as he'd finished eating, he was off again, eager to return to his fun.

Kneeling in front of the picnic basket, Lynn closed the lid and picked up the discarded bits of litter left over from her son's lunch.

"You're getting sun-burned," Ryder commented wryly.

She paused and glanced down at her arm, but didn't notice any appreciable difference.

"You'd better put on some sunscreen before you get burned." He reached for her hand, lifting her arm as if to examine it. "Let me put it on for you."

"No," she returned automatically. All day she'd taken pains to avoid any type of physical contact with Ryder, even the most innocent of touches. The thought of him sliding his hands up and down her shoulders and over her back was enough to flash huge red warning lights inside her head. This was something to be avoided at any cost.

"Lynn, you're being silly. You aren't used to all this sun."

"I'm fine," she said, fighting the tingling awareness of his fingers holding on to hers. She couldn't allow herself to get too close to Ryder, fearing the power he had to control her body's responses. She tugged at her hand, wanting to free herself before she sought a deeper contact. But Ryder wouldn't release her. Instead he lifted her hand to his mouth and pressed a soft, lingering kiss to its back. His tongue flickered out, moistening the tender skin there. Lynn's heart leaped into her throat at the sensual contact. His eyes, staring at her over her wrist, seemed to convey a thousand words. There were emotions he had yet to verbalize, matters she wasn't prepared to accept. Lynn found herself mesmerized by his dark brown eyes; she couldn't have pulled away had her life depended on it. The world she'd so carefully constructed since Ryder's absence was about to crumple at her feet and yet she dared to linger. Her heart was pounding so hard, she thought it might damage her rib cage.

She managed to pull her gaze from his, dropping it, but to her dismay, she encountered the crisp curling hairs and the hard muscles of his chest. The overwhelming desire to run her fingers through those dark hairs was akin to a physical blow. Ryder's uneven breathing told her he was equally affected by her merest touch. If anything, that increased Lynn's already heightened awareness of him and their situation. With an incredible surge of inner strength, she pulled away and stood abruptly—so abruptly, she nearly stumbled.

"I...think I'll go in the pool for a little bit," she said in a voice that trembled.

Lynn couldn't get away fast enough.

Ryder watched Lynn go with an overpowering sense of frustration. He'd tried being patient with her; he'd taken pains to make this outing as relaxed as possible. From the minute he'd arrived at the house, Ryder recognized that Lynn had carefully chosen to play the role of a good friend. It was obvious that she didn't want to experience the things he made her feel. Apparently she wanted to pretend they'd never kissed, and ignore the fact she'd come to life in his arms. Not once, but twice. It had been difficult, but Ryder had played along, falling into her scheme—for her sake, certainly not because that was the way he wanted it. All along, his intention had been to give Lynn the time she needed to relax and enjoy herself. He didn't want to spoil it by making emotional demands on her. Any kind of demands.

But she was driving him crazy. She'd worn a demure one-piece swimsuit, although he was certain she owned more than one bikini. But the modest suit did little to disguise her magnificent body. If anything, it boldly emphasized every luscious curve of her womanly shape. He hadn't thought it was possible to desire her any more than he already did, but watching her move in that swimsuit came close to driving him crazy.

Ryder's fingers ached with the need to caress her. When he'd reached for her hand, he felt her involuntary reaction to his touch. She'd shivered slightly. The ache in him increased with the memory and he drew a deep breath in an effort to minimize his body's response. The problem was she was so beautiful, with her wind tousled hair and her sweet face devoid of any makeup. There wasn't a woman alive who could compete with her.

Now, like a frightened rabbit, she was running away from him. His instinct was to reach out and grab her, keep her at his side, demand that she listen to all the love he had stored up in his heart for her. But he couldn't do that, couldn't express all this emotion that burned within his chest. To do so could frighten her into running blindly into the night and if he let that happen, he might never be able to catch her.

Patience, he told himself, repeating the word over and over in his mind.

Lynn's escape into the water had nothing to do with the sun. She'd gone swimming in an effort to cool down from being so close to Ryder. His touch, although light and impersonal, could be compared to falling into a lava bed, Lynn mused. She felt the heat rising in her all the way from the soles of her feet, sweeping through her body like a brushfire out of control. The only thing left for her to do was flee. There weren't nearly as many kids in the water as there had been earlier. She waded out until she was waist deep and still she didn't feel any of the cooling effect she sought. She went deeper and deeper until she had no choice but to dip her head beneath the water's churning surface. The liquid seemed to sizzle against her red-hot face. Dear heaven, if only she knew what was happening to her.

She swam underwater until her lungs felt as though they were about to burst. Breaking the surface, she drew in huge gulps of oxygen and brushed the long, wet strands of hair away from her face with both hands.

"Jason would be proud of you." The voice was all too familiar.

"Ryder." She opened her eyes and issued his name on

a husky murmur, surprised that he'd been able to find her in the huge pool.

"Lynn, don't keep running from me," his low voice pleaded with her.

Her eyes rounded and she stared at him so long she forgot to breathe. She opened her mouth to deny the fact she was trying to escape, but found she couldn't force the lie.

"Watch out."

Even before the words had completely left his mouth, Lynn was caught in a giant swell of water. Her feet flew out from under her and she was tossed about as easily as a leaf floating in an autumn breeze. A strong pair of hands slipped around her waist and righted her. Led by instinct, she reached out and held on.

Lynn and Ryder broke the surface together, clinging to each other.

"Are you all right?"

"Fine," she said automatically, not pausing to check otherwise.

"I didn't see it coming until the wave was on top of us."

He continued to hold her, bringing her so close to his body that Lynn was amazed the brief span of water between them wasn't boiling and spitting. She'd felt so strongly drawn to Ryder. In that moment, she had as much power to resist him as a stickpin would have against a magnet. Her hands were braced against the sides of his neck and she realized, too late, that she'd reached blindly for him, sensing she would be utterly safe in his arms.

Wordlessly he bent toward her, ever so slightly, and she began to stroke his neck, slipping her hands down the water-slickened muscles of his shoulders, reveling in the strength she sensed beneath her fingertips.

She was unsure of the exact moment it had happened, but

a warm, reeling awareness took control of her will, leaving her almost giddy in its wake. Without her knowing exactly how he'd managed to do it, Ryder wrapped his arms fully around her, pressing her to the long, hard length of him. She trembled, fitting snugly into his embrace, powerfully aware of the place where his fingers touched her skin. A tingling sensation spread out from his hands in rippling waves that flooded every cell of her body. Swamped with countless emotions, Lynn didn't know which one to respond to first. Confused, flustered and so completely lost in awareness, she buried her face in the hollow of his neck while she struggled within herself. She drew in several deep, shaking breaths, hoping those would help to clear her head.

While he held her firmly around her waist, he combed her hair away from her face in a slow, soothing action. "I'm never going to leave you again," he whispered. "I couldn't bear it a second time."

Lynn longed to tell him it wasn't his leaving that had confused her so much as his coming back. Her fuddled brain tried to formulate the words, but the thoughts cluttered in her mind. She couldn't think while he continued with his gentle caress. She gasped softly in protest when he slipped his hand from her hair down to her shoulders and back.

She opened her mouth and instantly became aware of his chest hair. The curly, dark hairs had fascinated her earlier and she now realized how close they were to her mouth. Common sense was highly overrated, Lynn decided recklessly, and let her tongue investigate the throbbing hollow of his neck. He tasted like salt and water, pleasant beyond belief. Her mouth opened further, hungrily exploring his skin as if he were a delectable feast, as indeed he was.

"Lynn." Her name was ground out between his teeth.

She ignored the plea in his voice. This was what he

wanted, why he'd swum out to find her. It was what she'd longed for all day and had tried desperately to avoid.

She continued pressing kisses up the strong cord of his neck, lapping him with her tongue, and giving him tiny love bites.

He tightened his arms around her. He was moving, carrying her through the water, but Lynn hardly noticed. When she happened to glance up, she noted that he'd found a secluded corner away from the rush of swimmers. She kissed the edge of his mouth to voice her approval. She nipped his earlobe, loving the way his body tensed with the action. He braced his feet farther apart as though expecting an assault.

Lynn gave him one.

She took his earlobe into her mouth, her tongue fluttering in and around, sucking, tasting, nibbling. A sense of hot pleasure flashed through her at the way his pulse exploded against her chest.

He groaned once, softly, and the sound excited her more than anything she'd ever known. He wove his fingers into her hair and she heard his harsh, ragged breath as he gently pulled her away from him. Lynn wasn't given more than a second to catch her breath before he took her mouth with a greed that defied anything she'd ever experienced.

Another wave assaulted them, but Lynn couldn't have cared less and apparently neither did Ryder. They were swept off their feet, tossed and rolled and still they relentlessly clung to each other. When they broke the surface, Ryder helped them back into a standing position. Briefly they broke apart, but he wouldn't allow it for long and kissed her again with a ravenous passion; he seemed to want to devour her whole. Lynn responded with everything that was in her. Her mouth opened to him like the sun coaxing open a flower bud. Lynn thought she would die from pure bliss.

He lifted her against his body, holding on to her as if her life were at stake. As her body slipped intimately over his, he groaned anew. "Oh, Lynn."

Her arms were completely around his neck, her fingers digging mindlessly into his tense shoulder muscles. "I know," she cried. "This isn't the time or the place." They were in a public place, although she doubted that anyone had noticed them.

"I want you," he growled into her ear.

She smiled and rubbed her foot down the back of his thigh. "Tell me you want me, too. I need to hear it."

What seemed like an eternity passed before she was willing to admit it. Why it should be so difficult to tell him what couldn't be any more obvious was beyond her comprehension.

"Lynn…"

"Yes," she groaned. "Yes, I want you."

He expelled his breath, then leaned his forehead against hers. "I don't dare kiss you," he whispered. "I'm afraid I won't be able to stop."

"I…feel the same way."

"I want to touch you so much. I swear there isn't a place on my whole body that isn't aching. If this is the flu, then it's the worst case I've ever had."

Lynn grinned and lightly brushed her lips over his mouth, needing to touch him, ignoring the consequences. "I'll have you know, Ryder Matthews, it's not very flattering to be compared to the flu."

"I don't suppose you'd care to being likened to the bubonic plague then, either?"

"That's even worse." Lynn was teasing him, but she was experiencing the same level of frustration. "Should we get out of the water?" she suggested next, looking for a means of easing this self-inflicted torture.

Ryder grinned. "I don't think we… I dare."

"Do you want to swim?"

"No," he growled. "I want to make love to you."

Having him say it so bluntly had a curious effect upon Lynn. The blood drained out of her face and she felt weak and shaky. Ryder must have noticed because his eyes searched her face, his love-thirsty eyes drinking from her.

"Certainly that doesn't shock you?" he asked gently.

"No," she lowered her gaze and took in a calming breath before explaining. "It's just that…it's been a long time for me. I feel like a virgin all over again. I suppose that sounds crazy considering the fact I was married several years and bore two children."

"When it comes to you, I *am* crazy."

Her eyes flew to him. "You are?"

He nodded. "But, Lynn, I already know how very good it's going to be for us."

Lynn did, too. After years of living without a husband, years in which she denied feeling anything sexual, she experienced an awesome passion building within her, like a volcano threatening to explode.

She couldn't keep her hands still. She stroked and caressed his face, loving the feel of his hard jaw, the gentle rasp of his beard and the moist heat of his mouth. When she couldn't hold back any longer, she nuzzled his throat, licking him with the fever that burned within her.

He kissed her again as though he'd been waiting years and was starving for the taste of her. "When?" she rasped when his mouth slid from hers. "Ryder, oh, please tell me when." She couldn't believe she was being so forward.

He went still. "When? What do you mean *when*?"

With her hands braced on each side of his jaw, she continued her loving assault. "I want to know how long it will be before we make love. Tonight?" She was shaking so badly that if Ryder hadn't been holding on to her she would have sank to the bottom of the pool. "Oh, no," she groaned, "what about the kids? We're going to have to be so careful." Her lips slid across his cheek and lightly brushed over his lips, darting her tongue in and out of his mouth. "Your place would be better. I think—"

"Lynn…"

"I'm not on the pill, either… I hadn't counted on anything like this…ever. What should we do?"

He tensed. "Why?"

"Oh, Ryder, please, think about it. There are going to be problems with this…minor ones, but we can solve them, I know we can." Once more she angled her mouth over his, feeding him with soft, nibbling kisses, feeding herself, unable to get enough of him. "First of all, I don't think it would be a good idea for Michelle and Jason to know what we're doing. They're young and impressionable and I—"

"Lynn, stop," he interrupted, his voice controlled enough for her to grow still.

Slowly she raised her head. It took her a couple of moments to realize how serious he was. She didn't understand. Some of the excitement and happiness drained from her. "What's wrong?"

"I want to know why you want to make love." he asked her, his gaze never wavering from her face.

"Why?" she repeated, stunned. "Do you always ask a woman that kind of question?" She didn't know what was happening, but whatever it was confused her.

"I know what your body is feeling, trust me, love, I feel

it, too. All I want you to do is give me one good reason why you're doing this."

"You know the answer to that." She loosened her hold from around his neck and braced her hands against his shoulders, feeling incredibly foolish now.

"I don't know the answer."

"Well…"

"Because it feels good?" he offered.

She leaped on that excuse and nodded eagerly. "Yes."

He closed his eyes as though she'd lashed out at him and when he opened them again an emotion she couldn't decipher flickered there.

"That's not enough for me," he told her with heavy reluctance. "I wish it was, but it isn't."

"Why isn't it?" she cried. It was enough for her…at least it had been until a few moments ago. She couldn't understand why Ryder was being so unreasonable. One minute he was whispering how much he wanted to make love to her and the next he was making her sound heartless and mercenary.

"I'm not looking for a woman to make me 'feel good.'"

He started to say more, but Lynn wouldn't let him, she dropped her arms and stepped back from him. Water lapped against her and when a large wave came on them, she rode it without a problem.

"If this is a joke, I'm not the least bit amused." Her intention was to sound sarcastic and flippant, but her voice broke. She jerked her chin a notch higher.

"Lynn, please," Ryder whispered, "don't look at me like that."

In response, she twisted away from him, feeling hurt and rejected. Only a minute before she'd come right out and admitted that there hadn't been anyone since Gary. Ryder knew she wasn't…loose, and yet he made her feel callous and coldhearted as if she made this type of arrangement with every man she felt the least bit attracted to.

"I don't know what you want from me," she murmured.

Several moments passed before he answered her, and when he did, his voice was filled with resignation. "No, I don't suppose you do. But you'll figure it out soon enough, and when you do I'll be waiting." That said, he swam away with clean, hard strokes.

Lynn watched him go and noted that he seemed to want to punish the water for what had just happened between them.

Exhausted, Ryder continued to pump his arms until his muscles quivvered and ached. He was as far away from Lynn as it was possible to get in the crowded swimming area. There wasn't any need to push himself further.

He loved Lynn, wanted her more than he'd ever longed for anything in his life. She'd wanted him, too. She was on fire for him. He hadn't dared to dream she would feel this strongly for him. But he didn't want a physical relationship with her that wasn't rooted in commitment. Her talk about keeping their affair a secret from the kids had been bad enough, but dragging up the subject of birth control was more than he could take. In the blink of an eye, he'd gone from aroused and eager to confused and irritated. He didn't want a casual affair with Lynn. He was looking for more from her than a few stolen moments together to ease the explosive physical need they felt for each other.

He wanted her, all right, but on his own terms. When they made love, there wouldn't be any questions left unanswered, nor would there be any secrets.

Soon enough, she would know what he wanted. Lynn

was too smart not to figure it out. He pleaded with heaven to make it soon because he couldn't take much more of this.

Lynn dried herself off with a thick beach towel, then reached for a light cotton blouse. Her fingers didn't want to cooperate and buttoning it seemed to take a half a lifetime. She was confused and angry and frustrated and excited. Each emotion demanded attention, and in response she ignored them all, making busywork around their picnic site. She folded the towels, and laid out the wet ones to dry, then she picked up a few pieces of litter. When she'd finished, she lay down on her stomach on the blanket and tried to sleep. Naturally that was impossible, but Ryder didn't need to know that. When he returned, she wanted him to think she'd simply forgotten what had happened in the water, and she'd put the entire incident behind her.

She heard him about ten minutes later and forcibly closed her eyes. He reached for a towel, that much she was able to ascertain by the sounds coming from behind her. Then she heard the cooler open and a soda can being opened. That was followed by the unmistakable rustle of him peeling the wrapping off a sandwich.

She frowned, marveling that he was able to overlook what had happened in the pool and sit down and eat. Her stomach was in turmoil and food was the last thing she cared about now.

When she couldn't stand it any longer, Lynn rolled onto her back. Shading her eyes with her forearm, she stared up to discover Michelle sitting at the picnic table.

"Hi, Mom. I thought you were asleep."

"Hi," Lynn greeted, feeling chagrined.

"This sure is a lot of fun. I've met some really awesome…people."

Lynn grinned, knowing exactly which sex these "people" probably were. "I'm glad, sweetie." She hadn't finished speaking when Ryder strolled up and reached for his towel, wiping the water from his face.

"I'm going back to my friends, now," Michelle said and stuffed the rest of her sandwich back inside the wicker basket.

"I'll be back in an hour," Michelle called and was off.

"Bye," Lynn called after her daughter, dreading the confrontation with Ryder more than anything she could remember. So much depended on what he was about to say.

Slowly he dropped the towel away from his face and gazed directly at her. "Are you all right?"

"Sure," she answered with a hysterical little laugh. "Why shouldn't I be?"

Twelve

A week passed and Ryder was amazed at all the ways Lynn invented in order to avoid him. She seemed absolutely determined to forget he existed. It would've been comical if Ryder didn't love her so much and long to put matters right between them. He knew beyond doubt the reason she was doing back flips in an effort to escape him. In the full light of reason, when her head wasn't muddled with passion and need, Lynn was probably thoroughly ashamed of their wanton behavior in the pool. Ryder had been delighted by her ready response. Her kisses had been ravenous, undisciplined and carnal. Every time Ryder thought about the way she blossomed in his arms, he trembled with aftershocks. The memory was like standing too close to an incinerator—he burned with a need she'd created in him.

Ryder cursed himself now for rejecting her offer to make love…for refusing himself. But he sought more than the release her body could give him, wanted more than to become Lynn's lover.

He yearned for her heart.

The realization had left him perplexed, and in some ways stunned him. Earlier—before the incident at the water park—he would gladly have accepted what she'd so guile-lessly offered him. She didn't love him, he realized, but she would soon enough. When it came right down to it, he didn't need the words. He loved her enough for the both of them.

But something powerful and deeply rooted within his conscience had stopped him from making love to Lynn, some sentiment he had yet to name. All he did know was that sleeping with her wouldn't be enough to satisfy him.

If Ryder was bewildered by the extent of his emotional need for Lynn, it was nothing compared to what she seemed to be experiencing. He hungered to talk to her, but when he'd phoned her at the salon and later at the house, she'd asked, both times, that a message be taken and then hadn't bothered to return his calls. He'd tried twice more, but on each occasion, she'd come up with a convenient excuse to avoid talking to him.

He'd gone so far as to stop in at her salon only to be told that she was too busy to see to him then. He was told that if he would be willing to wait a couple of hours, she would try to squeeze him in, but there weren't any guarantees. Frustrated and angry, he'd quickly left.

Next, Ryder phoned Michelle and Jason and took them to a movie, thinking he would surely see Lynn when he dropped them off at the house. But she'd exasperated him once more. When he'd gone to pick them up, Michelle had explained that they needed to be taken to Toni Morris's after the movie. His frustration had reached its peak that night.

Since Lynn seemed to require more time to sort out what was happening between them, Ryder reluctantly decided to give it to her. When she was ready, she would contact him. But there was a limit to his patience and it was fast running out.

* * *

Lynn parked her car outside Toni Morris's house and sat quietly for a couple of minutes, gathering her nerve before talking to her friend. Toni wouldn't let her pussyfoot around the issue, and Lynn knew that. She trusted Toni's insights, and sought her wisdom now.

Lynn's nervous fingers tightened around the steering wheel and she released her breath on a swell of anxiety and defeat.

"Lynn," Toni greeted, when she answered the door. "This is a pleasant surprise. Come in."

Lynn nervously brushed the hair from her forehead. "Have you got a minute? I mean if this is a bad time I could come back later."

Toni laughed. "I was looking for a reason not to mow the lawn. I should thank you for stopping by unexpectedly like this. At least I'll have an excuse when Joe gets home."

Lynn made a gallant effort to smile, followed Toni into the kitchen and nodded when the former policewoman motioned toward the coffeepot.

"So how are things developing with Ryder?"

Lynn nearly choked on the hot coffee. Leave it to Toni to cut through the small talk.

"Fine…he's been wonderful to the kids."

"I'm talking about *you* and Ryder," Toni pressed.

"Fine," she answered quickly…too quickly, calling herself the coward she was.

"I see." The two words were riddled with sarcasm. Toni pulled out the chair opposite Lynn and sat down. The air seemed to crackle with tension until Toni added, "How much longer are you planning to avoid him?"

Lynn's jaw flopped open. "How'd…you know?"

Toni's answering smile was fleeting. "Michelle made

some comment about not knowing why Ryder had to drop the two of them off at my place when you were supposed to be home. And frankly, you didn't do a good job of avoiding me that night, either."

"Why is it everything I do is so transparent?" Lynn asked, throwing her hands into the air. She felt like a witless adolescent.

"It's not as bad as you think," Toni answered with a saucy grin. "I know you, that's all." Toni took a couple of seconds to stir sugar into her coffee. "When was the last time you saw Ryder?"

"It's been over two weeks now."

"Did you argue?"

Lynn dropped her gaze so fast, she feared she'd strained her neck muscles. "In…a manner of speaking. He tried to call me several times, and stopped by the salon once, but I…I was busy."

Toni snickered softly at that bit of information. "When was the last time you heard from him?"

"Nine days ago."

"And you're ready to deal with whatever is happening?"

Lynn nodded. She'd been ready for almost a week, but Ryder hadn't contacted her. It was as if he'd dropped off the face of the earth. The first few days after their outing, she would have preferred death to confronting Ryder. Now she felt lost and terribly lonely without his friendship. Noise violated her from every direction, but the silence was killing her. In the past week, Lynn had been short-tempered with the kids, restless and uneasy at work. It was as though she'd walked into a giant void. Nothing felt right anymore. Nothing felt good.

"He's waiting for you to come to him."

The thought immobilized Lynn. She froze, the coffee cup

raised halfway to her mouth. It was one thing to be willing to talk to Ryder, but to contact him herself demanded a special kind of courage. If she knew what to say, and how to say it, it would help matters considerably, but all she could think about was how much heat there'd been in the way she'd kissed him and pleaded with him to make love to her.

Just the memory of that afternoon was enough to raise her body's temperature by several degrees. She'd practically begged Ryder to make love to her. She'd thought that was what he'd wanted, too, but then he'd told her that wasn't enough. The way he'd acted led her to believe she'd insulted him. She couldn't understand that, either. Ryder had admitted he wanted her, and yet he'd been totally unreasonable. When she'd brought up Michelle and Jason and the need for some form of birth control, he'd backed away as if she'd slapped him.

"Well?" Toni demanded.

"You think I should be the one to call him?"

"That's why you're here isn't it?"

"I…I don't know." She set down the mug and wiped a hand over her face, feeling tense and ill at ease. "Ryder makes me feel again and, Toni, that frightens me. Just thinking about him causes me to get all nervous and hyper. I wish he'd never come back and, in the same moment, I thank God he did. I'm so scared."

"Why?"

"If I knew that I wouldn't be sitting here with my knees knocking," Lynn cried, irritated by the way her friend continued to toss questions at her. "I don't like the way I feel around Ryder. I was comfortable the way things were before."

"You were miserable."

"I wasn't."

Toni's responding grin was off center. "That's not the story I got the day of the precinct picnic. You told me how you weren't sleeping well and how restless you'd become over the past several months."

Lynn tried to argue, but knew it was useless. Toni was right. Leaning back in her chair, her friend reached for the telephone receiver on the kitchen wall and handed it to Lynn. "Go ahead. I'll conveniently disappear and you can talk to your heart's content."

"But—"

"I hear the lawn calling to me now," Toni joked. She braced her hands against the table's edge and scooted back her seat. "I'm out of here."

"Toni, please, I don't know what to say."

"You'll think of something."

As it turned out, Lynn didn't need to come up with anything brilliant to start the conversation. Ryder was out of the office and when she tried his apartment, she got voice mail. She left a message on it, hating the way her voice wavered and pitched when she was trying so hard to sound cheerful and happy as though she'd contacted him every day of the week. She could only imagine what Ryder would think when he listened to it. Given the chance she would have gladly called back and erased the message, but it wasn't possible.

Toni glanced up expectantly and turned off the mower when Lynn came out of the house.

"He wasn't at the office or at his apartment," Lynn explained. "I…left a message so stop looking at me like I'm some kind of coward."

"If the shoe fits, my friend…" Toni laughed.

It was almost midnight and Ryder still hadn't returned her call. Hours before Lynn had given up expecting to hear from him. She was getting a taste of her own medicine and the flavor was definitely bitter. Depression settled over her shoulders like a heavy homemade quilt. Ryder was through with her and she had no one to blame but herself.

Forcing her attention away from the clock, Lynn focused on the ledger that was spread across the kitchen table. She tightened her fingers around the pencil until it threatened to snap in half. She'd gone over these figures so many times that the numbers had started to bleed together. No matter how many different ways she tried, nothing added up the way it should. Maintaining her own books for Slender, Too shouldn't be this complicated. She'd taken bookkeeping in high school and was familiar with the double-entry system, and yet...like everything else this summer, nothing was working out the way she planned.

Okay, so she'd blown it with Ryder. The disappointment was keen, but she'd suffered through disappointment before. It hurt, but it wasn't fatal. In many ways she was grateful to him. He'd waltzed into her life at a critical moment. She'd worked so hard in the past three years, seeking contentment in her children and her job, paying the price and never questioning the cost. In a few short weeks, Ryder had done something no other man had been able to do in a long time. He'd awakened her to the fact that she was a woman—a warm, generous woman made to feel and love. Since Gary's death, she'd done everything within her power to ignore that part of herself.

The sound of the front door opening caught her by surprise. Lynn leaped to her feet and met Ryder in the entryway. The sight of him bolted her to the floor.

"I would have knocked, but I didn't think you'd open the door once you saw it was me," he accused her, his voice filled with cynicism.

"That's not true—" She glanced up the stairs, grateful that Michelle and Jason were sound asleep.

"I doubt that," he shouted. "You've done everything you could to avoid me in the past two weeks and I'm fed up with it."

"There's no reason to shout." He'd been drinking, but he wasn't anywhere close to being drunk. He knew exactly what he was saying and doing, but that didn't reassure her any.

"I happen to feel there is. How much longer do you plan to bury your head in the sand?"

"If you think you can stand here and insult me, then let me assure you, you'd be doing us both a favor if you left."

"You can forget that."

Lynn refused to answer him. She whirled around and returned to the kitchen. She seated herself at the table and reached for the calculator. To her dismay, Ryder followed her inside.

He stood there silently for several moments, then twisted the ledger around and ran his gaze down the pale green sheet. "What's this?"

"The books for the salon. Not that it's any of your business."

"It's almost midnight."

"I'm well aware of the time, thank you," Lynn answered primly.

"Why are you working on those?"

She couldn't very well admit that she hadn't been able to sleep…hadn't even tried because she was mooning over her relationship with him. Working on balancing her books helped keep her mind off how she'd messed everything up between them.

"I'm not leaving until you answer me," Ryder demanded.

"I enjoy doing my own books."

He sniggered at that. "Sure you do. It's midnight."

"I…couldn't sleep."

"Why not?"

"That's none of your business." At all costs, she avoided looking in his direction.

"You don't need to answer that," he told her crisply. "I already know. You were thinking about me, weren't you? Regretting our day together and how you'd moved your body over mine in the water. You're wishing now you hadn't been so blatant in your wants. You're thinking that maybe I would have made love to you if you'd been a little more subtle."

His arrogance nettled her beyond belief. "Of all the nerve! You're vulgar, Ryder."

"Do you honestly believe I didn't know how much you wanted me?"

"Stop it," she cried, feeling her cheeks fill with flaming color.

"Honey, you wanted me so badly you practically burned me alive. I'm still smoldering two weeks later."

A husky denial burned on her lips. She *had* wanted him, but she would never admit it. Not now, when he was throwing the matter in her face, forcing her to deal with her body's response to him. Lynn preferred to forget the entire incident and go on with their relationship as though nothing had happened. But from the way he was looking at her, she realized the likelihood of that happening was slim.

Ryder turned her around, secured her jaw with one hand and lowered his mouth to hers.

Lynn struggled, but all her efforts only succeeded in exhausting her strength. When flinging her arms against his hard chest, and arching her back didn't help, she pressed her lips firmly together. When she relaxed ever so slightly, he outlined the shape of her lips with the tip of his tongue until her moans of anger and outrage became soft gasps of bliss. Finally, without any force from him, her mouth parted, and she gave herself over to his kiss.

"That's the way, Lynn," he praised her. "Enjoy it, love, enjoy it. Be honest, to yourself and to me."

His words were all the encouragement she needed. She folded her arms around his neck and without her being certain how he managed it, he lifted her from the chair and seated himself, setting her in his lap.

He broke off the kiss and his breath was warm and moist as it drifted over her upturned face. He smelled of expensive whiskey and she realized that was what she'd been tasting and loving. He didn't need to apply any pressure for her to welcome him a second time..

His breathing was as rapid and as unsteady as her own when Ryder finished kissing her. With his gaze holding hers, he worked at the buttons of her shirt. His fingers were trembling. "You wanted this the other day, too, and I wanted to give it to you."

Too late, Lynn realized his intent. "Ryder, please don't," she begged. "I don't like it when you touch me. We shouldn't be doing this—"

He ignored her small cry of protest, obviously recognizing her lie, and pushed the shirt from her shoulders. Her intention had been to tell him to stop, to deny the incredible sensations that washed over her like a tidal wave. He wanted her to own up to her feelings, and still she held back, furious with him for forcing her to confront her emotions and even more furious with herself for wanting him so much.

"You wanted me to do this the other day, didn't you?" he whispered, coaxing the truth from her.

Lynn refused to answer him.

"Didn't you?" he demanded a second time.

"No," she lied, denying him the satisfaction of the truth.

His eyes filled with disappointment, but he wouldn't be denied and it showed in the look he gave her. "Somehow, I don't believe you."

It wasn't until he spoke and his moist breath settled over her that Lynn whimpered.

"You want something more now too, don't you?" he asked her softly, then added, "I'll give it to you, Lynn, all you have to do is be honest with me."

She would die before she would tell him what she was feeling.

He must have seen the determination in her eyes because he laughed softly and tormented her with kisses up and down the side of her neck until she was squirming and rolling her head from side to side.

"Please," she begged, when she couldn't bear it any longer.

"Please what?"

She moaned.

"Ask me, Lynn." His own voice contained a thread of pleading.

"No," she whimpered her refusal.

"That's not what I want to hear. Do you want me, Lynn? Do you?"

"Yes, Ryder…yes." A sob tore through her throat while he poised his mouth over hers.

Thirteen

Somehow Ryder was able to move away from Lynn. He walked over to the kitchen sink, braced his hot hands against the cool ledge and closed his eyes to the torment that racked him. He hadn't wanted to push her like that, but he needed to force her to take responsibility for her own desires. She was an expert at avoiding her feelings. Every cell of his own body demanded release, every fiber of his being sought completion with her, but he couldn't allow himself to give in to his baser instincts. Not like this. Not now.

He'd been a fool to come to her this way. An angry fool. His actions may have caused him to lose the only woman he'd ever loved. Ever would love.

"Are you angry with me again?" Lynn asked, in a voice that trembled with distress.

Her soft pleading stabbed through his soul. Slowly he turned to face Lynn. "No."

She'd fastened her blouse, but her eyes were filled with despair and longing. Ryder tightened his hands into fists of resolve. "I shouldn't have come here tonight. If anyone deserves an apology, it's you. I had no right to say and do those things to you."

Slowly Lynn lowered her gaze. "You were right about me not being able to sleep because I was thinking of you. I spent half the night hoping you'd answer my call."

"Answer your call?"

Her face shot upward. "You mean you didn't get my message? I left you a voice mail."

Defeated, Ryder rubbed a hand across his weary face. All this hopelessness, this overwhelming sense of frustration could have been eliminated if he'd gone home when he was finished at the office the way he should have. Instead he'd walked along the Seattle waterfront, depressed and discouraged. Later he'd sat in some uptown bar and found courage at the bottom of a bottle. He felt sick with himself now. He'd come to Lynn for all the wrong reasons, intent on forcing her to accept her feelings for him—whatever they were.

Frustration filled his mouth. He couldn't look at her, didn't dare for fear of what he would see in her eyes. The only thing left to do was leave, and pray she would find it in her heart to forgive him.

He started for the front door when she called him.

"Ryder?"

He stopped, as though waiting for her instructions. He felt completely at her mercy. If she were to tell him to stay out of her life, he would have no recourse but to do as she asked. His intent had been to crush her, to bend her to his will. His higher intentions couldn't overcome his actions. When he remembered the way he'd tormented her, there could be no forgiveness. None.

He heard the sound of her chair as she stood. Still he didn't move, couldn't have even if the fate of the entire world rested on his actions.

She placed a hand on his elbow, then abruptly dropped it.

"I was wondering…" Her voice was little more than a whisper. "I know it's probably more than what you want, but…"

"Yes," he coaxed, almost afraid to hope.

"Would it be all right, if the two of us…you and me started dating?"

Ryder turned, his heart ready to burst with the generosity of the second chance she was offering him. For a long moment, all they did was stare at each other. Lynn was the first to look away.

His sigh of relief had a wounded quality. When he'd kissed and held her, his actions hadn't been completely prompted by love and concern the way he'd wanted to believe—the way she deserved. He'd trampled on her heart, dealing her emotions a crippling blow and all in the name of his stupid pride. "I should never have come," he told her, his face dark with self-anger.

"I'm glad you did."

"You're glad?" He couldn't believe what he was hearing.

"I'm such a coward, Ryder, in so many ways."

Lynn, a coward! She was possibly the most fearless woman he'd ever known. "No, honey, that's not true. I've been pushing you too hard and it hasn't worked. I just don't know what to do anymore."

She raised her gaze to his and looked straight at him. Her eyes were wide and filled with incredible longing. Ryder felt his knees weaken. If he were to press the issue, they would probably end up making love before the night was over. Clearly, it was what they both wanted.

"I think dating is a great idea," he said. "We'll get re-acquainted with each other the way other couples do." His words were more abrupt than he'd intended, but he had to turn his thoughts around before he and Lynn landed in bed and wondered how they'd gotten there so soon.

Lynn nodded.

"Can you go out with me tomorrow night? Dinner? Dancing? Anything you want."

"Dinner would be fine."

Her smile trembled on her lips and it took everything within him not to lean down and taste her once more. Briefly he wondered if a lifetime of her special brand of kisses would ever be enough to satisfy him. Somehow he doubted it.

"Do you want some coffee before you leave?"

Her offer surprised him and his look must have said as much.

"There's a pot already made," she explained. "I don't think it would be a good idea for you to drive when you've been drinking."

His actions had been sobering enough, but he couldn't refuse the excuse to be with her longer. "I'll take a cup— thanks for the offer."

She seemed almost glad as she moved out of the entry and back inside the kitchen. He joined her there and watched as she brought down two ceramic mugs and filled them both.

Ryder sat at the table and his gaze fell upon the ledger. He frowned once more. "Are you having problems?"

She nodded, sitting across from him. "Something's off. I can't get this sheet to balance for the life of me."

"Put it away," he suggested. "The mistake will be easier to find in the morning."

"That's what I thought yesterday."

For a long moment, Ryder resisted asking her, but he couldn't bear not knowing. "How long have you been struggling over this?"

"A week now," she admitted with some reluctance.

"Do you always do your own books?"

"I have from the beginning." A sense of pride lit up her eyes. "I like to keep my hands on every aspect of my business. It means a great deal to me."

"I don't suppose you've ever thought of hiring an accountant to balance your books," he made the suggestion lightly, although it troubled him to have Lynn drive herself to the edge, complicating her life with details others could handle far more efficiently.

"No."

Her answer was hot and automatic. He was treading on thin ice, and knew it, but still he couldn't keep himself from stepping out further. Lynn was stretching her endurance—there wasn't any need to push herself this way. He was doing them both a disservice to stand by and say nothing.

"A good accountant would save you countless hours of frustration."

"I prefer to do my own books, thank you. Besides, hiring a bookkeeper would be much too expensive."

Ryder bit his tongue to keep from telling her that she should at least check it out. She was wasting needless energy when an accountant could balance her books within a couple of hours, in addition to advising her about local and federal taxes, plus payroll.

"Slender, Too, is mine, Ryder. I handle my business affairs the way I want."

He raised both of his hands in surrender, backing off. It bothered him that Lynn was so prickly about taking his advice. He was only looking to help her, but it was obvious she didn't want him butting into her business. In the years since he'd been away, Lynn had gained a fierce independence and seemed to want to prove how capable she was at doing everything on her own. He didn't doubt that, but he fervently wished she were more open to suggestions.

Ryder gulped down the coffee. "What time tomorrow?"

"Does seven work for you?"

"That's fine."

He stood, and when he did, Lynn joined him. She walked him to the front door and stepped into his arms as though she'd been doing it half her life. He kissed her goodbye, making sure the kiss would last him until the following night.

"Hi, Mom." Michelle bounced herself down on top of the queen-size mattress in the master bedroom where Lynn was dressing. "So you're going out to dinner with Ryder?"

Methodically, Lynn finished fastening the tiny pearl buttons to her silk blouse. "I already told you that."

"Yeah, I know."

"Then why the comment now?" Lynn knew she was being defensive, but she couldn't help it. All day she'd been looking forward to this evening with Ryder and at the same time dreading it. They couldn't seem to be in the same room together without a type of spontaneous combustion exploding between them. "I thought you liked Ryder."

"I love him. He's been great. This summer would have been a real drag without him."

Lynn wasn't convinced she could accept that. "But you're not sure how you feel about the two of us going out…is that it?"

"I know how *I* feel and so does Jason. In fact, the two of us were talking and we decided—"

"What?" Lynn asked when her daughter stopped abruptly.

Michelle looked mildly shaken. "Never mind."

"Michelle, I want to know what you and your brother were talking about, especially if it concerns me and Ryder."

"It's nothing. Really."

"Michelle." Her voice lowered to a threatening cadence.

"Mom, I'm sorry, I can't tell you. Jason and I made a pact. I didn't want to go as far as to swear on my own life, but you know Jason. He's into this Incredible Hulk stuff so thick that he didn't give me any choice but to do what he said military style. Did you know commandos force their men to sign everything in fresh blood?"

Lynn managed to swallow a smile. "Did he make you do that?"

"He wanted to, but I refused. But he *did* manage to swear me to secrecy…so I can't say a word of what we talked about and decided."

"I understand."

Michelle heaved a giant sigh. "I will tell you this much, though," she admitted in a soft whisper. "Both Jason and I are real glad that you're going out to dinner with Ryder, even if it does mean we have to have a babysitter—which is completely unnecessary, you know?"

Lynn didn't. "The babysitter is for Jason's benefit, but don't tell him that, okay?"

"Okay," Michelle agreed, placated.

"And I'm pleased to hear you don't object to my going out with Ryder."

"Actually it isn't any real surprise after the day at Wild Waves."

Heat suffused Lynn's face until she was sure her color would rival a peeled beet's. It would have been too much to hope Michelle and Jason hadn't noticed the electricity between her and Ryder that afternoon.

The doorbell sounded from downstairs.

"I'll get it," Michelle cried, flying off the bed. "I think it must be Ryder."

Lynn knew it had to be. With her daughter gone, she took a couple of extra moments to check her appearance in the mirror. Only partially satisfied, she flattened her hands down the front of her outfit. Her heart was ramming against her ribs in anticipation. Ryder hadn't said where they would be dining and she prayed she'd dressed appropriately.

He was waiting for her at the bottom of the stairs, and when she started down the staircase, his eyes went directly to her. Dressed carefully in a stylish suit and tie, he'd never looked more handsome.

"Lynn." He made her name a caress. "You look lovely."

"Thank you." Lynn noticed the way Michelle poked her younger brother with her elbow. The two children looked at each other and nodded approvingly.

"Don't worry about coming home early," Michelle told Ryder excitedly. "Jason and I are watching videos and then going to bed early. Isn't that right, Jason?"

"Right." He offered Ryder a crisp military salute. "Sir," he added in afterthought.

A smile crowded Ryder's mouth and the edges of his lips quivered slightly. "At ease."

Jason dropped his arm and nodded. "Be sure to stay out as long as you want. Michelle and I want you to…there's no need to hurry home on our account."

While Ryder talked to her two kids, Lynn moved into the kitchen and gave a few instructions to the sitter. Ryder joined Lynn a couple of moments later with the phone number to the restaurant where they would be dining.

After a few choice instructions to the kids, Lynn reached for her purse and a light sweater. Ryder's hand, at the small of her back, directed her to his car, which was parked in front of the house. He held open the passenger door for her, and directed his gaze to her mouth. She thought he might want to kiss her and was mildly disappointed when he didn't. It wasn't until Lynn snapped her seat belt into place and she noticed Michelle and Jason studying her from the living-room window, that she understood Ryder's hesitancy.

They traveled the first five minutes in silence. "I've been thinking about you all day," Lynn spoke first, wishing she didn't feel like such a dunce in Ryder's company.

"I can't remember when I've looked forward to an evening more," he answered. He reached for her hand, raised it to his lips and kissed her fingertips.

The simple kiss went through her like an electric shock. Lynn sucked in her breath and bit into the soft flesh of her inner cheek. He entered the freeway and headed south toward Tacoma. "There's a new seafood restaurant someone was telling me about. I thought we'd try it."

Lynn folded her fingers around the strap of her purse, which rested in her lap. "I suppose you remember how much I love lobster."

"This place is said to serve huge portions."

Lynn couldn't help smiling. She remembered once when the three of them had gone out for dinner and she'd ordered lobster, but when her meal arrived, she'd been outraged at how tiny her serving had been. Disappointed, Lynn had muttered that it should be illegal to kill anything that small.

"We had so many good times, didn't we?" she asked casually.

Ryder nodded, but she noted that he didn't embellish on any memories. She didn't blame Ryder, because talking about the good times with Gary would put a damper on their evening. They'd both loved him so much and nothing could be said that would wipe out the past.

"I had a busy day today," she tried next.

"Oh? Did another of your employees phone in sick?"

"No… I took time off this afternoon to call an accountant."

Ryder's gaze flew from the roadway to Lynn.

"Don't get excited," she said, "my attitude was rotten. The only reason I contacted him was to prove how wrong you were. I knew an accountant would cost me an arm and a leg and I couldn't possibly afford one."

"And?"

"And…he actually sounded quite reasonable so I took everything in to him and we talked. What takes me two days to accomplish, he can do in about twenty minutes. Everything's done online these days. I wasn't keen on having him keep my books overnight… I'm always needing to write a check for one reason or another, but he doesn't need it. He makes copies of my ledger pages, assigned each account a number so that all I need do is write that figure on each check. It's so simple I could hardly believe it."

"Expensive?"

"Not at all. I should have done this in the beginning. He's helping me with my quarterly taxes, too, and with other things I didn't even know that I should be doing." She expelled a deep sigh when she finished.

"That wasn't so hard was it?"

"What?"

"Telling me you hired an accountant."

"No, it wasn't. You were right, Ryder, and I'm grateful you said something, although I'm sure my attitude last night didn't make it easy."

If he longed to remind her how difficult she had made it, he didn't, and Lynn was pleased. Ryder was a rare kind of man. More rare than she'd realized.

The restaurant was situated on Commencement Bay and they were seated by the window, which offered a spectacular view of the water. Sailboats with their boldly hued spinnakers floated past, adding dashes of bright color to the evening horizon. After their shaky beginning, Lynn was surprised at how easily they fell into conversation. Ryder told her about an important case he'd been assigned, listing the details for her, without using names, of course. As they were talking, Lynn noticed several women glancing toward them, their looks envious. She couldn't blame them, Ryder was incredibly handsome.

By the time they were served their dinner a band had started to play in the background. The music seemed to wrap itself around Lynn like a steel cable. She set her fork aside and briefly closed her eyes.

"I remember how much you like to dance."

"And I remember how much you don't."

His grin was filled with wry humor. "Right now, I'd use any excuse to hold you."

She lowered her gaze. "Oh, Ryder, don't say things like that."

"Why not?"

Lynn lowered her eyes. She didn't know how to tell him that it wasn't necessary. He didn't need to invent a reason to take her in his arms. She would go there willingly, happily. All he ever had to do was ask.

When the waiter carried away their plates, Ryder stood and offered her his hand. Lynn accepted it and when they reached the edges of the crowded dance floor, she felt as though she floated into his embrace. Ryder wrapped one arm around her waist and Lynn tucked the side of her head against his jaw, cherishing the feel of his hands, which were so gently securing her to him. She rarely danced anymore—

and yet it was as though she'd been partners with Ryder all her life. She fit into his arms as if she'd been handpicked for the position.

"You feel good against me," Ryder whispered close to her ear, and the tremble in his voice said far more than his words.

Lynn closed her eyes and nodded. He felt incredibly good, too. Warm, vital, alive and male...so very male. The music whirled around her like an early morning mist, touching her, caressing her soul with velvet.

The song ended and reluctantly, Lynn dropped her arms. "Thank you, Ryder." She started to move away, appreciating the generosity of him dancing with her once, but he caught her hand, stopping her.

"If you're willing to risk me stepping on your toes a second time, I'm game for another song."

She smiled up at him shyly and nodded. The music hadn't even started when she reached up and folded her arms around his neck.

"The last time you held me like this, we were in the water," Ryder whispered against her hair, his breath heavy. "It was torture then, too." He moved ever so slightly and she followed his lead. Her thighs slid intimately against his. Although her skirt and his pants barred her from experiencing the smooth satiny feel of their bare legs rubbing together, it didn't seem to matter—the sensation was there.

Ryder tightened his grip around her waist, pressing her stomach provocatively against his own. Her breasts were flattened over his torso and her body throbbed with the seductive movements of the impossibly slow dance.

"Lynn," he whispered her name in soft agony. "Either we get off this floor now or we're doomed to spend the rest of the night here."

Once outside, the evening air felt cool against her flushed cheeks. "I could have danced all night," she said with a meaningful sigh, chancing a look in his direction. Almost from the moment they'd stepped on the dance floor, it had been apparent that Ryder was distinctly uncomfortable holding her that intimately in such a public place.

Ryder groaned at her light teasing and shook his head. "You're a wicked woman, Lynn Danfort."

She grinned. "Nice of you to say so."

The ride back to Seattle was accomplished in companionable silence. Ryder held her hand as though he needed to feel her close. Lynn experienced the same need, and at the same time she found it essential to root herself in reality.

Ryder exited off the freeway, but instead of heading in the direction of her house, he pulled onto a side street, turned off the engine and braced both hands against the steering wheel.

"What's wrong?"

Ryder expelled his breath forcefully. "I don't know where to go."

Lynn frowned. "I don't understand."

"If I take you back to your place, Michelle and Jason will be all over us."

"Yes," she agreed, "they will."

"But if I take you to my apartment we're going to end up making love. There won't be any way either of us is going to be able to stop." He paused and looked at her, studying her as if expecting her to deny the obvious. "I'm right, aren't I?"

Lynn nearly swallowed her tongue, seeking a way to deny the truth, but she couldn't meet his gaze and lie. "Yes," she admitted in a choked whisper.

Silence seemed to throb between them.

"I'm ready to explode anytime I get near you." Inhaling

a slow, silent sigh, Ryder reached for her, taking her by the shoulders. He stared at her for a long moment, then cupped her chin in one hand and tilted back her head as he pressed his mouth over hers. His kiss was filled with hunger, passion and heat…such unbelievable heat. If a man could make love with his mouth, Ryder did so with that one kiss.

They broke apart, breathless. Feeling spineless, Lynn slumped against him and laid her cheek on his chest. No kiss had ever affected her more and she wondered if Ryder felt anything close to what she was experiencing.

"See what I mean," he whispered.

She nodded.

Ryder kissed her again, although she was sure he hadn't wanted to…at least not there on the dark street with cars buzzing past them.

Lynn laced her fingers through his hair, exalting in the feel of his mouth loving hers. He broke off the kiss and pressed his forehead against hers, taking in huge breaths as though to gain control of his needs.

Lynn felt as though she were about to incinerate. Ryder could do all this to her with a single kiss. She couldn't begin to imagine what would happen if they were to go to bed together. She trembled at the thought.

"Are you cold?" Ryder asked, rubbing his hands up and down the length of her arms.

"No. I'm burning up."

"Me, too. Sitting anywhere close to you I come away scorched."

"I'm sorry," she breathed.

"I'm not."

"You're not?"

"No, it tells me how good it's going to be for us."

Lynn frowned, not knowing how to comment. Ryder

utterly confused her. They couldn't get close to each other without threatening to ignite anything within a half-mile radius. And yet whenever the subject of making love came up, Ryder tensed and withdrew from her.

"We can't go on like this." He moved his hands over her throat and chest. Everywhere his fingers grazed her, Lynn tingled.

"What are we going to do?" she asked, on a husky whisper, hardly able to speak.

"The only thing we can." Whatever he suggested had to be better than this agony. She was about to melt at his feet.

"You aren't going to like it," he said, straightening, his look serious.

"What?"

"I think we should get married. The sooner the better."

Fourteen

"Married," Lynn echoed, stunned. "Married?"

He looked past her, refusing to meet her startled gaze. "I know this must come as something of a surprise. I didn't mean to blurt it out like this, but honestly, Lynn, I don't see any other way around it."

"I—"

"I love you. I love Michelle and Jason and they love me. I want the four of us to be a family…a real family. At night, when I crawl into bed, I want you at my side to love me and ease this ache of loneliness. When I'm old and gray, there's no one I'd rather have at my side."

"Oh, Ryder…" Her voice trailed off and she lowered her eyes. He was offering her the sun and the moon. Huge salty tears formed in the corners of her eyes.

He kissed her—a long, sensual kiss. When they broke apart, Lynn pressed the back of her head against the seat, closed her eyes and took in several calming breaths.

"Let's get out of here."

The only response she was capable of giving him was a weak nod. He started the engine and zoomed through the streets at breakneck speed as if he couldn't get her away from there fast enough. Lynn had no idea where he was driving. Her mind was whirling. Marriage. Ryder was offering her marriage because he couldn't see any way around it. Yet he claimed he loved her...loved the kids.

The biggest problem that Lynn faced was her feelings for Ryder. She hadn't had time to analyze what was happening between them. If he was looking to rescue her, she didn't need that. Nor did she want to negate any lingering guilt he was suffering over Gary's death.

Yet in her heart she loved Ryder...she always had. However, her feelings for him were deeply rooted in friendship from years past when she, Ryder and Gary had spent so much time together. In the years since Ryder had been away, her love for him had gone dormant. But now that he was back, it was as if he'd never left, although her love had been transformed from that between a sister for a brother to that between a woman and a man. Everything was magically different and had been from the moment he'd first kissed her. Her whole world had changed drastically.

"You don't seem to have much to say," he commented, his voice gruff. "Lynn, listen, I don't mean to rush you. When we started out tonight, I had no intention of proposing, but it seemed the right thing to do."

"In the heat of the moment?"

"No!"

"It isn't necessary, you know."

"What? Marrying you?"

"Yes." She couldn't believe she was admitting something like this. She'd held on to her virtue with steel manacles with every other man she'd dated, but one touch from Ryder and she'd never felt more alive. It was as if her whole body had been hibernating for three long years, and suddenly every cell had sprung to life.

"It's what I want."

Lynn couldn't understand why. His brief affairs had been legendary, but he didn't seem to want a short-term commitment from her. And from the dark scowl that covered his face, she realized he was offering her all or nothing.

"I'm not looking for an affair with you, Lynn."

That message had come through loud and clear the day at the waterworks park. "But, Ryder—"

"Do you or do you not want to get married?" The question was sharp with impatience.

Lynn squared her shoulders. "I'm not looking for anyone to rescue me."

His laugh was short and sarcastic. "You're telling me? Every time I so much as try, you bite my head off and calmly take control."

"And if you think you owe me something because of what happened to Gary—"

"Gary has nothing to do with this." Once more his words were sharp and abrupt.

Lynn gnawed on her bottom lip. Indecision boiled inside her. No clear direction presented itself.

"Are you going to marry me and put us both out of this misery?"

His voice was tender and warm, scattering Lynn's objections before she had a chance to assemble them. "I…think so." She would be a fool to turn him down and equally foolish to agree. She felt like laughing and crying at once. Good grief, what was she doing?

Ryder stepped on the brake, reached for her and kissed her soundly, ravaging her mouth. "I'll take that as a yes, then."

Lynn's mind was spinning. "We need to talk, though, don't you think?"

"Fine. A week from Saturday, okay?"

"You want to wait that long to talk?"

He cast her an astonished glance. "No, get married."

"So soon?" she gasped.

Ryder frowned. "As far as I'm concerned, it's a week longer than I want to wait. I'm going out of my head wanting you this way." He turned off the familiar thoroughfare and headed toward her house, easing the car into the driveway, out of sight of the house and hidden from the neighbors.

The engine had barely had time to stop humming before Ryder reached for her, closing his arms convulsively around her shoulders. Lynn wordlessly lifted her face to him, reaching out to him, parting her lips, shamelessly inviting his kiss. It was hot and possessive.

"Invite me inside," he muttered, nibbling on the edges of her lips.

"The kids?"

"We'll send them to bed."

She nodded, eager for his touch.

As it happened, both Michelle and Jason were upstairs asleep. Lynn paid the babysitter and walked the teenager to the door. She stood on the porch until the neighbor girl was safely inside her own house. By the time Lynn returned to the kitchen, Ryder was brewing a pot of coffee.

"I don't want that," she told him, slipping her arms around his middle, feeling brazen. When she accepted his proposal, she'd experienced a release of sorts. She was taking a chance marrying Ryder, but then life was full of them, and living dangerously entailed a good deal of excitement.

"You don't want any coffee?"

"Nope." She skillfully dealt with the buttons of his shirt. Once it was opened, she rubbed her palms up his firm chest, reveling in the feel of his nakedness.

Ryder's hands were equally busy. Their bodies were on fire for each other as they explored, beseeched and promised all at the same time.

"Say it," Ryder growled hoarsely. "I need to hear you say it."

At the moment, she would have agreed to verbalize anything he wanted. "What?" she asked, bewildered. "I'll marry you? I already said I would. Next week, tomorrow. Tonight, if you want."

"Not that." He kissed her repeatedly, slipping his hands down her backside.

She whimpered softly. "Ryder, what?"

"Tell me you love me. I need to hear the words… I need to know what you feel for me."

With her hands braced against the curve of his neck, she paused and slowly lifted her head. Her hungry gaze met his, and she was astonished at the uneasiness she saw there. He didn't know. He honestly didn't know.

Tenderness tore through her. This was a man who had often been recognized for his determination and arrogance. A man bold and persistent, volatile and tenacious. Yet he'd made himself vulnerable to her, opened himself up, exposed his inner self in a way she had never dreamed possible.

She slipped her hands up his neck and laced her fingers through his hair. His eyes held her, watching her, loving her. Tears boiled beneath the surface of her eyes.

"Lynn?"

She cocked her head at an angle to his mouth and slowly, patiently kissed him. He groaned, securing her against him.

"I love you," she told him when she'd finished the kiss. "I love you," she repeated obligingly when she witnessed a flicker of doubt flash into his gaze. "For now…for always."

"Lynn," he cried, and buried his face in her neck, crushing her in his embrace. "I need you so much."

Lynn doubted that she'd ever heard any words more beautiful in her life.

Lynn hardly slept that night and woke early the next morning, feeling rummy and out of sorts. A woman in love, a woman who had agreed to marry a man she'd loved and admired, shouldn't be feeling like this.

When the first light of dawn peeled across a cranky sky, Lynn climbed out of bed and stumbled into the kitchen for coffee.

By all rights, she should be the happiest woman alive. Between kisses and the building enthusiasm for this marriage, she'd agreed to a wedding date less than ten days away, although she couldn't understand the rush. But Ryder had been insistent and she couldn't find it in her heart to delay the ceremony any longer than he wanted. Yet she couldn't understand why he felt the need to bulldoze her into marriage.

Ryder had left her in the early morning hours when she'd been high on his love. She'd watched him leave and had reluctantly gone to bed. It was then that this melancholy mood had settled over her.

Their time together had been splurged on kisses and promises. They'd only brushed over the truly important issues. There were so many things that needed to be settled. Slender, Too, was a big concern. She didn't want to give up her business and she feared Ryder might insist upon certain changes. If he did, there could be problems. The children worried her, too. They loved Ryder, but he'd always played the role of an indulgent uncle with them. A father... stepfather was something entirely different, and she would personally feel more comfortable having him ease into that role instead of being thrust upon Michelle and Jason unexpectedly this way.

"Mom." Jason stood just inside the kitchen, looking surprised to see her. "What are you doing up so early?"

"Thinking," she answered with a smile. She held out her arms for a hug. He gave her one, although reluctantly. It was on her mind to tell him the Incredible Hulk hugged his mother, but she let the thought slide.

As for her answer to his question, he seemed to find the fact that she'd gotten up early to "think" acceptable. He dragged a chair across the kitchen floor, stood on it and opened the cupboard above the refrigerator, bringing down a cereal box. He then proceeded to pour himself a huge bowl.

"I thought we were out of Cap'n Crunch cereal?"

"That's what I wanted Michelle to think," he whispered. "A girl can't appreciate the finer qualities this cereal has to offer a man."

"So you've been holding out on her?"

He hesitated. "If that's the way you want to think of it."

At another time, Lynn would have scolded her son for his selfishness. Instead she decided to forego the lecture, determined to buy two boxes of the kids' favorite cereal the next time she went grocery shopping. That would settle that problem.

"So how'd the date go with Ryder?" Jason asked, carrying the impossibly full bowl over to the table and plopping himself down beside her.

"It…was nice."

"Nice?" Jason repeated, crunching his cereal at breakneck speed.

"Jason, please, don't talk with your mouth full."

"Sorry." He wiped the sleeve of his green camouflage pajamas across his mouth. "So you had a good time?"

"We had a very nice time."

"You like Ryder real well, don't you?" He paused and studied her, his dark brown eyes wide and curious.

"Yes…"

"Good," he said and nodded once, profoundly.

"Why is that good?"

His gaze darted across the room, skirting her probing one. "Because."

That didn't explain a whole lot. She was about to comment when Michelle appeared, looking sleepy and cross. "Good morning, sweetheart," Lynn greeted.

Michelle grunted in reply, walked past her mother and brother, crisscrossed her legs, plopped herself down in front of the sink and opened the cupboard. Lynn leaned backward in her chair to watch what her daughter was doing and nearly laughed out loud when Michelle extracted a box of Cap'n Crunch cereal from behind the pipes.

Jason's mouth dropped open. "She's been holding out on me," he fumed, glaring at his mother. "Aren't you going to say something?"

Lynn glanced from one child to the other and slowly shook her head. "No way—I'm staying out of this one."

Jason slouched forward, and muttered something under his breath about what kind of mother had God assigned him, anyway!

By midmorning, Lynn had come to a decision. She would agree to marry Ryder, but to do so within ten days was impossible. She would insist they set the date several weeks in the future, possibly in three or four months. Marriage was what they both wanted, but she couldn't understand Ryder's need to rush into a relationship this important. They had the rest of their lives to spend together, and lots of questions that needed to be answered before sealing their vows.

A niggling fear kept cropping up in the back of Lynn's mind. From the first day he'd returned, Ryder had resisted discussing Gary. Anytime Gary's name was mentioned, Ryder found a way to change the subject.

Although he'd assured her otherwise, Lynn couldn't dismiss the fear that Ryder was marrying her and taking on the responsibility of raising Michelle and Jason out of some kind of warped idea of duty to her dead husband. She honestly didn't believe that was the case, but the thought troubled her and she wanted the issue cleared.

At noon, she took the time to phone Ryder. She frowned when the honey-voiced receptionist answered. Whoever she was, the woman was efficient, and Lynn was connected with Ryder's office immediately.

"Lynn." Ryder sounded pleased to hear from her.

"Hi," she managed to swallow the question about the age of the receptionist. She was behaving like a jealous fool. Simply because the woman's voice sounded like black velvet didn't mean she looked like a beauty queen. "Would it be possible for you to stop over at the house tonight?"

"Of course. Any reason?"

"I…I think we have several things to discuss, don't you?"

He chuckled softly. "We don't seem to be able to do much of that, do we?"

Lynn blushed and whispered. "No, but I think we should try."

"I'll be out of here at about three. Do you want me to pick up Michelle and Jason for you?"

The way things were looking at the salon, that might be a good idea. "If you don't mind."

"I don't," he assured her.

"I'll be done around six."

"The kids and I'll be waiting for you," he paused. "Everything's all right, isn't it?"

Lynn couldn't see stirring up trouble over the phone. "Of course."

"We're going to have a good life, Lynn. A very good life."

Lynn didn't doubt Ryder, but she had her fears and she wanted them laid to rest. A lengthy engagement wouldn't hurt either of them.

By the time she arrived at the house, Ryder's car was parked out front. She pulled into the driveway and had no sooner climbed out of the driver's side when both kids and Ryder appeared.

"Why didn't you tell us?" Michelle cried, bouncing up and down with excitement.

"Tell you what, honey?" Ryder would know better than to say anything to the kids about their wedding plans. The task was for her and her alone. Nonetheless, she frowned, wondering.

She slapped her hands against her thighs. "About you and Ryder getting married next week. Mom, this is just wonderful."

Lynn's narrowed gaze flew to Ryder.

"I told you this would happen," Jason told his sister with a look of untainted righteousness. "Even when you wouldn't sign the pact in blood, it worked. They're getting married just the way we want them to."

Fifteen

"Ryder," Lynn whispered angrily. "What have you done?"

"We called and talked to the pastor," Michelle informed her mother with a cheerful grin. "He said next Saturday is fine with him, and then Ryder called the florist. You're really going to love all the roses and stuff."

Jason examined a caterpillar he was holding in the palm of his hand. "Grandma sounded surprised, though, don't you think, Michelle?"

"You've talked to your grandparents?"

"I know they're supposed to be on vacation, but I figured you'd want them to know. They're packing up the motor home and driving back to Seattle right away."

"Oh, dear." Lynn slumped against the side of her car.

"You're happy, aren't you, Mom?"

"I…"

"I think we may be moving too fast for your mother, but I didn't want to give her a chance to change her mind." Ryder's eyes reached out and gently caressed Lynn.

"She's not going to back out," Michelle quickly assured him. "We won't let her."

"I...I think Ryder and I've got several issues we need to settle first, though," she said through clenched teeth.

"Aren't you going to give her the ring?" Jason asked, tugging at Ryder's sleeve. Her son turned toward Lynn. "It's been in his family for seventy years. This is the engagement ring his grandfather gave his grandmother and his father his mother. I think this may mean you're going to have babies, right?"

Lynn opened her mouth, but she didn't know how to answer Jason. The subject of children was one in a long list she had yet to discuss with Ryder.

"I wouldn't mind a brother," Jason informed her, "but I don't know what I'd do with another sister. I wouldn't suppose there's any way you could order me a brother?"

"Jason," Michelle demanded, jerking him away. "Can't you see Mom and Ryder need time alone? He wants to give her the ring."

"I'm going to watch. It isn't every day a kid gets to see this kind of mushy stuff." The eight-year-old yanked his elbow from his sister's grasp and refused to budge. "Ryder's marrying us, too—we should get to see this if we want."

"I'd like more children." Ryder's dark eyes continued to hold Lynn's, his gaze filled with tenderness.

The word *more* was her undoing. Ryder honestly loved Michelle and Jason, as though he had actually fathered them. In the future she need never doubt that his actions weren't prompted by genuine concern for their welfare.

"Are you going to tell her about us moving into another house?" Michelle questioned.

"Another house?" Infuriated, Lynn swerved toward her daughter. She felt as if every aspect of her life had been taken over. "Do you have any *other* surprises for me?"

"I think I'd better do the talking now," Ryder said with a

halting smile. His hand at the small of Lynn's back directed her toward the front door, although Lynn tried to free herself. Rushing her into marriage was one thing, but making these kind of arrangements was going too far. Worlds too far. Her mind was whirling with outrage.

"Ryder, just what is going on?" She whirled around the instant she was inside the door. "You've contacted my parents in Minnesota, you've talked to the pastor and ordered flowers—"

"You object?"

"You're darn right I do." She was fighting like mad to quell her anger. The last thing she wanted was for her children to witness what she planned to say to him. Furious, now she was nearly foaming at the mouth. But Michelle and Jason worshiped the man and if she was going to have a heated argument with him, she would rather they were out of hearing distance. Besides, knowing her children, they would probably side with Ryder!

"I was only trying to help."

"You weren't," she shouted, unable to stop herself. "You're forcing me into this wedding and I don't like it."

Jason scooted a chair from the kitchen, twisted it around and straddled it as if it were a wild bronco. He propped his chin in his hands, his gaze shifting from Ryder to his mother and then back again.

"Jason, I need to talk to Ryder…alone."

"Sure." But he didn't budge.

"I think your mother wants you to leave, son," Ryder explained a minute later.

"Oh." Jason hopped off the chair, looking mildly chagrined. "Michelle told me you were going to fight, but she said that's something moms and dads do all the time and there wasn't any need to worry."

"There's nothing to be concerned about."

Ryder answered the youngster when Lynn didn't. As far as she was concerned, there was *plenty* to be worried about. She waited until Jason had vacated the entryway.

"The whole thing's off," she announced, her hands slicing the air like an umpire making a call, his decision final.

It took a minute for Ryder to react. "All right, if that's what you want."

It wasn't entirely, but Lynn wasn't going to be railroaded into marriage.

She opened her mouth to tell him exactly how furious she was, but he turned his back to her and calmly stated, "Then we'll just have to live in sin."

"What?" she exploded.

"With the way things are between us now, you don't honestly expect us to stay out of the bedroom? We can try— we've done it so far, but my restraint is at its limit. You're probably stronger than me."

"I…" She looked over her shoulder to make sure Jason wasn't spying on them. "That's the least of my concerns. We're talking about blending our lives together. There are going to be . . . difficulties."

"Like what?" He turned back to face her, hands in his pockets, the picture of nonchalance.

"Like…the kids. They love you now because you take them places, buy them things. You're like Santa Claus and the Easter Bunny all rolled into one wonderful person. But how are they going to feel when you start disciplining them?"

"That's something we're going to have to work out, isn't it?"

"In time, right."

"You mean you won't marry me if the kids balk when I send them to bed and they don't want to go?"

Lynn folded her arms tightly around her stomach. "I didn't suggest that…quit twisting everything I say to suit your own purpose."

"I'm only answering your questions. I don't understand the problem with the kids. They know I love them, they trust me to be fair. What's going to change if we get married?"

"What about children? Jason started asking me about a baby brother and I didn't know how to answer him."

"Do you want more children?"

"I think so…if you do."

"I do. That settles that. Is there anything else?"

"What about Slender, Too? I've put a lot of time and effort into building it up and I don't want to walk away from it now."

"You're asking me if I'm going to object if you keep working? Not in the least. That's your business and you have a right to be proud of what you've accomplished. I'm not going to take that away from you."

The hot wind that had buoyed the sails of her outrage started to slacken. What had once threatened to be a hurricane force diminished to a gentle breeze.

"But I don't want you to overdo it," Ryder warned. "When we decide it's time for you to get pregnant, I'd like you to consider taking time off to properly take care of yourself and the baby, but I'll leave that up to you."

Lynn blinked and nodded. "Naturally I'd want to do that."

"I love you, Lynn. I want you for my wife."

She stared at him mesmerized as he straightened and walked toward her. He was impossible to resist when he was looking at her with his eyes filled with such love. The only thing Lynn had to quell at the moment was the impulse to fall into his arms.

"You're going to marry me, aren't you?" he asked on a

husky murmur. "It's what we both want, but yet you keep fighting it. Why?"

"I'm afraid," she admitted.

"I frighten you that much?"

"Not you," she countered.

"What then?"

Now that she had the opportunity to voice her objections, she found them garbled and twisted in her mind. If she were to mention Gary's name, he would tell her how silly she was being in the same way that he'd assured her about everything else.

"Gary…"

Ryder frowned. "What about him?"

"You loved him?"

"You know I did."

As always when she mentioned Gary's name, Ryder tensed, but she had to know. "You're not marrying me out of a sense of duty, are you?"

His face twisted into a glower as if he resented her insinuating as much. "No," he answered abruptly. "I already told you I've dealt with the guilt of what happened. Loving you is completely separate from Gary's death."

"I…I had to be sure."

He reached for her, hauling her into his arms, his mouth seeking hers. She met his lips eagerly, returning the passion until she was weak and clinging. Because he'd turned her mind around so completely, she was frustrated they couldn't be married any sooner.

"You're going to marry me." This time it was a statement, not a question.

Lynn lowered her gaze and nodded. Heaven help her for being such a fool, but she loved this man. He was offering her a slice of paradise and it wasn't in her to refuse.

"Michelle." Jason cried and popped up from behind the living-room sofa. "It's working out just great."

Lynn slumped forward, securing her forehead against Ryder's chest. "He was listening the whole time."

"Hurry and come downstairs," Jason yelled. "We don't have anything to worry about…they're getting married just the way you said. We're going to be a real family in no time."

"Do you take this man to be your lawfully wedded husband?" Pastor Teed asked Lynn.

She stared up at Ryder, who was standing so confidently beside her, and felt her insides go soft, and her heart began to pound unnaturally hard. She was about to make a giant leap into a whole new life. She stood tall and proud, but on the inside she was a mass of quivering nerves.

"Lynn," the pastor prompted softly.

"I do," she returned, certain that she was doing the right thing.

Ryder smiled at her and although the man of God continued speaking, Lynn barely heard what he was saying. When Pastor Teed informed Ryder that he could kiss the bride, he did so gently, as if she were the most priceless piece of porcelain in the world and he feared breaking her. Silly tears gathered in the corners of her eyes. She had never expected to find such happiness and love a second time—she'd given up trying. Yet here she was standing before God and man, pledging her life to Ryder.

The reception was an intimate affair with only a handful of friends. Her parents were there, and Toni Morris, who was busy serving cake and coffee. Lynn's mother and father looked happy and proud. They knew Ryder from before and were pleased with her choice.

Michelle and Jason mingled with the guests, telling everyone who would listen how they'd known all along that their mother was going to marry Ryder.

All too soon the reception came to a close, and it was time for Lynn to change out of the pale silk dress she'd worn for the wedding ceremony and into one more suitable for traveling.

Toni Morris wiped a stray tear from her cheek and hugged Lynn after she'd changed outfits. It was unlike Toni to be demonstrative and Lynn hugged her friend back, squeezing her tightly.

"I'm happy for you, Lynn. Ryder loves you, don't ever doubt that."

Lynn nodded, grateful for all the moral support Toni had given her over the years, although she found her friend's words mildly disturbing. There wasn't any reason for her to doubt Ryder's love.

"You've got everything?" Toni asked.

"Yes. I've been through the list a dozen times."

"Your parents are keeping Michelle and Jason for the week."

"God bless parents," Lynn whispered, raising her eyes toward the heavens.

"Your suitcase is packed and ready."

Lynn grinned, it was packed all right, but Toni made it sound as though she was on her way to the maternity ward instead of her honeymoon.

"Work?"

"Sharon's the acting manager. If anything drastic happens, she has your phone number."

"Great." Toni hugged her once more. "Have a wonderful honeymoon, Mrs. Matthews."

Lynn giggled, reaching for her suitcase. "I intend to."

Sixteen

As bold as she'd been earlier in their courtship, Lynn felt like a blushing bride when she met Ryder in front of the reception hall at the country club.

"Bye, Mom," Michelle cried, hugging her mother tightly around the waist. "You'll bring me something back from Hawaii, won't you?"

"Of course."

In front of an audience, Jason wasn't as keen about showing his affection. He offered his mother his hand to shake, and Lynn politely shook it, then hugged him anyway.

"I'll bring you back something, too," she assured him before he could ask.

"Do you think you could find me a shark's jaw?"

Lynn cringed and nodded, knowing Jason would be delighted with the grisly bone. "I'll see what I can do."

Her mother and father stepped forward and Lynn gave them each a warm embrace, grateful, as always, for their unfailing love and support.

No more than a minute later, Lynn and Ryder were in his car on the way to a hotel close to the airport. Their flight was scheduled to leave for Honolulu early the following morning. Ryder had arranged for them to spend their first night in the honeymoon suite.

He reached for her hand and raised it to his mouth, kissing her fingertips. "You're a beautiful bride, Mrs. Matthews."

"Thank you." Once more she felt soft color flush into her cheeks. She was trembling and grateful that Ryder was too preoccupied with the traffic to notice her nervousness. There had only been one lover in her life and fears crowded the edges of her mind that she wouldn't be the kind of woman Ryder needed in bed. She would have preferred it if their lovemaking had happened more...naturally. She felt timid and shy and awkward with this man she had just married. It was right for them to wait, Lynn realized that much, but doubts confronted her at every turn. Not if she'd done the right thing by marrying Ryder, but if she was woman enough to satisfy him.

While Ryder registered them at the hotel desk, Lynn looked toward the four-star restaurant where several couples were dining by candlelight and champagne music. Ryder joined her a moment later.

"Hungry?"

She nodded eagerly, looking for a way to delay their lovemaking. She was being silly, she knew that, but she couldn't seem to shake her nervousness.

"We can order dinner from room service," Ryder suggested.

"Would you mind if we ate at the restaurant...here?" she asked quickly.

Ryder looked disappointed, but agreed.

Lynn ordered two glasses of wine with her meal and showed more interest in the chardonnay than the shrimp stuffed sole. She lingered over dessert, ignoring the fact that

Ryder preferred not to order any and glanced at his watch two or three times while she leisurely nibbled away at hers.

"There's nothing to worry about, you know," he whispered, after the waiter refilled her coffee cup for the third time.

Her head shot upward, her eyes round. "What…do you mean?"

"You know what I'm talking about."

"Ryder…my stomach feels like a nest of red ants are building a whole new colony in there. My palms are sweaty and I feel like an inexperienced girl. I want to make love with you so much it frightens me and yet I'm terrified of doing so."

"Honey, come on. There's only one way to face something like this."

"Maybe we should wait until we get to Hawaii…that's the real start of our honeymoon."

"Lynn, you're being ridiculous." He paid the bill and with his hand under her elbow, directing her, he led her to the elevator.

The whole way up to the twentieth floor, Lynn's mind floundered, seeking excuses. Never in a thousand years would she have believed she could be this anxious over something she'd been wanting for weeks. For heaven's sake, she'd practically seduced Ryder that day in the water.

Her husband opened the room and pushed open the door. He lifted her into his arms and, disregarding her protests, carried her into the opulent suite. Gently he set her back on the thick carpeting. Their suitcases were waiting for them on the floor next to the bed, but her gaze refused to go as far as the king-size mattress.

"Oh, look, they show movies," she said cheerfully, as though watching the latest release would be the highlight of this trip.

"We're going to take things nice and slow, Lynn. There won't be any time for movies."

She nodded, realizing how incredibly absurd she must have sounded.

Reaching for her, Ryder took her shoulders between his hands and drew her against him. "I love you."

"I love you, too." Lynn tried to smile, she honestly tried, but she failed utterly. Moistening her lips, she lifted her arms, bracing her hands against his chest. The heavy beat of his heart seemed to thunder against her palms and did little to reassure her.

"There's magic between us," he told her in a warm whisper. "I recognized it the first time we kissed."

Lynn had, too. She stared into his tanned, lean face, loving him all the more for his patience. He smiled at her so gently, so tenderly, the way a child does when petting a newborn kitten. Lynn felt the worst of the tension ease out of her stiff body.

He kissed her, lightly, making no demands on her, then pulled away, studying her. "That wasn't so terrible, was it?"

She shut her eyes. "I'm being foolish."

"No, you're not," he countered and kissed her again, more deeply this time, although he continued to hold her as though she were delicate and could easily break.

The taste of his mouth over hers was an awakening for Lynn, and as a brilliantly colored marigold does to the morning sun, Lynn opened to Ryder, flowering, seeking his warmth and love. There was nothing to be afraid of with this man. Nothing. The memory of his touch, the sound and taste of his lovemaking filled her mind. Thread by thread, the thoughts unwove her hesitation.

Ryder's gaze moved over her face. "Feeling better now?"

Lynn nodded. "Isn't it a little warm in here?" Before he

could answer, she reached up and started unfastening the buttons of his starched white shirt.

"Now that you mention it, yes." Eagerly he shucked his suit coat and let it fall heedlessly to the floor. Lynn smiled to herself, knowing how unlike Ryder it was to be messy or disorganized.

He reached for the zipper at the back of her dress, easing it down, slowly, cautiously as though he expected her to bolt and run from him at any time. His shirtfront was open and Lynn lifted her palms to his bare chest. His skin was hot to the touch and she longed to feel the kinky soft hairs matted there, against her face.

Ryder lifted his hands to her neck, easing the material of her dress over her shoulders and down her torso, past her hips. It disrupted her momentarily to step out of it and do away with her slip, bra and her other under-things, but they were disposed of soon enough.

She lifted her hands back to his chest. The need to taste him dominated her thoughts and she ran the tip of her tongue in a meandering path across his chest, savoring the hot, salty flavor of him.

Ryder shuddered and closed his arms around her waist, tugging her against his naked torso. She wrapped her arms around his neck, clinging to him, busying her fingers in the thick, dark hair at his nape. As she brushed her body against his, she could feel the gentle rasp of his body hair against her.

"Oh, Ryder," she whispered in rapturous awe.

Somehow he moved them onto the bed, lying above her, lowering himself just enough to brush his chest over her nakedness, tantalizing her. "Does that feel good, love?"

"Oh, yes…very good."

Ryder's mouth found hers in a kiss that was hard, hot and coaxing. He kissed her with a fierceness that robbed her of her breath and caused the blood to pound through her veins. She willingly parted her lips and arched her back until her tingling breasts encountered the hard, hairy wall of his chest once more.

"Ryder," she moaned, "I want you so much."

"Not yet, love."

Desire for him rocked through her until she was certain if he didn't take her soon, her bones would melt, longing for him the way she did. Her heart was pounding harder than it had at any other time in her life. Each staccato beat's echo was magnified a hundredfold in her ears.

His lips continued to torture her until the yearning was so potent she thought she would die from wanting him. It saturated every cell of her being and she lifted his head, and raised her mouth to his, longing to show him with her kiss how eager she was to be his wife. All her nervous reserve was gone, evaporating under his tender ministrations.

"Oh...please," she begged.

Lynn tangled her fingers in his hair and he dropped forward enough for her to plant a wild kiss on his lips. She gloried in the way his body trembled above hers.

"Lynn...oh, Lynn," he cried out. When they'd finished making love Lynn was replete, utterly enraptured by sensation.

They slept in each other's arms, and when she awoke the room was filled with dark shadows of night. She felt wonderful and, raising herself up on her elbow, she watched her husband's face, relaxed now in sleep. Ryder looked almost boyish and the surge of love that rocked through her brought a rush of tears to her eyes.

Slipping out of the sheet, she moved into the bathroom and ran water for a bath, luxuriating in the hot liquid.

"Lynn?" A thread of panic filled his voice.

"I'm in here." She climbed out of the tub and reached for a towel, holding it against her front.

Ryder stumbled into the room, looking mussed and sleepy, but he paused and relaxed when he saw her. "You're beautiful, Mrs. Matthews," he said, leaning against the door.

"I didn't mean to wake you."

"I'm glad you did."

"You are?"

He took a step toward her and gently pulled away the towel she was holding against her water-slickened body. "You're even more beautiful now."

Lynn lowered her head.

"You doubt me?"

"No," she told him softly. "Telling me that only assures me how much you really *do* love me." When she glanced at him, she read the confusion in his eyes. "I'm over thirty, Ryder, and I've borne two children…they've left their marks on my body. I'm not going to win any beauty pageants."

Instead of arguing, Ryder reached for her, folding her in his embrace. He led her back into the bedroom. "There isn't a woman on this earth more beautiful to me than you." His voice shook with sincerity.

Back in the bedroom, he sat on the edge of the mattress and pulled her down into his lap. He lifted his hands to her hair and tugged it loose from the carefully braided French roll the hairdresser had spent so long creating for her wedding. The length fell down the middle of her back. Ryder parted it over her shoulder and the dark length hung loosely, nearly covering her shoulders.

He paused and seemed to stop breathing as he lifted it away from her head with widespread fingers, letting the softness flow through his hands like spilled coffee. "I've dreamed of you kissing me with your hair falling over my face."

With her hands at his shoulders, she gently pressed him back against the mattress, securing him there. He watched her with curious eyes as she positioned herself above her husband.

Slowly, very slowly, she leaned forward, letting her hair fall over him. But Ryder surprised her even more by raising his head and clamping his hands at each side of her waist. Lynn whimpered with the explosive desire that pitched through her.

"Oh, Lynn," he breathed "Oh, baby, you haven't got a clue what you do to me."

Lynn smiled softly to herself. Actually she had a very good idea of what she did to him.

Ryder scooted his chair away from his desk. He should be going over a brief, but his mind refused to focus on the case he was studying. Instead, his thoughts drifted to his wife. They'd been married for several weeks now and it was as if they'd always been together. Every time he thought about Lynn his throat filled with such strong emotion that he could hardly breathe. He couldn't get enough of her and her special brand of lovemaking. Every time he felt her body, all soft and athletic beside him, it affected him. He had to have her. Sometimes once a night wasn't enough. Lynn seemed as eager as he was for this side of their marriage and that pleased him immeasurably. He would reach for her and she would come into his arms with an enthusiasm that caused his blood to boil.

Loving and craving Lynn the way he did frightened him. He'd never expected to experience this deep a commitment in his life. The need he felt just to know she was close clawed at him and the thought of losing her was enough to drive him over the edge of sanity.

He glanced at his watch, troubled by his thoughts. Lynn would be home by now. He decided to read the brief that night. With that decided, he shoved the papers inside his briefcase and headed out of the office.

Lynn's car was parked in the driveway when he pulled up in front of the house and he exhaled sharply.

"You're home early," she greeted, when he stepped into the kitchen. She wore an apron around her waist and was slicing thin strips of beef for their dinner.

"Where are Michelle and Jason?" he asked, and slipped his arms around her waist, nuzzling her neck.

"Michelle's helping Janice babysit and will be home at five-thirty, and Jason's at soccer practice."

"Good." He unknotted the apron strings and let it drop to the kitchen floor.

"Ryder?"

Next, he fiddled with the buttons on her blouse, peeling it open with an excitement that caused his hands to shake. Ryder had only meant to touch her, but the minute his hands experienced the silky softness of her skin he knew there was no stopping him. A melting sort of ecstasy grew within him that would be satisfied only by making love to Lynn.

"Now?" she breathed the question.

He answered her with an ardent kiss.

"Dinner's going to be late," she whispered.

"We'll order pizza," he answered, leading her toward the stairs.

Lynn giggled. "Ryder, we're too old for this! We can't keep this up and live beyond forty."

"Talk for yourself, woman."

"Married life certainly seems to suit you," Toni commented over lunch a few days later.

The lunch was Toni's treat. But Lynn wasn't fooled; her friend wanted to gloat. When Lynn had announced to Toni that she was marrying Ryder, Toni had asked what took her so long to figure out why Ryder had come back to Seattle.

"I'm so much in love I can hardly stand it," Lynn admitted almost shyly. "It's funny really… I'd given up dating. As far as I could see the world was filled with… I don't know."

"I think the term you used earlier this summer was warthogs."

Lynn smiled. "That about says it. Ryder came into my life when I least expected to fall in love again."

"I'd like to say I told you so, but Joe wouldn't let me say one word to you about Ryder loving you."

Lynn would have doubted her friend, anyway.

"Everything's working out with the kids?"

"It's too good to be true. They turn to him just as if he were their father. From day one they've both been on their best behavior."

"You don't expect that to last, do you?"

"No. Ryder knows that, too."

"Now what's this I hear about you buying a new house?"

Lynn focused her attention on the chef salad and slowly exhaled, hoping her friend didn't notice her hesitation. "Ryder wants to move."

"Is that so difficult to understand?"

It wasn't, but Lynn still had trouble letting go of the house. She'd lived in that colonial since shortly after she and Gary were married. Both children had been born while they lived there. The house was filled with happy memories of a life she treasured and revered. It was convenient to the salon and shopping. The school was only a few blocks away and the neighbors were good friends. At Ryder's insistence, they'd looked at several new homes, but Lynn couldn't find one that suited her.

"Is it?" Toni pressed.

"I can't seem to find anything I like."

"And Ryder?"

"He's found several he thinks we'll fit into nicely. We're leaning toward a five-bedroom place a couple of miles from where we live now."

"Five bedrooms?" Toni gasped, mocking Lynn with her eyes.

"Ryder wants one for a den."

"And later one for the baby?"

Lynn blushed. "There isn't going to be any baby for a year or more, so get that snide look off your face."

"But not from lack of trying, if what I see in your face is true. Good grief Lynn, it isn't any wonder Ryder's got circles under his eyes and you walk around wearing that silly grin."

"Toni, stop it, you're embarrassing me." But she *was* wearing a smile these days, a contented one, and nothing seemed to dampen her good spirits.

"How's the salon doing?"

Lynn shrugged. "Good. I've got a membership campaign in the works. I'm training a couple of new girls who seem to be working out nicely—no pun intended. Things couldn't be better."

"And Ryder doesn't object to you spending so much time at the salon?"

Lynn shrugged. There wasn't any reason for him to complain. She was home every night, usually before he was. He did offer a suggestion or two, which she'd taken into consideration. He liked to know what was going on in her business and she enjoyed sharing that part of her life with him.

"I hope you're not going to kill yourself over this membership campaign," Toni said with a sigh. "I know you and it's difficult for you to delegate responsibility. You can't do everything yourself, so don't make the mistake of trying."

The two chatted for several minutes more, then parted. Lynn went back to the salon, checked in with Sharon, then took the rest of the afternoon off, stopping at a couple of stores on the way home to do errands.

On impulse, she bought a negligee, wondering how long she would be able to keep it on once she modeled it for Ryder.

The house was quiet when she unlocked the door. Once inside the entryway, she turned, feeling that something wasn't right, but couldn't put her finger on it. She looked around, but didn't notice anything different. Ryder was still at the office and both kids were in school. She set down the grocery bags and placed the milk inside the refrigerator.

"Hi, Mom." Jason shouted as he came through the front door. The screen door slammed in his wake. "What's for snack?"

"Milk and—"

"Are we having pizza for dinner again tonight?"

Lynn tried to hide a smile. "Why?"

"Joey wants to come over for dinner if we are. He said he didn't know anyone in the whole world who had pizza four nights in a row."

"Actually I thought I'd serve spaghetti and meatballs tonight. Is that all right?"

"Sure," he shrugged and reached for an apple. "I'm going outside, okay?"

"What about your homework?"

"I don't have any and if I did, I'd do it after dinner."

Lynn walked him to the front door and again was assailed with the fact that something was out of place. She turned and strolled through the living room, paused, and turned around.

Her gaze fell on the television and she gasped. Gary's picture, which had rested there for over three years was gone. She whirled around and looked at the fireplace. *All* the pictures of him were missing from there, too. Only the ones of her and Michelle and Jason remained.

There was only one person who would have removed them, and that was Ryder.

Lynn knew it was time for a talk.

Seventeen

"Hi, Mom," Michelle greeted when Lynn walked in the house the following week. Lynn had yet to confront Ryder about the missing photos of Gary. She was afraid, she suspected. Still it troubled her greatly. Her daughter's gaze was glued to the television where a popular rock group was crooning out the unintelligible words to a top-ten hit.

Lynn ripped the sweatband from her forehead and hurried toward the kitchen, tossing her purse on the counter and rubbing the pain in the small of her back. "Where're Ryder and Jason?"

"Soccer practice."

Lynn heaved a sigh of relief—she should have remembered that. This was the third night in a row that she was late getting out of the salon and she'd been worried about confronting Ryder. He hadn't said anything about the extra hours she was putting in, but she knew it bothered him.

"What's for dinner?" Michelle yelled. "I'm starved."

Lynn rubbed her hand over her face and sighed. "I don't know yet."

"Mom…is it going to be another one of those nights?"

Lynn paused. "What do you mean by that?"

"The only time we have a decent meal anymore is when Ryder orders out."

Lynn wanted to argue, but she hadn't a leg to stand on, as the old saying went. Things had been hectic at Slender, Too, since the first of the month. Lynn had started a membership campaign with local newspaper and radio advertisement. The response had been greater than she'd dared to hope, but consequently she was left to deal with a ton of paperwork plus individual exercise programs to calculate for her newest customers. To complicate matters, Lynn had come up with the brilliant idea of hanging a star from the salon ceiling for every inch lost in the month of September. It sounded like such a good suggestion at the time. But her fingers ached from working with scissors and the salon was quickly beginning to resemble another planet.

"How does bacon, eggs and pancakes sound?" Lynn asked her daughter, forcing some enthusiasm into her voice.

"Like something you should serve for breakfast."

"Sometimes a breakfast meal can be fun at dinnertime." Rooting through the refrigerator didn't offer her any other suggestions. The shelves were bare. What leftovers there were had long been eaten.

"How about tacos?"

Jason would love that, and Lynn sighed her regret. "I don't have any hamburger thawed out."

"Use the microwave...what have you got in the freezer, anyway?"

"Bacon and that's it." Lynn had been so busy over the weekend that she hadn't had time to buy groceries. It was already Wednesday and she still hadn't gotten to the market.

"You mean to tell me all we've got is bacon?"

"I'm sorry," she snapped, "I'll get to the store tomorrow."

"That's what you said last night."

The front door banged open and Jason stormed inside like a Texas whirlwind. "I scored two goals and made an assist and Mr. Lawson said I did the best ever."

Lynn hugged her son and brushed the sweat-heavy hair from his flushed brow. "That's great."

"Ryder's going to be the assistant coach now."

Lynn's gaze found her husband's. "I didn't know you played soccer."

"He doesn't," Jason answered automatically, dismissing that detail as minor. "I have to teach him."

"But..." Lynn was about to question Ryder about the unexpectedness of his offer, when Jason jerked open the refrigerator and groaned.

"You haven't got any pop yet?"

"I...didn't get a chance to get to the store."

Jason wailed in protest. "Mom, you promised. I'm dying of thirst...you don't honestly expect me to drink *water*, do you?"

"I didn't promise. I told you I'd *try* to get to the store," she barked, feeling pressured and angry. "Why do I have to be the one to do everything around here? I work, too, you know. If I lazed around some luxurious office all day reading court papers then I'd probably have more time for other things, too." Lynn couldn't believe what she was saying, how unfair she was being, but once she got started, she couldn't seem to stop. Ryder was the one having fun with her children while she was stuck in her office cutting out stupid gold stars. Tears filled her eyes and when she wiped them aside, she found Michelle, Jason and Ryder all staring at her in stunned silence.

Both children stood frozen, their eyes wide with shock and horror. Ryder's gaze was spitting and angry, but outwardly, at least, he remained calm.

"I think your mother and I need some time alone," he told Michelle and Jason, his hands on their shoulders. Gently he guided them toward the stairs. There was a quick exchange of whispers before Ryder returned to the kitchen.

"That's it, Lynn," he told her when he returned.

She slammed a package of microwave-thawed bacon on the counter. "All right, I shouldn't have said that. I apologize." Her hands were furiously at work trying to peel the thick slices of meat apart and place them in the frying pan.

"That's not good enough." He took a step closer.

"Don't accept my apology, then." She refused to look at him, fearing she would burst into tears if she did. The ache in the small of her back intensified.

"It's been weeks since we returned from Hawaii. At first everything was wonderful, but it's been a nightmare ever since."

"How can you say that?" she cried. She'd been trying so hard to be a good wife to him. Not once had she turned him down when he wanted to make love…and heaven knew that was every night. She kept the house spotless, managed the laundry and everything else that kept the house running smoothly. Okay, she hadn't gotten groceries in a few days, but that was only a minor thing.

"For the past two weeks, you fly in here after six, throw something together for dinner and then collapse."

"I work hard." She felt like weeping, tears churned just below the surface and the knot forming in her throat was large enough to choke her. No one seemed to appreciate all she did—they simply took it for granted that she could keep up with everything. Well, she couldn't.

"We all work hard—Michelle and Jason, too, in their own way. I just don't like what you're doing to yourself and everyone close to you."

Ryder wasn't the only one with complaints. She had a few of her own. She hadn't even mentioned anything about Gary's pictures being missing. Nor had she said anything about how she felt Ryder was trying to buy Michelle's and Jason's love. He couldn't seem to do enough for them. This latest thing—agreeing to help coach Jason's soccer team when he knew next to nothing about the sport was a perfect example.

"You're exhausted," he complained. "Look at you. You can hardly stand, you're so tired. You keep driving yourself and pretty soon you're going to crack. I can't allow that, Lynn. You're too important to us."

"If you didn't keep me up half the night with your lusty demands, then I might get a decent night's sleep."

Ryder's face drained of color. Lynn had never seen a man look more furious. His eyes were as cold as glaciers and when they narrowed on her, she realized she'd stepped over the line of his patience.

"Come here, Lynn," he demanded in a voice that would have shattered diamonds.

"No."

He took the bacon out of her hand so fast that Lynn whirled around and gasped. The meat fell to the floor with a slapping sound that seemed to echo around the kitchen.

"Now look what you've done," she cried, backing away from him.

He cornered her against the counter, pinning her there with the full length of his body. Lynn glared at him, her chin raised, her eyes spitting with defiance. Tears continued to sting her eyes, but she would die before she let them fall.

"So it's my 'lusty demands' that are responsible for keeping you up all night?"

"Yes," she cried.

"Then it's all my fault that you're so cranky and unreasonable."

She nodded, knowing it was a lie, but too proud to admit it. "You force me night after night. If I'm exhausted it's because of you…"

To her surprise, Ryder laughed at her. She knew she was being unreasonable and ridiculous, but he'd made her so angry and lashing out at him helped ease her frustration. But when he found her words humorous, that infuriated her all the more.

"You're lying to yourself if you believe that. You want to make love as much as I do, even more."

"No," she insisted, shaking her head.

"Oh, yes, you do."

He kissed her then, his lips moist and seductive. Her traitorous body sprang to life, responding to him the way a child does to praise. Soon her gasps of anger became tiny moans of pleasure.

"Stop it, Ryder," she cried when he broke off the kiss, pushing at him, wanting out of his arms before she begged him to make love to her.

"Why?"

"I don't like it."

"Oh, but you do," he returned with supreme arrogance; his eyes continued to laugh at her. "Do you really want me to show you how much you like it?"

"No." She pushed again at his shoulders once more.

He smiled and kissed her again. Within seconds every part of her was throbbing.

Lynn swallowed a weak groan and sank her teeth into her bottom lip when Ryder caught her earlobe between his lips and tugged on it. "I don't suppose you like this, either?"

"No." Her hands fell lifelessly to her sides. Even a token protest was more than she could muster.

"I thought not," he returned in a husky murmur..

Lynn was convinced it was a miracle she didn't sink to the floor. Every fiber of her being was alive and singing, demanding the release he'd made so remarkably familiar to her.

He slipped his hand to her backside, dragging her even closer until they were glued together.

"Want me?"

She nodded, her whole body weak with longing.

He rewarded her with a kiss that liquified anything that was left of her defenses.

"That's too bad," he whispered, his own voice shaking. She opened her eyes slowly and discovered him staring at her, his gaze clouded with passion. "I want you, too, but you need your rest."

It took a moment for his words to sink in to her consciousness and when they did, she wanted to cry out in frustration. it felt as if she'd suffered a blow to her midsection. She scooted past him and brushed the hair from her flushed face. With deliberate movements, she picked up the bacon off the floor, her hands shaking so badly it was a wonder she could manage that.

Ryder slowly moved away from her. "I'll go get us something for dinner," he told her in a voice that was filled with strain. "Take a hot bath and go to bed. You're exhausted— I'll take care of everything here."

"You don't need to do that, Ryder. I'll fix dinner."

His answering sigh was filled with defeat. "Do what you want, then."

The sound of the front door closing sounded like thunder. Lynn stretched out her hand and grabbed hold of the counter, needing it to remain upright.

"Can we come down now?" Jason called from the top of the stairs.

"Sure." It took effort to keep her voice from pitching and wobbling.

"Where'd Ryder go?" Michelle wanted to know when she joined her mother in the kitchen. She looked around suspiciously as though she expected to find him hiding under the table.

"He…he's going to bring us back something to eat."

"I wish he'd taken me with him," Jason said, whining just a little. "We haven't had hamburgers in a long time and I was hoping for a little variety."

"Ryder didn't need to leave," Michelle pointed out. "He could've ordered pizza. We haven't had that in a while either—not like we used to when you first came back from Hawaii. What's he bringing us?"

"I don't know." Lynn turned back to the sink, not wanting her children to know how close she was to bursting into tears.

"I thought you guys were going to have a big fight," Michelle said, "We listened, but we didn't even hear you shout."

"We…didn't. I think I'll go up and take a shower if you two don't need me."

"Sure, Mom, go ahead."

She raced up the stairs, undressed and turned on the water spigots. Tears scalded her cheeks as she heaved in giant gulps of oxygen. The water didn't ease any of the ache she was experiencing, but then she'd known it wouldn't. When she was finished, she dressed in her pajamas and stood at the top of the stairs.

"Michelle, would you tell Ryder when he gets back that I'm tired and I've decided to go to bed?"

"Okay," she answered with some reluctance.

"But, Mom, it's not even seven," Jason objected.

"I'm really exhausted tonight," she said and turned away to swallow a sob. "He'll understand."

Since that was exactly where he'd sent her, she doubted that Ryder would object. Although she listened for him, Ryder didn't come upstairs until several hours later. Lynn had snoozed off and on for most of the evening, but she was instantly awake the minute Ryder entered the bedroom. The illuminated dial on the clock radio revealed it was after eleven.

He didn't turn on the light, but she heard him undressing in the dark, taking pains to be quiet.

"I'm awake," she whispered. "Do you want to talk?"

"Not particularly."

If her mood had improved, his hadn't. Sullen silence filled the room.

"I'll stop on my way home tomorrow night and buy groceries," she offered a couple of minutes later, regretting the things she'd said and done and looking for a way to show him how sorry she was.

"While I was out earlier, I picked up a few essentials, so there's no rush." Ryder lifted the sheets and climbed into the bed, staying as far away from her as space would allow.

"I promise I'll do it tomorrow."

"Before or after you put in a ten-hour day?"

Lynn let that comment slide. "It's this membership campaign. You know it won't be like this every week, I promise. By the end of the month things will have settled back to normal."

He bunched up the pillow and rolled onto his side, presenting her with a clear view of his back.

More tortuous seconds passed.

"I'm sorry for the things I said earlier—none of them were true." She tried again, feeling more wretched by the minute, desperate to repair the damage her pride had inflicted.

He didn't respond and she felt a growing desolation. "Ryder, I love you so much, please don't do this... I can't bear it."

She felt him stiffen as though a battle were raging within him. It seemed like an eternity passed before he shifted his weight and turned onto his back. Lynn eagerly scooted into his arms, looping her arm around his waist and burying her face between his shoulder and his neck. It felt like coming home after being away a long while, his arms a shelter from the worst storms. Only this hurricane had been one of her own making.

"You can't go on like this," he whispered into her hair, tenderly brushing it away from her face. "I refuse to let you do this to yourself, to your family."

She could only agree. "I've been doing a lot of thinking, between catnaps tonight," she admitted. "I think I understand what's been happening with Slender, Too, the last few months, and why I've pushed myself the way I have."

"You do?"

Lynn nodded. "The first couple of years after Gary was gone, I floundered terribly. Everything in my life was dictated by other people while I struggled for some kind of control. Bit by bit, I gained my independence in small ways. When I was ready to really break free and soar on my own, I bought the franchise. It was the first time in my life that I'd invested in something that was completely mine. I was the one in charge. Slender, Too, was a tiny piece of life that I could govern and the success or failure rested entirely on my shoulders. That first sample of accomplishment was powerful and the taste of independence addictive. I've clung on to it, refusing to let go of even the most mundane aspects of the business, despite the fact that the children didn't have as much attention as they'd wanted. I needed the time for *me*."

"But you're willing to now?"

"Yes, I have to, because I've learned how important my family is in my life. And…"

"Yes?"

"You did that, Ryder."

Then he kissed her until her heart was pounding out of control. "Ah, Lynn, you know exactly what to say to turn my head."

She giggled, loving the feel of his hands as they sought her.

"I want to change things, Ryder, but I'm not sure I know how."

"What you need is a manager to take some of the responsibility off your shoulders."

"But I still want to maintain some control," she inserted, knowing the role of observer would never satisfy her.

"You will have, honey, just not all the hours. Try it out and see how it works."

She nodded, knowing he was right, but still having trouble admitting it—she always *did* have problems owning up to that.

He closed his arms more securely around her. "About what happened in the kitchen," he murmured, flicking his tongue over her ear, nibbling on her lobe.

"Yes?"

Ryder's hand lifted her breast. "Don't you think it's time we finished what we started?"

Eighteen

"Ryder," Lynn purred, utterly content. She slid her bare leg seductively down his much longer one and toyed with the soft hairs at his nape. She was resting on her back and he was lying on his stomach with his hand draped over her middle. "I love you."

"Hmm… I know." He raised himself up on one elbow and kissed her in a leisurely exercise. "But if anyone should complain about being kept awake nights, it's me."

"Very funny." She rubbed her hands over his back, pausing at the dip below his waist, then hesitated. "I want to talk to you about something important."

He caught her lower lip between his teeth and sucked gently. "What?"

"Gary."

Ryder went completely still. She felt his breath lodge in his throat and his body tense. "Why?"

"Because every time I mention his name, you freeze up and change the subject."

His mouth descended over hers while he rooted through her long hair as though to punish her for bringing Gary's name into their conversation. Lynn gave a painful yelp and he relaxed his grip and lifted his head. His lungs made a soft rustling sound. "That's because I don't want to talk about him."

She smiled gently, and whispered, "I guessed as much, but, Ryder, I don't think that's healthy." Except for their initial discussion at the picnic, from the time he'd returned from Boston, Ryder had gone to great lengths to avoid talking about his best friend.

Again and again he'd assured Lynn that his love for her had nothing to do with what had happened to Gary or any guilt associated with the tragedy of his death. Perhaps because she'd wanted to believe it so badly, she'd held on to the assumption. But lately little things had started to add up and she didn't like the sum total she was seeing. Tonight seemed to be the one to settle their qualms. This problem with Gary was important and she wanted to lay it to rest.

"He's dead, Lynn."

"But that shouldn't mean—"

"You're my wife now."

"I'm not contesting that."

"It's a good thing." He tried the playful approach in an effort to beset her, planting kisses on the edges of her mouth in a teasing game that would have easily turned her mind an hour earlier.

"Ryder, please," she begged.

He emitted a low guttural sound and chuckled. "I love it when you say that."

"You're impossible!"

He slipped his gaze his down her stomach and the amusement drained from his eyes.

Emotion flickered through them as he eased himself up and over her. "You're doing it again," she said, stopping him.

"I plan to do it every day of our married life."

"Ryder…"

"I want a baby," he announced without warning. "I know we agreed to wait, but I need to get you pregnant now. Tonight. Right now. I can't wait a minute more to feel my son moving inside you."

The plea that came into his voice was almost desperate. "I've thought about it a good deal this past month. Living with Michelle and Jason has taught me so much," he continued, holding her gaze. "I often wondered what kind of a father I'd be. I've even worried about it, but now I know I'm going to love having children."

"Oh, Ryder." She was eager, too, but a little afraid.

His face, poised above her own, filled with wonder. His jaw was clenched tight, but not with anger—some other emotion, restraint, she decided. His eyes shone with more vulnerability than she had ever seen in him. Just gazing up at this man she had married, and her heart felt as if it would burst.

"I remember how you had morning sickness with Michelle and Jason. I only want one baby…just one," he said, and laid his hand against her cheek, rubbing his thumb over her lower lip. "But promise me you'll throw out those damn birth control pills."

Tears gathered in the corners of her eyes as she nodded. "Ryder, I love you. I'll give you a dozen children if that's what you want."

"Oh Lynn, will I ever get enough of you?"

"I sincerely hope not." She twisted around, so that she was on her stomach, and reached for the knot behind her head that would unravel the long plait of hair. Ryder watched her movements with wide-eyed wonder, as though he couldn't believe what she was preparing to do. Coming to a kneeling position, she pressed his shoulders back against the mattress before staddling him.

It wasn't until Lynn was dressing the following morning that she discovered Gary's uniform hat and badge were missing. She'd kept them stored on the shelf above the closet in their bedroom, carefully packed away in a box she planned to give Jason when he turned eighteen.

She paused, uncertain. Removing Gary's photo from the living room was one thing, but for Ryder to take away something that was a part of her son's inheritance was another. After a short search, she found Gary's photos and several other items stored in the garage, tucked away in a secluded corner.

Lynn exhaled sharply, remembering how she'd tried to talk to Ryder about Gary just the night before. But Ryder had done it to her again. Now that she gave the matter thought, Lynn realized that Michelle and Jason rarely mentioned their deceased father anymore, either. They, too, had apparently sensed Ryder's uneasiness over the subject and had eliminated Gary's name from casual conversation.

Following that episode with the missing hat and badge, Lynn was more determined than ever to have this out with Ryder. It was paramount that they discuss Gary and the role he now played in their lives. Ryder seemed to want to shove him aside and pretend he'd never existed. The only reason she could figure why he would do something like that wasn't one she was eager to face. If Ryder continued to carry a burden of guilt over Gary's death, then she could never be fully certain of his motive for marrying her and taking on the responsibility of raising Michelle and Jason.

She loved him. The children loved him. Ryder had made certain of that. He'd done everything humanly possible to garner their affection. He spoiled Michelle and Jason, taking his duty as stepfather far beyond what anyone would have expected. In analyzing the situation, Lynn realized it was as if Ryder was trying to make up to them for all the years they'd gone without a father figure.

The knot in her stomach twisted into a tighter knot.

When it came to proving his devotion to her, Ryder had seemed determined to be the model husband. He brought her gifts, made love to her frequently, and spoiled her in much the same way he did the children, as if he needed to compensate her for the loss of Gary.

A week passed, and although Lynn tried twice more to talk about her dead husband, Ryder wouldn't allow it. He was never abrupt or angry in his efforts to avoid the subject, but firmly subtle. She would carefully plan the discussion, wait for a quiet moment, usually after Michelle and Jason were in bed, and fifteen minutes later she would marvel at just how skillful Ryder's methods were of dodging the issue.

The problem was that they were both so busy. Ryder's caseload was increasing, which meant he left for work earlier and arrived home later. On her end, Lynn had offered the job of manager, with an appropriate increase in salary, to her assistant, Sharon. Her employee seemed both pleased and surprised and had eagerly accepted the promotion. That same week, Lynn hired another new assistant and left her training in Sharon's capable hands.

Lynn was still needed at the salon, but much of the day-to-day responsibility fell onto Sharon, which surprisingly pleased Lynn. She thought she would miss the control, but her life was so full that it was a relief not to worry about Slender, Too along with everything else.

On Wednesday, Lynn decided to try once more to talk to Ryder. This time, she wouldn't be put off so easily.

"I'm going to lunch now," Sharon informed Lynn, sticking her head into the office. "Judy's taking the noon class, but this is her first time going solo, so you might want to keep an eye on her."

"Will do," Lynn answered with a smile. She was reviewing the work schedule, penciling in names and times for the following week.

Sharon left the door to the office ajar, and the upbeat melody for the aerobics class drifted into the room. Absently Lynn tapped her foot, but the action stopped abruptly as her eyes fell on the following Monday's date.

It was silly that such a minor thing would trouble her so— Gary's birthday—or what would have been his birthday. He would have been thirty-seven, only Gary would remain thirty-three forever.

The remainder of the day was melancholy. Lynn found herself pensive and blue. She wouldn't change her life from the way it was now—she had no regrets—but a certain sadness permeated her being. One she couldn't shake or fully understand.

She was home before the kids, which was unusual. She left the salon early, telling Sharon she had a headache.

"Mom, I'm going over to Marcy's. Okay?" Michelle asked ten minutes after she was in the door.

"That's fine, honey."

Jason was holding an apple and a banana in one hand and a box of graham crackers in the other. "Do we have any chocolate chip cookies left?" He must have noticed her frown because he added, "I'm a growing boy—I need my afternoon snack."

"Take the apple and a few of the crackers, I don't want you ruining your dinner."

"Oh, Mom."

He may not have agreed, but he willingly obeyed her.

The pork chops were ready for the oven and the house was quiet. The real-estate agent they'd been working with phoned to tell Lynn about a large colonial that had just come on the market.

"Would you like to make an appointment to see it this evening?"

Lynn's gaze scooted around the kitchen and family room, falling lovingly on each wall and each piece of furniture. She didn't want to move, she never had. Ryder had been the one who insisted they start looking for another home right away. The day they returned from their honeymoon, he'd contacted a Realtor. At least Lynn had been able to convince him not to put their house on the market until they found something suitable.

"Mrs. Matthews?"

"Not tonight," she answered abruptly, realizing she'd left the woman hanging. "Perhaps tomorrow... I'm not feeling well." Considering her mood, that wasn't so far from the truth.

When she finished with the phone conversation, Lynn sat and covered her face with her hands. In the bottom drawer of the china cabinet was her and Gary's wedding album. She felt drawn to that. Reverently she removed the bulky book and folded back the cover and the first thick page as though turning something fragile. The picture of her and Gary, standing with their wedding party, both so young and so much in love, greeted her like an old friend.

Tears flooded Lynn's eyes. Tears she couldn't fully comprehend.

She loved Ryder...she loved Gary.

The front door opened and thinking it was one of the children, Lynn wiped the moisture from her cheek and forced a smile.

Instead Ryder sauntered into the room. It was hours before he was due home. "Did the Realtor call to set an appointment for us to see that new house?"

"I...I told her we'd look at it another day," she answered abruptly, quickly closing the picture album.

Ryder frowned. "I called the salon, but Sharon told me you'd gone home because of a headache."

Feeling incredibly guilty, Lynn stood abruptly and moved in front of the table. "I'm fine." She rubbed her palms together in an agitated movement and stepped across the room, praying Ryder wouldn't notice the picture album.

Ryder hesitated. "You've been crying."

"Not really...something must have gotten into my eye."

"Lynn, what's wrong?"

"Nothing." She moved to the kitchen counter and brewed herself a cup of coffee, although she already had one. When she turned back, she found Ryder standing at the round oak table, his hand on the wedding portfolio. He lifted back the cover.

Watching him, Lynn wanted to cry out for him to stop, but she knew it wouldn't do any good. His narrowed gaze rested on the picture she had been studying. He seemed to stop breathing. She looked on helplessly as he clenched his jaw, but the action wasn't directed by anger. Somehow, she'd expected him to become irate, but the look on his face revealed far more pain than irritation.

"You're still in love with him, aren't you?"

Nineteen

"Yes," Lynn admitted. "I love Gary."

The blood drained from Ryder's face as though she'd physically punched him. After the initial shock, he wore a look that claimed he'd known it all along, and wasn't the least bit surprised.

"Ryder... I was married to the man for nine years. Michelle and Jason are his children. I'm not the kind of woman who can conveniently forget that. Yes, I love Gary and as much as you don't want to hear it, I'm not likely to ever forget him."

"Gary is dead."

"You're making it sound like I'm being unfaithful to you by remembering him. I can't pretend the man never existed and neither can you."

"Thinking about him is one thing, but do you have to moon over his pictures, grieving your terrible loss?"

"His death *was* a terrible loss," she cried, losing patience. "And I wasn't mooning!"

"I find you weeping while looking over pictures of your wedding to another man and you try to feed me some line about there being something in your eye. You don't even have to say it. I can tell you regret the fact we're married."

"I don't. How can you ever think such a thing?"

"You honestly expect me to answer that? How many other times have you taken out that wedding album and cried over Gary?"

"This is the first time…in months. I don't even remember the last time I felt like this. He was my husband, I have the right to look at these pictures and feel sad."

"Not when you're married to me."

"I will if I want," she cried defensively.

Ryder's mouth thinned. "I'm your husband, Lynn."

"I know that." His attitude was infuriating her more every minute.

"What possible reason would you have to drag out those old pictures and weep over him now?"

Lynn's hands knotted in defense, knowing Ryder wasn't going to like her answer. "It's his birthday."

Ryder took three abrupt steps away from her, halted and jerked his fingers through his hair. "The man is dead. He doesn't have birthdays."

"I'm well aware of that. But I can't forget the fact he lived and breathed and loved."

Ryder began pacing and seemed to mull over her words. "The loving part is the crux of the problem, isn't it?"

"Of course," she cried. "I know that bothers you, and I'm sorry, but I can't change the past anymore than I could raise Gary from the dead. He was an important part of my life and I don't plan on forgetting him because you can't bear the mention of his name."

Ryder went still as if a new thought had flashed into his mind. His dark eyes hardened. "You blame me for his death, too, don't you? I'd always feared you would, and then I chose to overlook the obvious."

"Oh, Ryder, honestly," she whispered, wanting to weep, "I don't blame you. I never did—I couldn't have married you if there'd been doubt in my heart."

He shook his head, discounting her answer. "The revenge would be sweet. If you'd planned to torture me, you couldn't have chosen a more painful method."

"Stop talking like that. It's crazy—I love you. Hasn't the past month taught you that much?"

"I did this to myself," he murmured, defeated. "There's no one else to blame." He inhaled a long, slow breath, and continued thoughtfully. "I rushed you into the marriage, using every trick I could think of, and like a fool, I didn't even consider the fact you planned to hold on to Gary with both hands."

"I'm not holding on to Gary—you're being utterly ridiculous."

"Am I?"

The fight seemed to have died in him, Lynn noticed. He was resolved now, subdued, as if he'd lost the most important battle of his life.

"I honestly thought I could step into Michelle's and Jason's lives and fill the void left by Gary's death. Only there wasn't one. You've carried his image in your heart and on your lips all these years. They didn't need a father, not when the memory of Gary remained so strong. You made sure of that."

"Ryder…"

"You didn't need a husband, either."

"You're right," she cried, her patience gone. "I didn't *need* one, but I *wanted* you…"

"In bed."

"In my life," she cried. Tears of anger and frustration brimmed in her eyes and she wiped them aside, furious that she couldn't hold back the emotion.

His smile was unbelievably sad. "I knew you loved Gary in the beginning, but I thought once we were married that would change."

"Change?"

He ignored her question and walked over to the kitchen window, looking out onto the back patio, although Lynn felt certain he was blind to the glory of the late summer afternoon. "The Realtor has taken us to look at how many houses now?"

He was jumping from one subject to another, without any logical reason that she could decipher. "What has that got to do with anything?"

"Ten homes? Fifteen? And yet you've never been able to find one you like. The house may be perfect for us, but you've always managed to come up with a convenient excuse why we shouldn't buy it."

"I—"

"Have you ever considered the reason all those homes didn't suit you? Why you've continued to drag your feet again and again? It's getting to the point now that you delay even setting up the appointment with the Realtor."

She wanted to shout at him, tell him how wrong he was, but as far as the Realtor went, she was guilty of everything he claimed. "I...oh, Ryder, I never *did* want to move. I'm trying, but there are so many happy memories associated with this place. I love it here, I'm comfortable."

"And I'm not."

She dipped her head and eased her breath out on a disheartened sigh. "I know."

"Gary's ghost is here, in every room, and he's haunted

me from the minute we returned from Hawaii. Every time I walk through the front door, I feel his presence, every time I turn around, his face is looking at me, accusing me. I tried to ignore him, tried to pretend he wasn't there. I went so far as to remove his pictures and a few other things, thinking that would help, but it didn't."

Lynn wasn't sure what to say. She could understand his feelings, although that didn't help their situation any.

"But a new house isn't going to solve that, is it, Lynn?"

"How do you mean?"

"Gary's a part of you in the same way that he's a part of Michelle and Jason. We won't ever be able to escape him, because wherever you are, he'll be there, too."

She opened her mouth to deny that, then realized what he said was true.

"I notice you're not bothering to repudiate that fact."

Lynn drooped her head as the defeat worked its way through her tired limbs. "No, I don't think I can. You're right."

"I thought as much." If he experienced any elation at correctly deciphering her actions, it wasn't evident in his voice. What *did* come through was a heavy note of despair. "I can't continue to fool myself any longer and neither can you. Nothing's going to change."

"I don't understand why it should," she cried. "You're asking me to wipe out a decade of my life, and I find that unreasonable. It's just not going to happen."

"You don't need to tell me that, I figured it out already." He reached out and touched her, lightly grazing her cheek with his fingertips, his eyes filled with an agony of regret. "I won't take second place in your life, Lynn."

The action tugged at Lynn's heart and she caught his hand in her own, wanting to weep and beg him to understand. She managed to hold all the emotion boiling within her at bay; she longed to find the words that would reassure him, but was at a loss.

"I love you, Ryder."

He nodded, sadly. "But not enough."

With that he turned and slowly climbed the stairs.

Lynn followed him a couple of minutes later and was shocked to see him packing his suitcases.

"What are you doing?"

"Giving us both some needed space to think things out."

"But you're moving out. Why?" Tears gushed down her face—she didn't even try to hold them inside.

"I was wrong to have married you," Ryder said, busily filling his luggage, hardly stopping to look at her.

"Well, that's just wonderful," she cried and slumped onto the edge of the mattress. Her legs felt incredibly weak. "So you're going to walk out on me. It's getting to be a habit with you, Ryder. A bad habit. When the going gets tough, the tough move on, is that it? Where are you going this time? Europe? Do you think that'll be far enough away to forget?"

He whirled around. "You've already admitted you still love Gary, what else do you expect me to do?"

"I also admitted that I love *you*! Love me back, accept me for who I am—love Michelle and Jason. I want you to give me the child you've talked about so much, and build a good life with me and our children."

"And play second fiddle to a dead man? No thanks." He slammed the top closed on the first suitcase and reached for the second.

"Why are you doing this?" she cried.

He hesitated. "You already know the answer to that. There isn't any need to discuss it further."

Desperate now, Lynn scooted off the bed and walked

over to the window. She closed her eyes and covered her mouth with her hand. "Aren't I even allowed to keep the memories?"

He didn't respond, which was answer enough.

"Can't I?" she tried again, tears drenching her face, dripping onto her chin. She brushed them off with the heel of her hand, and held her head high, the action dictated by an abundance of pride.

"Go ahead and leave me, Ryder. Walk out on me. I got along without you the first time, I'll do it again." She marched across the room to the closet and ripped his dress shirts off the hangers one by one in a disorderly fashion. "I wouldn't want you to forget anything," she sobbed. "Take it all."

He carelessly stuffed the pressed shirts in the bottom of the garment bag, paused and glance around. "I'll send someone for whatever else is left."

"Fine." She didn't dare look at him, for fear she would break down completely and beg him to stay. "Just be sure this is what you really want."

He hesitated, his gaze mirroring her own agony. "It isn't, but I think a separation will give us both time to sort through our feelings."

"How long? One year? Three? Or should we try to break a record this time?"

Ryder closed his eyes, as though her words were a physical assault. Lynn frantically wiped the moisture from her face. "I tried to talk to you about Gary," she sobbed. "You know, I tried, but you'd never let me. The minute I mentioned his name you did cartwheels in an effort to change the subject."

"The reason should have been obvious."

"If we'd been able to clear the air before…then maybe

none of this would be necessary. But oh no, you insisted on sweeping everything under the carpet—ignore it and it'll go away. But Gary isn't going and neither am I!"

"I didn't want to hear what you were so bound and determined to tell me," he shouted. "In this instance, ignorance was bliss." He swung the suitcases off the mattress with such force it tugged the bedspread onto the floor.

Lynn righted it as though that was of the utmost importance.

Ryder left the bedroom, walking away from her with ground-devouring steps, as if he couldn't get away fast enough. Lynn remained in the bedroom, and flinched at the sound of the front door closing as it echoed up the stairway.

The silence that followed was as profound as it was deafening.

Lynn didn't know how long she stood there, immobile and numb. The floor seemed to sway and buckle under her feet and she lowered herself onto the edge of the bed, her fingers biting into the mattress.

The tears had dried against the flushed skin of her cheeks long before she was composed enough to go downstairs and confront Michelle and Jason.

"When's dinner?" Jason asked as he barged in the front door a few minutes later with Michelle close behind him.

"I'm…just putting it on now." She quietly put the pork chops into the oven, all the time knowing she wouldn't be able to gag down a single bite of the evening meal.

"You haven't even started yet?"

"It's only five," Michelle said indignantly.

"I need something to carry me through," Jason cried. He opened the cookie jar and stuck in his hand. The bowl had been empty all week, but her son managed to gain a pawful of crumbs and took delight in licking them from his hand a finger at a time as he walked out of the kitchen.

"I don't suppose you thought to wash your hands before you did that?" Michelle commented, having gone to position herself in front of the television. "Aren't you going to tell him to wash, Mom? He could be bringing in germs that will infect us all."

"It would be like closing the gate after the horse gets loose," she said, doing her best to pretend everything was normal.

"When's Ryder getting home?" Jason asked, opening the refrigerator and peering inside.

"He's…going to be away on a business trip for a while," she said as nonchalantly as possible, trying to play down the fact he was missing without arousing their suspicions.

The door to the refrigerator closed with a bang. "When did he tell you this?"

She glanced at the clock. "An hour ago."

"How long is he going to be gone?" Jason asked anxiously. "What about soccer? What am I going to tell the coach when Ryder doesn't show up… I'm counting on him and so is everyone else. I play better when Ryder's there watching me."

"I…don't know what you should tell Mr. Lawson…tell him Ryder had to go out of town."

"He could have said something to us, don't you think?" Michelle said with a pout. "I need him to help me with math. We're dividing fractions and some of those problems are too hard for me and a simple calculator. I've got to have massive help."

"You can do it, Michelle, I'll be around to lend a hand."

"Thanks, but no thanks," she said, on a sarcastic note.

"I remember the last time you decided to tutor me in fractions. I'm lucky I made it out of fifth grade."

"Why would Ryder leave on a business trip?" Jason wanted to know, his eyes curious. "I thought all his cases were in Seattle."

Lynn hated to lie to her children, but she didn't want to alarm them unnecessarily. She would tell them the truth, but not now when it was difficult enough for her to face.

The dinner was one of the best Lynn had fixed all week, but no one seemed to have much of an appetite.

"Ryder's coming back, isn't he, Mom?" Michelle whispered the question while Lynn removed their plates from the table. Jason was talking to Brad on the telephone.

"Of course he is," she returned with an encouraging grin that took all her reserve of strength. She didn't know what had prompted the question and prayed her daughter didn't notice the way her hands shook as she placed their dinner dishes in the dishwasher.

Michelle relaxed. "It's been good having a dad again."

"I know." It had been good having a husband, too. But Lynn had the crippling feeling that this problem with Ryder wasn't going to be settled overnight.

"Ryder's going to phone us, isn't he?" Jason asked, once he was finished talking to his friend. "Brad's father goes on business trips sometimes and he calls every night. Brad says it's really great because when his dad comes home, he brings him and his little sister gifts."

"I don't know if Ryder will have a chance to call," Lynn said, making busywork around the sink, scrubbing it extra hard. Her eyes blurred with fresh tears.

"He'll bring us back a present, won't he?"

"I...don't know that, either."

Jason uttered a disgruntled sound. "What's the use of

having him go away, if he doesn't bring us back something?"

"Maybe he doesn't know he's supposed to," Michelle murmured thoughtfully. "He didn't have any kids until us. Maybe we should all write him and drop the hint. I'm sure he'd want to know what his duties are to me and Jason."

Lynn couldn't endure another minute of their exchange. Ryder claimed Gary's ghost filled their house and that their children held on to his memory. If Ryder were there to hear this conversation now, he would know how untrue that was.

The evening seemed to drag. Although Michelle claimed she didn't want Lynn's help with her math, after several minutes of grumbling over her assignment, she succumbed and took everything to her mother. When Lynn wasn't much help, Michelle suggested they call Lynn's accountant.

As expected, Jason put up a fuss about taking a bath, but that was normal. Lynn's patience was stretched to its limit. Jason must have known that because after voicing the usual arguments, he went upstairs and bathed in world-record time. Lynn wondered if he'd managed to get his entire body wet, but hadn't the fight in her to question him.

The kids were in their rooms when the front door opened.

"Ryder," Jason cried from the top of the stairs, racing into his arms. "What happened on your business trip? Did you know when you go away you're supposed to bring back presents for your kids? It's the expected thing."

"You're not supposed to blurt it out like that!" Michelle stormed. "You can be such a nerd, sometimes."

"Who's calling who a nerd?"

"Children, please," Lynn cried moving into the entryway. She sought Ryder's gaze, but he avoided meeting hers.

"How come you're home?" Michelle asked. "You haven't even been gone a single night."

"The plane was late," Ryder told her. He glanced at his watch. "Now go back upstairs, it's long past your bed time."

"Okay."

"Do we have to?"

"Yes, you do," Lynn answered for Ryder. "Good night to you both."

"You missed a great dinner," Jason added, hugging him one last time. "Mom cooked her special pork chops."

If pork chops would have kept Ryder home, Lynn would cook them every night.

"I'll see you in the morning," Jason said on the tail end of a yawn. "I hope you stay home...it's not right when you're gone."

Both Michelle and Jason had returned to their bedrooms before Ryder spoke. "I apologize for dropping in like this, but I forgot my briefcase. There are some papers I'll need in the morning, otherwise I wouldn't have troubled you."

Twenty

Ryder scooted past Lynn and retrieved his briefcase. Lynn stood frozen, her heart jackhammering against her rib cage, but she dared not move for fear she would break down and weep before he left.

Ryder returned, and paused in front of the door. "I take it you told the kids I was going away on a business trip?"

She nodded. "I probably shouldn't have lied, but I didn't know what else to say."

"That explanation is as good as any. Once they get used to the idea of me being gone, you can tell them the truth."

"Which is?"

"Which is," he repeated and drew in an unsteady breath, "I needed to get away for a while...to think things through."

"I'm sure they'll understand that readily enough." Her voice dipped sarcastically. "And what should I tell them you're thinking about? They'll ask me that, you know. Exactly what do you want me to tell them?"

"You know the answer to that," he snapped.

"I don't."

"I'm trying to decide if I can continue to live with a woman who's in love with another man."

Lynn crossed her arms over her middle to ward off a chill that descended over her like an October frost. "You make it sound so vile, as though I'm committing adultery by honoring Gary's memory."

"You do more than honor his memory, despite what we have, you won't let him go."

"No..." Her voice cracked, and she whirled around, unable to face him any longer. "I love you, Ryder, and it's going to break my heart to lose you, but I don't know what I can do to make things right for us."

He was silent for so long, Lynn wondered if he'd slipped out the door without her hearing him move, but she didn't turn around to investigate.

Suddenly the tension of the day overwhelmed her. Tears flooded her eyes and she sobbed so hard her shoulders shook violently.

A bedroom door opened upstairs. "Mom?"

"It's all right, Jason," Ryder answered.

"I can hear Mom crying." Her son started down the stairs, pausing halfway down. "She *is* crying."

Lynn wiped the moisture from her face as best she could. "I'm fine, honey."

"Ryder," Jason shouted. "Do something...hold her or kiss her or do that other stuff women like. You can't let her stand there like that, bawling her head off."

Ryder hesitated, then walked over to Lynn's side. He didn't want to touch her, she could feel his reluctance, but they both knew Jason wouldn't be appeased until he was assured his mother was receiving the comfort she needed. Ryder wrapped his arms around her and Lynn buried her face in his shoulder, her arms hanging limply at her sides.

"You've got to hold on to him, too, Mom," Jason instructed impatiently.

Lynn complied, awkwardly. Her raised arms loosely circled Ryder's waist. Being this close to him demanded a steep fee and she quivered, wondering how she would ever adjust to a life where there wouldn't be someone to love her the way Ryder did. Her whole body felt as if it were trembling from the inside out.

"I don't think you should be taking this business trip," Jason announced, marching the rest of the way down the stairs, with a military crispness that would have pleased an Army officer.

Lynn backed out of Ryder's arms and made an effort to compose herself. "Honey, listen—"

"Ryder didn't say anything about going away on business trips when he married us."

"I'm sorry, son, but I have to leave." Ryder's own voice was dark and heavy.

"But we need you here. Mom tried not to show it, but Michelle and I noticed how miserable she was all night. She misses you a whole bunch already and you've only been gone a little while."

Ryder's gaze fell on Lynn and a weary sadness invaded his eyes.

"Michelle and I need you, too. Mom had to help Michelle with her math tonight and it didn't go very well."

"I'm sure your mother did just fine."

"Not according to Michelle," Jason murmured, tossing Lynn an apologetic glance. "I don't think Mom's into fractions."

"What are you guys talking about down there?" Michelle shouted testily. "I thought we were supposed to be in bed, asleep."

"Mom's crying," Jason shot back at his sister.

"I knew something like this was going to happen," Michelle blurted out and raced down the stairs like an avenging angel of mercy. "I hope you know this is all your fault, Ryder."

"Michelle," Lynn warned.

"Mom's been a basket case all night. How can you leave the woman who loves you alone like this?"

So much for the gallant effort she'd made to hide her distress from the kids. Knowing how woefully she'd failed, Lynn's lower lip quivered and she was forced to take in several deep breaths to hold back a fresh batch of tears. "Michelle and Jason, it's time for you to go back upstairs."

"Are you going to cry again?" Jason wanted reassurance before he returned to his bedroom.

Lynn shook her head, then realized she couldn't make that guarantee. "I'll try not to."

Michelle and Jason shared a meaningful glance and then by unspoken agreement, headed toward their bedrooms. Lynn stopped them at the foot of the stairs, hugging them separately, loving her children so much her heart felt as if it would burst with the weight of the emotion. Gary had given her these precious two and if there had been no other grounds than that, she would always love him. As it was there were so many reasons to love and remember Gary Danfort.

"You want a hug, too, Ryder?" Michelle asked, yawning out the question with her hand in front of her face.

He nodded, holding Michelle close. Lynn noted the way his eyes closed and his jaw tightened.

"Next time when you need to go away on business," Michelle murmured, "try to tell us sooner so we won't all feel so lonely without you. It's bad when you leave and we haven't had time to—" she paused and dragged a huge breath through her lungs "—prepare for it."

"You're not still going, are you?" Jason cried, shocked. "After all this?"

"Jason, to bed!" Lynn pointed up the stairs, her voice more solid.

"He made you cry and Michelle could flunk math, and Ryder is still going to catch that stupid plane, anyway? Doesn't he know he's got responsibilities…like taking out the garbage and helping coach soccer—"

"We're going to be just fine without Ryder," Lynn interrupted her son's outburst, but her voice lacked any real conviction.

"No, we won't!" Jason proclaimed under his breath. He paused and his eyes flashed with concern. "You'll be back in time for Saturday's game, won't you?"

"I'm not sure."

With that, Jason tossed his arms into the air. "What's the use of having a new dad if he can't come to my soccer games?"

"Jason!"

He muttered something unintelligible under his breath and vanished inside his bedroom.

Lynn straightened her shoulders and tried to offer Ryder a smile to make up for the disruption, but her mouth wouldn't cooperate. It was unlikely that Ryder even noticed since his gaze was centered on the empty hallway upstairs, from where both children had disappeared.

"They love you," Lynn told him softly, wondering if he fully understood how much.

Ryder nodded and reluctantly reached for his briefcase.

Lynn closed her eyes, unable to bear the pain of his leaving. It had been difficult enough the first time. The words to ask him to stay burned on the tip of her tongue, but she was forced to swallow them. The taste of acid filled her dry mouth.

Ryder hesitated in front of the door and then turned back to her. "I don't know that I can do it." Each word seemed to be painfully pulled from his heart, his voice strained and low.

Lynn bowed her head. "I don't know that I can let you."

"By all rights, you should throw me out of here, but I'd like to try to sort this out if we can. Let's reason this out."

Lynn felt her body go weak with relief, and led the way into the kitchen. She automatically put on a pot of coffee. Ryder stepped behind her, his hands resting lightly on her shoulders as if he needed to touch her.

"I didn't really need the briefcase," he admitted, "I was looking for a convenient excuse to come back and make things right, although heaven knows, I can't see any solution to this."

Lynn sucked part of her bottom lip with her teeth. It had cost Ryder a good deal of pride to be so honest and she was grateful.

When the coffee had finished dripping into the glass pot, she poured them each a mug and carried them to the table, where Ryder was waiting. She sat across from him.

Ryder cupped his hands around the steaming mug, his eyes downcast. "After what just happened with Michelle and Jason, I realize what a jealous fool I'm being. How can I feel resentful toward a man I loved...a man who's been dead for over three years?"

"But, Ryder you don't have any reason to be jealous of Gary."

Ryder looked away from her, refusing to meet her eyes. "Please let me finish, Lynn. It's not a pleasant emotion to have to admit to myself, let alone confess to you. I realized while I was driving around tonight that undiluted, hard-core jealousy was exactly what I was feeling."

"But, Ryder, I love you so much."

"I know that, too, but as damning as it sounds, I begrudge every minute of the life you shared with Gary." He stopped and ran his hand over his jaw as if the action would erase the guilt charted across the tight lines of his face. "Admitting it to you this way makes me feel like I've got to be the pettiest man alive. How can I even think like this? What kind of man am I to feel these things? I look around me and this crushing weight of shame is pressed upon me. I loved Gary—he was the best kind of police officer and human being I'm ever likely to know. He was everything that was good…honorable and generous…he was my friend and yet I'm harboring all these negative emotions toward him."

Lynn reached for Ryder's hand, intertwining their fingers. "You love Gary and you resent Gary…it isn't any wonder you haven't wanted to talk about him."

"If he hadn't died, I wouldn't have you and the kids and so there's an incredible amount of guilt involved as well." He sucked in a sigh and slowly shook his head as though the magnitude of his emotions was more than he could fully comprehend. "I honestly believed I'd dealt with all my feelings for him while I was in law school, but I can see now that you were right. I was sweeping all these painful emotions under a carpet, avoiding confronting them because I've been so confused. In fact, I'm still confused." The rugged lines in his face were testament enough to the turmoil churning inside his soul. "I packed my bags and was running away from you and the kids…that was so stupid, so illogical, I can't believe the thought so much as entered my mind. The only place in the world I want to be is with you and Michelle and Jason. My heart is here…my soul is here… there's no leaving, no running away."

Tears bled down the side of Lynn's face. Unable to maintain this distance from her husband any longer, she stood and walked around the table. Ryder scooted out his chair and lowered her into his lap, folding her in his embrace, sighing as her arms circled him.

"I've been doing some thinking tonight myself," Lynn told him, her throat thick with emotion. "And like you, I realize I've made a lot of mistakes. Looking over those wedding pictures was one of them… I can understand how you must have felt when you found me."

"Deep down inside, I know how completely unreasonable I'm being to ask you to forget Gary, but I can't seem to put that behind me."

"Can *you* forget him?" she asked quietly, cupping his face in her hands.

Ryder's mouth twisted with the question and Lynn could feel the tension in his taut body. "No," he admitted with a strangled breath. "And I'm not sure I want to."

"I can't either. You loved him. I loved him. Michelle and Jason loved him. We can't conveniently forget he lived and touched our lives. We can't pretend a part of him won't always be with us. You love Michelle and Jason—you have from the time they were born—they're a part of Gary, too."

"I know… I know." But that insight didn't seem to ease Ryder's distress. "Maybe we're going about this all wrong."

Lynn frowned. "How do you mean?"

His arms circled her waist and he pressed his forehead against her shoulder. "For the past few months, I've done everything I could to cast him from our lives. I've resented his intrusion into what I consider my family, but I've been wrong, because you and the kids are his family, too."

"Yes," she answered, not sure she was following his line of reasoning.

"I've tried everything within my power to make everyone forget him. You didn't. Michelle and Jason didn't. And neither did I."

Lynn nodded.

"I can't ignore him any longer, Lynn. If he were here now, we could sit down and talk this out. Man to man."

"But he isn't here."

For the first time that evening, Ryder smiled. "I think he is...not in any ghostly form or anything like that, but his spirit is here, his essence. He's a large part of Michelle and Jason...and a part of you."

"If Gary were here," she murmured, "and you could talk to him, what would you say?"

Ryder frowned thoughtfully. "I'm not sure. One thing I'd do is tell him how much I love you and explain that I know he felt the same deep commitment to you. I think he'd understand and approve of me marrying you." Some of the weary tautness left his limbs as soon as he'd voiced the thought.

"If Gary had handpicked the man to take his place in our lives, it would have been you."

Ryder relaxed even more with that. "I'd tell him how proud he'd be of his children, and of you," he paused to kiss her lightly.

Some of the strain eased from his eyes and Lynn leaned forward enough to plant a simple kiss on his lips. She ran her fingers through his hair, toying with it because she needed to keep touching and feeling him. "You know what we're doing, don't you?"

Ryder's responding glance confirmed that he didn't.

"We're inviting Gary's memory back into our lives, because excluding him would be futile."

"And wrong," Ryder added in a voice that trembled slightly.

They stared at each other, both sets of eyes glistening with unshed tears. Words weren't necessary now, they would have been superfluous at that moment. Lynn and Ryder had emptied their hearts of any emotion except the gift Gary Danfort had given them—each other.

Lynn wrapped her arms around Ryder's neck and hugged him close, cradling his head against her breast. "Don't you think it's time to unpack those bags?"

He was too busy toying with the front of her blouse. "I think it's time for other things, too."

"Sleep?"

"If you think you're going upstairs to rest, think again, woman."

Slowly their mouths merged, and when they kissed their hearts were open, free from the chains of the past, free to soar in their love.

* * * * *

YOURS AND MINE

Debbie Macomber

One

"Mom, I forgot to tell you, I need two dozen cupcakes for tomorrow morning."

Joanna Parsons reluctantly opened her eyes and lifted her head from the soft feather pillow, squinting at the illuminated dial of her clock radio. "Kristen, it's after eleven."

"I know, Mom, I'm sorry. But I've *got* to bring cupcakes."

"No, you don't," Joanna said hopefully. "There's a package of Oreos on the top shelf of the cupboard. You can take those."

"Oreos! You've been hiding Oreos from me again! Just what kind of mother are you?"

"I was saving them for an emergency—like this."

"It won't work." Crossing her arms over her still-flat chest, eleven-year-old Kristen sat on the edge of the mattress and heaved a loud, discouraged sigh.

"Why not?"

"It's got to be cupcakes, home-baked chocolate ones."

"That's unfortunate, since you seem to have forgotten to mention the fact earlier. And now it's about four hours too late for baking anything. Including chocolate cupcakes."

Joanna tried to be fair with Kristen, but being a single parent wasn't easy.

"Mom, I know I forgot," Kristen cried, her young voice rising in panic, "but I've got to bring cupcakes to class tomorrow. It's important! Really important!"

"Convince me." Joanna used the phrase often. She didn't want to seem unyielding and hard-nosed. After all, she'd probably forgotten a few important things in her thirty-odd years, too.

"It's Mrs. Eagleton's last day as our teacher—remember I told you her husband got transferred and she's moving to Denver? Everyone in the whole class hates to see her go, so we're throwing a party."

"Who's *we*?"

"Nicole and me," Kristen answered quickly. "Nicole's bringing the napkins, cups and punch, and I'm supposed to bring homemade cupcakes. Chocolate cupcakes. Mom, I've just got to. Nicole would never forgive me if I did something stupid like bring store-bought cookies for a teacher as wonderful as Mrs. Eagleton."

Kristen had met Nicole almost five months before at the beginning of the school year, and the two girls had been as thick as gnats in August from that time on. "Shouldn't the room mother be organizing this party?" That made sense to Joanna; surely there was an adult who would be willing to help.

"We don't have one this year. Everyone's mother is either too busy or working."

Joanna sighed. Oh, great, she was going to end up baking cupcakes until the wee hours of the morning. "All right," she muttered, giving in to her daughter's pleading. Mrs. Eagleton *was* a wonderful teacher, and Joanna was as sorry as Kristen to see her leave.

"We just couldn't let Mrs. Eagleton move to Denver without doing something really nice for her," Kristen pressed.

Although Joanna agreed, she felt that Oreos or Fig Newtons should be considered special enough, since it was already after eleven. But Kristen obviously had her heart set on home-baked cupcakes.

"Mom?"

Even in the muted light, Joanna recognized the plea in her daughter's dark brown eyes. She looked so much like Davey that a twinge of anguish worked its way through Joanna's heart. They'd been divorced six years now, but the pain of that failure had yet to fade. Sometimes, at odd moments like these, she still recalled how good it had felt to be in his arms and how much she'd once loved him. Mostly, though, Joanna remembered how naive she'd been to trust him so completely. But she'd come a long way in the six years since her divorce. She'd gained a new measure of independence and self-respect, forging a career for herself at Columbia Basin Savings and Loan. And now she was close to achieving her goal of becoming the first female senior loan officer.

"All right, honey." Joanna sighed, dragging her thoughts back to her daughter. "I'll bake the cupcakes. Only next time, please let me know before we go to bed, okay?"

Kristen's shoulders slumped in relief. "I owe you one, Mom."

Joanna resisted the urge to remind her daughter that the score was a lot higher than one. Tossing aside the thick warm blankets, she climbed out of bed and reached for her long robe.

Kristen, flannel housecoat flying behind her like a flag unfurling, raced toward the kitchen, eager to do what she could to help. "I'll turn on the oven and get everything ready," she called.

"All right," Joanna said with a yawn as she sent her foot searching under the bed for her slippers. She was mentally scanning the contents of her cupboards, wondering if she had a chocolate cake mix. Somehow she doubted it.

"Trouble, Mom," Kristen announced when Joanna entered the well-lighted kitchen. The eleven-year-old stood on a chair in front of the open cupboards above the refrigerator, an Oreo between her teeth. Looking only mildly guilty, she ate the cookie whole, then shook her head. "We don't have cake mix."

"I was afraid of that."

"I guess we'll have to bake them from scratch," Kristen suggested, reaching for another Oreo.

"Not this late, we won't. I'll drive to the store." There was an Albertson's that stayed open twenty-four hours less than a mile away.

Kristen jumped down from the chair. The pockets of her bathrobe were stuffed full of cookies, but her attempt to conceal them failed. Joanna pointed toward the cookie jar, and dutifully Kristen emptied her pockets.

When Kristen had finished, Joanna yawned again and ambled back into her bedroom.

"Mom, if you're going to the store, I suppose I should go with you."

"No, honey, I'm just going to run in and out. You stay here."

"Okay," Kristen agreed quickly.

The kid wasn't stupid, Joanna thought wryly. Winters in eastern Washington were often merciless, and temperatures in Spokane had been well below freezing all week. To be honest, she wasn't exactly thrilled about braving the elements herself. She pulled on her calf-high boots over two pairs of heavy woolen socks. Because the socks were so thick, Joanna could only zip the boots up to her ankles.

"Mom," Kristen said, following her mother into the bedroom, a thoughtful expression on her face. "Have you ever thought of getting married again?"

Surprised, Joanna looked up and studied her daughter. The question had come from out of nowhere, but her answer was ready. "Never." The first time around had been enough. Not that she was one of the walking wounded, at least she didn't think of herself that way. Instead, her divorce had made her smart, had matured her. Never again would she look to a man for happiness; Joanna was determined to build her own. But the unexpectedness of Kristen's question caught her off guard. Was Kristen telling her something? Perhaps her daughter felt she was missing out because there were only the two of them. "What makes you ask?"

The mattress dipped as she sat beside Joanna. "I'm not exactly sure," she confessed. "But you could remarry, you know. You've still got a halfway decent figure."

Joanna grinned. "Thanks... I think."

"I mean, it's not like you're really old and ugly."

"Coming from you, that's high praise indeed, considering that I'm over thirty."

"I'm sure if you wanted to, you could find another man. Not like Daddy, but someone better."

It hurt Joanna to hear her daughter say things like that about Davey, but she couldn't disguise from Kristen how selfish and hollow her father was. Nor could she hide Davey's roving eye when it came to the opposite sex. Kristen spent one month every summer with him in Seattle and saw for herself the type of man Davey was.

After she'd finished struggling with her boots, Joanna clumped into the entryway and opened the hall cupboard.

"Mom!" Kristen cried, her eyes round with dismay.

"What?"

"You can't go out looking like that!" Her daughter was pointing at her, as though aghast at the sight.

"Like what?" Innocently Joanna glanced down at the dress-length blue wool coat she'd slipped on over her rose-patterned flannel pajamas. Okay, so the bottoms showed, but only a little. And she was willing to admit that the boots would look better zipped up, but she was more concerned with comfort than fashion. If the way she looked didn't bother her, then it certainly shouldn't bother Kristen. Her daughter had obviously forgotten why Joanna was venturing outside in the first place.

"Someone might see you."

"Don't worry, I have no intention of taking off my coat." She'd park close to the front door of the store, run inside, head for aisle three, grab a cake mix and be back at the car in four minutes flat. Joanna didn't exactly feel like donning tights for the event.

"You might meet someone," Kristen persisted.

"So?" Joanna stifled a yawn.

"But your hair… Don't you think you should curl it?"

"Kristen, listen. The only people who are going to be in the grocery store are insomniacs and winos and maybe a couple of pregnant women." It was highly unlikely she'd run into anyone from the bank.

"But what if you got in an accident? The policeman would think you're some kind of weirdo."

Joanna yawned a second time. "Honey, anyone who would consider making cupcakes in the middle of the night has a mental problem as it is. I'll fit right in with everyone else, so quit worrying."

"Oh, all right," Kristen finally agreed.

Draping her bag strap over her shoulder, Joanna opened the front door and shivered as the arctic wind of late January wrapped itself around her. Damn, it was cold. The grass was so white with frost that she wondered, at first, if it had snowed. To ward off the chill, she wound Kristen's purple striped scarf around her neck to cover her ears and mouth and tied it loosely under her chin.

The heater in her ten-year-old Ford didn't have a chance to do anything but spew out frigid air as she huddled over the steering wheel for the few minutes it took to drive to the grocery store. According to her plan, she parked as close to the store as possible, turned off the engine and dashed inside.

Just as she'd predicted, the place was nearly deserted, except for a couple of clerks working near the front, arranging displays. Joanna didn't give them more than a fleeting glance as she headed toward the aisle where baking goods were shelved.

She was reaching for the first chocolate cake mix to come into sight when she heard footsteps behind her.

"Mrs. Parsons! Hello!" The shrill excited voice seemed to ring like a Chinese gong throughout the store.

Joanna hunched down as far as she could and cast a furtive glance over her shoulder. Dear Lord, Kristen had been right. She was actually going to bump into someone who knew her.

"It's me—Nicole. You remember me, don't you?"

Joanna attempted a smile as she turned to face her daughter's best friend. "Hi, there," she said weakly, and raised her right hand to wave, her wrist limp. "It's good to see you again." So she was lying. Anyone with a sense of decency would have pretended not to recognize her and casually looked the other way. Not Nicole. It seemed as though all the world's eleven-year-olds were plotting against her tonight. One chocolate cake mix; that was all she wanted. That and maybe a small tub of ready-made frosting. Then she could return home, get those cupcakes baked and climb back into bed where most sane people were at this very moment.

"You look different," Nicole murmured thoughtfully, her eyes widening as she studied Joanna.

Well, that was one way of putting it.

"When I first saw you, I thought you were a bag lady."

Loosening the scarf that obscured the lower half of her face, Joanna managed a grin.

"What are you doing here this late?" the girl wanted to know next, following Joanna as she edged her way to the checkout stand.

"Kristen forgot to tell me about the cupcakes."

Nicole's cheerful laugh resounded through the store like a yell echoing in an empty sports stadium. "I was watching 60 Minutes with my dad when I remembered I hadn't bought the juice and stuff for the party. Dad's waiting for me in the car right now."

Nicole's father allowed her to stay up that late on a school night? Joanna did her utmost to hide her disdain. From what Kristen had told her, she knew Nicole's parents were also divorced and her father had custody of Nicole. The poor kid probably didn't know what the word *discipline* meant. No doubt her father was one of those weak-willed liberal parents so involved in their own careers that they didn't have any time left for their children. Imagine a parent letting an eleven-year-old wander around a grocery store at this time of night! The mere thought was enough to send chills of parental outrage racing up and down Joanna's backbone. She placed her arm around Nicole's shoulders as if to protect her from life's harsher realities. The poor sweet kid.

The abrupt whoosh of the automatic door was followed by the sound of someone striding impatiently into the store. Joanna glanced up to discover a tall man, wearing a well-cut dark coat, glaring in their direction.

"Nicole, what's taking so long?"

"Dad," the girl said happily, "this is Mrs. Parsons—Kristen's mom."

Nicole's father approached, obviously reluctant to acknowledge the introduction, his face remote and unsmiling.

Automatically Joanna straightened, her shoulders stiffening with the action. Nicole's father was exactly as she'd pictured him just a few moments earlier. Polished, worldly, and too darn handsome for his own good. Just like Davey. This was exactly the type of man she went out of her way to avoid. She'd been burned once, and no relationship was worth what she'd endured. This brief encounter with Nicole's father told Joanna all she needed to know.

"Tanner Lund," he announced crisply, holding out his hand.

"Joanna Parsons," Joanna said, and gave him hers for a brisk cold shake. She couldn't take her hand away fast enough.

His eyes narrowed as they studied her, and the look he gave her was as disapproving as the one she offered him. Slowly his gaze dropped to the unzipped boots flapping at her ankles and the worn edges of the pajamas visible below her wool coat.

"I think it's time we met, don't you?" Joanna didn't bother to disguise her disapproval of the man's attitude toward child-rearing. She'd had Nicole over after school several times, but on the one occasion Kristen had visited her friend, the child was staying with a babysitter.

A hint of a smile appeared on his face, but it didn't reach his eyes. "Our meeting is long overdue, I agree."

He seemed to be suggesting that he'd made a mistake in allowing his daughter to have anything to do with someone who dressed the way she did.

Joanna's gaze shifted to Nicole. "Isn't it late for you to be up on a school night?"

"Where's Kristen?" he countered, glancing around the store.

"At home," Joanna answered, swallowing the words that said home was exactly where an eleven-year-old child belonged on a school night—or any other night for that matter.

"Isn't she a bit young to be left alone while you run to a store?"

"N-not in the least."

Tanner frowned and his eyes narrowed even more. His disapproving gaze demanded to know what kind of mother left a child alone in the house at this time of night.

Joanna answered him with a scornful look of her own.

"It's a pleasure to meet you, Mr. Lund," she said coolly, knowing her eyes relayed a conflicting message.

"The pleasure's mine."

Joanna was all the more aware of her disheveled appearance. Uncombed and uncurled, her auburn hair hung limply to her shoulders. Her dark eyes were nice enough, she knew, fringed in long curling lashes. She considered them her best asset, and purposely glared at Tanner, hoping her eyes were as cold as the blast from her car heater had been.

Tanner placed his hands on his daughter's shoulders and drew her protectively to his side. Joanna was infuriated by the action. If Nicole needed shielding, it was from an irresponsible father!

Okay, she reasoned, so her attire was a bit outlandish. But that couldn't be helped; she was on a mission that by rights should win her a nomination for the mother-of-the-year award. The way Tanner Lund had implied that *she* was the irresponsible parent was something Joanna found downright insulting.

"Well," Joanna said brightly, "I have to go. Nice to see you again, Nicole." She swept two boxes of cake mix into her arms and grabbed what she hoped was some frosting.

"You, too, Mrs. Parsons," the girl answered, smiling up at her.

"Mr. Lund."

"Mrs. Parsons."

The two nodded politely at each other, and, clutching her packages, Joanna walked regally to the checkout stand. She made her purchase and started back toward the car. The next time Kristen invited Nicole over, Joanna mused on the short drive home, she intended to spend lots of extra time with the girls. Now she knew how badly Nicole needed someone to nurture her, to give her the firm but loving guidance every child deserved.

The poor darling.

Two

Joanna expertly lowered the pressure foot of her sewing machine over the bunched red material, then used both hands to push the fabric slowly under the bobbing needle. Straight pins, tightly clenched between her lips, protruded from her mouth. Her concentration was intense.

"Mom." A breathless Kristen bounded into the room.

Joanna intercepted her daughter with one upraised hand until she finished stitching the seam.

Kristen stalked around the kitchen table several times, like a shark circling its kill. "Mom, hurry, this is really important."

"Wlutt?" Joanna asked, her teeth still clamped on the pins.

"Can Nicole spend the night?"

Joanna blinked. This wasn't the weekend, and Kristen knew the rules; she had permission to invite friends over only on Friday and Saturday nights. Joanna removed the pins from her mouth before she answered. "It's Wednesday."

"I know what day it is." Kristen rolled her eyes towards the ceiling and slapped the heel of her hand against her forehead.

Allowing his daughter to stay over at a friend's house on

a school night was exactly the kind of irresponsible parenting Joanna expected from Tanner Lund. Her estimation of the man was dropping steadily, though that hardly seemed possible. Earlier in the afternoon, Joanna had learned that Nicole didn't even plan to tell her father she and Kristen were going to be performing in the school talent show. The man revealed absolutely no interest in his daughter's activities. Joanna felt so bad about Tanner Lund's attitude that she'd volunteered to sew a second costume so Nicole would have something special to wear for this important event. And now it seemed that Tanner was in the habit of farming out his daughter on school nights, as well.

"Mom, hurry and decide. Nicole's on the phone."

"Honey, there's school tomorrow."

Kristen gave her another scornful look.

"The two of you will stay up until midnight chattering, and then in the morning class will be a disaster. The answer is no!"

Kristen's eager face fell. "I promise we won't talk. Just this once, Mom. Oh, please!" She folded her hands prayerfully, and her big brown eyes pleaded with Joanna. "How many times do I ask you for something?"

Joanna stared incredulously at her daughter. The list was endless.

"All right, forget I asked that. But this is important, Mom, real important—for Nicole's sake."

Every request was argued as urgent. But knowing what she did about the other little girl's home life made refusing all the more difficult. "I'm sorry, Kristen, but not on a school night."

Head drooping, Kristen shuffled toward the phone. "Now Nicole will have to spend the night with Mrs. Wagner, and she hates that."

"Who's Mrs. Wagner?"

Kristen turned to face her mother and released a sigh intended to evoke sympathy. "Her babysitter."

"Her father makes her spend the night at a babysitter's?"

"Yes. He has a business meeting with Becky."

Joanna stiffened and felt a sudden chill. "Becky?"

"His business partner."

I'll just bet! Joanna's eyes narrowed with outrage. Tanner Lund was a lowlife, kicking his own daughter out into the cold so he could bring a woman over. The man disgusted her.

"Mrs. Wagner is real old and she makes Nicole eat health food. She has a black-and-white TV, and the only programs she'll let Nicole watch are nature shows. Wouldn't you hate that?"

Joanna's mind was spinning. Any child would detest being cast from her own bed and thrust upon the not always tender mercies of a babysitter. "How often does Nicole have to spend the night with Mrs. Wagner?"

"Lots."

Joanna could well believe it. "How often is 'lots'?"

"At least twice a month. Sometimes even more often than that."

That poor neglected child. Joanna's heart constricted at the thought of sweet Nicole being ruthlessly handed over to a woman who served soybean burgers.

"Can she, Mom? Oh, please?" Again Kristen folded her hands, pleading with her mother to reconsider.

"All right," Joanna conceded, "but just this once."

Kristen ran across the room and hurled her arms around Joanna's neck, squeezing for all she was worth. "You're the greatest mother in the whole world."

Joanna snorted softly. "I've got to be in the top ten percent, anyway," she said, remembering the cupcakes.

* * *

"Absolutely not," Tanner said forcefully as he laid a neatly pressed shirt in his open suitcase. "Nicole, I won't hear of it."

"But, Dad, Kristen is my very best friend."

"Believe me, sweetheart, I'm pleased you've found a soulmate, but when I'm gone on these business trips I need to know you're being well taken care of." And supervised, he added mentally. What he knew about Kristen's mother wasn't encouraging. The woman was a scatterbrain who left her young daughter unattended while she raided the supermarket for nighttime goodies—and then had the nerve to chastise him because Nicole was up a little late. In addition to being a busybody, Joanna Parsons dressed like a fruitcake.

"Dad, you don't understand what it's like for me at Mrs. Wagner's."

Undaunted, Tanner continued packing his suitcase. He wasn't any happier about leaving Nicole than she was, but he didn't have any choice. As a relatively new half owner of Spokane Aluminum, he was required to do a certain amount of traveling. More these first few months than would be necessary later. His business trips were essential, since they familiarized him with the clients and their needs. He would have to absorb this information as quickly as possible in order to determine if the plant was going to achieve his and John Becky's five-year goal. In a few weeks, he expected to hire an assistant who would assume some of this responsibility, but for now the task fell into his hands.

Nicole slumped onto the edge of the bed. "The last time I spent the night at Mrs. Wagner's she served baked beef heart for dinner."

Involuntarily Tanner cringed.

"And, Dad, she made me watch a special on television that was all about fungus."

Tanner gritted his teeth. So the old lady was a bit eccentric, but she looked after Nicole competently, and that was all that mattered.

"Do you know what Kristen's having for dinner?"

Tanner didn't care to guess. It was probably something like strawberry ice cream and caramel-flavored popcorn. "No, and I don't want to know."

"It isn't sweet-and-sour calf liver, I can tell you that."

Tanner's stomach turned at the thought of liver in any kind of sauce. "Nicole, the subject is closed. You're spending the night with Mrs. Wagner."

"It's spaghetti and meatballs and three-bean salad and milk and French bread, that's what. And Mrs. Parsons said I could help Kristen roll the meatballs—but that's all right, I'll call and tell her that you don't want me to spend the night at a home where I won't be properly looked after."

"Nicole—"

"Dad, don't worry about it, I understand."

Tanner sincerely doubted that. He placed the last of his clothes inside the suitcase and closed the lid.

"At least I'm *trying* to understand why you'd send me to someplace like Mrs. Wagner's when my very best friend *invited* me to spend the night with her."

Tanner could feel himself weakening. It was only one night and Kristen's weird mother wasn't likely to be a dangerous influence on Nicole in that short a time.

"Spaghetti and meatballs," Nicole muttered under her breath. "My all-time favorite food."

Now that was news to Tanner. He'd thought pizza held that honor. He'd never known his daughter to turn down pizza at any time of the day or night.

"And they have a twenty-inch color television set."

Tanner hesitated.

"With remote control."

Would wonders never cease? "Will Kristen's mother be there the entire night?" he asked.

"Of course."

His daughter was looking at him as though he'd asked if Mrs. Parsons were related to ET. "Where will you sleep?"

"Kristen has a double bed." Nicole's eyes brightened. "And we've already promised Mrs. Parsons that we'll go straight to bed at nine o'clock and hardly talk."

It was during times such as this that Tanner felt the full weight of parenting descend upon his shoulders. Common sense told him Nicole would be better off with Mrs. Wagner, but he understood her complaints about the older woman as well. "All right, Nicole, you can stay at Kristen's."

His daughter let out a whoop of sheer delight.

"But just this once."

"Oh, Dad, you're the greatest." Her arms locked around his waist, and she squeezed with all her might, her nose pressed against his flat stomach.

"Okay, okay, I get the idea you're pleased with my decision," Tanner said with a short laugh.

"Can we leave now?"

"Now?" Usually Nicole wanted to linger at the apartment until the last possible minute.

"Yes. Mrs. Parsons really did say I could help roll the meatballs, and you know what else?"

"What?"

"She's sewing me and Kristen identical costumes for the talent show."

Tanner paused—he hadn't known anything about his daughter needing a costume. "What talent show?"

"Oops." Nicole slapped her hand over her mouth. "I wasn't

going to tell you because it's on Valentine's Day and I know you won't be able to come. I didn't want you to feel bad."

"Nicole, it's more important that you don't hide things from me."

"But you have to be in Seattle."

She was right. He'd hate missing the show, but he was scheduled to meet with the Foreign Trade Commission on the fourteenth regarding a large shipment of aluminum to Japan. "What talent do you and Kristen have?" he asked, diverting his disappointment for the moment.

"We're lip-synching a song from Heart. You know, the rock group?"

"That sounds cute. A fitting choice, too, for a Valentine's Day show. Perhaps you two can be persuaded to give me a preview before the grand performance."

Her blue eyes became even brighter in her excitement. "That's a great idea! Kristen and I can practice while you're away, and we'll show you when you come back."

It was an acceptable compromise.

Nicole dashed out of his bedroom and returned a couple of minutes later with her backpack. "I'm ready anytime you are," she announced.

Tanner couldn't help but notice that his daughter looked downright cheerful. More cheerful than any of the other times he'd been forced to leave her. Normally she put on a long face and moped around, making him feel guilty about abandoning her to the dreaded Mrs. Wagner.

By the time he picked up his briefcase and luggage, Nicole was waiting at the front door.

"Are you going to come in and say hello to Mrs. Parsons?" Nicole asked when Tanner eased his Mercedes into Kristen's driveway fifteen minutes later. Even in the fading late-afternoon light, he could see that the house was newly painted, white with green shutters at the windows. The lawn and flower beds seemed well maintained. He could almost picture rose bushes in full bloom. It certainly wasn't the type of place he'd associated with Kristen's loony mother.

"Are you coming in or not?" Nicole asked a second time, her voice impatient.

Tanner had to mull over the decision. He wasn't eager to meet that unfriendly woman who wore unzipped boots and flannel pajamas again.

"Dad!"

Before Tanner could answer, the door opened and Kristen came bowling out of the house at top speed. A gorgeous redhead followed sedately behind her. Tanner felt his jaw sag and his mouth drop open. No, it couldn't be! Tall, cool, sophisticated, this woman looked as though she'd walked out of the pages of a fashion magazine. It couldn't be Joanna Parsons—no way. A relative perhaps, but certainly not the woman he'd met in the grocery store that night.

Nicole had already climbed out of the car. She paused as though she'd forgotten something, then ran around to his side of the car. When Tanner rolled down his window, she leaned over and gave him one of her famous bear hugs, hurling her arms around his neck and squeezing enthusiastically. "Bye, Dad."

"Bye, sweetheart. You've got the phone number of my hotel to give Mrs. Parsons?"

Nicole patted her jeans pocket. "It's right here."

"Be good."

"I will."

When Tanner looked up, he noted that Joanna was standing behind her daughter, her hands resting on Kristen's shoulders. Cool, disapproving eyes surveyed him. Yup, it was the same woman all right. Joanna Parsons's gaze could freeze watermelon at a Fourth of July picnic.

Three

"Would you like more spaghetti, Nicole?" Joanna asked for the second time.

"No, thanks, Mrs. Parsons."

"You asked her that already," Kristen commented, giving her mother a puzzled look. "After we've done the dishes, Nicole and I are going to practice our song."

Joanna nodded. "Good idea, but do your homework first."

Kristen exchanged a knowing look with her friend, and the two grinned at each other.

"I'm really glad you're letting me stay the night, Mrs. Parsons," Nicole said, as she carried her empty plate to the kitchen sink. "Dinner was great. Dad tries, but he isn't much of a cook. We get take-out food a lot." She wandered back to the table and fingered the blue-quilted place mat. "Kristen told me you sewed these, too. They're pretty."

"Thank you. The pattern is really very simple."

"They have to be," Kristen added, stuffing the last slice of toasted French bread into her mouth. "'Cause Mom let me do a couple of them."

"You made two of these?"

"Yeah," Kristen said, after she'd finished chewing. Pride

beamed from her dark brown eyes. "We've made lots of things together since we bought the house. Do you have any idea how expensive curtains can be? Mom made the entire set in my room—that's why everything matches."

"The bedspread, too?"

"Naturally." Kristen made it sound like they'd whipped up the entire set over a weekend, when the project had actually taken the better part of two weeks.

"Wow."

From the way Nicole was staring at her, Joanna half expected the girl to fall to her knees in homage. She felt a stab of pity for Nicole, who seemed to crave a mother's presence. But she had to admit she was thrilled by her own daughter's pride in their joint accomplishments.

"Mom sews a lot of my clothes," Kristen added, licking the butter from her fingertips. "I thought you knew that."

"I... No, I didn't."

"She's teaching me, too. That's the best part. So I'll be able to make costumes for our next talent show." Kristen's gaze flew from Nicole to her mother then back to Nicole. "I bet my mom would teach you how to sew. Wouldn't you, Mom?"

"Ah..."

"Would you really, Mrs. Parsons?"

Not knowing what else to say, Joanna agreed with a quick nod of her head. "Why not? We'll have fun learning together." She gave an encouraging smile, but she wondered a bit anxiously if she was ready for a project like this.

"That would be great." Nicole slipped her arm around Kristen's shoulders. Her gaze dropped as she hesitated. "Dinner was really good, too," she said again.

"I told you what a great cook my mom is," Kristen boasted.

Nicole nodded, but kept her eyes trained to the floor. "Could I ask you something, Mrs. Parsons?"

"Of course."

"Like I said, Dad tries real hard, but he just isn't a very good cook. Would it be rude to ask you for the recipe for your spaghetti sauce?"

"Not at all. I'll write it out for you tonight."

"Gee, thanks. It's so nice over here. I wish Dad would let me stay here all the time. You and Kristen do such neat things, and you eat real good, too."

Joanna could well imagine the kind of meals Tanner Lund served his daughter. She already knew that he frequently ordered out, and the rest probably came from the frozen-food section of the local grocery. That was if he didn't have an array of willing females who did his cooking for him. Someone like this Becky person, the woman he was with now.

"Dad makes great tacos, though," Nicole was saying. "They're his specialty. He said I might be able to have a slumber party for my birthday in March, and I want him to serve tacos then. But I might ask him to make spaghetti instead—if he gets the recipe right."

"You get to have a slumber party?" Kristen cried, her eyes widening. "That's great! My mom said I could have two friends over for the night on my birthday, but only two, because that's all she can mentally handle."

Joanna pretended an interest in her leftover salad, stirring her fork through the dressing that sat in the bottom of the bowl. It was true; there were limits to her mothering abilities. A house full of screaming eleven-and twelve-year-olds was more than she dared contemplate on a full stomach.

While Nicole finished clearing off the table, Kristen

loaded the dishwasher. Working together, the two completed their tasks in only a few minutes.

"We're going to my room now. Okay, Mom?"

"Sure, honey, that's fine," Joanna said, placing the leftovers in the refrigerator. She paused, then decided to remind the pair a second time. "Homework before anything else."

"Of course," answered Kristen.

"Naturally," added Nicole.

Both vanished down the hallway that led to Kristen's bedroom. Watching them, Joanna grinned. The friendship with Nicole had been good for Kristen, and Joanna intended to shower love and attention on Nicole in the hope of compensating her for her unsettled home life.

Once Joanna had finished wiping down the kitchen counters, she made her way to Kristen's bedroom. Dutifully knocking—since her daughter made emphatic comments about privacy these days—she let herself in. Both girls were sitting cross-legged on the bed, spelling books open on their laps.

"Need any help?"

"No, thanks, Mom."

Still Joanna lingered, looking for an excuse to stay and chat. "I was placed third in the school spelling bee when I was your age."

Kristen glanced speculatively toward her friend. "That's great, Mom."

Warming to her subject, Joanna hurried to add, "I could outspell every boy in the class."

Kristen closed her textbook. "Mrs. Andrews, our new teacher, said the school wasn't going to have a spelling bee this year."

Joanna walked into the room and sat on the edge of the bed. "That's too bad, because I know you'd do well."

"I only got a B in spelling, Mom. I'm okay, but it's not my best subject."

A short uneasy silence followed while both girls studied Joanna, as though waiting for her to either leave or make a formal announcement.

"I thought we'd pop popcorn later," Joanna said, flashing a cheerful smile.

"Good." Kristen nodded and her gaze fell pointedly to her textbook. This was followed by another long moment of silence.

"Mom, I thought you said you wanted us to do our homework."

"I do."

"Well, we can't very well do it with you sitting here watching us."

"Oh." Joanna leapt off the bed. "Sorry."

"That's all right."

"Let me know when you're done."

"Why?" Kristen asked, looking perplexed.

Joanna shrugged. "I... I thought we might all sit around and chat. Girl talk, that sort of thing." Without being obvious about it, she'd hoped to offer Nicole maternal advice and some much needed affection. The thought of the little girl's father and what he was doing that very evening was so distasteful that Joanna had to force herself not to frown.

"Mom, Nicole and I are going to practice our song once we've finished our homework. Remember?"

"Oh, right. I forgot." Sheepishly, she started to walk away.

"I really appreciate your sewing my costume, Mrs. Parsons," Nicole added.

"It's no trouble, Nicole. I'm happy to do it."

"Speaking of the costumes," Kristen muttered, "didn't

you say something about wanting to finish them before the weekend?"

"I did?" The look Kristen gave her suggested she must have. "Oh, right, now I remember."

The girls, especially her daughter, seemed relieved when Joanna left the bedroom. This wasn't going well. She'd planned on spending extra time with them, but it was clear they weren't keen on having her around. Taking a deep breath, Joanna headed for the living room, feeling a little piqued. Her ego should be strong enough to handle rejection from two eleven-year-old girls.

She settled in the kitchen and brought out her sewing machine again. The red costumes for the talent show were nearly finished. She ran her hand over the polished cotton and let her thoughts wander. She and Kristen had lived in the house only since September. For the six years following the divorce, Joanna had been forced to raise her daughter in a small apartment. Becoming a home owner had been a major step for her and she was proud of the time and care that had gone into choosing their small one-story house. It had required some repairs, but nothing major, and the sense of accomplishment she'd experienced when she signed her name to the mortgage papers had been well worth the years of scrimping. The house had only two bedrooms, but there was plenty of space in the backyard for a garden, something Joanna had insisted on. She thought that anyone studying her might be amused. On the one hand, she was a woman with basic traditional values, and on the other, a goal-setting businesswoman struggling to succeed in a male-dominated field. Her boss would have found it difficult to understand that the woman who'd set her sights on the position of senior loan officer liked the feel of wet dirt under her fingernails. And he would have been surprised to learn that she could take a simple piece of bright red cotton and turn it into a dazzling costume for a talent show.

An hour later, when Joanna was watching television and finishing up the hand stitching on the costumes, Kristen and Nicole rushed into the living room, looking pleased about something.

"You girls ready for popcorn?"

"Not me," Nicole said, placing her hands over her stomach. "I'm still full from dinner."

Joanna nodded. The girl obviously wasn't accustomed to eating nutritionally balanced meals.

"We want to do our song for you."

"Great." Joanna scooted close to the edge of the sofa, eagerly awaiting their performance. Kristen plugged in her MP3 player, then hurried to her friend's side, striking a pose until the music started.

"I can tell already that you're going to be great," Joanna said, clapping her hands to the lively beat.

She was right. The two did astonishingly well, and when they'd finished Joanna applauded loudly.

"We did okay?"

"You were fabulous."

Kristen and Nicole positively glowed.

When they returned to Kristen's bedroom, Joanna followed them. Kristen turned around and seemed surprised to find her mother there.

"Mom," she hissed between clenched teeth, "what's with you tonight? You haven't been yourself since Nicole arrived."

"I haven't?"

"You keep following us around."

"I do?"

"Really, Mom, we like you and everything, but Nicole

and I want to talk about boys and stuff, and we can't very well do that with you here."

"Oh, Mrs. Parsons, I forgot to tell you," Nicole inserted, obviously unaware of the whispered conversation going on between Kristen and her mother. "I told my dad about you making my costume for the talent show, and he said he wants to pay you for your time and expenses."

"You told your dad?" Kristen asked, and whirled around to face her friend. "I thought you weren't going to because he'd feel guilty. Oh, I get it! That's how you got him to let you spend the night. Great idea!"

Joanna frowned. "What exactly does that mean?"

The two girls exchanged meaningful glances and Nicole looked distinctly uncomfortable.

"What does what mean?" Kristen repeated the question in a slightly elevated voice Joanna recognized immediately. Her daughter was up to one of her schemes again.

Nicole stepped in front of her friend. "It's my fault, Mrs. Parsons. I wanted to spend the night here instead of with Mrs. Wagner, so I told Dad that Kristen had invited me."

"Mom, you've got to understand. Mrs. Wagner won't let Nicole watch anything but educational television, and you know there are special shows we like to watch."

"That's not the part I mean," Joanna said, dismissing their rushed explanation. "I want to know what you meant by not telling Mr. Lund about the talent show because he'd feel guilty."

"Oh...that part." The two girls glanced at each other, as though silently deciding which one would do the explaining.

Nicole raised her gaze to Joanna and sighed, her thin shoulders moving up and down expressively. "My dad won't be able to attend the talent show because he's got a business meeting in Seattle, and I knew he'd feel terrible about it. He really likes it when I do things like the show. It gives him something to tell my grandparents about, like I was going to be the next Madonna or something."

"He has to travel a lot to business meetings," Kristen added quickly.

"Business meetings?"

"Like tonight," Kristen went on to explain.

"Dad has to fly someplace with Mr. Becky. He owns half the company and Dad owns the other half. He said it had to do with getting a big order, but I never listen to stuff like that, although Dad likes to explain every little detail so I'll know where he's at and what he's doing."

Joanna felt a numbing sensation creeping slowly up her spine. "Your dad owns half a company?"

"Spokane Aluminum is the reason we moved here from West Virginia."

"Spokane Aluminum?" Joanna's voice rose half an octave. "Your dad owns half of Spokane Aluminum?" The company was one of the largest employers in the Northwest. A shockingly large percentage of their state's economy was directly or indirectly tied to this company. A sick feeling settled in Joanna's stomach. Not only was Nicole's father wealthy, he was socially prominent, and all the while she'd been thinking… Oh, dear heavens. "So your father's out of town tonight?" she asked, feeling the warmth invade her face.

"You knew that, Mom." Kristen gave her mother another one of those searching gazes that suggested Joanna might be losing her memory—due to advanced age, no doubt.

"I… I thought—" Abruptly she bit off what she'd been about to say. When Kristen had said something about Tanner being with Becky, she'd assumed it was a woman. But of course it was *John* Becky, whose name was familiar to everyone in that part of the country. Joanna remembered reading in the *Review* that Becky had taken on a partner, but she hadn't made the connection. Perhaps she'd misjudged Tanner Lund, she reluctantly conceded. Perhaps she'd been a bit too eager to view him in a bad light.

"Before we came to Spokane," Nicole was saying now, "Dad and I had a long talk about the changes the move would make in our lives. We made a list of the good things and a list of the bad things, and then we talked about them. One bad thing was that Dad would be gone a lot, until he can hire another manager. He doesn't feel good about leaving me with strangers, and we didn't know a single person in Spokane other than Mr. Becky and his wife, but they're real old—over forty, anyway. He even went and interviewed Mrs. Wagner before I spent the night there the first time."

The opinion Joanna had formed of Tanner Lund was crumbling at her feet. Evidently he wasn't the irresponsible parent she'd assumed.

"Nicole told me you met her dad in the grocery store when you bought the mix for the cupcakes." Kristen shook her head as if to say she was thoroughly disgusted with her mother for not taking her advice that night and curling her hair before she showed her face in public.

"I told my dad you don't dress that way all the time," Nicole added, then shifted her gaze to the other side of the room. "But I don't think he believed me until he dropped me off tonight."

Joanna began to edge her way toward the bedroom door. "Your father and I seem to have started off on the wrong foot," she said weakly.

Nicole bit her lower lip. "I know. He wasn't real keen on me spending the night here, but I talked him into it."

Debbie Macomber

"Mom?" Kristen asked, frowning. "What did you say to Mr. Lund when you met him at the store?"

"Nothing," she answered, taking a few more retreating steps.

"She asked my dad what I was doing up so late on a school night, and he told me later that he didn't like her attitude," Nicole explained. "I didn't get a chance to tell you that I'm normally in bed by nine thirty, but that night was special because Dad had just come home from one of his trips. His plane was late and I didn't remember to tell him about the party stuff until after we got home from Mrs. Wagner's."

"I see," Joanna murmured, and swallowed uncomfortably.

"You'll get a chance to settle things with Mr. Lund when he picks up Nicole tomorrow night," Kristen stated, and it was obvious that she wanted her mother to make an effort to get along with her best friend's father.

"Right," Joanna muttered, dreading the confrontation. She never had been particularly fond of eating crow.

Four

Joanna was breading pork chops the following evening when Kristen barreled into the kitchen, leaving the door swinging in her wake. "Mr. Lund's here to pick up Nicole. I think you should invite him and Nicole to stay for dinner... and explain about, you know, the other night."

Oh, sure, Joanna mused. She often invited company owners and acting presidents over for an evening meal. Pork chops and mashed potatoes weren't likely to impress someone like Tanner Lund.

Before Kristen could launch into an argument, Joanna shook her head and offered the first excuse that came to mind. "There aren't enough pork chops to ask him tonight. Besides, Mr. Lund is probably tired from his trip and anxious to get home."

"I bet he's hungry, too," Kristen pressed. "And Nicole thinks you're a fabulous cook, and—"

A sharp look from her mother cut her off. "Another night, Kristen!"

Joanna brushed the bread crumbs off her fingertips and untied her apron. Inhaling deeply, she paused long enough to run a hand through her hair and check her reflection in the window above the sink. No one was going to mistake her for Miss America, but her appearance was passable. Okay, it was time to hold her head high, spit the feathers out of her mouth and get ready to down some crow.

Joanna forced a welcoming smile onto her lips as she stepped into the living room. Tanner stood awkwardly just inside the front door, as though prepared to beat a hasty retreat if necessary. "How was your trip?" she ventured, straining to make the question sound cheerful.

"Fine. Thank you." His expression didn't change.

"Do you have time for a cup of coffee?" she asked next, doing her best to disguise her unease. She wondered quickly if she'd unpacked her china cups yet. After their shaky beginning, Joanna wasn't quite sure if she could undo the damage. But standing in the entryway wouldn't work. She needed to sit down for this.

He eyed her suspiciously. Joanna wasn't sure she should even try to explain things. In time he'd learn she wasn't a candidate for the loony bin—just as she'd stumbled over the fact that he wasn't a terrible father. Trying to tell him that she was an upstanding member of the community after he'd seen her dressed in a wool coat draped over pajamas, giving him looks that suggested he be reported to Children's Protective Services, wasn't exactly a task she relished.

Tanner glanced at his wristwatch and shook his head. "I haven't got time to visit tonight. Thanks for the invitation, though."

Joanna almost sighed aloud with relief.

"Did Nicole behave herself?"

Joanna nodded. "She wasn't the least bit of trouble. Nicole's a great kid."

A smile cracked the tight edges of his mouth. "Good."

Kristen and Nicole burst into the room. "Is Mr. Lund going to stay, Mom?"

"He can't tonight..."

"Another time..."

They spoke simultaneously, with an equal lack of enthusiasm.

"Oh." The girls looked at each other and frowned, their disappointment noticeable.

"Have you packed everything, Nicole?" Tanner asked, not hiding his eagerness to leave.

The eleven-year-old nodded reluctantly. "I think so."

"Don't you think you should check my room one more time?" Kristen suggested, grabbing her friend's hand and leading her back toward the hallway.

"Oh, right. I suppose I should." The two disappeared before either Joanna or Tanner could call them back.

The silence between them hummed so loudly Joanna swore she could have waltzed to it. But since the opportunity had presented itself, she decided to get the unpleasant task of explaining her behavior out of the way while she still had her nerve.

"I think I owe you an apology," she murmured, her face flushing.

"An apology?"

"I thought...you know... The night we met, I assumed you were an irresponsible parent because Nicole was up so late. She's now told me that you'd just returned from a trip."

"Yes, well, I admit I did feel the sting of your disapproval."

This wasn't easy. Joanna swallowed uncomfortably and laced her fingers together forcing herself to meet his eyes. "Nicole explained that your flight was delayed and she forgot to mention the party supplies when you picked her up at the babysitter's. She said she didn't remember until you got all the way home."

Tanner's mouth relaxed a bit more. "Since we're both being truthful here, I'll admit that I wasn't overly impressed with you that night, either."

Joanna dropped her gaze. "I can imagine. I hope you realise I don't usually dress like that."

"I gathered as much when I dropped Nicole off yesterday afternoon."

They both paused to share a brief smile and Joanna instantly felt better. It hadn't been easy to blurt all this out, but she was relieved that they'd finally cleared the air.

"Since Kristen and Nicole are such good friends, I thought, well, that I should set things right between us. From everything Nicole's said, you're doing an excellent job of parenting."

"From everything she's told me, the same must be true of you."

"Believe me, it isn't easy raising a preteen daughter," Joanna announced. She rubbed her palms together a couple of times, searching for something brilliant to add.

Tanner shook his head. "Isn't that the truth?"

They laughed then, and because they were still awkward with each other the sound was rusty.

"Now that you mention it, maybe I could spare a few minutes for a cup of coffee."

"Sure." Joanna led the way into the kitchen. While Tanner sat down at the table, she filled a mug from the pot keeping warm on the plate of the automatic coffeemaker and placed it carefully in front of him. Now that she knew him a bit better, she realized he'd prefer that to a dainty china cup. "How do you take it?"

"Just black, thanks."

She pulled out the chair across the table from him, still feeling a little ill at ease. Her mind was whirling. She didn't want to give Tanner a second wrong impression now that she'd managed to correct the first one. Her worry was that he might interpret her friendliness as a sign of romantic interest, which it wasn't. Building a new relationship was low on her priority list. Besides, they simply weren't on the same economic level. She worked for a savings-and-loan institution and he was half owner of the largest employer in the area. The last thing she wanted was for Tanner to think of her as a gold digger.

Joanna's thoughts were tumbling over themselves as she struggled to find a diplomatic way of telling him all this without sounding like some kind of man hater. And without sounding presumptuous.

"I'd like to pay you," Tanner said, cutting into her reflections. His chequebook was resting on the table, Cross pen poised above it.

Joanna blinked, not understanding. "For the coffee?"

He gave her an odd look. "For looking after Nicole."

"No, please." Joanna shook her head dismissively. "It wasn't the least bit of trouble for her to stay the night. Really."

"What about the costume for the talent show? Surely I owe you something for that."

"No." Once more she shook her head for emphasis. "I've had that material tucked away in a drawer for ages. If I hadn't used it for Nicole's costume, I'd probably have ended up giving it away later."

"But your time must be worth something."

"It was just as easy to sew up two as one. I was happy to do it. Anyway, there'll probably be a time in the future when I need a favor. I'm worthless when it comes to electrical outlets and even worse with plumbing."

Joanna couldn't believe she'd said that. Tanner Lund wasn't the type of man to do his own electrical repairs.

"Don't be afraid to ask," he told her. "If I can't fix it, I'll find someone who can."

"Thank you," she said, relaxing. Now that she was talking to Tanner, she decided he was both pleasant and forthright, not at all the coldly remote or self-important man his wealth might have led her to expect.

"Mom," Kristen cried as she charged into the kitchen, "did you ask Mr. Lund yet?"

"About what?"

"About coming over for dinner some time."

Joanna felt the heat shoot up her neck and face until it reached her hairline. Kristen had made the invitation sound like a romantic tryst the three of them had been planning the entire time Tanner was away.

Nicole, entering the room behind her friend, provided a timely interruption.

"Dad, Kristen and I want to do our song for you now."

"I'd like to see it. Do you mind, Joanna?"

"Of course not."

"Mom finished the costumes last night. We'll change and be back in a minute," Kristen said, her voice high with excitement. The two scurried off. The minute they were out of sight, Joanna stood up abruptly and refilled her cup. Actually she was looking for a way to speak frankly to Tanner, without embarrassing herself—or him. She thought ironically that anyone looking at her now would be hard put to believe she was a competent loan officer with a promising future.

"I think I should explain something," she began, her voice unsteady.

"Yes?" Tanner asked, his gaze following her movements around the kitchen.

Joanna couldn't seem to stand in one place for long. She moved from the coffeepot to the refrigerator, finally stopping in front of the stove. She linked her fingers behind her back and took a deep breath before she trusted herself to speak. "I thought it was important to clear up any misunderstanding between us, because the girls are such good friends. When Nicole's with Kristen and me, I want you to know she's in good hands."

Tanner gave her a polite nod. "I appreciate that."

"But I have a feeling that Kristen—and maybe Nicole, too—would like for us to get to know each other, er, better, if you know what I mean." Oh Lord, that sounded so stupid. Joanna felt herself grasping at straws. "I'm not interested in a romantic relationship, Tanner. I've got too much going on in my life to get involved, and I don't want you to feel threatened by the girls and their schemes. Forgive me for being so blunt, but I'd prefer to have this out in the open." She'd blurted it out so fast, she wondered if he'd understood. "This dinner invitation was Kristen's idea, not mine. I don't want you to think I had anything to do with it."

"An invitation to dinner isn't exactly a marriage proposal."

"True," Joanna threw back quickly. "But you might think… I don't know. I guess I don't want you to assume I'm interested in you—romantically, that is." She slumped back into the chair, pushed her hair away from her forehead and released a long sigh. "I'm only making matters worse, aren't I?"

"No. If I understand you correctly, you're saying you'd like to be friends and nothing more."

"Right." Pleased with his perceptiveness, Joanna straightened. Glad he could say in a few simple words what had left her breathless.

"The truth of the matter is, I feel much the same way," Tanner went on to explain. "I was married once and it was more than enough."

Joanna found herself nodding enthusiastically. "Exactly. I like my life the way it is. Kristen and I are very close. We just moved into this house and we've lots of plans for redecorating. My career is going nicely."

"Likewise. I'm too busy with this company to get involved in a relationship, either. The last thing I need right now is a woman to complicate my life."

"A man would only come between Kristen and me at this stage."

"How long have you been divorced?" Tanner asked, folding his hands around his coffee mug.

"Six years."

The information appeared to satisfy him, and he nodded slowly, as though to say he trusted what she was telling him. "It's been five for me."

She nodded, too. Like her, he hadn't immediately jumped into another relationship, nor was he looking for one. No doubt he had his reasons; Joanna knew she had hers.

"Friends?" Tanner asked, and extended his hand for her to shake.

"And nothing more," Joanna added, placing her hand in his.

They exchanged a smile.

"Since Mr. Lund can't be here for the talent show on Wednesday, he wants to take Nicole and me out for dinner next Saturday night," Kristen announced. "Nicole said to ask you if it was all right."

"That's fine," Joanna returned absently, scanning the front page of the Saturday evening newspaper. It had been more than a week since she'd spoken to Tanner. She felt good about the way things had gone that afternoon; they understood each other now, despite their rather uncertain start.

Kristen darted back into the kitchen, returning a minute later. "I think it would be best if you spoke to Mr. Lund yourself, Mom."

"Okay, honey." She'd finished reading Dear Abby and had just turned to the comics section, looking for Garfield, her favourite cat.

"Mom!" Kristen cried impatiently. "Mr. Lund's on the phone now. You can't keep him waiting like this. It's impolite."

Hurriedly Joanna set the paper aside. "For heaven's sake, why didn't you say so earlier?"

"I did. Honestly, Mom, I think you're losing it."

Whatever *it* was sounded serious. The minute Joanna was inside the kitchen, Kristen thrust the telephone receiver into her hand.

"This is Joanna," she said.

"This is Tanner," he answered right away. "Don't feel bad. Nicole claims I'm losing *it*, too."

"I'd take her more seriously if I knew what *it* was."

"Yeah, me, too," Tanner said, and she could hear the laughter in his voice. "Listen, is dinner next Saturday evening all right with you?"

"I can't see a problem at this end."

"Great. The girls suggested that ice-cream parlor they're always talking about."

"The Pink Palace," Joanna said, and managed to swallow a chuckle. Tanner was really letting himself in for a crazy night with those two. Last year Kristen had talked Joanna into dinner there for her birthday. The hamburgers had been as expensive as T-bone steaks, and tough as rawhide. The music was so loud it had impaired Joanna's hearing for an entire week afterward. And the place was packed with teenagers. On the bright side, though, the ice cream was pretty good.

"By the way," Joanna said, "Nicole's welcome to stay here when you're away next week."

"Joanna, that's great. I didn't want to ask, but the kid's been at me ever since the last time. She was worried I was going to send her back to Mrs. Wagner."

"It'll work best for her to stay here, since that's the night of the talent show."

"Are you absolutely sure?"

"Absolutely. It's no trouble at all. Just drop her off—and don't worry."

"Right." He sounded relieved. "And don't wear anything fancy next Saturday night."

"Saturday night?" Joanna asked, lost for a moment.

"Yeah. Didn't you just tell me it was all right for the four of us to go to dinner?"

Five

"I really appreciate this, Joanna," Tanner said. Nicole stood at his side, overnight bag clenched in her hand, her eyes round and sad.

"It's no problem, Tanner. Really."

Tanner hugged his daughter tightly. He briefly closed his eyes and Joanna could feel his regret. He was as upset about missing his daughter's talent-show performance as Nicole was not to have him there.

"Be good, sweetheart."

"I will."

"And I want to hear all the details about tonight when I get back, okay?"

Nicole nodded and attempted a smile.

"I'd be there if I could."

"I know, Dad. Don't worry about it. There'll be plenty of other talent shows. Kristen and I were thinking that if we do really good, we might take our act on the road, the way Daisy Gilbert does."

"Daisy who?" Tanner asked, and raised questioning eyes to Joanna, as if he expected her to supply the answer.

"A singer," was the best Joanna could do. Kristen had as

many albums as Joanna had runs in her tights. She found it impossible to keep her daughter's favorite rock stars straight. Apparently Tanner wasn't any more knowledgeable than she was.

"Not just *any* singer, Mom," Kristen corrected impatiently. "Daisy's special. She's only a little older than Nicole and me, and if she can be a rock star at fifteen, then so can we."

Although Joanna hated to squelch such optimism, she suspected that the girls might be missing one minor skill if they hoped to find fame and fortune as professional singers. "But you don't sing."

"Yeah, but we lip-synch real good."

"Come on, Nicole," Kristen said, reaching for her friend's overnight bag. "We've got to practice."

The two disappeared down the hallway and Joanna was left alone with Tanner.

"You have the telephone number for the hotel and the meeting place?" he asked.

"I'll call if there's a problem. Don't worry, Tanner, I'm sure everything's going to be fine."

He nodded, but a tight scowl darkened his face.

"For heaven's sake, stop looking so guilty."

His eyes widened in surprise. "It shows?"

"It might as well be flashing from a marquee."

Tanner grinned and rubbed the side of his jaw with his left hand. "There are only two meetings left that I'll have to deal with personally. Becky's promised to handle the others. You know, when I bought into the company and committed myself to these trips, I didn't think leaving Nicole would be this traumatic. We both hate it—at least, she did until she spent the night here with you and Kristen the last time."

"She's a special little girl."

"Thanks," Tanner said, looking suitably proud. It was obvious that he worked hard at being a good father, and Joanna felt a twinge of conscience for the assumptions she'd made about him earlier.

"Listen," she murmured, then took a deep breath, wondering how best to approach the subject of dinner. "About Saturday night…"

"What about it?"

"I thought, well, it would be best if it were just you and the girls."

Already he was shaking his head, his mouth set in firm lines of resolve. "It wouldn't be the same without you. I owe you, Joanna, and since you won't accept payment for keeping Nicole, then the least you can do is agree to dinner."

"But—"

"If you're worried about this seeming too much like a date—don't. We understand each other."

Her responding smile was decidedly weak. "Okay, if that's the way you want it. Kristen and I'll be ready Saturday at six."

"Good."

Joanna was putting the finishing touches to her makeup before the talent show when the telephone rang.

"I'll get it," Kristen yelled, racing down the hallway as if answering the phone before the second ring was a matter of life and death.

Joanna rolled her eyes toward the ceiling at the importance telephone conversations had recently assumed for Kristen. She half expected the call to be from Tanner, but then she heard Kristen exclaim, "Hi, Grandma!" Joanna smiled softly, pleased that her mother had remembered the talent show. Her parents were retired and lived in Colville, a town about sixty miles north of Spokane. She knew they would have attended the talent show themselves had road conditions been better. In winter, the families tended to keep in touch by phone because driving could be hazardous. No doubt her mother was calling now to wish Kristen luck.

Bits and pieces of the conversation drifted down the hall-way as Kristen chatted excitedly about the show, Nicole's visit and their song.

"Mom, it's Grandma!" Kristen yelled. "She wants to talk to you."

Joanna finished blotting her lipstick and hurried to the phone. "Hi, Mom," she said cheerfully. "It's nice of you to call."

"What's this about you going out on a date Saturday night?"

"Who told you that?" Joanna demanded, groaning silently. Her mother had been telling her for years that she ought to remarry. Joanna felt like throttling Kristen for even mentioning Tanner's name. The last thing she needed was for her parents to start pressuring her about this relationship.

"Why, Kristen told me all about it, and sweetie, if you don't mind my saying so, this man sounds just perfect for you. You're both single parents. He has a daughter, you have a daughter, and the girls are best friends. The arrangement is ideal."

"Mother, please, I don't know what Kristen told you, but Tanner only wants to thank me for watching Nicole while he's away on business. Dinner on Saturday night is not a date!"

"He's taking you to dinner?"

"Me and Kristen and his daughter."

"What was his name again?"

"Tanner Lund," Joanna answered, desperate to change

the subject. "Hasn't the weather been nasty this week? I'm really looking forward to spring. I was thinking about planting some annuals along the back fence."

"Tanner Lund," her mother repeated, slowly drawling out his name. "Now that has a nice solid feel to it. What's he like, sweetie?"

"Oh, honestly, Mother, I don't know. He's a man. What more do you want me to say?"

Her mother seemed to approve that piece of information. "I find it interesting that that's the way you view him. I think he could be the one, Joanna."

"Mother, please, how many times do I have to tell you? I'm not going to remarry. Ever!"

A short pause followed her announcement. "We'll see, sweetie, we'll see."

"Aren't you going to wear a dress, Mom?" Kristen gave her another of those scathing glances intended to melt a mother's confidence into puddles of doubt. Joanna had deliberated for hours on what to wear for this evening out with Tanner and the girls. If she chose a dress, something simple and classic like the ones she wore to the office, she might look too formal for a casual outing. The only other dresses she owned were party dresses, and those were so outdated they were almost back in style.

Dark wool pants and a wheat-colored Irish cable-knit sweater had seemed the perfect solution. Or so Joanna had thought until Kristen looked at her and frowned.

"Mom, tonight is important."

"We're going to the Pink Palace, not the Spokane House."

"I know, but Mr. Lund is so nice." Her daughter's gaze fell on the bouquet of pink roses on the dining-room table, and she reverently stroked a bloom. Tanner had arranged for the flowers to be delivered to Nicole and Kristen the night of the talent show. "You can't wear slacks to dinner with the man who sent me my first real flowers," she announced in tones of finality.

Joanna hesitated. "I'm sure this is what Mr. Lund expects," she said with far more confidence than she felt.

"You think so?"

She hoped so! She smiled, praying that her air of certainty would be enough to appease her sceptical daughter. Still, she had to agree with Kristen: Tanner *was* nice. More than nice—that was such a weak word. With every meeting, Joanna's estimation of the man grew. He'd called on Friday to thank her for minding Nicole, who'd gone straight home from school on Thursday afternoon since her father was back, and mentioned he was looking forward to Saturday. He was thoughtful, sensitive, personable and a wonderful father. Not to mention one of the best-looking men she'd ever met. It was unfortunate, really, that she wasn't looking for a husband, because Tanner Lund could easily be a prime candidate.

The word *husband* bounced in Joanna's mind like a ricocheting bullet. She blamed her mother for that. What she'd told her was true—Joanna was finished with marriage, finished with love. Davey had taught her how difficult it was for most men to remain faithful, and Joanna had no intention of repeating those painful lessons. Besides, if a man ever did become part of her life again, it would be someone on her own social and economic level. Not like Tanner Lund. But that didn't mean she was completely blind to male charms. On the contrary, she saw handsome men every day, worked with several, and had even dated a few. However, it was Tanner Lund she found herself thinking about lately, and that bothered Joanna. It bothered her a lot.

The best thing to do was nip this near relationship in the bud. She'd go to dinner with him this once, but only this once, and that would be the end of it.

"They're here!" The drape swished back into place as Kristen bolted away from the large picture window.

Calmly Joanna opened the hall closet and retrieved their winter coats. She might appear outwardly composed, but her fingers were shaking. The prospect of seeing Tanner left her trembling, and that fact drained away what little confidence she'd managed to accumulate over the past couple of days.

Both Tanner and Nicole came to the front door. Kristen held out her hands, and Nicole gripped them eagerly. Soon the two were jumping up and down like pogo sticks gone berserk.

"I can tell we're in for a fun evening," Tanner muttered under his breath.

He looked wonderful, Joanna admitted grudgingly. The kind of man every woman dreams about—well, almost every woman. Joanna longed to think of herself as immune to the handsome Mr. Lund. Unfortunately she wasn't.

Since their last meeting, she'd tried to figure out when her feelings for Tanner had changed. The roses had done it, she decided. Ordering them for Kristen and Nicole had been so thoughtful, and the girls had been ecstatic at the gesture.

When they'd finished lip-synching their song, they'd bowed before the auditorium full of appreciative parents. Then the school principal, Mr. Holliday, had stood at their side and presented them each with a beautiful bouquet of long-stemmed pink roses. Flowers Tanner had wired because he couldn't be there to watch their act.

"Are you ready?" Tanner asked, holding open the door for Joanna.

She nodded. "I think so."

Although it was early, a line had already begun to form outside the Pink Palace when they arrived. The minute they pulled into the parking lot, they were accosted by a loud, vibrating rock-and-roll song that might have been an old Jerry Lee Lewis number.

"It looks like we'll have to wait," Joanna commented. "That lineup's getting longer by the minute."

"I had my secretary make reservations," Tanner told her. "I heard this place really grooves on a Saturday night."

"Grooves!" Nicole repeated, smothering her giggles behind her cupped palm. Kristen laughed with her.

Turner leaned his head close to Joanna's. "It's difficult to reason with a generation that grew up without Janis and Jimi!"

Janis Joplin and Jimi Hendrix were a bit before Joanna's time, too, but she knew what he meant.

The Pink Palace was exactly as Joanna remembered. The popular ice-cream parlor was decorated in a fifties theme, with old-fashioned circular booths and outdated jukeboxes. The waitresses wore billowing pink skirts with a French poodle design and roller-skated between tables, taking and delivering orders. Once inside, Joanna, Tanner and the girls were seated almost immediately and handed huge menus. Neither girl bothered to read through the selections, having made their choices in the car. They'd both decided on cheeseburgers and banana splits.

By the time the waitress, chewing on a thick wad of bubble gum, skated to a stop at their table, Joanna had made her selection, too.

"A cheeseburger and a banana split," she said, grinning at the girls.

"Same here," Tanner said, "and coffee, please."

"I'll have a cup, too," Joanna added.

The teenager wrote down their order and glided toward the kitchen.

Joanna opened her purse and brought out a small wad of cotton wool.

"What's that for?" Tanner wanted to know when she pulled it apart into four fluffy balls and handed two of them to him, keeping the other pair for herself.

She pointed to her ears. "The last time I was here, I was haunted for days by a ringing in my ears that sounded suspiciously like an old Elvis tune."

Tanner chuckled and leaned across the table to shout, "It does get a bit loud, doesn't it?"

Kristen and Nicole looked from one parent to the other then shouted together, "If it's too loud, you're too old!"

Joanna raised her hand. "Guilty as charged."

Tanner nodded and shared a smile with Joanna. The smile did funny things to her stomach, and Joanna pressed her hands over her abdomen in a futile effort to quell her growing awareness of Tanner. A warning light flashed in her mind, spelling out danger.

Joanna wasn't sure what had come over her, but whatever it was, she didn't like it.

Their meal arrived, and for a while, at least, Joanna could direct her attention to that. The food was better than she remembered. The cheeseburgers were juicy and tender and the banana splits divine. She promised herself she'd eat cottage cheese and fruit every day at lunch for the next week to balance all the extra calories from this one meal.

While Joanna and Tanner exchanged only the occasional remark, the girls chattered happily throughout dinner. When the waitress skated away with the last of their empty plates, Tanner suggested a movie.

"Great idea!" Nicole cried, enthusiastically seconded by Kristen.

"What do you think, Joanna?" asked Tanner.

She started to say that the evening had been full enough—until she found two eager young faces looking hopefully at her. She couldn't finish her sentence; it just wasn't in her to dash their good time.

"Sure," she managed instead, trying to insert a bit of excitement into her voice.

"*Teen Massacre* is showing at the mall," Nicole said, shooting a glance in her father's direction. "Donny Rosenburg saw it and claims it scared him out of his wits, but then Donny doesn't have many."

Kristen laughed and nodded, apparently well-acquainted with the witless Donny.

Without the least bit of hesitation, Tanner shook his head. "No way, Nicole."

"Come on, Dad, everyone's seen it. The only reason it got an adult rating is because of the blood and gore, and I've seen that lots of times."

"Discussion is closed." He spoke without raising his voice, but the authority behind his words was enough to convince Joanna she'd turn up the loser if she ever crossed Tanner Lund. Still, she knew she wouldn't hesitate if she felt he was wrong, but in this case she agreed with him completely.

Nicole's lower lip jutted out rebelliously, and for a minute Joanna thought the girl might try to argue her case. But she wasn't surprised when Nicole yielded without further argument.

Deciding which movie to see involved some real negotiating. The girls had definite ideas of what was acceptable, as did Tanner and Joanna. Like Tanner, Joanna wasn't about to allow her daughter to see a movie with an adult rating, even if it was "only because of the blood and gore."

They finally compromised on a comedy that starred a popular teen idol. The girls thought that would be "all right," but they made it clear that *Teen Massacre* was their first choice.

Half an hour later they were inside the theater, and Tanner asked, "Anyone for popcorn?"

"Me," Kristen said.

"Me, too, and could we both have a Coke and chocolate-covered raisins, too?" Nicole asked.

Tanner rolled his eyes and, grinning, glanced toward Joanna. "What about you?"

"Nothing." She didn't know where the girls were going to put all this food, but she knew where it would end up if she were to consume it. Her hips! She sometimes suspected that junk food didn't even pass through her stomach, but attached itself directly to her hip bones.

"You're sure?"

"Positive."

Tanner returned a moment later with three large boxes of popcorn and other assorted treats.

As soon as they'd emptied Tanner's arms of all but one box of popcorn, the girls started into the auditorium.

"Hey, you two, wait for us," Joanna called after them, bewildered by the way they'd hurried off without waiting for her and Tanner.

Kristen and Nicole stopped abruptly and turned around, a look of pure horror on their young faces.

"You're not going to sit with us, are you, Mom?" Kristen wailed. "You just can't!"

"Why not?" This was news to Joanna. Sure, it had been

a while since she'd gone to a movie with her daughter, but Kristen had always sat with her in the past.

"Someone might see us," her daughter went on to explain, in tones of exaggerated patience. "No one sits with their parents anymore. Not even woosies."

"Woosies?"

"Sort of like nerds, only worse!" Kristen said.

"Sitting with us is obviously a social embarrassment to be avoided at all costs," Tanner muttered.

"Can we go now, Mom?" Kristen pleaded. "I don't want to miss the previews."

Joanna nodded, still a little stunned. She enjoyed going out to a movie now and again, usually accompanied by her daughter and often several of Kristen's friends. Until tonight, no one had openly objected to sitting in the same row with her. However, now that Joanna thought about it, Kristen hadn't been interested in going to the movies for the past couple of months.

"I guess this is what happens when they hit sixth grade," Tanner said, holding the auditorium door for Joanna.

She walked down the center aisle and paused by an empty row near the back, checking with Tanner before she entered. Neither of them sat down, though, until they'd located the girls. Kristen and Nicole were three rows from the front and had slid down so far that their eyes were level with the seats ahead of them.

"Ah, the joys of fatherhood," Tanner commented, after they'd taken their places. "Not to mention motherhood."

Joanna still felt a little taken aback by what had happened. She thought she had a close relationship with Kristen, and yet her daughter had never said a word about not wanting to be anywhere near her in a movie theater. She knew this might sound like a trivial concern to some, but she couldn't help worrying that the solid foundation she'd spent a decade reinforcing had started to crumble.

"Joanna?"

She turned to Tanner and tried to smile, but the attempt was unconvincing.

"What's wrong?"

Joanna fluttered her hand weakly, unable to find her voice. "Nothing." That came out sounding as though she might burst into tears any second.

"Is it Kristen?"

She nodded wildly.

"Because she didn't want to sit with us?"

Her hair bounced against her shoulders as she nodded again.

"The girls wanting to be by themselves bothers you?"

"No... Yes. I don't know what I'm feeling. She's growing up, Tanner, and I guess it just hit me right between the eyes."

"It happened to me last week," Tanner said thoughtfully. "I found Nicole wearing a pair of tights. Hell, I didn't even know they made them for girls her age."

"They do, believe it or not," Joanna informed him. "Kristen did the same thing."

He shook his head as though he couldn't quite grasp the concept. "But they're only eleven."

"Going on sixteen."

"Has Kristen tried pasting on those fake fingernails yet?" Tanner shuddered in exaggerated disgust.

Joanna covered her mouth with one hand to hold back an attack of giggles. "Those press-on things turned up every place imaginable for weeks afterward."

Tanner turned sideways in his seat. "What about makeup?" he asked urgently.

"I caught her trying to sneak out of the house one morning last month. She was wearing the brightest eye shadow I've ever seen in my life. Tanner, I swear if she'd been standing on a shore, she could have guided lost ships into port."

He smiled, then dropped his gaze, looking uncomfortable. "So you do let her wear makeup?"

"I'm holding off as long as I can," Joanna admitted. "At the very least, she'll have to wait until seventh grade. That was when my mother let me. I don't think it's so unreasonable to expect Kristen to wait until junior high."

Tanner relaxed against the back of his seat and nodded a couple of times. "I'm glad to hear that. Nicole's been after me to 'wake up and smell the coffee,' as she puts it, for the past six months. Hell, I didn't know who to ask about these things. It really isn't something I'm comfortable discussing with my secretary."

"What about her mother?"

His eyes hardened. "She only sees Nicole when it's convenient, and it hasn't been for the past three years."

"I... I didn't mean to pry."

"You weren't. Carmen and I didn't exactly part on the best of terms. She's got a new life now and apparently doesn't want any reminders of the past—not that I totally blame her. We made each other miserable. Frankly, Joanna, my feelings about getting married again are the same as yours. One failed marriage was enough for me."

The theater lights dimmed then, and the sound track started. Tanner leaned back and crossed his long legs, balancing one ankle on the opposite knee.

Joanna settled back, too, grateful that the movie they'd selected was a comedy. Her emotions were riding too close to the surface this evening. She could see herself bursting into tears at the slightest hint of sadness—for that matter, joy. Bambi traipsing through the woods would have done her in just then.

Joanna was so caught up in her thoughts that when Tanner and the others around her let out a boisterous laugh, she'd completely missed whatever had been so hilarious.

Without thinking, she reached over and grabbed a handful of Tanner's popcorn. She discovered that the crunchiness and the buttery, salty flavor suited her mood. Tanner held the box on the arm between them to make sharing easier.

The next time Joanna sent her fingers digging, they encountered Tanner's. "Sorry," she murmured, pulling her hand free.

"No problem," he answered, tilting the box her way.

Joanna munched steadily. Before she knew it, the popcorn was gone and her fingers were laced with Tanner's, her hand firmly clasped in his.

The minute he reached for her hand, Joanna lost track of what was happening on the screen. Holding hands seemed such an innocent gesture, something teenagers did. He certainly didn't mean anything by it, Joanna told herself. It was just that her emotions were so confused lately, and she wasn't even sure why.

She liked Tanner, Joanna realised anew, liked him very much. And she thoroughly enjoyed Nicole. For the first time since her divorce, she could imagine getting involved with another man, and the thought frightened her. All right, it terrified her. This man belonged to a different world. Besides, she wasn't ready. Good grief, six years should have given her ample time to heal, but she'd been too afraid to lift the bandage.

When the movie was over, Tanner drove them home. The girls were tired, but managed to carry on a lively backseat conversation. The front seat was a different story. Neither Tanner nor Joanna had much to say.

"Would you like to come in for coffee?" Joanna asked when Tanner pulled into her driveway, although she was silently wishing he'd decline. Her nerves continued to clamor from the hand holding, and she wanted some time alone to organise her thoughts.

"Can we, Dad? Please?" Nicole begged. "Kristen and I want to watch the Saturday night videos together."

"You're sure?" Tanner looked at Joanna, his brow creased with concern.

She couldn't answer. She wasn't sure of anything just then. "Of course," she forced herself to say. "It'll only take a minute or two to brew a pot."

"All right, then," Tanner said, and the girls let out whoops of delight.

Occasionally Joanna wondered if their daughters would ever get tired of one another's company. Probably, although they hadn't shown any signs of it yet. As far as she knew, the two girls had never had a serious disagreement.

Kristen and Nicole disappeared as soon as they got into the house. Within seconds, the television could be heard blaring rock music, which had recently become a familiar sound in the small one-storey house.

Tanner followed Joanna into the kitchen and stood leaning against the counter while she filled the automatic coffeemaker with water. Her movements were jerky and abrupt. She felt awkward, ungraceful—as though this was the first time she'd ever been alone with a man. And that was a ridiculous way to feel, especially since the girls were practically within sight.

"I enjoyed tonight," Tanner commented, as she removed two cups from the cupboard.

"I did, too." She tossed him a lazy smile over her shoulder. But Tanner's eyes held hers, and it was as if she was seeing him for the first time. She half turned toward him, suddenly aware of how tall and lean he was, how thick and soft his dark hair. With an effort, Joanna looked from those mesmerising blue eyes and returned to the task of making coffee, although her fingers didn't seem willing to cooperate.

She stood waiting for the dark liquid to filter its way into the glass pot. Never had it seemed to take so long.

"Joanna."

Judging by the loudness of his voice, Tanner was standing directly behind her. A beat of silence followed before she turned around to face him.

Tanner's hands grasped her shoulders. "It's been a long time since I've sat in a movie and held a girl's hand."

She lowered her eyes and nodded. "Me, too."

"I felt like a kid again."

She'd been thinking much the same thing herself.

"I want to kiss you, Joanna."

She didn't need an analyst to inform her that kissing Tanner was something best avoided. She was about to tell him so when his hands gripped her waist and pulled her away from the support of the kitchen counter. A little taken aback, Joanna threw up her hands, as if to ward him off. But the minute they came into contact with the muscled hardness of his chest, they lost their purpose.

The moment Tanner's warm mouth claimed her lips, she felt an excitement that was almost shocking in its intensity. Her hands clutched the collar of his shirt as she eagerly gave herself up to the forgotten sensations. It had been so long since a man had kissed her like this.

The kiss was over much too soon. Far sooner than Joanna would have liked. The fire of his mouth had ignited a response in her she'd believed long dead. She was amazed at how readily it had sprung back to life. When Tanner dropped his arms and released her, Joanna felt suddenly weak, barely able to remain upright.

Her hand found her chest and she heaved a giant breath. "I…don't think that was a good idea."

Tanner's brows drew together, forming a ledge over his narrowed eyes. "I'm not sure I do, either, but it seemed right. I don't know what's happening between us, Joanna, and it's confusing the hell out of me."

"You? I'm the one who made it abundantly clear from the outset that I wasn't looking for a romantic involvement."

"I know, and I agree, but—"

"I'm more than pleased Kristen and Nicole are good friends, but I happen to like my life the way it is, thank you."

Tanner's frown grew darker, his expression both baffled and annoyed. "I feel the same way. It was a kiss, not a suggestion we live in sin."

"I…really wish you hadn't done that, Tanner."

"I apologize. Trust me, it won't happen again," he muttered, and buried his hands deep inside his pockets. "In fact it would probably be best if we forgot the entire incident."

"I agree totally."

"Fine then." He stalked out of the kitchen, but not before Joanna found herself wondering if she *could* forget it.

Six

A kiss was really such a minor thing, Joanna mused, slowly rotating her pencil between her palms. She'd made a criminal case out of nothing, and embarrassed both Tanner and herself.

"Joanna, have you had time to read over the Osborne loan application yet?" her boss, Robin Simpson asked, strolling up to her desk.

"Ah, no, not yet," Joanna said, her face flushing with guilt.

Robin frowned as he studied her. "What's been with you today? Every time I see you, you're gazing at the wall with a faraway look in your eye."

"Nothing's wrong." Blindly she reached toward her In basket and grabbed a file, although she hadn't a clue which one it was.

"If I didn't know better, I'd say you were daydreaming about a man."

Joanna managed a short, sarcastic laugh meant to deny everything. "Men are the last thing on my mind," she said flippantly. It was a half-truth. Men in the plural didn't interest her, but *man*, as in Tanner Lund, well, that was another matter.

Over the years Joanna had gone out of her way to avoid men she was attracted to—it was safer. She dated occasionally, but usually men who might be classified as pleasant, men for whom she could never feel anything beyond a mild friendship. Magnetism, charm and sex appeal were lost on her, thanks to a husband who'd possessed all three and systematically destroyed her faith in the possibility of a lasting relationship. At least, those qualities hadn't piqued her interest again, until she met Tanner. Okay, so her dating habits for the past few years had been a bit premeditated, but everyone deserved a night out now and again. It didn't seem fair to be denied the pleasure of a fun evening simply because she wasn't in the market for another husband. So she'd dated, not a lot, but some and nothing in the past six years had affected her as much as those few short hours with Nicole's father.

"Joanna!"

She jerked her head up to discover her boss still standing beside her desk. "Yes?"

"The Osborne file."

She briefly closed her eyes in a futile effort to clear her thoughts. "What about it?"

Robin glared at the ceiling and paused, as though pleading with the light fixture for patience. "Read it and get back to me before the end of the day—if that isn't too much to ask?"

"Sure," she grumbled, wondering what had put Robin in such a foul mood. She picked up the loan application and was halfway through it before she realized the name on it wasn't Osborne. Great! If her day continued like this, she could blame Tanner Lund for getting her fired.

When Joanna arrived home three hours later she was exhausted and short-tempered. She hadn't been herself all day, mainly because she'd been so preoccupied with thoughts of Tanner Lund and the way he'd kissed her. She was overreacting—she'd certainly been kissed before, so it shouldn't be such a big deal. But it was. Her behaviour demonstrated all the maturity of someone Kristen's age, she chided herself. She'd simply forgotten how to act with men; it was too long since she'd been involved with one. The day wasn't a complete waste, however. She'd made a couple of important decisions in the last few hours, and she wanted to clear the air with her daughter before matters got completely out of hand.

"Hi, honey."

"Hi."

Kristen's gaze didn't waver from the television screen where a talk-show host was interviewing a man whose brilliant red hair was so short on top it stuck straight up and so messy in front it fell over his face, almost reaching his left eye and part of his nose.

"Who's that?"

Kristen gave a deep sigh of wonder and adolescent love. "You mean you don't know? I've been in love with Ed Sheeran for a whole year and you don't even know him when you see him?"

"No, I can't say that I do."

"Oh, Mom, honestly, get with it."

There *it* was again. First she was losing *it* and now she was supposed to get with *it*. Joanna wished her daughter would decide which she wanted.

"We need to talk."

Kristen reluctantly dragged her eyes away from her idol. "Mom, this is important. Can't it wait?"

Frustrated, Joanna sighed and muttered, "I suppose."

"Good."

Kristen had already tuned her out. Joanna strolled into the kitchen and realised she hadn't taken the hamburger out of the freezer to thaw. Great. So much for the tacos she'd planned to make for dinner. She opened and closed cupboard doors, rummaging around for something interesting. A can of tuna fish wasn't likely to meet with Kristen's approval. One thing about her daughter that the approach of the teen years hadn't disrupted was her healthy appetite.

Joanna stuck her head around the corner. "How does tuna casserole sound for dinner?"

Kristen didn't even look in her direction, just held out her arm and jerked her thumb toward the carpet.

"Soup and sandwiches?"

Once more Kristen's thumb headed downward, and Joanna groaned.

"Bacon, lettuce and tomato on toast with chicken noodle soup," she tried. "And that's the best I can do. Take it or leave it."

Kristen sighed. "If that's the final offer, I'll take it. But I thought we were having tacos."

"We were. I forgot to take out the hamburger."

"All right, BLTs," Kristen muttered, reversing the direction of her thumb.

Joanna was frying the bacon when Kristen joined her, sitting on a stool while her mother worked. "You wanted to talk to me about something?"

"Yes." Joanna concentrated on spreading mayonnaise over slices of whole-wheat toast, as she made an effort to gather her scattered thoughts. She cast about for several moments, trying to come up with a way of saying what needed to be said without making more of it than necessary.

"It must be something big," Kristen commented. "Did my teacher phone you at work or something?"

"No, should she have?" She raised her eyes and scrutinised Kristen's face closely.

Kristen gave a quick denial with a shake of her head.

"No way. I'm a star pupil this year. Nicole and I are both doing great. Just wait until report-card time, then you'll see."

"I believe you." Kristen had been getting top marks all year, and Joanna was proud of how well her daughter was doing. "What I have to say concerns Nicole and—" she hesitated, swallowing tightly "—her father."

"Mr. Lund sure is good-looking, isn't he?" Kristen said enthusiastically, watching for Joanna's reaction.

Reluctantly Joanna nodded, hoping to sound casual. "I suppose."

"Oh, come on, Mom, he's a hunk."

"All right," Joanna admitted slowly. "I'll grant you that Tanner has a certain amount of…appeal."

Kristen grinned, looking pleased with herself.

"Actually it was Mr. Lund I wanted to talk to you about," Joanna continued, placing a layer of tomato slices on the toast.

"Really?" The brown eyes opened even wider.

"Yes, well, I wanted to tell you that I… I don't think it would be a good idea for the four of us to go on doing things together."

Abruptly Kristen's face fell with surprise and disappointment. "Why not?"

"Well…because he and I are both really busy." Even to her own ears, the statement sounded illogical, but it was difficult to tell her own daughter that she was frightened of her attraction to the man. Difficult to explain why nothing could come of it.

"Because you're both busy? Come on, Mom, that doesn't make any sense."

"All right, I'll be honest." She wondered whether an eleven-year-old could grasp the complexities of adult relationships. "I don't want to give Nicole's dad the wrong idea," she said carefully.

Kristen leaned forward, setting her elbows on the kitchen counter and resting her face in both hands. Her gaze looked sharp enough to shatter diamonds. "The wrong idea about what?" she asked.

"Me," Joanna said, swallowing uncomfortably.

"You?" Kristen repeated thoughtfully, a frown creasing her smooth brow. She relaxed then and released a huge sigh. "Oh, I see. You think Mr. Lund might think you're in the marriage market."

Joanna pointed a fork at her daughter. "Bingo!"

"But, Mom, I think it would be great if you and Nicole's dad got together. In fact, Nicole and I were talking about it just today. Think about all the advantages. We could all be a real family, and you could have more babies... I don't know if I ever told you this, but I'd really like a baby brother, and so would Nicole. And if you married Mr. Lund we could take family vacations together. You wouldn't have to work, because... I don't know if you realize this, but Mr. Lund is pretty rich. You could stay home and bake cookies and sew and stuff."

Joanna was so surprised that it took her a minute to find her voice. Openmouthed, she waved the fork jerkily around. "No way, Kristen." Joanna's knees felt rubbery, and before she could slip to the floor, she slumped into a chair. All this time she'd assumed she was a good mother, giving her daughter everything she needed physically and emotionally, making up to Kristen as much as she could for her father's absence. But she apparently hadn't done enough. And Kristen and Nicole were scheming to get Joanna and Tanner together. As in married!

Something had to be done.

She decided to talk to Tanner, but an opportunity didn't present itself until much later that evening when Kristen was in bed, asleep. At least Joanna hoped her daughter was asleep. She dialled his number and prayed Nicole wouldn't answer.

Thankfully she didn't.

"Tanner, it's Joanna," she whispered, cupping her hand over the mouthpiece, taking no chance that Kristen could overhear their conversation.

"What's the matter? Have you got laryngitis?"

"No," she returned hoarsely, straining her voice. "I don't want Kristen to hear me talking to you."

"I see. Should I pretend you're someone else so Nicole won't tell on you?" he whispered back.

"Please." She didn't appreciate the humor in his voice. Obviously he had yet to realize the seriousness of the situation. "We need to talk."

"We do?"

"Trust me, Tanner. You have no idea what I just learned. The girls are planning on us getting married."

"Married?" he shouted.

That, Joanna had known, would get a reaction out of him.

"When do you want to meet?"

"As soon as possible." He still seemed to think she was joking, but she couldn't blame him. If the situation were reversed, no doubt she would react the same way. "Kristen said something about the two of them swimming Wednesday night at the community pool. What if we meet at Denny's for coffee after you drop Nicole off?"

"What time?" He said it as though they were planning a reconnaissance mission deep into enemy territory.

"Seven ten." That would give them both a few extra minutes to make it to the restaurant.

"Shall we synchronise our watches?"

"This isn't funny, Tanner."

"I'm not laughing."

But he was, and Joanna was furious with him. "I'll see you then."

"Seven-ten, Wednesday night at Denny's," he repeated. "I'll be there."

On the evening of their scheduled meeting, Joanna arrived at the restaurant before Tanner. She already regretted suggesting they meet at Denny's, but it was too late to change that now. There were bound to be other customers who would recognise either Tanner or her, and Joanna feared that word of their meeting could somehow filter back to the girls. She'd been guilty of underestimating them before; she wouldn't make the same mistake a second time. If Kristen and Nicole did hear about this private meeting, they'd consider it justification for further interference.

Tanner strolled into the restaurant and glanced around. He didn't seem to recognise Joanna, and she moved her sunglasses down her nose and gave him an abrupt wave.

He took one look at her, and even from the other side of the room she could see he was struggling to hold in his laughter.

"What's with the scarf and sunglasses?"

"I'm afraid someone might recognize us and tell the girls." It made perfect sense to her, but obviously not to him. Joanna forgave him since he didn't know the extent of the difficulties facing them.

But all he said was, "I see." He inserted his hands in the pockets of his overcoat and walked lazily past her, whistling. "Should I sit here or would you prefer the next booth?"

"Don't be silly."

"I'm not going to comment on that."

"For heaven's sake," Joanna hissed, "sit down before someone notices you."

"Someone notices me? Lady, you're wearing sunglasses at night, in the dead of winter, and with that scarf tied around your chin you look like an old woman."

"Tanner," she said, "this is not the time to crack jokes."

A smile lifted his features as he slid into the booth opposite her. He reached for a menu. "Are you hungry?"

"No." His attitude was beginning to annoy her. "I'm just having coffee."

"Nicole cooked dinner tonight, and frankly I'm starving."

When the waitress appeared he ordered a complete dinner. Joanna asked for coffee.

"Okay, what's up, Sherlock?" he asked, once the coffee had been poured.

"To begin with I... I think Kristen and Nicole saw you kiss me the other night."

He made no comment, but his brow puckered slightly.

"It seems the two of them have been talking, and from what I gather they're interested in getting us, er, together."

"I see."

To Joanna's dismay, Tanner didn't seem to be the slightest bit concerned by her revelation.

"That troubles you?"

"Tanner," she said, leaning toward him, "to quote my daughter, 'Nicole and I have been talking and we thought it would be great if you and Mr. Lund got together. You could have more babies and we could go on vacations and be a real family and you could stay home and bake cookies and stuff.'" She waited for his reaction, but his face remained completely impassive.

"What kind of cookies?" he asked finally.

"Tanner, if you're going to turn this into a joke, I'm leaving." As far as Joanna was concerned, he deserved to be tormented by two dedicated eleven-year-old matchmakers! She started to slide out of the booth, but he stopped her with an upraised hand.

"All right, I'm sorry."

He didn't sound too contrite, and she gave a weak sigh of disgust. "You may consider this a joking matter, but I don't."

"Joanna, we're both mature adults," he stated calmly. "We aren't going to let a couple of eleven-year-old girls manipulate us!"

"Yes, but—"

"From the first, we've been honest with each other. That isn't going to change. You have no interest in remarriage—to me or anyone else—and I feel the same way. As long as we continue as we are now, the girls don't have a prayer."

"It's more than that," Joanna said vehemently. "We need to look past their schemes to the root of the problem."

"Which is?"

"Tanner, obviously we're doing something wrong as single parents."

He frowned. "What makes you say that?"

"Isn't it obvious? Kristen, and it seems equally true for Nicole, wants a complete family. What Kristen is really saying is that she longs for a father. Nicole is telling you she'd like a mother."

The humour drained out of Tanner's eyes, replaced with a look of real concern. "I see. And you think this all started because Kristen and Nicole saw us kissing?"

"I don't know," she murmured, shaking her head. "But I do know my daughter, and when she wants something, she goes after it with the force of a bulldog and won't let up. Once she's got it in her head that you and I are destined for each other, it's going to be pretty difficult for her to accept that all we'll ever be is friends."

"Nicole can get that way about certain things," he said thoughtfully.

The waitress delivered his roast beef sandwich and refilled Joanna's coffee cup.

Maybe she'd overreacted to the situation, but she couldn't help being worried. "I suppose you think I'm making more of a fuss about this than necessary," she said, flustered and a little embarrassed.

"About the girls manipulating us?"

"No, about the fact that we've both tried so hard to be good single parents, and obviously we're doing something wrong."

"I will admit that part concerns me."

"I don't mind telling you, Tanner, I've been in a panic all week, wondering where I've failed. We've got to come to terms with this. Make some important decisions."

"What do you suggest?"

"To start with, we've got to squelch any hint of personal involvement. I realize a certain amount of contact will be unavoidable with the girls being such close friends." She paused and chewed on her bottom lip. "I don't want to disrupt their relationship."

"I agree with you there. Being friends with Kristen has meant a good deal to Nicole."

"You and I went months without talking to each other," Joanna said, recalling that they'd only recently met. "There's no need for us to see each other now, is there?"

"That won't work."

"Why not?"

"Nicole will be spending the night with you again next Thursday—that is, unless you'd rather she didn't."

"Of course she can stay."

Tanner nodded, looking relieved. "To be honest, I don't think she'd go back to Mrs. Wagner's anymore without raising a big fuss."

"Taking care of Nicole is one thing, but the four of us doing anything together is out of the question."

Once more he nodded, but he didn't look pleased with the suggestion. "I think that would be best, too."

"We can't give them any encouragement."

Pushing his plate aside, Tanner reached for his water glass, cupping it with both hands. "You know, Joanna, I think a lot of you." He paused, then gave her a teasing smile. "You have a habit of dressing a little oddly every now and then, but other than that I respect your judgment. I'd like to consider you a friend."

She decided to let his comment about her choice of clothing slide. "I'd like to be your friend, too," she told him softly.

He grinned, and his gaze held hers for a long uninterrupted moment before they both looked away. "I know you think that kiss the other night was a big mistake, and I suppose you're right, but I'm not sorry it happened." He hesitated, as though waiting for her to argue with him, and when she didn't, he continued. "It's been a lot of years since I held a woman's hand at a movie or kissed her the way I did you. It was good to feel that young and innocent again."

Joanna dropped her gaze to her half-filled cup. It had felt right for her, too. So right that she'd been frightened out of her wits ever since. She could easily fall in love with Tanner, and that would be the worst possible thing for her. She just wasn't ready to take those risks again. They came from different worlds, too, and she'd never fit comfortably in his. Yet every time she thought about that kiss, she started to shake from the inside out.

"In a strange sort of way we need each other," Tanner went on, his look thoughtful. "Nicole needs a strong loving woman to identify with, to fill a mother's role, and she thinks you're wonderful."

"And Kristen needs to see a man who can be a father, putting the needs of his family before his own."

"I think it's only natural for the two of them to try to get us together," Tanner added. "It's something we should be prepared to deal with in the future."

"You're right," Joanna agreed, understanding exactly what he meant. "We need each other to help provide what's lacking in our daughters' lives. But we can't get involved with each other." She didn't know any other way to say it but bluntly.

"I agree," he said, with enough conviction to lay aside any doubt Joanna might still hold.

They were silent for a long moment.

"Why?"

Strangely, Joanna knew immediately what he was asking. She had the same questions about what had happened between him and Nicole's mother.

"Davey was—is—the most charming personable man I've ever met. I was fresh out of college and so in love with him I didn't stop to think." She paused and glanced away, not daring to look at Tanner. Her voice had fallen so low it was almost a whisper. "We were engaged when my best friend, Carol, told me Davey had made a pass at her. Fool that I was, I didn't believe her. I thought she was jealous that Davey had chosen me to love and marry. I was sick that my friend would stoop to anything so underhand. I always knew Carol found him attractive—most women did—and I was devastated that she would lie that way. I trusted Davey so completely that I didn't even ask him about the incident.

Later, after we were married, there were a lot of times when he said he was working late, a lot of unexplained absences, but I didn't question those, either. He was building his career in real estate, and if he had to put in extra hours, well, that was understandable. All those nights I sat alone, trusting him when he claimed he was working, believing with all my heart that he was doing his utmost to build a life for us…and then learning he'd been with some other woman."

"How'd you find out?"

"The first time?"

"You mean there was more than once?"

She nodded, hating to let Tanner know how many times she'd forgiven Davey, how many times she'd taken him back after he'd pleaded and begged and promised it would never happen again.

"I was blind to his wandering eye for the first couple of years. What they say about ignorance being bliss is true. When I found out, I was physically sick. When I realised how I'd fallen for his lies, it was even worse, and yet I stuck it out with him, trusting that everything would be better, everything would change…someday. I wanted so badly to believe him, to trust him, that I accepted anything he told me, no matter how implausible it sounded.

"The problem was that the more I forgave him, the lower my self-esteem dropped. I became convinced it was all my fault. I obviously lacked something, since he…felt a need to seek out other women."

"You know now that's not true, don't you?" His voice was so gentle, so caring, that Joanna battled down a rush of emotion.

"There'd never been a divorce in my family," she told him quietly. "My parents have been married nearly forty years, and my brothers all have happy marriages. I think that was one of the reasons I held on so long. I just didn't know how to let go. I'd be devastated and crushed when I learned about his latest affair, yet I kept coming back for more. I suppose I believed Davey would change. Something magical would happen and all our problems would disappear. Only it never did. One afternoon—I don't even know what prompted it… All I knew was that I couldn't stay in the marriage any longer. I packed Kristen's and my things and walked out. I've never been back, never wanted to go back."

Tanner reached for her hand, and his fingers wrapped warmly around hers. A moment passed before he spoke, and when he did, his voice was tight with remembered pain. "I thought Carmen was the sweetest, gentlest woman in the world. As nonsensical as it sounds, I think I was in love with her before I even knew her name. She was a college cheerleader and a homecoming queen, and I felt like a nobody. By chance, we met several years after graduation when I'd just begun making a name for myself. I'd bought my first company, a small aluminum window manufacturer back in West Virginia. And I was working night and day to see it through those first rough weeks of transition.

"I was high on status," Tanner admitted, his voice filled with regret. "Small-town boy makes good—that kind of stuff. She'd been the most popular girl in my college year, and dating her was the fulfilment of a fantasy. She'd recently broken up with a guy she'd been involved with for two years and had something to prove herself, I suppose." He focused his gaze away from Joanna. "Things got out of hand and a couple of months later Carmen announced she was pregnant. To be honest, I was happy about it, thrilled. There was never any question whether I'd marry her. By then I was so in love with her I couldn't see straight. Eight months after the wedding, Nicole was born…" He hesitated, as though gathering his thoughts. "Some women are meant to be mothers, but not Carmen. She didn't even like to hold Nicole, didn't want anything to do with her. I'd come home at night and find that Carmen had neglected Nicole most of the day. But I made excuses for her, reasoned everything out in my own mind—the unexplained bruises on the baby, the fear I saw in Nicole's eyes whenever her mother was around. It got so bad that I started dropping Nicole off at my parents', just so I could be sure she was being looked after properly."

Joanna bit the corner of her lip at the raw pain she witnessed in Tanner's eyes. She was convinced he didn't speak of his marriage often, just as she rarely talked about Davey, but this was necessary if they were to understand each other.

"To be fair to Carmen, I wasn't much of a husband in those early months. Hell, I didn't have time to be. I was feeling like a big success when we met, but that didn't last long. Things started going wrong at work and I damn near lost my shirt.

"Later," he continued slowly, "I learned that the entire time I was struggling to hold the company together, Carmen was seeing her old boyfriend, Sam Dailey."

"Oh, Tanner."

"Nicole's my daughter, there was no doubting that. But Carmen had never really wanted children, and she felt trapped in the marriage. We separated when Nicole was less than three years old."

"I thought you said you'd only been divorced five years?"

"We have. It took Carmen a few years to get around to the legal aspect of things. I wasn't in any rush, since I had no intention of ever marrying again."

"What's happened to Carmen since? Did she remarry?"

"Eventually. She lived with Sam for several years, and the last thing I heard was they'd split up and she married a professional baseball player."

"Does Nicole ever see her mother?" Joanna remembered that he'd said his ex-wife saw Nicole only when it was convenient.

"She hasn't in the past three years. The thing I worry about most is having Carmen show up someday, demanding that Nicole come to live with her. Nicole doesn't remember anything about those early years—thank God—and she seems to have formed a rosy image of her mother. She keeps Carmen's picture in her bedroom and every once in a while I'll see her staring at it wistfully." He paused and glanced at his watch. "What time were we supposed to pick up the kids?"

"Eight."

"It's five after now."

"Oh, good grief." Joanna slung her bag over her shoulder as they slid out of the booth and hurried toward the cash register. Tanner insisted on paying for her coffee, and Joanna didn't want to waste time arguing.

They walked briskly toward their cars, parked beside each other in the lot. "Joanna," he called, as she fumbled with her keys. "I'll wait a couple of minutes so we don't both arrive at the same time. Otherwise the girls will probably guess we've been together."

She flashed him a grateful smile. "Good thinking."

"Joanna." She looked at him questioningly as he shortened the distance between them. "Don't misunderstand this," he said softly. He pulled her gently into the circle of his arms, holding her close for a lingering moment. "I'm sorry for what Davey did to you. The man's a fool." Tenderly he brushed his lips over her forehead, then turned and abruptly left her.

It took Joanna a full minute to recover enough to get into her car and drive away.

Seven

"**M**om," Kristen screeched, "the phone's for you."

Joanna was surprised. A call for her on a school night was rare enough, but one that actually got through with Kristen and Nicole continually on the line was a special occasion.

"Who is it, honey?" No doubt someone interested in cleaning her carpets or selling her a cemetery plot.

"I don't know," Kristen said, holding the phone to her shoulder. She lowered her voice to whisper, "But whoever it is sounds weird."

"Hello." Joanna spoke into the receiver as Kristen wandered toward her bedroom.

"Can you talk?" The husky male voice was unmistakably Tanner's.

"Y-yes." Joanna looked toward Kristen's bedroom to be certain her daughter was out of earshot.

"Can you meet me tomorrow for lunch?"

"What time?"

"Noon at the Sea Galley."

"Should we synchronize our watches?" Joanna couldn't resist asking. It had been a week since she'd last talked to

Tanner. In the meantime she hadn't heard a word from Kristen about getting their two families together again. That in itself was suspicious, but Joanna had been too busy at work to think about it.

"Don't be cute, Joanna. I need help."

"Buy me lunch and I'm yours." She hadn't meant that quite the way it sounded and was grateful Tanner didn't comment on her slip of the tongue.

"I'll see you tomorrow then."

"Right."

A smile tugged at the edges of her mouth as she replaced the telephone receiver. Her hand lingered there for a moment as an unexpected tide of happiness washed over her.

"Who was that, Mom?" Kristen asked, poking her head around her bedroom door.

"A…friend, calling to ask if I could meet…her for lunch."

"Oh." Kristen's young face was a study in scepticism. "For a minute there I thought it sounded like Mr. Lund trying to fake a woman's voice."

"Mr. Lund? That's silly," Joanna said with a forced little laugh, then deftly changed the subject. "Kristen, it's nine thirty. Hit the hay, kiddo."

"Right, Mom. 'Night."

"'Night, sweetheart."

"Enjoy your lunch tomorrow."

"I will."

Joanna hadn't had a chance to walk away from the phone before it pealed a second time. She gave a guilty start and reached for it.

"Hello," she said hesitantly, half expecting to hear Tanner's voice again.

But it was her mother's crisp clear voice that rang over the wire. "Joanna, I hope this isn't too late to call."

"Of course not, Mom," Joanna answered quickly. "Is everything all right?"

Her mother ignored the question and asked one of her own instead. "What was the name of that young man you're dating again?"

"Mother," Joanna said with an exasperated sigh, "I'm not seeing anyone. I told you that."

"Tanner Lund, wasn't it?"

"We went out to dinner *once* with both our daughters, and that's the extent of our relationship. If Kristen let you assume anything else, it was just wishful thinking on her part. One dinner, I swear."

"But, Joanna, he sounds like such a nice young man. He's the same Tanner Lund who recently bought half of Spokane Aluminum, isn't he? I saw his name in the paper this morning and recognised it right away. Sweetie, your dad and I are so pleased you're dating such a famous successful man."

"Mother, please!" Joanna cried. "Tanner and I are friends. How many times do I have to tell you, we're not dating? Kristen and Tanner's daughter, Nicole, are best friends. I swear that's all there is to—"

"Joanna," her mother interrupted. "The first time you mentioned his name, I heard something in your voice that's been missing for a good long while. You may be able to fool yourself, but not me. You like this Tanner." Her voice softened perceptively.

"Mother, nothing could possibly come of it even if I was attracted to him—which I'm not." Okay, so that last part wasn't entirely true. But the rest of it certainly was.

"And why couldn't it?" her mother insisted.

"You said it yourself. He's famous, in addition to being wealthy. I'm out of his league."

"Nonsense," her mother responded in a huff.

Joanna knew better than to get into a war of words with her stubborn parent.

"Now don't be silly. You like Tanner Lund, and I say it's about time you let down those walls you've built around yourself. Joanna, sweetie, you've been hiding behind them for six years now. Don't let what happened with Davey ruin your whole life."

"I'm not going to," Joanna promised.

There was a long pause before her mother sighed and answered, "Good. You deserve some happiness."

At precisely noon the following day, Joanna drove into the Sea Galley parking lot. Tanner was already there, waiting for her by the entrance.

"Hi," she said with a friendly grin, as he walked toward her.

"What, no disguises?"

Joanna laughed, embarrassed now by that silly scarf and sunglasses she'd worn when they met at Denny's. "Kristen doesn't know anyone who eats here."

"I'm grateful for that."

His smile was warm enough to tunnel through snow drifts, and as much as Joanna had warned herself not to be affected by it, she was.

"It's good to see you," Tanner added, taking her arm to escort her into the restaurant.

"You, too." Although she hadn't seen him in almost a week, Tanner was never far from her thoughts. Nicole had stayed with her and Kristen when Tanner flew to New York for two days in the middle of the previous week. The Spokane area had been hit by a fierce snowstorm the evening he left. Joanna had felt nervous the entire time about his traveling in such inclement weather, yet she hadn't so much as asked him about his flight when he arrived to pick up Nicole. Their conversation had been brief and pleasantly casual, but her relief that he'd got home safely had kept her awake for hours. Later, she'd been furious with herself for caring so much.

The Sea Galley hostess seated them right away and handed them thick menus. Joanna ordered a shrimp salad and coffee. Tanner echoed her choice.

"Nicole's birthday is next week," he announced, studying her face carefully. "She's handing out the party invitations today at school."

Joanna smiled and nodded. But Tanner's eyes held hers, and she saw something unidentifiable flicker there.

"In a moment of weakness, I told her she could have a slumber party."

Joanna's smile faded. "As I recall, Nicole did mention something about this party," she said, trying to sound cheerful. The poor guy didn't know what he was in for. "You're obviously braver than I am."

"You think it was a bad move?"

Joanna made a show of closing her eyes and nodding vigorously.

"I was afraid of that," Tanner muttered, and he rearranged the silverware around his place setting a couple of times. "I know we agreed it probably wouldn't be a good idea for us to do things together. But I need some advice— from a friend."

"What can I do?"

"Joanna, I haven't the foggiest idea about entertaining a whole troop of girls. I can handle contract negotiations and make split-second business decisions, but I panic at the thought of all those squealing little girls sequestered in my apartment for all those hours."

"How do you want me to help?"

"Would you consider…" He gave her a hopeful look, then shook his head regretfully. "No. I can't ask that of you. Besides, we don't want to give the girls any more ideas about the two of us. What I really need is some suggestions for keeping all these kids occupied. What do other parents do?"

"Other parents know better."

Tanner wiped a lock of dark brown hair from his brow and frowned. "I was afraid of that."

"What time are the girls supposed to arrive?"

"Six."

"Tanner, that's too early."

"I know, but Nicole insists I serve my special tacos, and she has some screwy idea about all the girls crowding into the kitchen to watch me."

Now it was Joanna's turn to frown. "That won't work. You'll end up with ten different pairs of hands trying to help. There'll be hamburger and cheese from one end of the place to the other."

"I thought as much. Good Lord, Joanna, how did I get myself into this mess?"

"Order pizza," she tossed out, tapping her index finger against her bottom lip. "Everyone loves that."

"Pizza. Okay. What about games?"

"A scavenger hunt always comes in handy when things get out of hand. Release the troops on your unsuspecting neighbours."

"So far we've got thirty minutes of the first fourteen hours filled."

"Movies," Joanna suggested next. "Lots of movies. You can go on Netflix and browse for something, maybe pick an old favourite like *Pretty in Pink*, and the girls will be in seventh heaven."

His eyes brightened. "Good idea."

"And if you really feel adventurous, take them roller-skating."

"Roller-skating? You think they'd like that?"

"They'd love it, especially if word leaked out that they were going to be at the rink Friday night. That way, several of the boys from the sixth-grade class can just happen to be there, too."

Tanner nodded, and a smile quirked the corners of his mouth. "And you think that'll keep everyone happy?"

"I'm sure of it. Wear 'em out first, show a movie or two second, with the lights out, of course, and I guarantee you by midnight everyone will be sound asleep."

Their salads arrived and Tanner stuck his fork into a fat succulent shrimp, then paused. "Now what was it you said last night about buying you lunch and making you mine?"

"It was a slip of the tongue," she muttered, dropping her gaze to her salad.

"Just my luck."

They laughed, and it felt good. Joanna had never had a relationship like this with a man. She wasn't on her guard the way she normally was, fearing that her date would put too much stock in an evening or two out. Because their daughters were the same age, they had a lot in common. They were both single parents doing their damnedest to raise their daughters right. The normal dating rituals and practised moves were unnecessary with him. Tanner was her friend, and it renewed Joanna's faith in the opposite sex to know there were still men like him left. Their friendship reassured her—but the undeniable attraction between them still frightened her.

"I really appreciate your suggestions," he said, after they'd both concentrated on their meals for several moments. "I've had this panicky feeling for the past three days. I suppose it wasn't a brilliant move on my part to call you at home, but I was getting desperate."

"You'll do fine. Just remember, it's important to keep the upper hand."

"I'll try."

"By the way, when *is* Hell Night?" She couldn't resist teasing him.

He gave a heartfelt sigh. "Next Friday."

Joanna slowly ate a shrimp. "I think Kristen figured out it was you on the phone last night."

"She did?"

"Yeah. She started asking questions the minute I hung up. She claimed my 'friend' sounded suspiciously like Mr. Lund faking a woman's voice."

Tanner cleared his throat and answered in a high falsetto. "That should tell you how desperate I was."

Joanna laughed and speared another shrimp. "That's what friends are for."

Eight

"Mom, hurry or we're going to be late." Kristen paced the hallway outside her mother's bedroom door while Joanna finished dressing.

"Have you got Nicole's gift?"

"Oh." Kristen dashed into her bedroom and returned with a gaily wrapped oblong box. They'd bought the birthday gift the night before, a popular board game, which Kristen happened to know Nicole really wanted.

"I think Mr. Lund is really nice to let Nicole have a slumber party, don't you?"

"Really brave is a more apt description. How many girls are coming?"

"Fifteen."

"Fifteen!" Joanna echoed in a shocked voice.

"Nicole originally invited twenty, but only fifteen could make it."

Joanna slowly shook her head. He'd had good reason to feel panicky. With all these squealing, giddy preadolescent girls, the poor man would be certifiable by the end of the night. Either that or a prime candidate for extensive counseling.

When they arrived, the parking area outside Tanner's apartment building looked like the scene of a rock concert. There were enough parents dropping off kids to cause a minor traffic jam.

"I can walk across the street if you want to let me out here," Kristen suggested, anxiously eyeing the group of girls gathering outside the building.

"I'm going to find a parking place," Joanna said, scanning the side streets for two adjacent spaces—so that she wouldn't need to struggle to parallel park.

"You're going to find a place to leave the car? Why?" Kristen wanted to know, her voice higher pitched and more excited than usual. "You don't have to come in, if you don't want. I thought you said you were going to refinish that old chair Grandpa gave us last summer."

"I was," Joanna murmured with a short sigh, "but I have the distinct impression that Nicole's father is going to need a helping hand."

"I'm sure he doesn't, Mom. Mr. Lund is a really organized person. I'm sure he's got everything under control."

Kristen's reaction surprised Joanna. She would have expected her daughter to encourage the idea of getting the two of them together.

She finally found a place to park and they hurried across the street, Kristen apparently deep in thought.

"Actually, Mom, I think helping Mr. Lund might be a good idea," she said after a long pause. "He'll probably be grateful."

Joanna wasn't nearly as confident by this time. "I have a feeling I'm going to regret this later."

"No, you won't." Joanna could tell Kristen was about to launch into another one of her little speeches about babies, vacations and homemade cookies. Thankfully she didn't get the chance, since they'd entered the building and encountered a group of Kristen's other friends.

Tanner was standing in the doorway of his apartment, already looking frazzled when Joanna arrived. Surprise flashed through his eyes when he saw her.

"I've come to help," she announced, peeling off her jacket and pushing up the sleeves of her thin sweater. "This group is more than one parent can reasonably be expected to control."

He looked for a moment as though he wanted to fall to the ground and kiss her feet. "Bless you."

"Believe me, Tanner, you owe me for this." She glanced around at the chaos that dominated the large apartment. The girls had already formed small groups and were arguing loudly with each other over some subject of earth-shattering importance—like Adam Levine's age, or the real color of Niall Horan's hair.

"Is the pizza ready?" Joanna asked him, raising her voice in order to be heard over the din of squeals, shouts and rock music.

Tanner nodded. "It's in the kitchen. I ordered eight large ones. Do you think that'll be enough?"

Joanna rolled her eyes. "I suspect you're going to be eating leftover pizza for the next two weeks."

The girls proved her wrong. Never had Joanna seen a hungrier group. They were like school of piranha attacking a hapless victim, and within fifteen minutes everyone had eaten her fill. There were one or two slices left of four of the pizzas, but the others had vanished completely.

"It's time for a movie," Joanna decided, and while the girls voted on which film to see first Tanner started dumping dirty paper plates and pop cans into a plastic garbage sack. When the movie was finished, Joanna calculated, it would be time to go skating.

Peace reigned once Tom Cruise appeared on the television screen and Joanna joined Tanner in the bright cheery kitchen.

He was sitting dejectedly at the round table, rubbing a hand across his forehead. "I feel a headache coming on."

"It's too late for that," she said with a soft smile. "Actually I think everything is going very well. Everyone seems to be having a good time, and Nicole is a wonderful hostess."

"You do? She is?" He gave her an astonished look. "I keep having nightmares about pillow fights and lost dental appliances."

"Hey, it isn't going to happen." Not while they maintained control. "Tanner, I meant what I said about the party going well. In fact, I'm surprised at how smoothly everything is falling into place. The kids really are having a good time, and as long as we keep them busy there shouldn't be any problems."

He grinned, looking relieved. "I don't know about you, but I could use a cup of coffee."

"I'll second that."

He poured coffee into two pottery mugs and carried them to the table. Joanna sat across from him, propping her feet on the opposite chair. Sighing, she leaned back and cradled the steaming mug.

"The pizza was a good idea." He reached for a piece and shoved the box in her direction.

Now that she had a chance to think about it, Joanna realized she'd been so busy earlier, serving the girls, she hadn't managed to eat any of the pizza herself. She straightened enough to reach for a napkin and a thick slice dotted with pepperoni and spicy Italian sausage.

"What made you decide to give up your evening to help me out?" Tanner asked, watching her closely. "Kristen told Nicole that you had a hot date tonight. You were the last person I expected to see."

Joanna wasn't sure what had changed her mind about tonight and staying to help Tanner. Pity, she suspected. "If the situation were reversed, you'd lend me a hand," she replied, more interested in eating than conversation at the moment.

Tanner frowned at his pizza. "You missed what I was really asking."

"I did?"

"I was trying to be subtle about asking if you had a date tonight."

Joanna found that question odd. "Obviously I didn't."

"It isn't so obvious to me. You're a single parent, so there aren't that many evenings you can count on being free of responsibility. I would have thought you'd use this time to go out with someone special, flap your wings and that sort of thing." His frown grew darker.

"I'm too old to flap my wings," she said with a soft chuckle. "Good grief, I'm over thirty."

"So you aren't dating anyone special?"

"Tanner, you know I'm not."

"I don't know anything of the sort." Although he didn't raise his voice, Joanna could sense his disquiet.

"All right, what's up?" She didn't like the looks he was giving her. Not one bit.

"Nicole."

"Nicole?" she repeated.

"She was telling me that other day that you'd met someone recently. 'A real prince' is the phrase she used. Someone rich and handsome who was crazy about you—she claimed you were seeing a lot of this guy. Said you were falling madly in love."

Joanna dropped her feet to the floor with a loud thud and bolted upright so fast she nearly tumbled out of the chair. She was furiously chewing her pepperoni-and-sausage pizza, trying to swallow it as quickly as she could. All the while, her finger was pointing, first toward the living room where the girls were innocently watching *Top Gun* and then at Tanner who was staring at her in fascination.

"Hey, don't get angry with me," he said. "I'm only repeating what Kristen supposedly told Nicole and what Nicole told me."

She swallowed the piece of pizza in one huge lump. "They're plotting again, don't you see? I should have known something was up. It's been much too quiet lately. Kristen and Nicole are getting devious now, because the direct approach didn't work." Flustered, she started pacing the kitchen floor.

"Settle down, Joanna. We're smarter than a couple of school kids."

"That's easy for you to say." She pushed her hair away from her forehead and continued to pace. Little wonder Kristen hadn't been keen on the idea of her helping Tanner tonight. Joanna whirled around to face him. "Well, aren't you going to say something?" To her dismay, she discovered he was doing his best not to chuckle. "This isn't a laughing matter, Tanner Lund. I wish you'd take this seriously!"

"I am."

Joanna snorted softly. "You are not!"

"We're mature adults, Joanna. We aren't going to allow two children to dictate our actions."

"Is that a fact?" She braced both hands against her hips

and glared at him. "I'm pleased to hear you're such a tower of strength, but I'll bet a week's pay that it wasn't your idea to have this slumber party. You probably rejected the whole thing the first time Nicole suggested it, but after having the subject of a birthday slumber party brought up thirty times in about thirty minutes you weakened, and that was when Nicole struck the fatal blow. If your daughter is anything like mine, she probably used every trick in the book to talk you into this party idea. Knowing how guilty you felt about all those business trips, I suppose Nicole brought them up ten or twelve times. And before you knew what hit you, there were fifteen little girls spending the night at your apartment."

Tanner paled.

"Am I right?" she insisted.

He shrugged and muttered disparagingly, "Close enough."

Slumping into the chair, Joanna pushed the pizza box aside and forcefully expelled her breath. "I don't mind telling you, I'm concerned about this. If Kristen and Nicole are plotting against us, then we've got to form some kind of plan of our own before they drive us out of our minds. We can't allow them to manipulate us like this."

"I think you may be right."

She eyed him hopefully. "Any suggestions?" If he was smart enough to manage a couple of thousand employees, surely he could figure out a way to keep two eleven-year-olds under control.

Slouched in his chair, his shoulders sagging, Tanner shook his head. "None. What about you?"

"Communication is the key."

"Right."

"We've got to keep in touch with each other and keep

tabs on what's going on with these two. Don't believe a thing they say until we check it out with the other."

"We've got another problem, Joanna," Tanner said, looking in every direction but hers.

"What?"

"It worked."

"What worked?" she asked irritably. Why was he speaking in riddles?

"Nicole's telling me that you'd been swept off your feet by this rich guy."

"Yes?" He still wasn't making any sense.

"The purpose of that whole fabrication was to make me jealous—and it worked."

"It worked?" An icy numb feeling swept through her. Swallowing became difficult.

Tanner nodded. "I kept thinking about how much I liked you. How much I enjoyed talking to you. And then I decided that when this slumber party business was over, I was going to risk asking you out to dinner."

"But I've already told you I'm not interested in a romantic relationship. One marriage was more than enough for me."

"I don't think that's what bothered me."

"Then what did?"

It was obvious from the way his eyes darted around the room that he felt uncomfortable. "I kept thinking about another man kissing you, and frankly, Joanna, that's what bothered me most."

The kitchen suddenly went so quiet that Joanna was almost afraid to breathe. The only noise was the faint sound of the movie playing in the other room.

Joanna tried to put herself in Tanner's place, wondering how she'd feel if Kristen announced that he'd met a gorgeous blonde and was dating her. Instantly she felt her stomach muscles tighten. There wasn't the slightest doubt in Joanna's mind that the girls' trick would have worked on her, too. Just the thought of Tanner's kissing another woman produced a curious ache, a pain that couldn't be described—or denied.

"Kissing you that night was the worst thing I could have done," Tanner conceded reluctantly. "I know you don't want to talk about it. I don't blame you—"

"Tanner," she interjected in a low hesitant voice, which hardly resembled her own. "It would have worked with me, too."

His eyes were dark and piercing. "Are you certain?"

She nodded, feeling utterly defeated yet strangely excited. "I'm afraid so. What are we going to do now?"

The silence returned as they stared at one another.

"The first thing I think we should do is experiment a little," he suggested in a flat emotionless voice. Then he released a long sigh. "Almost three weeks have passed since the night we took the girls out, and we've both had plenty of time to let that kiss build in our minds. Right?"

"Right," Joanna agreed. She'd attempted to put that kiss completely out of her mind, but it hadn't worked, and there was no point in telling him otherwise.

"It seems to me," Tanner continued thoughtfully, "that we should kiss again, for the sake of research, and find out what we're dealing with here."

She didn't need him to kiss her again to know she was going to like it. The first time had been ample opportunity for her to recognise how strongly she was attracted to Tanner Lund, and she didn't need another kiss to remind her.

"Once we know, we can decide where to go from there. Agreed?"

"Okay," she said impulsively, ignoring the small voice that warned of danger.

He stood up and held out his hand. She stared at it for a moment, uncertain. "You want to kiss right now?"

"Do you know of a better time?"

She shook her head. Good grief, she couldn't believe she was doing this. Tanner stretched out his arms and she walked into them with all the finesse of tumbleweed. The way she fit so snugly, so comfortably into his embrace worried her already. And he hadn't even kissed her yet.

Tanner held her lightly, his eyes wide and curious as he stared down at her. First he cocked his head to the right, then abruptly changed his mind and moved it to the left.

Joanna's movements countered his until she was certain they looked like a pair of ostriches who couldn't make up their minds.

"Are you comfortable?" he asked, and his voice was slightly hoarse.

Joanna nodded. She wished he'd hurry up and do it before one of the girls came crashing into the kitchen and found them. With their luck, it would be either Kristen or Nicole. Or both.

"You ready?" he asked.

Joanna nodded again. He was looking at her almost anxiously as though they were waiting for an imminent explosion. And that was exactly the way it felt when Tanner's mouth settled on hers, even though the kiss was infinitely gentle, his lips sliding over hers like a soft summer rain, barely touching.

They broke apart, momentarily stunned. Neither spoke, and then Tanner kissed her again, moving his mouth over her parted lips in undisguised hunger. His hand clutched the thick hair at her nape as she raised her arms and tightened them around his neck, leaning into him, absorbing his strength.

Tanner groaned softly and deepened the kiss until it threatened to consume Joanna. She met his fierce urgency with her own, arching closer to him, holding onto him with everything that was in her.

An unabating desire flared to life between them as he kissed her again and again, until they were both breathless and shaking.

"Joanna," he groaned, and dragged in several deep breaths. After taking a long moment to compose himself, he asked, "What do you think?" The question was murmured into her hair.

Joanna's chest was heaving, as though she'd been running and was desperate for oxygen. "I... I don't know," she lied, silently calling herself a coward.

"I do."

"You do?"

"Good Lord, Joanna, you taste like heaven. We're in trouble here. Deep trouble."

Nine

The pop music at the roller-skating rink blared from huge speakers and vibrated around the room. A disc jockey announced the tunes from a glass-fronted booth and joked with the skaters as they circled the polished hardwood floor.

"I can't believe I let you talk me into this," Joanna muttered, sitting beside Tanner as she laced up her rented high-top white skates.

"I refuse to be the only one over thirty out there," he replied, but he was smiling, obviously pleased with his persuasive talents. No doubt he'd take equal pleasure in watching her fall flat on her face. It had been years since Joanna had worn a pair of roller skates. *Years*.

"It's like riding a bicycle," Tanner assured her with that maddening grin of his. "Once you know how, you never forget."

Joanna grumbled under her breath, but she was actually beginning to look forward to this. She'd always loved roller-skating as a kid, and there was something about being with Tanner that brought out the little girl in her. *And the woman*, she thought, remembering their kiss.

Nicole's friends were already skating with an ease that

made Joanna envious. Slowly, cautiously, she joined the crowd circling the rink.

"Hi, Mom." Kristen zoomed past at the speed of light.

"Hi, Mrs. Parsons," Nicole shouted, following her friend.

Staying safely near the side, within easy reach of the handrail, Joanna concentrated on making her feet work properly, wheeling them back and forth as smoothly as possible. But instead of the gliding motion achieved by the others, her movements were short and jerky. She didn't acknowledge the girls' greetings with anything more than a raised hand and was slightly disconcerted to see the other skaters giving her a wide berth. They obviously recognized danger when they saw it.

Tanner glided past her, whirled around and deftly skated backward, facing Joanna. She looked up and threw him a weak smile. She should have known Tanner would be as confident on skates as he seemed to be at everything else—except slumber parties for eleven-year-old girls. Looking at him, one would think he'd been skating every day for years, although he claimed it was twenty years since he'd been inside a rink. It was clear from the expert way he soared across the floor that he didn't need to relearn anything—unlike Joanna, who felt as awkward as a newborn foal attempting to stand for the first time.

"How's it going?" he asked, with a cocky grin.

"Great. Can't you tell?" Just then, her right foot jerked out from under her and she groped desperately for the rail, managing to get a grip on it seconds before she went crashing to the floor.

Tanner was by her side at once. "You okay?"

"About as okay as anyone who has stood on the edge and looked into the deep abyss," she muttered.

"Come on, what you need is a strong hand to guide you."

Joanna snorted. "Forget it, fellow. I'll be fine in a few minutes, once I get my sea legs."

"You're sure?"

"Tanner, for heaven's sake, at least leave me with my pride intact!" Keeping anything intact at the moment was difficult, with her feet flaying wildly as she tried to pull herself back into an upright position.

"Okay, if that's what you want," he said shrugging, and sailed away from her with annoying ease.

Fifteen minutes later, Joanna felt steady enough to join the main part of the crowd circling the rink. Her movements looked a little less clumsy, a little less shaky, though she certainly wasn't in complete control.

"Hey, you're doing great," Tanner said, slowing down enough to skate beside her.

"Thanks," she said breathlessly, studying her feet in an effort to maintain her balance.

"You've got a gift for this," he teased.

She looked up at him and laughed outright. "Isn't that the truth! I wonder if I should consider a new career as a roller-skating waitress at the Pink Palace."

Amusement lifted the edge of his sensuous mouth. "Has anyone ever told you that you have an odd sense of humor?"

Looking at Tanner distracted Joanna, and her feet floundered for an instant. "Kristen does at least once a day."

Tanner chuckled. "I shouldn't laugh. Nicole tells me the same thing."

The disc jockey announced that the next song was for couples only. Joanna gave a sigh of relief and aimed her body toward the nearest exit. She could use the break; her calf muscles were already protesting the unaccustomed exercise. She didn't need roller-skating to remind her she wasn't a kid.

"How about it, Joanna?" Tanner asked, skating around her.

"How about what?"

"Skating together for the couples' dance. You and me and fifty thousand preteens sharing center stage." He offered her his hand. The lights had dimmed and a mirrored ball hanging in the middle of the ceiling cast speckled shadows over the floor.

"No way, Tanner," she muttered, ignoring his hand.

"I thought not. Oh well, I'll see if I can get Nicole to skate with her dear old dad." Effortlessly he glided toward the group of girls who stood against the wall flirtatiously challenging the boys on the other side with their eyes.

Once Joanna was safely off the rink, she found a place to sit and rest her weary bones. Within a couple of minutes, Tanner lowered himself into the chair beside her, looking chagrined.

"I got beat out by Tommy Spenser," he muttered.

Joanna couldn't help it—she was delighted. Now Tanner would understand how she'd felt when Kristen announced she didn't want her mother sitting with her at the movies. Tanner looked just as dejected as Joanna had felt then.

"It's hell when they insist on growing up, isn't it?" she said, doing her best not to smile, knowing he wouldn't appreciate it.

He heaved an expressive sigh and gave her a hopeful look before glancing out at the skating couples. "I don't suppose you'd reconsider?"

The floor was filled with kids, and Joanna knew the minute she moved onto the hardwood surface with Tanner, every eye in the place would be on them.

He seemed to read her mind, because he added, "Come on, Joanna. My ego has just suffered a near-mortal wound. I've been rejected by my own flesh and blood."

She swallowed down a comment and awkwardly rose to her feet, struggling to remain upright. "When my ego got shot to bits at the movie theatre, all you did was share your popcorn with me."

He chuckled and reached for her hand. "Don't complain. This gives me an excuse to put my arm around you again." His right arm slipped around her waist, and she tucked her left hand in his as they moved side by side. She had to admit it felt incredibly good to be this close to him. Almost as good as it had felt being in his arms for those few moments in his kitchen.

Tanner must have been thinking the same thing, because he was unusually quiet as he directed her smoothly across the floor to the strains of a romantic ballad. They'd circled the rink a couple of times when Tanner abruptly switched position, skating backward and holding onto her as though they were dancing.

"Tanner," she said, surprise widening her eyes as he swept her into his arms. "The girls will start thinking… things if we skate like this."

"Let them."

His hands locked at the base of her spine and he pulled her close. Very close. Joanna drew a slow breath, savoring the feel of Tanner's body pressed so intimately against her own.

"Joanna, listen," he whispered. "I've been thinking."

So had she. Hard to do when she was around Tanner.

"Would it really be such a terrible thing if we were to start seeing more of each other? On a casual basis—it doesn't have to be anything serious. We're both mature adults. Neither of us is going to allow the girls to manipulate us into anything we don't want. And as far as the past is concerned, I'm not Davey and you're not Carmen."

Why, Joanna wondered, was the most important discussion she'd had in years taking place in a roller-skating rink with a top-forty hit blaring in one ear and Tanner whispering in the other? Deciding to ignore the thought, she said, "But the girls might start making assumptions, and I'm afraid we'd only end up disappointing them."

Tanner disagreed. "I feel our seeing each other might help more than it would hinder."

"How do you mean?" Joanna couldn't believe she was actually entertaining this suggestion. Entertaining was putting it mildly; her heart was doing somersaults at the prospect of seeing Tanner more often. She was thrilled, excited... and yet hesitant. The wounds Davey had inflicted went very deep.

"If we see each other more often we could include the girls, and that should lay to rest some of the fears we've had over their matchmaking efforts. And spending time with you will help satisfy Nicole's need for a strong mother figure. At the same time, I can help Kristen, by being a father figure."

"Yes, but—"

"The four of us together will give the girls a sense of belonging to a whole family," Tanner added confidently.

His arguments sounded so reasonable, so logical. Still, Joanna remained uncertain. "But I'm afraid the girls will think we're serious."

Tanner lifted his head enough to look into her eyes, and Joanna couldn't remember a time they'd ever been bluer or more intense. "I am serious."

She pressed her forehead against his collarbone and willed her body to stop trembling. Their little kissing experiment had affected her far more than she dared let him know. Until tonight, they'd both tried to disguise or deny their attraction for each other, but the kiss had exposed everything.

"I haven't stopped thinking about you from the minute we first met," he whispered, and touched his lips to her temple. "If we were anyplace else right now, I'd show you how crazy I am about you."

If they'd been anyplace else, Joanna would have let him. She wanted him to kiss her, needed him to, but she was more frightened by her reaction to this one man than she'd been by anything else in a very long while. "Tanner, I'm afraid."

"Joanna, so am I, but I can't allow fear to rule my life." Gently he brushed the loose wisps of curls from the side of her face. His eyes studied her intently. "I didn't expect to feel this way again. I've guarded against letting this happen, but here we are, and Joanna, I don't mind telling you, I wouldn't change a thing."

Joanna closed her eyes and listened to the battle raging inside her head. She wanted so badly to give this feeling between them a chance to grow. But logic told her that if she agreed to his suggestion, she'd be making herself vulnerable again. Even worse, Tanner Lund wasn't just any man—he was wealthy and successful, the half owner of an important company. And she was just a loan officer at a small local bank.

"Joanna, at least tell me what you're feeling."

"I… I don't know," she hedged, still uncertain.

He gripped her hand and pressed it over his heart, holding it there. "Just feel what you do to me."

Her own heart seemed about to hammer its way out of her chest. "You do the same thing to me."

He smiled ever so gently. "I know."

The music came to an end and the lights brightened. Reluctantly Tanner and Joanna broke apart, but he still kept her close to his side, tucking his arm around her waist.

"You haven't answered me, Joanna. I'm not going to hurt you, you know. We'll take it nice and easy at first and see how things develop."

Joanna's throat felt constricted, and she couldn't answer him one way or the other, although it was clear that he was waiting for her to make a decision.

"We've got something good between us," he continued, "and I don't want to just throw it away. I think we should find out whether this can last."

He wouldn't hurt her intentionally, Joanna realised, but the probability of her walking away unscathed from a relationship with this man was remote.

"What do you think?" he pressed.

She couldn't refuse him. "Maybe we should give it a try," she said after a long pause.

Tanner gazed down on her, bathing her in the warmth of his smile. "Neither of us is going to be sorry."

Joanna wasn't nearly as confident. She glanced away and happened to notice Kristen and Nicole. "Uh-oh," she murmured.

"What's wrong?"

"I just saw Kristen zoom over to Nicole and whisper into her ear. Then they hugged each other like long-lost sisters."

"I can deal with it if you can," he said, squeezing her hand.

Tanner's certainty lent her courage. "Then so can I."

Ten

Joanna didn't sleep well that night, or the following two. Tanner had suggested they meet for dinner the next weekend. It seemed an eternity, but there were several problems at work that demanded his attention. She felt as disappointed as he sounded that their first real date wouldn't take place for a week.

Joanna wished he hadn't given her so much time to think about it. If they'd been able to casually go to a movie the afternoon following the slumber party, she wouldn't have been so nervous about it.

When she arrived at work Monday morning, her brain was so muddled she felt as though she were walking in a fog. Twice during the weekend she'd almost called Tanner to suggest they call the whole thing off.

"Morning," her boss murmured absently, hardly looking up from the newspaper. "How was your weekend?"

"Exciting," Joanna told Robin, tucking her purse into the bottom drawer of her desk. "I went roller-skating with fifteen eleven-year-old girls."

"Sounds adventurous," Robin said, his gaze never leaving the paper.

Joanna poured herself a cup of coffee and carried it to

her desk to drink black. The way she was feeling, she knew she'd need something strong to clear her head.

"I don't suppose you've been following what's happening at Spokane Aluminum?" Robin asked, refilling his own coffee cup.

It was a good thing Joanna had set her mug down when she did, otherwise it would have tumbled from her fingers. "Spokane Aluminum?" she echoed.

"Yes." Robin sat on the edge of her desk, allowing one leg to dangle. "There's another news item in the paper this morning on Tanner Lund. Six months ago, he bought out half the company from John Becky. I'm sure you've heard of John Becky?"

"Of…course."

"Apparently Lund came into this company and breathed new life into its sagging foreign sales. He took over management himself and has completely changed the company's direction…all for the better. I've heard nothing but good about this guy. Every time I turn around, I'm either reading how great he is, or hearing people talk about him. Take my word, Tanner Lund is a man who's going places."

Joanna couldn't agree more. And she knew for a fact where he was going Saturday night. He was taking her to dinner.

"Mr. Lund's here," Kristen announced the following Saturday, opening Joanna's bedroom door. "And does he ever look handsome!"

A dinner date. A simple dinner date, and Joanna was more nervous than a college graduate applying for her first job. She smoothed her hand down her red-and-white flowered dress and held in her breath so long her lungs ached.

Kristen rolled her eyes. "You look fine, Mom."

"I do?"

"As nice as Mr. Lund."

For good measure, Joanna paused long enough to dab more cologne behind her ears, then she squared her shoulders and turned to face the long hallway that led to the living room. "Okay, I'm ready."

Kristen threw open the bedroom door as though she expected royalty to emerge. By the time Joanna had walked down the hallway to the living room where Tanner was waiting, her heart was pounding and her hands were shaking. Kristen was right. Tanner looked marvellous in a three-piece suit and silk tie. He smiled when she came into the room, and stood up, gazing at her with an expression of undisguised delight.

"Hi."

"Hi." Their eyes met, and everything else faded away. Just seeing him again made Joanna's pulse leap into overdrive. No week had ever dragged more.

"Sally's got the phone number of the restaurant, and her mother said it was fine if she stayed here late," Kristen said, standing between them and glancing from one adult to the other. "I don't have any plans myself, so you two feel free to stay out as long as you want."

"Sally?" Joanna forced herself to glance at the babysitter.

"Yes, Mrs. Parsons?"

"There's salad and leftover spaghetti in the refrigerator for dinner, and some microwave popcorn in the cupboard for later."

"Okay."

"I won't be too late."

"But, Mom," Kristen cut in, a slight whine in her voice, "I just got done telling you that it'd be fine if you stayed out till the wee hours of the morning."

"We'll be back before midnight," Joanna informed the babysitter, ignoring Kristen.

"Okay," the girl said, as Kristen sighed expressively. "Have a good time."

Tanner escorted Joanna out to the car, which was parked in front of the house, and opened the passenger door. He paused, his hand still resting on her shoulder. "I'd like to kiss you now, but we have an audience," he said, nodding toward the house.

Joanna chanced a look and discovered Kristen standing in the living-room window, holding aside the curtain and watching them intently. No doubt she was memorising everything they said and did to report back to Nicole.

"I couldn't believe it when she agreed to let Sally come over. She's of the opinion lately that she's old enough to stay by herself."

"Nicole claims the same thing, but she didn't raise any objections about having a babysitter, either."

"I guess we should count our blessings."

Tanner drove to an expensive downtown restaurant overlooking the Spokane River, in the heart of the city.

Joanna's mouth was dry and her palms sweaty when the valet opened her door and helped her out. She'd never eaten at such a luxurious place in her life. She'd heard that their prices were outrageous. The amount Tanner intended to spend on one meal would probably outfit Kristen for an entire school year. Joanna felt faint at the very idea.

"Chez Michel is an exceptionally nice restaurant, Tanner, if you get my drift," she muttered under her breath after he handed the car keys to the valet. As a newcomer to town, he might not have been aware of just how expensive this place actually was.

"Yes, that's why I chose it," he said nonchalantly. "I was

quite pleased with the food and the service when I was here a few weeks ago." He glanced at Joanna and her discomfort must have shown. "Consider it a small token of my appreciation for your help with Nicole's birthday party," he added, offering her one of his bone-melting smiles.

Joanna would have been more than content to eat at Denny's, and that thought reminded her again of how different they were.

She wished now that she'd worn something a little more elegant. The waiters seemed to be better dressed than she was. For that matter, so were the menus.

They were escorted to a table with an unobstructed view of the river. The maître d' held out Joanna's chair and seated her with flair. The first thing she noticed was the setting of silverware, with its bewildering array of forks, knives and spoons. After the maître d' left, she leaned forward and whispered to Tanner, "I've never eaten at a place that uses three teaspoons."

"Oh, quit complaining."

"I'm not, but if I embarrass you and use the wrong fork, don't blame me."

Unconcerned, Tanner chuckled and reached for the shiny gold menu.

Apparently Chez Michel believed in leisurely dining, because nearly two hours had passed by the time they were served their after-dinner coffee. The entire meal was everything Joanna could have hoped for, and more. The food was exceptional, but Joanna considered Tanner's company the best part of the evening. She'd never felt this much at ease with a man before. He made her smile, but he challenged her ideas, too. They talked about the girls and about the demands of being a parent. They discussed Joanna's career goals and Tanner's plans for his company. They covered a lot of different subjects, but didn't focus their conversation on any one.

Now that the meal was over, Joanna was reluctant to see the evening end. She lifted the delicate china cup, admiring its pattern, and took a sip of fragrant coffee. She paused, her cup raised halfway to her mouth, when she noticed Tanner staring at her. "What's wrong?" she asked, fearing part of her dessert was on her nose or something equally disastrous.

"Nothing."

"Then why are you looking at me like that?"

Tanner relaxed, leaned back in his chair, and grinned. "I'm sorry. I was just thinking how lovely you are, and how pleased I am that we met. It seems nothing's been the same since. I never thought a woman could make me feel the way you do, Joanna."

She looked quickly down, feeling a sudden shyness— and a wonderful warmth. Her life had changed, too, and she wasn't sure she could ever go back to the way things had been before. She was dreaming again, feeling again, trusting again, and it felt so good. And so frightening.

"I'm pleased, too," was her only comment.

"You know what the girls are thinking, don't you?"

Joanna could well imagine. No doubt those two would have them engaged after one dinner date. "They're probably expecting us to announce our marriage plans tomorrow morning," Joanna said, trying to make a joke of it.

"To be honest, I find some aspects of married life appealing."

Joanna smiled and narrowed her eyes suspiciously. "Come on, Tanner, just how much wine have you had?"

"Obviously too much, now that I think about it," he said, grinning. Then his face sobered. "All kidding aside, I want you to know how much I enjoy your company. Every time

I'm with you, I come away feeling good about life—you make me laugh again."

"I'd make anyone laugh," she said, "especially if I'm wearing a pair of roller skates." She didn't know where their conversation was leading, but the fact that Tanner spoke so openly and honestly about the promise of their relationship completely unnerved her. She felt exactly the same things, but didn't have the courage to voice them.

"I'm glad you agreed we should start seeing each other," Tanner continued.

"Me, too." But she fervently hoped her mother wouldn't hear about it, although Kristen had probably phoned her grandmother the minute Joanna was out the door. Lowering her gaze, Joanna discovered that a bread crumb on the linen tablecloth had become utterly absorbing. She carefully brushed it onto the floor, an inch at a time. "It's worked out fine...so far. Us dating, I mean." It was more than fine. And now he was telling her how she'd brightened his life, as though *he* was the lucky one. That someone like Tanner Lund would ever want to date her still astonished Joanna.

She gazed up at him, her heart shining through her eyes, telling him without words what she was feeling.

Tanner briefly shut his eyes. "Joanna, for heaven's sake, don't look at me like that."

"Like what?"

"Like...that."

"I think you should kiss me," Joanna announced, once again staring down at the tablecloth. The instant the words slipped out she longed to take them back. She couldn't believe she'd said something like that to him.

"I beg your pardon?"

"Never mind," she said quickly, grateful he hadn't heard her. He had. "Kiss you? Now? Here?"

Joanna shook her head, forcing a smile. "Forget I said that. It just slipped out. Sometimes my mouth disconnects itself from my brain."

Tanner didn't remove his gaze from hers as he raised his hand. Their waiter appeared almost immediately, and still looking at Joanna, he muttered, "Check, please."

"Right away, sir."

They were out of the restaurant so fast Joanna's head was spinning. Once they were seated in the car, Tanner paused, frowning, his hands clenched on the steering wheel.

"What's the matter?" Joanna asked anxiously.

"We goofed. We should have shared a babysitter."

The thought had fleetingly entered her mind earlier, but she'd discounted the idea because she didn't want to encourage the girls' scheming.

"I can't take you back to my place because Nicole will be all over us with questions, and it'll probably be the same story at your house with Kristen."

"You're right." Besides, her daughter would be sorely disappointed if they showed up this early. It wasn't even close to midnight.

"Just where am I supposed to kiss you, Joanna Parsons?"

Oh Lord, he'd taken her seriously. "Tanner…it was a joke."

He ignored her comment. "I don't know of a single look-out point in the city."

"Tanner, please." Her voice rose in embarrassment, and she could feel herself blushing.

Tanner leaned over and brushed his lips against her cheek. "I've got an idea for something we can do, but don't laugh."

"An idea? What?"

"You'll see soon enough." He eased his car onto the street and drove quickly through the city to the freeway on-ramp and didn't exit until they were well into the suburbs.

"Tanner?" Joanna said, looking around her at the unfamiliar streets. "What's out here?" Almost as soon as she'd spoken a huge white screen appeared in the distance. "A drive-in?" she whispered in disbelief.

"Have you got any better ideas?"

"Not a one." Joanna chuckled; she couldn't help it. He was taking her to a drive-in movie just so he could kiss her.

"I can't guarantee this movie. This is its opening weekend, and if I remember the ad correctly, they're showing something with lots of blood and gore."

"As long as it isn't *Teen Massacre*. Kristen would never forgive me if I saw it when she hadn't."

"If the truth be known, I don't plan to watch a whole lot of the movie." He darted an exaggerated leer in her direction and wiggled his eyebrows suggestively.

Joanna returned his look by demurely fluttering her lashes. "I don't know if my mother would approve of my going to a drive-in on a first date."

"With good reason," Tanner retorted. "Especially if she knew what I had in mind."

Although the weather had been mild and the sky was cloudless and clear, only a few cars were scattered across the wide lot.

Tanner parked as far away from the others as possible. He connected the speaker, but turned the volume so low it was almost inaudible. When he'd finished, he placed his arm around Joanna's shoulders, pulling her closer.

"Come here, woman."

Joanna leaned her head against his shoulder and pretended to be interested in the cartoon characters leaping across the large screen. Her stomach was playing jumping jacks with the dinner she'd just eaten.

"Joanna?" His voice was low and seductive.

She tilted her head to meet his gaze, and his eyes moved slowly over her upturned face, searing her with their intensity. The openness of his desire stole her breath away. Her heart was pounding, although he hadn't even kissed her yet. One hungry look from Tanner and she was melting at his feet.

Her first thought was to crack a joke. That had saved her in the past, but whatever she might have said or done was lost as Tanner lowered his mouth and tantalized the edges of her trembling lips, teasing her with soft, tempting nibbles, making her ache all the way to her toes for his kiss. Instinctively her fingers slid up his chest and around the back of his neck. Tanner created such an overwhelming need in her that she felt both humble and elated at the same time. When her hands tightened around his neck, his mouth hardened into firm possession.

Joanna thought she'd drown in the sensations that flooded her. She hadn't felt this kind of longing in years, and she trembled with the wonder of it. Tanner had awakened the deep womanly part of her that had lain dormant for so long. And suddenly she felt all that time without love come rushing up at her, overtaking her. Years of regret, years of doubt, years of rejection all pressed so heavily on her heart that she could barely breathe.

A sob was ripped from her throat, and the sound of it broke them apart. Tears she couldn't explain flooded her eyes and ran unheeded down her face.

"Joanna, what's wrong? Did I hurt you?"

She tried to break away, but Tanner wouldn't let her go. He brushed the hair from her face and tilted her head to lift her eyes to his, but she resisted.

He must have felt the wetness on her face, because he

paused and murmured, "You're crying," in a tone that sounded as shocked as she felt. "Dear Lord, what did I do?"

Wildly she shook her head, unable to speak even if she'd been able to find the words to explain.

"Joanna, tell me, please."

"J-just hold me." Even saying that much required all her reserves of strength.

He did as she asked, wrapping his arms completely around her, kissing the crown of her head as she buried herself in his strong, solid warmth.

Still, the tears refused to stop, no matter how hard she tried to make them. They flooded her face and seemed to come from the deepest part of her.

"I can't believe I'm doing this," she said between sobs. "Oh, Tanner, I feel like such a fool."

"Go ahead and cry, Joanna. I understand."

"You do? Good. You can explain it to me."

She could feel his smile as he kissed the corner of her eye. She moaned a little and he lowered his lips to her cheek, then her chin, and when she couldn't bear it any longer, she turned her face, her mouth seeking his. Tanner didn't disappoint her, kissing her gently again and again until she was certain her heart would stop beating if he ever stopped holding her and kissing her.

"Good Lord, Joanna," he whispered after a while, gently extricating himself from her arms and leaning against the car seat, his eyes closed. His face was a picture of desire struggling for restraint. He drew in several deep breaths.

Joanna's tears had long since dried on her face and now her cheeks flamed with confusion and remorse.

A heavy silence fell between them. Joanna searched frantically for something witty to say to break the terrible tension.

"Joanna, listen—"

"No, let me speak first," she broke in, then hesitated. Now that she had his attention, she didn't know what to say. "I'm sorry, Tanner, really sorry. I don't know what came over me, but you weren't the one responsible for my tears. Well, no, you were, but not the way you think."

"Joanna, please," he said and his hands bracketed her face. "Don't be embarrassed by the tears. Believe me when I say I'm feeling the same things you are, only they come out in different ways."

Joanna stared up at him, not sure he could possibly understand.

"It's been so long for you—it has for me, too," Tanner went on. "I feel like a teenager again. And the drive-in has nothing to do with it."

Her lips trembled with the effort to smile. Tanner leaned his forehead against hers. "We need to take this slow. Very, very slow."

That was a fine thing for him to say, considering they'd been as hot as torches for each other a few minutes ago. If they continued at this rate, they'd end up in bed together by the first of the week.

"I've got a company party in a couple of weeks—I want you there with me. Will you do that?"

Joanna nodded.

Tanner drew her closer to his side and she tucked her head against his chest. His hand stroked her shoulder, as he kissed the top of her head.

"You're awfully quiet," he said after several minutes. "What are you thinking?"

Joanna sighed and snuggled closer, looping one arm around his middle. Her free hand was laced with his. "It just occurred to me that for the first time in my life I've met a real prince. Up until now, all I've done is make a few frogs happy."

Eleven

Kneeling on the polished linoleum floor of the kitchen, Joanna held her breath and tentatively poked her head inside the foam-covered oven. Sharp, lemon-scented fumes made her grimace as she dragged the wet sponge along the sides, peeling away a layer of blackened crust. She'd felt unusually ambitious for a Saturday and had worked in the yard earlier, planning her garden. When she'd finished that, she'd decided to tackle the oven, not questioning where this burst of energy had come from. Spring was in the air, but instead of turning her fancy to thoughts of love, it filled her mind with zucchini seeds and rows of tomato seedlings.

"I'm leaving now, Mom," Kristen called from behind her.

Joanna jerked her head free, gulped some fresh air and twisted toward her daughter. "What time will you be through at the library?" Kristen and Nicole were working together on a school project, and although they complained about having to do research, they'd come to enjoy it. Their biggest surprise was discovering all the cute junior-high boys who sometimes visited the library. In Kristen's words, it was an untapped gold mine.

"I don't know when we'll be through, but I'll call. And remember, Nicole is coming over afterwards."

"I remember."

Kristen hesitated, then asked, "When are you going out with Mr. Lund again?"

Joanna glanced over at the calendar. "Next weekend. We're attending a dinner party his company's sponsoring."

"Oh."

Joanna rubbed her forearm across her cheek, and glanced suspiciously at her daughter. "What does that mean?"

"What?"

"That little 'oh.'"

Kristen shrugged. "Nothing… It's just that you're not seeing him as often as Nicole and I think you should. You like Mr. Lund, don't you?"

That was putting it mildly. "He's very nice," Joanna said cautiously. If she admitted to anything beyond a casual attraction, Kristen would assume much more. Joanna wanted her relationship with Tanner to progress slowly, one careful step at a time, not in giant leaps—though slow and careful didn't exactly describe what had happened so far!

"Nice?" Kristen exclaimed.

Her daughter's outburst caught Joanna by surprise.

"Is that all you can say about Mr. Lund?" Kristen asked, hands on her hips. "I've given the matter serious consideration and I think he's a whole lot more than just nice. Really, Mother."

Taking a deep breath, Joanna plunged her head back inside the oven, swiping her sponge furiously against the sides.

"Are you going to ignore me?" Kristen demanded.

Joanna emerged again, gasped and looked straight at her daughter. "Yes. Unless you want to volunteer to clean the oven yourself."

"I would, but I have to go to the library with Nicole."

Joanna noted the soft regret that filled her daughter's voice and gave her a derisive snort. The kid actually sounded sorry that she wouldn't be there to do her part. Kristen was a genius at getting out of work, and she always managed to give the impression of really wishing she could help her mother—if only she could fit it into her busy schedule.

A car horn beeped out front. "That's Mr. Lund," Kristen said, glancing toward the living room. "I'll give you a call when we're done."

"Okay, honey. Have a good time."

"I will."

With form an Olympic sprinter would envy, Kristen tore out of the kitchen. Two seconds later, the front door slammed. Joanna was only mildly disappointed that Tanner hadn't stopped in to chat. He'd phoned earlier and explained that after he dropped the girls off at the library, he was driving to the office for a couple of hours. An unexpected problem had arisen, and he needed to deal with it right away.

Actually Joanna had to admit she was more grateful than disappointed that Tanner hadn't stopped in. It didn't look as though she'd get a chance to see him before the company party. She needed this short separation to pull together her reserves. Following their dinner date and the drive-in movie afterward, Joanna felt dangerously close to falling in love with Tanner. Every time he came to mind, and that was practically every minute of every day, a rush of warmth and happiness followed. Without too much trouble, she could envision them finding a lifetime of happiness together. For the first time since her divorce she allowed herself the luxury of dreaming again, and although the prospect of remarriage excited and thrilled her, it also terrified her.

Fifteen minutes later, with perspiration beaded on her

forehead and upper lip, Joanna heaved a sigh and sat back on her heels. The hair she'd so neatly tucked inside a scarf and tied at the back of her head, had fallen loose. She swiped a grimy hand at the auburn curls that hung limply over her eyes and ears. It was all worth it, though, since the gray-speckled sides of the oven, which had been encrusted with black grime, were now clearly visible and shining.

Joanna emptied the bucket of dirty water and hauled a fresh one back to wipe the oven one last time. She'd just knelt down when the doorbell chimed.

"Great," she muttered under her breath, casting a glance at herself. She looked like something that had crawled out of the bog in some horror movie. Pasting a smile on her face, she peeled off her rubber gloves and hurried to the door.

"Davey!" Finding her ex-husband standing on the porch was enough of a shock to knock the breath from Joanna's lungs.

"May I come in?"

"Of course." Flustered, she ran her hand through her hair and stepped aside to allow him to pass. He looked good— really good—but then Davey had never lacked in the looks department. From the expensive cut of his three-piece suit, she could tell that his real-estate business must be doing well, and of course that was precisely the impression he wanted her to have. She was pleased for him; she'd never wished him ill. They'd gone their separate ways, and although both the marriage and the divorce had devastated Joanna, she shared a beautiful child with this man. If he had come by to tell her how successful he was, well, she'd just smile and let him.

"It's good to see you, Joanna."

"You, too. What brings you to town?" She struggled to keep her voice even and controlled, hoping to hide her discomfort at being caught unawares.

"I'm attending a conference downtown. I apologize for dropping in unexpectedly like this, but since I was going to be in Spokane, I thought I'd stop in and see how you and Kristen are doing."

"I wish you'd phoned first. Kristen's at the library." Joanna wasn't fooled—Davey hadn't come to see their daughter, although he meant Joanna to think so. It was all part of the game he played with her, wanting her to believe that their divorce had hurt him badly. Not calling to let her know he planned to visit was an attempt to catch her off guard and completely unprepared—which, of course, she was. Joanna knew Davey, knew him well. He'd often tried to manipulate her this way.

"I should have called, but I didn't know if I'd have the time, and I didn't want to disappoint you if I found I couldn't slip away."

Joanna didn't believe that for a minute. It wouldn't have taken him much time or trouble to phone before he left the hotel. But she didn't mention the fact, couldn't see that it would have done any good.

"Come in and have some coffee." She led him into the kitchen and poured him a mug, automatically adding the sugar and cream she knew he used. She handed it to him and was rewarded with a dazzling smile. When he wanted, Davey Parsons could be charming, attentive and generous. The confusing thing about her ex-husband was that he wasn't all bad. He'd gravely wounded her with his unfaithfulness, but in his own way he'd loved her and Kristen—as much as he could possibly love anybody beyond himself. It had taken Joanna a good many years to distance herself enough to appreciate his good points and to forgive him for the pain he'd caused her.

"You've got a nice place here," he commented, casually

glancing around the kitchen. "How long have you lived here now?"

"Seven months."

"How's Kristen?"

Joanna was relieved that the conversation had moved to the only subject they still had in common—their daughter. She talked for fifteen minutes nonstop, telling him about the talent show and the other activities Kristen had been involved in since the last time she'd seen her father.

Davey listened and laughed, and then his gaze softened as he studied Joanna. "You're looking wonderful."

She grinned ruefully. "Sure I am," she scoffed. "I've just finished working in the yard and cleaning the oven."

"I wondered about the lemon perfume you were wearing."

They both laughed. Davey started to tease her about their early years together and some of the experimental meals she'd cooked and expected him to eat and praise. Joanna let him and even enjoyed his comments, for Davey could be warm and funny when he chose. Kristen had inherited her friendly, easygoing confidence from her father.

The doorbell chimed and still chuckling, Joanna stood up. "It's probably one of the neighborhood kids. I'll just be a minute." She never ceased to be astonished at how easy it was to be with Davey. He'd ripped her heart in two, lied to her repeatedly, cheated on her and still she couldn't be around him and not laugh. It always took him a few minutes to conquer her reserve, but he never failed. She was mature enough to recognise her ex-husband's faults, yet appreciate his redeeming qualities.

For the second time that day, Joanna was surprised by the man who stood on her front porch. "Tanner."

"Hi," he said with a sheepish grin. "The girls got off okay and I thought I'd stop in for a cup of coffee before heading to the office." His eyes smiled softly into hers. "I heard you laughing from out here. Do you have company? Should I come back later?"

"N-no, come in," she said, her pulse beating as hard and loud as jungle drums. Lowering her eyes, she automatically moved aside. He walked into the living room and paused, then raised his hand and gently touched her cheek in a gesture so loving that Joanna longed to fall into his arms. Now that he was here, she found herself craving some time alone with him.

Tanner's gaze reached out to her, but Joanna had trouble meeting it. A frown started to form, and his eyes clouded. "This is a bad time, isn't it?"

"No...not really." When she turned around, Davey was standing in the kitchen doorway watching them. The smile she'd been wearing felt shaky as she stood between the two men and made the introductions. "Davey, this is Tanner Lund. Tanner, this is Davey—Kristen's father."

For a moment, the two men glared at each other like angry bears who had claimed territory and were prepared to do battle to protect what was theirs. When they stepped towards each other, Joanna held her breath for fear neither one would make the effort to be civil.

Stunned, she watched as they exchanged handshakes and enthusiastic greetings.

"Davey's in town for a real-estate conference and thought he'd stop in to see Kristen," Joanna explained, her words coming out in such a rush that they nearly stumbled over themselves.

"I came to see you, too, Joanna," Davey added in a low sultry voice that suggested he had more on his mind than a chat over a cup of coffee.

She flashed him a heated look before marching into the

kitchen, closely followed by both men. She walked straight to the cupboard, bringing down another cup, then poured Tanner's coffee and delivered it to the table.

"Kristen and my daughter are at the library," Tanner announced in a perfectly friendly voice, but Joanna heard the undercurrents even if Davey didn't.

"Joanna told me," Davey returned.

The two men remained standing, smiling at each other. Tanner took a seat first, and Davey promptly did the same.

"What do you do?" her ex-husband asked.

"I own half of Spokane Aluminum."

It was apparent to Joanna that Davey hadn't even bothered to listen to Tanner's reply because he immediately fired back in an aggressive tone, "I recently opened my own real-estate brokerage and have plans to expand within the next couple of years." He announced his success with a cocky slant to his mouth.

Watching the change in Davey's features as Tanner's identity began to sink in was so comical that Joanna nearly laughed out loud. Davey's mouth sagged open, and his eyes flew from Joanna to Tanner and then back to Joanna.

"Spokane Aluminum," Davey repeated slowly, his face unusually pale. "I seem to remember reading something about John Becky taking on a partner."

Joanna almost felt sorry for Davey. "Kristen and Tanner's daughter, Nicole, are best friends. They were in the Valentine's Day show together—the one I was telling you about…"

To his credit, Davey regrouped quickly. "She gets all that performing talent from you."

"Oh, hardly," Joanna countered, denying it with a vigorous shake of her head. Of the two of them, Davey was the entertainer—crowds had never intimidated him. He could walk into a room full of strangers, and anyone who didn't know better would end up thinking Davey Parsons was his best friend.

"With the girls being so close, it seemed only natural for Joanna and me to start dating," Tanner said, turning to smile warmly at Joanna.

"I see," Davey answered. He didn't appear to have recovered from Tanner's first announcement.

"I sincerely hope you do understand," Tanner returned, all pretence of friendliness dropped.

Joanna resisted rolling her eyes toward the ceiling. Both of them were behaving like immature children, battling with looks and words as if she were a prize to be awarded the victor.

"I suppose I'd better think about heading out," Davey said after several awkward moments had passed. He stood up, noticeably eager to make his escape.

As a polite hostess, Joanna stood when Davey did. "I'll walk you to the door."

He sent Tanner a wary smile. "That's not necessary."

"Of course it is," Joanna countered.

To her dismay, Tanner followed them and stood conspicuously in the background while Davey made arrangements to phone Kristen later that evening. The whole time Davey was speaking, Joanna could feel Tanner's eyes burning into her back. She didn't know why he'd insisted on following her to the door. It was like saying he couldn't trust her not to fall into Davey's arms the minute he was out of sight, and that irritated her no end.

Once her ex-husband had left, she closed the door and whirled around to face Tanner. The questions were jammed in her mind. They'd only gone out on one date, for heaven's sake, and here he was, acting as though…as though they were engaged.

"I thought he broke your heart," Tanner said, in a cutting voice.

Joanna debated whether or not to answer him, then decided it would be best to clear the air. "He did."

"I heard you laughing when I rang the doorbell. Do you often have such a good time with men you're supposed to hate?"

"I don't hate Davey."

"Believe me, I can tell."

"Tanner, what's wrong with you?" That was a silly question, and she regretted asking it immediately. She already knew what was troubling Tanner. He was jealous. And angry. And hurt.

"Wrong with me?" He tossed the words back at her. "Nothing's wrong with me. I happen to stumble upon the woman I'm involved with cozying up to her ex-husband, and I don't mind telling you I'm upset. But nothing's wrong with me. Not one damn thing. If there's something wrong with anyone, it's you, lady."

Joanna held tightly onto her patience. "Before we start arguing, let's sit down and talk this out." She led him back into the kitchen, then took Davey's empty coffee mug and placed it in the sink, removing all evidence of his brief visit. She searched for a way to reassure Tanner that Davey meant nothing to her anymore. But she had to explain that she and her ex-husband weren't enemies, either; they couldn't be for Kristen's sake.

"First of all," she said, as evenly as her pounding heart would allow, "I could never hate Davey the way you seem to think I should. As far as I'm concerned, that would only be counterproductive. The people who would end up suffering are Kristen and me. Davey is incapable of being faithful to one woman, but he'll always be Kristen's father, and if for no other reason than that, I prefer to remain on friendly terms with him."

"But he cheated on you...used you."

"Yes." She couldn't deny it. "But, Tanner, I lived a lot of years with Davey. He's not all bad—no one is—and scattered between all the bad times were a few good ones. We're divorced now. What good would it do to harbor ill will toward him? None that I can see."

"He let it be known from the moment I walked into this house that he could have you back any time he wanted."

Joanna wasn't blind; she'd recognized the looks Davey had given Tanner, and the insinuations. "He'd like to believe that. It helps him deal with his ego."

"And you let him?"

"Not the way you're implying."

Tanner mulled that over for a few moments. "How often does he casually drop in unannounced like this?"

She hesitated, wondering whether she should answer his question. His tone had softened, but he was obviously still angry. She could sympathize, but she didn't like having to defend herself or her attitude toward Davey. "I haven't seen him in over a year. This is the first time he's been to the house."

Tanner's hands gripped the coffee mug so tightly that Joanna was amazed it remained intact. "You still love him, don't you?"

The question hit her square between the eyes. Her mouth opened and closed several times as she struggled for the words to deny it. Then she realized she couldn't. Lying to Tanner about this would be simple enough and it would keep the peace, but it would wrong them both. "I suppose in a way I do," she began slowly. "He's the father of my child. He was my first love, Tanner. And the only lover I've ever had. Although I'd like to tell you I don't feel a thing for him, I can't do that and be completely honest. But please, try to understand—"

"You don't need to say anything more." He stood abruptly, his back stiff. "I appreciate the fact that you told me the truth. I won't waste any more of your time. I wish you and Kristen a good life." With that he stalked out of the room, headed for the door.

Joanna was shocked. "Tanner…you make it sound like I'll never see you again."

"I think that would be best for everyone concerned," he replied, without looking at her.

"But…that's silly. Nothing's changed." She snapped her mouth closed. If Tanner wanted to act so childishly and ruin everything, she wasn't about to argue with him. He was the one who insisted they had something special, something so good they shouldn't throw it away because of their fears. And now he was acting like this! Fine. If that was the way he wanted it. It was better to find out how unreasonable he could be before anything serious developed between them. Better to discover now how quick-tempered he could be, how hurtful.

"I have no intention of becoming involved with a woman who's still in love with her loser of an ex-husband," he announced, his hands clenched at his sides. His voice was calm, but she recognized the tension in it. And the resolve.

Unable to restrain her anger any longer, Joanna marched across the room and threw open the front door. "Smart move, Tanner," she said, her words coated with sarcasm. "You made a terrible mistake getting involved with a woman who refuses to hate." Now that she had a better look at him, she decided he wasn't a prince after all, only another frog.

Tanner didn't say a word as he walked past her, his strides filled with purpose. She closed the door and leaned against it, needing the support. Tears burned in her eyes and clogged her throat, but she held her head high and hurried back into the kitchen, determined not to give in to the powerful emotions that racked her, body and soul.

She finished cleaning up the kitchen, and took a long hot shower afterward. Then she sat quietly at the table, waiting for Kristen to phone so she could pick up the two girls. The call came a half hour later, but by that time she'd already reached for the cookies, bent on self-destruction.

On the way home from the library, Joanna stopped off at McDonald's and bought the girls cheeseburgers and chocolate milk shakes to take home for dinner. Her mind was filled with doubts. In retrospect, she wished she'd done a better job of explaining things to Tanner. The thought of never seeing him again was almost too painful to endure.

"Aren't you going to order anything, Mom?" Kristen asked, surprised.

"Not tonight." Somewhere deep inside, Joanna found the energy to smile.

She managed to maintain a lighthearted facade while Kristen and Nicole ate their dinner and chattered about the boys they'd seen at the library and how they were going to shock Mrs. Andrews with their well-researched report.

"Are you feeling okay?" Kristen asked, pausing in midsentence.

"Sure," Joanna lied, looking for something to occupy her hands. She settled for briskly wiping down the kitchen counters. Actually, she felt sick to her stomach, but she couldn't blame Tanner; she'd done that to herself with all those stupid cookies.

It was when she was putting the girls' empty McDonald's containers in the garbage that the silly tears threatened to spill over. She did her best to hide them and quickly carried out the trash. Nicole went to get her MP3 player from Kristen's bedroom, but Kristen followed her mother outside.

"Mom, what's wrong?"

"Nothing, sweetheart."

"You have tears in your eyes."

"It's nothing."

"You never cry," Kristen insisted.

"Something must have got into my eye to make it tear like this," she said, shaking her head. The effort to smile was too much for her. She straightened and placed her hands on Kristen's shoulders, then took a deep breath. "I don't want you to be disappointed if I don't see Mr. Lund again."

"He did this?" Kristen demanded, in a high shocked voice.

"No," Joanna countered immediately. "I already told you, I got something in my eye."

Kristen studied her with a frown, and Joanna tried to meet her daughter's gaze. If she was fool enough to make herself vulnerable to a man again, then she deserved this pain. She'd known better than to get involved with Tanner, but her heart had refused to listen.

A couple of hours later, Tanner arrived to pick up Nicole. Joanna let Kristen answer the door and stayed in the kitchen, pretending to be occupied there.

When the door swung open, Joanna assumed it was her daughter and asked, "Did Nicole get off all right?"

"Not yet."

Joanna jerked away from the sink at the husky sound of Tanner's voice. "Where are the girls?"

"In Kristen's room. I want to talk to you."

"I can't see how that would do much good."

"I've reconsidered."

"Bravo for you. Unfortunately so have I. You're absolutely right about it being better all around if we don't see each other again."

Tanner dragged his fingers through his hair and stalked to the other side of the room. "Okay, I'll admit it. I was jealous as hell when I walked in and found you having coffee with Davey. I felt you were treating him like some conquering hero returned from the war."

"Oh, honestly, it wasn't anything like that."

"You were laughing and smiling."

"Grievous sins, I'm sure."

Tanner clamped down his jaw so hard that the sides of his face went white. "All I can do is apologise, Joanna. I've already made a fool of myself over one woman who loved someone else, and frankly that caused me enough grief. I'm not looking to repeat the mistake with you."

A strained silence fell between them.

"I thought I could walk away from you and not feel any regrets, but I was wrong," he continued a moment later. "I haven't stopped thinking about you all afternoon. Maybe I overreacted. Maybe I behaved like a jealous fool."

"Maybe?" Joanna challenged. "Maybe? You were unreasonable and hurtful and…and I ate a whole row of Oreo cookies over you."

"What?"

"You heard me. I stuffed down a dozen cookies and now I think I'm going to be sick and it was all because of you. I've come too far to be reduced to that. One argument with you and I was right back into the Oreos! If you think you're frightened—because of what happened with Carmen—it's nothing compared to the fears I've been facing since the day we met. I can't deal with your insecurities, Tanner. I've got too damn many of my own."

"Joanna, I've already apologized. If you can honestly tell me there isn't any chance that you'll ever get back together with Davey, I swear to you I'll drop the subject and never bring it up again. But I need to know that much. I'm sorry, but I've got to hear you say it."

"I had a nice quiet life before you paraded into it," she went on, as though she hadn't heard him.

"Joanna, I asked you a question." His intense gaze cut straight through her.

"You must be nuts! I'd be certifiably insane to ever take Davey back. Our marriage—our entire relationship—was over the day I filed for divorce, and probably a lot earlier than that."

Tanner relaxed visibly. "I wouldn't blame you if you decided you never wanted to see me again, but I'm hoping you'll be able to forget what happened this afternoon so we can go back to being…friends again."

Joanna struggled against the strong pull of his magnetism for as long as she could, then nodded, agreeing to place this quarrel behind them.

Tanner walked toward her and she met him halfway, slipping easily into his embrace. She felt as if she belonged here, as if he were the man she would always be content with. He'd once told her he wouldn't ever hurt her the way her ex-husband had, but caring about him, risking a relationship with him, left her vulnerable all over again. She'd realised that this afternoon, learned again what it was to give a man the power to hurt her.

"I reduced you to gorging yourself with Oreos?" Tanner whispered the question into her hair.

She nodded wildly. "You fiend. I didn't mean to eat that many, but I sat at the table with the Oreos package and a glass of milk and the more I thought about what happened, the angrier I became, and the faster I shoved those cookies into my mouth."

"Could this mean you care?" His voice was still a whisper.

She nodded a second time. "I hate fighting with you. My stomach was in knots all afternoon."

"Good Lord, Joanna," he said, dropping several swift kisses on her face. "I can't believe what fools we are."

"We?" She tilted back her head and glared up at him, but her mild indignation drained away the moment their eyes met. Tanner was looking down at her with such tenderness, such concern, that every negative emotion she'd experienced earlier that afternoon vanished like rain falling into a clear blue lake.

He kissed her then, with a thoroughness that left her in no doubt about the strength of his feelings. Joanna rested against this warmth, holding on to him with everything that was in her. When he raised his head, she looked up at him through tear-filled eyes and blinked furiously in a futile effort to keep them at bay.

"I'm glad you came back," she said, when she could find her voice.

"I am, too." He kissed her once more, lightly this time, sampling her lips, kissing the tears from her face. "I wasn't worth a damn all afternoon." Once more he lowered his mouth to hers, creating a delicious sensation that electrified Joanna and sent chills racing down her spine.

Tanner's arms tightened as loud voices suddenly erupted from the direction of the living room.

"I never want to see you again," Joanna heard Kristen declare vehemently.

"You couldn't possibly want to see me any less than I want to see you," Nicole returned with equal volume and fury.

"What's that all about?" Tanner asked, his eyes searching Joanna's.

"I don't know, but I think we'd better find out."

Tanner led the way into the living room. They discovered Kristen and Nicole standing face to face, glaring at each other in undisguised antagonism.

"Kristen, stop that right now," Joanna demanded. "Nicole is a guest in our home and I won't have you talking to her in that tone of voice."

Tanner moved to his daughter's side. "And you're Kristen's guest. I expect you to be on your best behaviour whenever you're here."

Nicole crossed her arms over her chest and darted a venomous look in Kristen's direction. "I refuse to be friends with her ever again. And I don't think you should have anything more to do with Mrs. Parsons."

Joanna's eyes found Tanner's.

"I don't want my mother to have anything to do with Mr. Lund, either." Kristen spun around and glared at Tanner and Nicole.

"I think we'd best separate these two and find out what happened," Joanna suggested. She pointed toward Kristen's bedroom. "Come on, honey, let's talk."

Kristen averted her face. "I have nothing to say!" she declared melodramatically and stalked out of the room without a backward glance.

Joanna raised questioning eyes to Tanner, threw up her hands and followed her daughter.

Twelve

"**K**risten, what's wrong?" Joanna sat on the end of her daughter's bed and patiently waited for the eleven-year-old to repeat the list of atrocities committed by Nicole Lund.

"Nothing."

Joanna had seen her daughter wear this affronted look often enough to recognize it readily, and she felt a weary sigh work its way through her. Hell hath no fury like a sixth-grader done wrong by her closest friend.

"I don't ever want to see Nicole again."

"But, sweetheart, she's your best friend."

"*Was* my best friend," Kristen announced theatrically. She crossed her arms over her chest with all the pomp of a queen who'd made her statement and expected unquestioning acquiescence.

With mounting frustration, Joanna folded her hands in her lap and waited, knowing better than to try to reason with Kristen when she was in this mood. Five minutes passed, but Kristen didn't utter another word. Joanna wasn't surprised.

"Does your argument have to do with something that happened at school?" she asked as nonchalantly as possible, examining the fingernails on her right hand.

Kristen shook her head. She pinched her lips as if to suggest that nothing Joanna could say would force the information out of her.

"Does it involve a boy?" Joanna persisted.

Kristen's gaze widened. "Of course not."

"What about another friend?"

"Nope."

At the rate they were going, Joanna would soon run out of questions. "Can't you just tell me what happened?"

Kristen cast her a look that seemed to question her mother's intelligence. "No!"

"Does that mean we're going to sit here all night while I try to guess?"

Kristen twisted her head and tilted it at a lofty angle, then pantomimed locking her lips.

"All right," Joanna said with an exaggerated sigh, "I'll simply have to ask Nicole, who will, no doubt, be more than ready to tell all. Her version should be highly interesting."

"Mr. Lund made you cry!" Kristen mumbled, her eyes lowered.

Joanna blinked back her astonishment. "You mean to say this whole thing has to do with Tanner and me?"

Kristen nodded once.

"But—"

"Nicole claims that whatever happened was obviously your fault, and as far as I'm concerned that did it. From here on out, Nicole is no longer my friend and I don't think you should have anything to do with...with that man, either."

"That man?"

Kristen sent her a sour look. "You know very well who I mean."

Joanna shifted farther onto the bed, brought up her knees and rested her chin on them. She paused to carefully measure her words. "What if I told you I was beginning to grow fond of 'that man'?"

"Mom, no!" Her daughter's eyes widened with horror, and she cast her mother a look of sheer panic. "That would be the worst possible thing to happen. You might marry him and then Nicole and I would end up being sisters!"

Joanna made no attempt to conceal her surprise. "But, Kristen, from the not-so-subtle hints you and Nicole have been giving me and Mr. Lund, I thought that was exactly what you both wanted. What you'd planned."

"That was before."

"Before what?"

"Before...tonight, when Nicole said those things she said. I can't forgive her, Mom, I just can't."

Joanna stayed in the room a few more silent minutes, then left. Tanner and Nicole were talking in the living room, and from the frustrated look he gave her, she knew he hadn't been any more successful with his daughter than Joanna had been with hers.

When he saw Joanna, Tanner got to his feet and nodded toward the kitchen, mutely suggesting they talk privately and compare stories.

"What did you find out?" she asked the minute they were alone.

Tanner shrugged, then gestured defeat with his hands. "I don't understand it. She keeps saying she never wants to see Kristen again."

"Kristen says the same thing. Adamantly. She seems to think she's defending my honour. It seems this all has to do with our misunderstanding earlier this afternoon."

"Nicole seems to think it started when you didn't order anything at McDonalds," Tanner said, his expression confused.

"What?" Joanna's question escaped on a short laugh.

"From what I can get out of Nicole, Kristen claims you didn't order a Big Mac, which is supposed to mean something. Then later, before I arrived, there was some mention of your emptying the garbage when it was only half-full?" He paused to wait for her to speak. When she simply nodded, he continued, "I understand that's unusual for you, as well?"

Once more Joanna nodded. She'd wanted to hide her tears from the girls, so taking out the garbage had been an excuse to escape for a couple of minutes while she composed herself.

Tanner wiped his hand across his brow in mock relief. "Whew! At least neither of them learned about the Oreos!"

Joanna ignored his joke and slumped against the kitchen counter with a long slow sigh of frustration. "Having the girls argue is a problem neither of us anticipated."

"Maybe I should talk to Kristen and you talk to Nicole?" Tanner suggested, all seriousness again.

Joanna shook her head. "Then we'd be guilty of interfering. We'd be doing the same thing they've done to us—and I don't think we'd be doing them any favors."

"What do you suggest then?" Tanner asked, looking more disgruntled by the minute.

Joanna shrugged. "I don't know."

"Come on, Joanna, we're intelligent adults. Surely we can come up with a way to handle a couple of preadolescent egos."

"Be my guest," Joanna said, and laughed aloud at the comical look that crossed Tanner's handsome face.

"Forget it."

Joanna brushed the hair away from her face. "I think

our best bet is to let them work this matter out between themselves."

Tanner's forehead creased in concern, then he nodded, his look reluctant. "I hope this doesn't mean you and I can't be friends." His tender gaze held hers.

Joanna was forced to lower her eyes so he couldn't see just how important his friendship had become to her. "Of course we can."

"Good." He walked across the room and gently pulled her into his arms. He kissed her until she was weak and breathless. When he raised his head, he said in a husky murmur, "I'll take Nicole home now and do as you suggest. We'll give these two a week to settle their differences. After that, you and I are taking over."

"A week?" Joanna wasn't sure that would be long enough, considering Kristen's attitude.

"A week!" Tanner repeated emphatically, kissing her again.

By the time he'd finished, Joanna would have agreed to almost anything. "All right," she managed. "A week."

"How was school today?" Joanna asked Kristen on Monday evening while they sat at the dinner table. She'd waited as long as she could before asking. If either girl was inclined to make a move toward reconciliation, it would be now, she reasoned. They'd both had ample time to think about what had happened and to determine the value of their friendship.

Kristen shrugged. "School was fine, I guess."

Joanna took her time eating her salad, focusing her attention on it instead of her daughter. "How'd you do on the math paper I helped you with?"

Kristen rolled her eyes. "You showed me wrong."

"Wrong!"

"The answers were all right, but Mrs. Andrews told me they don't figure out equations that way anymore."

"Oh. Sorry about that."

"You weren't the only parent who messed up."

That was good to hear.

"A bunch of other kids did it wrong. Including Nicole."

Joanna slipped her hand around her water glass. Kristen sounded far too pleased that her ex-friend had messed up the assignment. That wasn't encouraging. "So you saw Nicole today?"

"I couldn't very well not see her. Her desk is across the aisle from mine. But if you're thinking what I think you're thinking, you can forget it. I don't need a friend like Nicole Lund."

Joanna didn't comment on that, although she practically had to bite her tongue. She wondered how Tanner was doing. Staying out of this argument between the two girls was far more difficult than she'd imagined. It was obvious to Joanna that Kristen was miserable without her best friend, but saying as much would hurt her case more than help it. Kristen needed to recognize the fact herself.

The phone rang while Joanna was finishing up the last of the dinner dishes. Kristen was in the bath, so Joanna grabbed the receiver, holding it between her hunched shoulder and her ear while she squirted detergent into the hot running water.

"Hello?"

"Joanna? Good Lord, you sounded just like Kristen there. I was prepared to have the phone slammed in my ear," Tanner said. "How's it going?"

Her heart swelled with emotion. She hadn't talked to him since Saturday, and it felt as though months had passed since she'd heard his voice. It wrapped itself around her now, warm and comforting. "Things aren't going too well. How are they at your end?"

"Not much better. Did you know Kristen had the nerve to eat lunch with Nora this afternoon? In case you weren't aware of this, Nora is Nicole's sworn enemy."

"Nora?" Joanna could hardly believe her ears. "Kristen doesn't even like the girl." If anything, this war between Kristen and Nicole was heating up.

"I hear you bungled the math assignment," Tanner said softly, amused.

"Apparently you did, too."

He chuckled. "Yeah, this new math is beyond me." He paused, and when he spoke, Joanna could hear the frustration in his voice. "I wish the girls would hurry and patch things up. Frankly, Joanna, I miss you like crazy."

"It's only been two days." She should talk—the last forty-eight hours had seemed like an eternity.

"It feels like two years."

"I know," she agreed softly, closing her eyes and savoring Tanner's words. "But we don't usually see each other during the week anyway." At least not during the past couple of weeks.

"I've been thinking things over and I may have come up with an idea that will put us all out of our misery."

"What?" By now, Joanna was game for anything.

"How about a movie?" he asked unexpectedly, his voice eager.

"But Tanner—"

"Tomorrow night. You can bring Kristen and I'll bring Nicole, and we could accidentally-on-purpose meet at the theater. Naturally there'll be a bit of acting on our part and some huffing and puffing on theirs, but if things work out the way I think they will, we won't have to do a thing. Nature will take its course."

Joanna wasn't convinced this scheme of his would work. The whole thing could blow up in their faces, but the thought of being with Tanner was too enticing to refuse. "All right," she agreed. "As long as you buy the popcorn and promise to hold my hand."

"You've got yourself a deal."

On Tuesday evening, Kristen was unusually quiet over dinner. Joanna had fixed one of her daughter's favorite meals—macaroni-and-cheese casserole—but Kristen barely touched it.

"Do you feel like going to a movie?" Joanna asked, her heart in her throat. Normally Kristen would leap at the idea, but this evening Joanna couldn't predict anything.

"It's a school night, and I don't think I'm in the mood to see a movie."

"But you said you didn't have any homework, and it sounds like a fun thing to do...and weren't you saying something about wanting to see Tom Cruise's latest film?" Kristen's eyes momentarily brightened, then faded. "And don't worry," Joanna added cheerfully, "you won't have to sit with me."

Kristen gave a huge sigh. "I don't have anyone else to sit with," she said, as though Joanna had suggested a trip to the dentist.

It wasn't until they were in the parking lot at the theater that Kristen spoke. "Nicole likes Tom Cruise, too."

Joanna made a noncommittal reply, wondering how easily the girls would see through her and Tanner's scheme.

"Mom," Kristen cried. "I see Nicole. She's with her dad. Oh, no, it looks like they're going to the same movie."

"Oh, no," Joanna echoed, her heart acting like a Ping-Pong ball in her chest. "Does this mean you want to skip the whole thing and go home?"

"Of course not," Kristen answered smugly. She practically bounded out of the car once Joanna turned off the engine, glancing anxiously at Joanna when she didn't walk across the parking lot fast enough to suit her.

They joined the line, about eight people behind Tanner and Nicole. Joanna was undecided about what to do next. She wasn't completely sure that Tanner had even seen her. If he had, he was playing his part perfectly, acting as though this whole thing had happened by coincidence.

Kristen couldn't seem to stand still. She peeked around the couple ahead of them several times, loudly humming the song of Heart's that she and Nicole had performed in the talent show.

Nicole whirled around, standing on her tiptoes and staring into the crowd behind her. She jerked on Tanner's sleeve and, when he bent down, whispered something in his ear. Then Tanner turned around, too, and pretended to be shocked when he saw Joanna and Kristen.

By the time they were inside the theater, Tanner and Nicole had disappeared. Kristen was craning her neck in every direction while Joanna stood at the refreshment counter.

"Do you want any popcorn?"

"No. Just some of those raisin things. Mom, you said I didn't have to sit with you. Did you really mean that?"

"Yes, honey, don't worry about it, I'll find a place by myself."

"You're sure?" Kristen looked only mildly concerned.

"No problem. You go sit by yourself."

"Okay." Kristen collected her candy and was gone before Joanna could say any more.

Since it was still several minutes before the movie was scheduled to start, the theater auditorium was well lit. Joanna found a seat toward the back and noted that Kristen was two rows from the front. Nicole sat in the row behind her.

"Is this seat taken?"

Joanna smiled up at Tanner as he claimed the seat next to her, and had they been anyplace else she was sure he would have kissed her. He handed her a bag of popcorn and a cold drink.

"I sure hope this works," he muttered under his breath, "because if Nicole sees me sitting with you, I could be hung as a traitor." Mischief brightened his eyes. "But the risk is worth it. Did anyone ever tell you how kissable your mouth looks?"

"Tanner," she whispered frantically and pointed toward the girls. "Look."

Kristen sat twisted around and Nicole leaned forward. Kristen shook a handful of her chocolate-covered raisins into Nicole's outstretched hand. Nicole offered Kristen some popcorn. After several of these exchanges, both girls stood up, moved from their seats to a different row entirely, sitting next to each other.

"That looks promising," Joanna whispered.

"It certainly does," Tanner agreed, slipping his arm around her shoulder.

They both watched as Kristen and Nicole tilted their heads toward each other and smiled at the sound of their combined giggles drifting to the back of the theater.

Thirteen

After their night at the movies, Joanna didn't give Tanner's invitation to the dinner party more than a passing thought until she read about the event on the society page of Wednesday's newspaper. The *Review* described the dinner, which was being sponsored by Spokane Aluminum, as the gala event of the year. Anyone who was anyone in the eastern half of Washington state would be attending. Until Joanna noticed the news article, she'd thought it was a small intimate party; that was the impression Tanner had given her.

From that moment on, Joanna started worrying, though she wasn't altogether sure why. As a loan officer, she'd attended her share of business-related social functions...but never anything of this scope. The problem, she decided, was one she'd been denying since the night of Nicole's slumber party. Tanner's social position and wealth far outdistanced her own. He was an important member of their community, and she was just a spoke in the wheel of everyday life.

Now, as she dressed for the event, her uneasiness grew, because she knew how important this evening was to Tanner—although he hadn't told her in so many words. The reception and dinner were all part of his becoming half owner of a major corporation and, according to the newspaper article, had been in the planning stages for several months after his arrival. All John Becky's way of introducing Tanner to the community leaders.

Within the first half hour of their arrival, Joanna recognized the mayor and a couple of members from the city council, plus several other people she didn't know, who nonetheless looked terribly important.

"Here," Tanner whispered, stepping to her side and handing her a glass of champagne.

Smiling up at him, she took the glass and held the dainty stem in a death grip, angry with herself for being so unnerved. It wasn't as though she'd never seen the mayor before—okay, only in pictures, but still… "I don't know if I dare have anything too potent," she admitted.

"Why not?"

"If you want the truth, I feel out of it at this affair. I'd prefer to fade into the background, mingle among the draperies, get acquainted with the wallpaper. That sort of thing."

Tanner's smile was encouraging. "No one would know it to look at you."

Joanna had trouble believing that. The smile she wore felt frozen on her lips, and her stomach protested the fact that she'd barely managed to eat all day. Tonight was important, and for Tanner's sake she'd do what she had to.

The man who owned the controlling interest in Columbia Basin Savings and Loan strolled past them and paused when he recognized her. Joanna nodded her recognition, and when he continued on she swallowed the entire glass of champagne in three giant gulps.

"I feel better," she announced.

"Good."

Tanner apparently hadn't noticed how quickly she'd downed the champagne, for which Joanna was grateful.

"Come over here. There are some people I want you to meet."

More people! Tanner had already introduced her to so many that the names were swimming around in her head like fish crowded in a small pond. She'd tried to keep them all straight, and it had been simple in the beginning when he'd started with his partner, John Becky, and John's wife, Jean, but from that point on her memory had deteriorated steadily.

Tanner pressed his hand to the middle of her spine and steered her across the room to where a small group had gathered.

Along the way, Joanna picked up another glass of champagne, just so she'd have something to do with her hands. The way she was feeling, she had no intention of drinking it.

The men and women paused in the middle of their conversation when Tanner approached. After a few words of greeting, introductions were made.

"Pleased to meet all of you," Joanna said, forcing some life into her fatigued smile. Everyone seemed to be looking at her, expecting something more. She nodded toward Tanner. "Our daughters are best friends."

The others smiled.

"I didn't know you had a daughter," a voluptuous blonde said, smiling sweetly up at Tanner.

"Nicole just turned twelve."

The blonde seemed fascinated with this information. "How very sweet. My niece is ten and I know she'd just love to meet Nicole. Perhaps we could get the two of them together. Soon."

"I'm sure Nicole would like that."

"It's a date then." She sidled as close to Tanner as she possibly could, practically draping her breast over his forearm.

Joanna narrowed her gaze and took a small sip of the champagne. The blonde, whose name was—she searched her mind—Blaise, couldn't have been any more obvious had she issued an invitation to her bed.

"Tanner, there's someone you must meet—that is, if I can drag you away from Joanna for just a little minute." The blonde cast a challenging look in Joanna's direction.

"Oh, sure." Joanna gestured with her hand as though to let Blaise know Tanner was free to do as he wished. She certainly didn't have any claims on him.

Tanner frowned. "Come with us," he suggested.

Joanna threw him what she hoped was a dazzling smile. "Go on. You'll only be gone a little minute," she said sweetly, purposely echoing Blaise's words.

The two left, Blaise clinging to Tanner's arm, and Joanna chatted with the others in the group for a few more minutes before fading into the background. Her stomach was twisted in knots. She didn't know why she'd sent Tanner off like that, when it so deeply upset her. Something in her refused to let him know that; it was difficult enough to admit even to herself.

Hoping she wasn't being obvious, her gaze followed Tanner and Blaise until she couldn't endure it any longer, and then she turned and made her way into the ladies' room. Joanna was grateful that the outer room was empty, and she slouched onto the sofa. Her heart was slamming painfully against her rib cage, and when she pressed her hands to her cheeks her face felt hot and feverish. Joanna would gladly have paid the entire three hundred and fifteen dollars in her savings account for a way to gracefully disappear.

It was then that she knew.

She was in love with Tanner Lund. Despite all the warnings she'd given herself. Despite the fact that they were worlds apart, financially and socially.

With the realisation that she loved Tanner came another. The night had only begun—they hadn't even eaten yet. The ordeal of a formal dinner still lay before her.

"Hello again," Jean Becky said, strolling into the ladies' room. She stopped for a moment, watching Joanna, then sat down beside her.

"Oh, hi." Joanna managed the semblance of a smile to greet the likeable older woman.

"I just saw Blaise Ferguson walk past clinging to Tanner. I hope you're not upset."

"Oh heavens, no," Joanna lied.

"Good. Blaise, er, has something of a reputation, and I didn't want you to worry. I'm sure Tanner's smart enough not to be taken in by someone that obvious."

"I'm sure he is, too."

"You're a sensible young woman," Jean said, looking pleased.

At the moment, Joanna didn't feel the least bit sensible. The one emotion she was experiencing was fear. She'd fallen in love again, and the first time had been so painful she had promised never to let it happen again. But it had. With Tanner Lund, yet. Why couldn't she have fallen for the mechanic who'd worked so hard repairing her car last winter, or someone at the office? Oh, no, she had to fall—and fall hard—for the most eligible man in town. The man every single woman in the party had her eye on this evening.

"It really has been a pleasure meeting you," Jean continued. "Tanner and Nicole talk about you and your daughter so often. We've been friends of Tanner's for several years now, and it gladdens our hearts to see him finally meet a good woman."

"Thank you." Joanna wasn't sure what to think about being classified as a "good woman." It made her wonder who Tanner had dated before he'd met her. She'd never asked him about his social life before he'd moved to Spokane—or even after. She wasn't sure she wanted to know. No doubt he'd made quite a splash when he came to town. Rich, handsome, available men were a rare commodity these days. It was a wonder he hadn't been snatched up long before now.

Five minutes later, Joanna had composed herself enough to rejoin the party. Tanner was at her side within a few seconds, noticeably irritable and short-tempered.

"I've been searching all over for you," he said, frowning heavily.

Joanna let that remark slide. "I thought you were otherwise occupied."

"Why'd you let that she-cat walk off with me like that?" His eyes were hot with fury. "Couldn't you tell I wanted out? Good Lord, woman, what do I have to do, flash flags?"

"No." A waiter walked past with a loaded tray, and Joanna deftly reached out and helped herself to another glass of champagne.

Just as smoothly, Tanner removed it from her fingers. "I think you've had enough."

Joanna took the glass back from him. She might not completely understand what was happening to her this evening, but she certainly didn't like his attitude. "Excuse me, Tanner, but I am perfectly capable of determining my own limit."

His frown darkened into a scowl. "It's taken me the last twenty minutes to extract myself from her claws. The least you could have done was stick around instead of doing a disappearing act."

"No way." Being married to Davey all those years had taught her more than one valuable lesson. If her ex-husband, Tanner, or any other man, for that matter, expected her to make a scene over another woman, it wouldn't work. Joanna was through with those kinds of destructive games.

"What do you mean by that?"

"I'm just not the jealous type. If you were to go home with Blaise, that'd be fine with me. In fact, you could leave with her right now. I'll grab a cab. I'm really not up to playing the role of a jealous girlfriend because another woman happens to show some interest in you. Nor am I willing to find a flimsy excuse to extract you from her clutches. You look more than capable of doing that yourself."

"You honestly want me to leave with Blaise?" His words were low and hard.

Joanna made a show of shrugging. "It's entirely up to you—you're free to do as you please. Actually you might be doing me a favor."

Joanna couldn't remember ever seeing a man more angry. His eyes seemed to spit fire at her. His jaws clamped together tightly, and he held himself with such an unnatural stiffness, it was surprising that something in his body didn't crack. She observed all this in some distant part of her mind, her concentration focused on preserving her facade of unconcern.

"I'm beginning to understand Davey," he said, his tone as cold as an arctic wind. "Has it ever occurred to you that your ex-husband turned to other women out of a desperate need to know you cared?"

Tanner's words hurt more than any physical blow could have. Joanna's breath caught in her throat, though she did her best to disguise the pain his remark had inflicted. When she was finally able to breathe, the words tumbled from her lips. "No. Funny, I never thought of that." She paused and searched the room. "Pick a woman then, any woman will do, and I'll slug it out with her."

"Joanna, stop it," Tanner hissed.

"You mean you don't want me to fight?"

He closed his eyes as if seeking patience. "No."

Dramatically, Joanna placed her hand over her heart. "Thank goodness. I don't know how I'd ever explain a black eye to Kristen."

Dinner was about to be served, and, tucking his hand under her elbow, Tanner led Joanna into the banquet room, which was quickly filling up.

"I'm sorry, I didn't mean that about Davey," Tanner whispered as they strolled toward the dining room. "I realize you're nervous, but no one would ever know it—except me. We'll discuss this Blaise thing later."

Joanna nodded, feeling subdued now, accepting his apology. She realized that she'd panicked earlier, and not because this was an important social event, either. She'd attended enough business dinners in her career to know she hadn't made a fool of herself. What disturbed her so much was the knowledge that she'd fallen in love with Tanner.

To add to Joanna's dismay, she discovered that she was expected to sit at the head table between Tanner and John Becky. She trembled at the thought, but she wasn't about to let anyone see her nervousness.

"Don't worry," Tanner said, stroking her hand after they were seated. "Everyone who's met you has been impressed."

His statement was meant to lend her courage; unfortunately it had the opposite effect. What had she said or done to impress anyone?

When the evening was finally over, Tanner appeared to

be as eager to escape as she was. With a minimum of fuss, they made their farewells and were gone.

Once in the car, Tanner didn't speak. But when he parked in front of the house, he turned off the car engine and said quietly, "Invite me in for coffee."

It was on the tip of Joanna's tongue to tell him she had a headache, which was fast becoming the truth, but delaying the inevitable wouldn't help either of them.

"Okay," she mumbled.

The house was quiet, and Sally was asleep on the sofa. Joanna paid her and waited on the front porch while the teenager ran across the street to her own house. Gathering her courage, she walked into the kitchen. Tanner had put the water and ground coffee into the machine and taken two cups down from the cupboard.

"Okay," he said, turning around to face her, "I want to know what's wrong."

The bewilderment in his eyes made Joanna raise her chin an extra notch. Then she remembered Kristen doing the same thing when she'd questioned her about her argument with Nicole, and the recollection wasn't comforting.

Joanna was actually surprised Tanner had guessed anything was wrong. She thought she'd done a brilliant job of disguising her distress. She'd done her best to say and do all the right things. When Tanner had stood up, after the meal, to give his talk, she'd whispered encouragement and smiled at him. Throughout the rest of the evening, she'd chatted easily with both Tanner and John Becky.

Now she had to try to explain something she barely understood herself.

"I don't think I ever realized what an important man you are," she said, struggling to find her voice. "I've always seen you as Nicole's father, the man who was crazy enough to agree to a slumber party for his daughter's birthday. The man who called and disguised his voice so Kristen wouldn't recognise it. That's the man I know, not the one tonight who stood before a filled banquet room and promised growth and prosperity for our city. Not the man who charts the destiny of an entire community."

Tanner glared at her. "What has that got to do with anything?"

"You play in the big league. I'm in the minors."

Tanner's gaze clouded with confusion. "I'm talking about our relationship and you're discussing baseball!"

Pulling out a kitchen chair, Joanna sat in it and took a deep breath. The best place to start, she decided, was the beginning. "You have to understand that I didn't come away from my marriage without a few quirks."

Tanner started pacing, clearly not in the mood to sit still. "Quirks? You call what happened with Blaise a quirk? I call it loony. Some woman I don't know from Adam comes up to me—"

"Eve," Joanna inserted, and when he stared at her, uncomprehending, she elaborated. "Since Blaise Ferguson's a woman, you don't know her from Eve."

"Whatever!"

"Well, it does make a difference." The coffee had finished filtering into the pot, so Joanna got up and poured them each a cup. Holding hers in both hands, she leaned against the counter and took a tentative sip.

"Some woman I don't know from Eve," Tanner tried again, "comes up to me, and you act as if you can't wait to get me out of your hair."

"*You* acted as if you expected me to come to your rescue. Honestly, Tanner, you're a big boy. I assumed you could take care of yourself."

"You looked more than happy to see me go with her."

"That's not true. I was content where I was." Joanna knew they were sidestepping the real issue, but this other business seemed to concern Tanner more.

"You were content to go into hiding."

"If you're looking for someone to fly into a jealous rage every time another woman winks at you, you'll need to look elsewhere."

Tanner did some more pacing, his steps growing longer and heavier with each circuit of the kitchen. "Explain what you meant when you said you didn't come away from your marriage without a few quirks."

"It's simply really," she said, making light of it. "Davey used to get a kick out of introducing me to his women friends. Everyone in the room knew what he was doing, except me. I was so stupid, so blind, that I just didn't know any better. Once the scales fell from my eyes, I was astonished at what a complete fool I'd been. But when I became wise to his ways, it was much worse. Every time he introduced me to a woman, I'd be filled with suspicion. Was Davey involved with her, or wasn't he? The only thing left for me to do was hold my head high and smile." Her voice was growing tighter with every word, cracking just as she finished.

Tanner walked toward her and reached out his hands as though to comfort her. "Joanna, listen—"

"No." She set her coffee aside and wrapped her arms around her middle. "I feel honored, Tanner, that you would ask me to attend this important dinner with you tonight. I think we both learned something valuable from the experience. At least, I know I did."

"Joanna—"

"No," she cut in again, "let me finish, please. Although it's difficult to say this, it needs to be said. We're not right for each other. We've been so caught up in everything we had in common and what good friends the girls are and how wonderful it felt to…be together, we didn't stop to notice that we live in different worlds." She paused and gathered her resolve before continuing. "Knowing you and becoming your friend has been wonderful, but anything beyond that just isn't going to work."

"The only thing I got carried away with was you, Joanna. The girls have nothing to do with it."

"I feel good that you would say that, I really do, but we both lost sight of the fact that neither one of us wants to become involved. That had never been our intention. Something happened, and I'm not sure when or why, but suddenly everything is so intense between us. It's got to stop before we end up really hurting each other."

Tanner seemed to mull over her words. "You're so frightened of giving another man the power to hurt you that you can't see anything else, can you?" His brooding, confused look was back. "I told you this once, but it didn't seem to sink into that head of yours—I'm never going to do the things Davey did. We're two entirely different men, and it's time you realized that."

"What you say may very well be true, Tanner, but I don't see what difference it's going to make. Because I have no intention of involving myself in another relationship."

"In case you hadn't noticed, Joanna, we're already involved."

"Roller-skating in the couples round doesn't qualify as being involved to me," she said, in a futile attempt at humor. It fell flat.

Tanner was the first to break the heavy silence that followed. "You've obviously got some thinking to do," he said wearily. "For that matter, so do I. Call me, Joanna, when you're in the mood to be reasonable."

Fourteen

"Hi, Mom," Kristen said, slumping down on the sofa beside Joanna. "I hope you know I'm bored out of my mind," she said, and sighed deeply.

Joanna was busy counting the stitches on her knitting needle and didn't pause to answer until she'd finished. "What about your homework?"

"Cute, Mom, real cute. It's spring break—I don't have any homework."

"Right. Phone Nicole then. I bet she'll commiserate with you." And she might even give Kristen some information about Tanner. He'd walked out of her house, and although she'd thought her heart would break she'd let him go. Since then, she'd reconsidered. She was dying to hear something from Tanner. Anything. But she hadn't—not since the party more than a week earlier, and each passing day seemed like a lifetime.

"Calling Nicole is a nothing idea."

"I could suggest you clean your room."

"Funny, Mom, real funny."

"Gee, I'm funny and cute all in one evening. How'd I get so lucky?"

Not bothering to answer, Kristen reached for a magazine and idly thumbed through the pages, not finding a single picture or article worth more than a fleeting glance. She set it aside and reached for another. By the time she'd gone through the four magazines resting on top of the coffee table, Joanna was losing her patience.

"Call Nicole."

"I can't."

"Why not?"

"Because I can't."

That didn't make much sense to Joanna. And suggesting that Kristen phone Nicole was another sign of her willingness to settle this rift between her and Tanner. It had been so long since she'd last seen or heard from him. Ten interminable days, and with each one that passed she missed him more. She'd debated long and hard about calling him, wavering with indecision, battling with her pride. What she'd told him that night had been the truth—they did live in different worlds. But she'd overreacted at the dinner party, and now she felt guilty about how the evening had gone. When he'd left the house, Tanner had suggested she call him when she was ready to be reasonable. Well, she'd been ready the following morning, ready to acknowledge her fault. And her need. But pride held her back. And with each passing day, it became more difficult to swallow that pride.

"You know I can't call Nicole," Kristen whined.

"Why not? Did you have another argument?" Joanna asked without looking at her daughter. Her mind was preoccupied with counting stitches. She always knitted when she was frustrated with herself; it was a form of self-punishment, she suspected wryly.

"We never fight. Not anymore. Nicole's in West Virginia."

Joanna paused and carefully set the knitting needles down on her lap. "Oh? What's she doing there?"

"I think she went to visit her mother."

"Her mother?" It took some effort to keep her heart from exploding in her throat. According to Tanner, Nicole hadn't seen or heard from Carmen in three years. His biggest worry, he'd told her, was that someday his ex-wife would develop an interest in their daughter and steal her away from him. "Nicole is with her mother?" Joanna repeated, to be certain she'd heard Kristen correctly.

"You knew that."

"No, I didn't."

"Yes, you did. I told you she was leaving last Sunday. Remember?"

Vaguely, Joanna recalled the conversation—she'd been peeling potatoes at the sink—but for the last week, every time Kristen mentioned either Tanner or Nicole, Joanna had made an effort to tune her daughter out. Now she was hungry for information, starving for every tidbit Kristen was willing to feed her.

The eleven-year-old straightened and stared at her mother. "Didn't Mr. Lund mention Nicole was leaving?"

"Er, no."

Kristen sighed and threw herself against the back of the sofa. "You haven't been seeing much of him lately, have you?"

"Er, no."

Kristen picked up Joanna's hand and patted it gently. "You two had a fight?"

"Not exactly."

Her daughter's hand continued its soothing action. "Okay, tell me all about it. Don't hold back a single thing— you need to talk this out. Bare your soul."

"Kristen!"

"Mom, you need this. Releasing your anger and frustration will help. You've got to work out all that inner agitation and responsive turbulence. It's disrupting your emotional poise. Seriously, Mom, have you ever considered Rolfing?"

"Emotional poise? Responsive turbulence? Where'd you hear about that? Where'd you hear about Rolfing?"

Kristen blinked and cocked her head to one side, doing her best to look concerned and sympathetic. "Oprah Winfrey."

"I see," Joanna muttered, and rolled her eyes.

"Are you or are you not going to tell me all about it?"

"No, I am not!"

Kristen released a deep sigh that expressed her keen disappointment. "I thought not. When it comes to Nicole's dad, you never want to talk about it. It's like a deep dark secret the two of you keep from Nicole and me. Well, that's all right—we're doing our best to understand. You don't want us to get our hopes up that you two might be interested in each other. I can accept that, although I consider it grossly unfair." She stood up and gazed at her mother with undisguised longing, then loudly slapped her hands against her sides. "I'm perfectly content to live the way we do…but it sure would be nice to have a baby sister to dress up. And you know how I've *always* wanted a brother."

"Kristen!"

"No, Mom." She held up her hand as though she were stopping a freight train. "Really, I do understand. You and I get along fine the way we are. I guess we don't need to complicate our lives with Nicole and her dad. That could even cause real problems."

For the first time, her daughter was making sense.

"Although heaven knows, I can't remember what it's like to be part of a *real* family."

"Kristen, that's enough," Joanna cried, shaking her head. Her daughter was invoking so much guilt that Joanna was beginning to hear violins in the background. "You and I *are* a real family."

"But, Mom, it could be so much better." Kristen sank down beside Joanna again and crossed her legs. Obviously her argument had long since been prepared, and without pausing to breathe between sentences, she proceeded to list the advantages of joining the two families.

"Kristen—"

Once more her daughter stopped her with an outstretched hand, as she started on her much shorter list of possible disadvantages. There was little Joanna could do to stem the rehearsed speech. Impatiently she waited for Kristen to finish.

"I don't want to talk about Tanner again," Joanna said in a no-nonsense tone of voice reserved for instances such as this. "Not a single word. Is that clearly understood?"

Kristen turned round sad eyes on her mother. The fun and laughter seemed to drain from her face as she glared back at Joanna. "Okay—if that's what you really want."

"It is, Kristen. Not a single word."

Banning his name from her daughter's lips and banning his name from her own mind were two entirely different things, Joanna decided an hour later. The fact that Nicole was visiting Carmen concerned her—not that she shared Tanner's worries. But knowing Tanner, he was probably beside himself worrying that Carmen would want their daughter to come and live with her.

It took another half hour for Joanna to build up enough courage to phone Tanner. He answered on the second ring.

"Hello, Tanner...it's Joanna." Even that was almost more than she could manage.

"Joanna." Just the way he said her name revealed his delight in hearing from her.

Joanna was grateful that he didn't immediately bring up the dinner party and the argument that had followed. "How have you been?"

"Good. How about you?"

"Just fine," she returned awkwardly. She leaned against the wall, crossing and uncrossing her ankles. "Listen, the reason I phoned is that Kristen told me Nicole was with her mother, and I thought you might be in need of a divorced-parent prep talk."

"What I really need is to see you. Lord, woman, it took you long enough. I thought you were going to make me wait forever. Ten days can be a very long time, Joanna. Ten whole days!"

"Tanner—"

"Can we meet someplace?"

"I'm not sure." Her mind struggled with a list of excuses, but she couldn't deny how lonely and miserable she'd been, how badly she wanted to feel his arms around her. "I'd have to find someone to sit with Kristen, and that could be difficult at the last minute like this."

"I'll come to you then."

It was part question, part statement, and again, she hesitated. "All right," she finally whispered.

The line went oddly silent. When Tanner spoke again there was a wealth of emotion in his words, although his voice was quiet. "I'm glad you phoned, Joanna."

She closed her eyes, feeling weak and shaky. "I am, too," she said softly.

"I'll be there within half an hour."

"I'll have coffee ready."

When she replaced the receiver, her hand was trembling,

and it was as though she were twenty-one again. Her heart was pounding out of control just from the sound of his voice, her head swimming with the knowledge that she'd be seeing him in a few minutes. How wrong she'd been to assume that if she put him out of her sight and mind she could keep him out of her heart, too. How foolish she'd been to deny her feelings. She loved this man, and it wouldn't matter if he owned the company or swept the floors.

Joanna barely had time to refresh her makeup and drag a brush through her hair. Kristen had been in her room for the past hour without a sound; Joanna sincerely hoped she was asleep.

She'd just poured water into the coffeemaker when the doorbell chimed.

The bedroom door flew open, and Kristen appeared in her pajamas, wide awake. "I'll get it," she yelled.

Joanna started to call after her, but it was too late. With a resigned sigh, she stood in the background and waited for her daughter to admit Tanner.

Kristen turned to face her mother, wearing a grin as wide as the Mississippi River. "It's that man whose name I'm not supposed to mention ever again."

"Yes, I know."

"You know?"

Joanna nodded.

"Good. Talk it out with him, Mom. Relieve yourself of all that inner stuff. Get rid of that turmoil before it eats you alive."

Joanna cast a weak smile in Tanner's direction, then turned her attention to Kristen. "Isn't it your bedtime, young lady?"

"No."

Joanna's eyes narrowed. "Yes, it is."

"But, Mom, it's spring break, so I can sleep in tomorrow—Oh, I get it, you want me out of here."

"In your room reading or listening to music should do nicely."

Kristen beamed her mother a broad smile. "'Night, Mom. 'Night... Nicole's dad."

"'Night."

With her arms swinging at her sides, Kristen strolled out of the living room. Tanner waited until they heard her bedroom door shut, then he started across the carpet toward Joanna. He stopped suddenly, frowning. "She wasn't supposed to say my name?"

Joanna gave a weak half shrug, her gaze holding his. No man had ever looked better. His eyes seemed to caress her with a tenderness and aching hunger that did crazy things to her equilibrium.

"It's so good to see you," she said, her voice unsteady. She took two steps towards him.

When Tanner reached for her, a heavy sigh broke from his lips and the tension left his muscles. "Dear Lord, woman, ten days you left me dangling." He said more, but his words were muffled in the curve of her neck as he crushed her against his chest.

Joanna soaked up his warmth, and when his lips found hers she surrendered with a soft sigh of joy. Being in Tanner's arms was like coming home after a long journey and discovering the comfort in all that's familiar. It was like walking in sunshine after a bad storm, like holding the first rose of summer in her hand.

Again and again his mouth sought hers in a series of passionate kisses, as though he couldn't get enough of the taste of her.

The creaky sound of a bedroom door opening caused

Joanna to break away from him. "It's Kristen," she murmured, her voice little more than a whisper.

"I know, but I don't care." Tanner kept her close for a moment longer. "Okay," he breathed, and slowly stroked the top of her head with his chin. "We need to settle a few things. Let's talk."

Joanna led him into the kitchen, since they were afforded the most privacy there. She automatically took down two cups and poured them each some coffee. They sat at the small table, directly across from each other, but even that seemed much too far.

"First, tell me about Nicole," she said, her eyes meeting his. "Are you worried now that she's with Carmen?"

A sad smile touched the edges of Tanner's mouth. "Not particularly. Carmen, who prefers to be called Rama Sheba now, contacted my parents at the end of last week. According to my mother, the reason we haven't heard from her in the past three years is that Carmen's been on a long journey in India and Nepal. Apparently Carmen went halfway around the world searching for herself. I guess she found what she was looking for, because she's back in the United States and inquiring about Nicole."

"Oh, dear. Do you think she wants Nicole to come live with her?"

"Not a chance. Carmen, er, Rama Sheba, doesn't want a child complicating her life. She never did. Nicole wanted to see her mother and that's understandable, so I sent her back to West Virginia for a visit with my parents. While she's there, Carmen will spend an afternoon with her."

"What happened to… Rama Sheba and the baseball player?"

"Who knows? He may have joined her in her wanderings, for all I know. Or care. Carmen plays such a minor role in my life now that I haven't the energy to second-guess her. She's free to do as she likes, and I prefer it that way. If she wants to visit Nicole, fine. She can see her daughter—she has the right."

"Do you love her?" The question sounded abrupt and tactless, but Joanna needed to know.

"No," he said quickly, then grinned. "I suppose I feel much the same way about her as you do about Davey."

"Then you don't hate her?" she asked next, not looking at him.

"No."

Joanna ran a fingertip along the rim of her cup and smiled. "Good."

"Why's that good?"

She lifted her eyes to meet his and smiled a little shyly. "Because if you did have strong feelings for her it would suggest some unresolved emotion."

Tanner nodded. "As illogical as it sounds, I don't feel anything for Carmen. Not love, not hate—nothing. If something bad were to happen to her, I suppose I'd feel sad, but I don't harbor any resentments toward her."

"That's what I was trying to explain to you the afternoon you dropped by when Davey was here. Other people have a hard time believing this, especially my parents, but I honestly wish him success in life. I want him to be happy, although I doubt he ever will be." Davey wasn't a man who would ever be content. He was always looking for something more, something better.

Tanner nodded.

Once more, Joanna dropped her gaze to the steaming coffee. "Calling you and asking about Nicole was only an excuse, you know."

"Yes. I just wish you'd come up with it a few days earlier. As far as I'm concerned, waiting for you to come to your senses took nine days too long."

"I—"

"I know, I know," Tanner said before she could list her excuses. "Okay, let's talk."

Joanna managed a smile. "Where do we start?"

"How about with what happened the night of the party?"

Instantly Joanna's stomach knotted. "Yes, well, I guess I should be honest and let you know I was intimidated by how important you are. It shook me, Tanner, really shook me. I'm not used to seeing you as chairman of the board. And then later, when you strolled off with Blaise, those old wounds from my marriage with Davey started to bleed."

"I suppose I did all the wrong things. Maybe I should have insisted you come with me when Blaise dragged me away, but—"

"No, that wouldn't have worked, either."

"I should have guessed how you'd feel after being married to Davey."

"You had no way of knowing." Now came the hard part. "Tanner," she began, and was shocked at how thin and weak her voice sounded, "I was so consumed with jealousy that I just about went crazy when Blaise wrapped her arms around you. It frightened me to have to deal with those negative emotions again. I know I acted like an idiot, hiding like that, and I'd like to apologize."

"Joanna, it isn't necessary."

She shook her head. "I don't mean this as an excuse, but you need to understand why I was driven to behave the way I did. I'd thought I was beyond that—years beyond acting like a jealous fool. I promised myself I'd never allow a man to do it to me again." In her own way, Joanna was trying to tell him how much she loved him, but the words weren't coming out right.

He frowned at that. "Jealous? You were jealous? Good Lord, woman, you could have fooled me. You handed me over to Blaise without so much as a hint of regret. From the way you were behaving, I thought you *wanted* to be rid of me."

The tightness in Joanna's throat made talking difficult. "I already explained why I did that."

"I know. The way I acted when I saw your ex here was the other kind of jealous reaction—the raging-bull kind. I think I see now where *your* kind of reaction came from. I'm not sure which one is worse, but I think mine is." He smiled ruefully, and a silence fell between them.

"Could this mean you have some strong feelings for me, Joanna Parsons?"

A smile quirked at the corners of her mouth. "You're the only man I've ever eaten Oreos over."

The laughter in Tanner's eyes slowly faded. "We could have the start of something very important here, Joanna. What do you think?"

"I… I think you may be right."

"Good." Tanner looked exceedingly pleased with this turn of events. "That's exactly what I wanted to hear."

Joanna thought—no, hoped—that he intended to lean over and kiss her. Instead his brows drew together darkly over brooding blue eyes. "Okay, where do we go from here?"

"Go?" Joanna repeated, feeling uncomfortable all of a sudden. "Why do we have to go anywhere?"

Tanner looked surprised. "Joanna, for heaven's sake, when a man and a woman feel about each other the way we do, they generally make plans."

"What do you mean 'feel about each other the way we do'?"

Tanner's frown darkened even more. "You love me."

Only a few moments before, Joanna would have willingly admitted it, but silly as it sounded, she wanted to hear Tanner say the words first. "I... I..."

"If you have to think about it, then I'd say you obviously don't know."

"But I do know," she said, lifting her chin a notch higher. "I'm just not sure this is the time to do anything about it. You may think my success is insignificant compared to yours, but I've worked damn hard to get where I am. I've got the house I saved for years to buy, and my career is starting to swing along nicely, and Robin—he's my boss—let me know that I was up for promotion. My goal of becoming the first female senior loan officer at the branch is within sight."

"And you don't want to complicate your life right now with a husband and second family?"

"I didn't say that."

"It sure sounded like it to me."

Joanna swallowed. The last thing in the world she wanted to do was argue with Tanner. Craziest of all, she wasn't even sure what they were arguing about. They were in love with each other and both just too damn proud. "I don't think we're getting anywhere with this conversation."

Tanner braced his elbows on the table and folded his hands. "I'm beginning to agree with you. All week, I've been waiting for you to call me, convinced that once you did, everything between us would be settled. I wanted us to start building a life together, and all of a sudden you're Ms. Career Woman, and about as independent as they come."

"I haven't changed. You just didn't know me."

His lips tightened. "I guess you're right. I don't know you at all, do I?"

* * *

"Mom, Mom, come quick!"

Joanna's warm cozy dream was interrupted by Kristen's shrieks. She rolled over and glared at the digital readout on her clock radio. Five. In the morning. "Kristen?" She sat straight up in bed.

"Mom!"

The one word conveyed such panic that Joanna's heart rushed to her throat and she threw back her covers, running barefoot into the hallway. Almost immediately, her feet encountered ice-cold water.

"Something's wrong," Kristen cried, hopping up and down. "The water won't stop."

That was the understatement of the year. From the way the water was gushing out of the bathroom door and into the hallway, it looked as though a dam had burst.

"Grab some towels," Joanna cried, pointing toward the hallway linen closet. The hems of her long pajamas were already damp. She scooted around her daughter, who was standing in the doorway, still hopping up and down like a crazed kangaroo.

Further investigation showed that the water was escaping from the cabinet under the sink.

"Mom, Mom, here!" Dancing around, Kristen threw her a stack of towels that separated in midair and landed in every direction.

"Kristen!" Joanna snapped, squatting down in front of the sink. She opened the cabinet and was immediately hit by a wall of foaming bubbles. The force of the flowing water had knocked over her container of expensive bubble bath and spilled its contents. "You were in my bubble bath!" Joanna cried.

"I… How'd you know?"

"The cap's off, and now it's everywhere!"

"I just used a little bit."

Three bars of Ivory soap, still in their wrappers, floated past Joanna's feet. Heaven only knew what else had been stored under the sink or where it was headed now.

"I'm sorry about the bubble bath," Kristen said defensively. "I figured you'd get mad if you found out, but a kid needs to know what luxury feels like, too, you know."

"It's all right, we can't worry about that now." Joanna waved her hands back and forth trying to disperse the bubbles enough to assess the damage. It didn't take long to determine that a pipe had burst. With her forehead pressing against the edge of the sink, Joanna groped inside the cabinet for the knob to turn off the water supply. Once she found it, she twisted it furiously until the flowing water dwindled to a mere trickle.

"Kristen!" Joanna shouted, looking over her shoulder. Naturally, when she needed her, her daughter disappeared. "Get me some more towels. Hurry, honey!"

A couple of minutes later, Kristen reappeared, her arms loaded with every towel and washcloth in the house. "Yuck," she muttered, screwing her face into a mask of sheer disgust. "What a mess!"

"Did any water get into the living room?"

Kristen nodded furiously. "But only as far as the front door."

"Great." Joanna mumbled under her breath. Now she'd need to phone someone about coming in to dry out the carpet.

On her hands and knees, sopping up as much water as she could, Joanna was already soaked to the skin herself.

"You need help," her daughter announced.

The child was a master of observation. "Change out of

those wet things first, Kristen, before you catch your death of cold."

"What about you?"

"I'll dry off as soon as I get some of this water cleaned up."

"Mom—"

"Honey, just do as I ask. I'm not in any mood to argue with you."

Joanna couldn't remember ever seeing a bigger mess in her life. Her pajamas were soaked; bubbles were popping around her head—how on earth had they got into her hair? She sneezed violently, and reached for a tissue that quickly dissolved in her wet hands.

"Here, use this."

The male voice coming from behind her surprised Joanna so much that when she twisted around, she lost her footing and slid down into a puddle of the coldest water she'd ever felt.

"Tanner!" she cried, leaping to her feet. "What are you doing here?"

Fifteen

Dumbfounded, Joanna stared at Tanner, her mouth hanging open and her eyes wide.

"I got this frantic phone call from Kristen."

"Kristen?"

"The one and only. She suggested I hurry over here before something drastic happened." Tanner took one step toward her and lovingly brushed a wet tendril away from her face. "How's it going, Tugboat Annie?"

"A pipe under the sink broke. I've got it under control now—I think." Her pajamas hung limply at her ankles, dripping water onto her bare feet. Her hair fell in wet spongy curls around her face, and Joanna had never felt more like bursting into tears in her life.

"Kristen shouldn't have phoned you," she said, once she found her voice.

"I'm glad she did. It's nice to know I can be useful every now and again." Heedless of her wet state, he wrapped his arms around Joanna and brought her close, gently pressing her damp head to his chest.

A chill went through her and she shuddered. Tanner felt so warm and vital, so concerned and loving. She'd let him think she was this strong independent woman, and normally she was, but when it came to broken pipes and floods and things like that, she crumbled into bite-sized pieces. When it came to Tanner Lund, well...

"You're soaked to the skin," he whispered, close to her ear.

"I know."

"Go change. I'll take over here."

The tears started then, silly ones that sprang from somewhere deep inside her and refused to be stopped. "I can't get dry," she sobbed, wiping furiously at the moisture that rained down her face. "There aren't any dry towels left in this entire house."

Tanner jerked his water-blotched tan leather jacket off and placed it around her shoulders. "Honey, don't cry. Please. Everything's going to be all right. It's just a broken pipe, and I can have it fixed for you before noon—possibly sooner."

"I can't help it," she bellowed, and to her horror, hiccuped. She threw a hand over her mouth and leaned her forehead against his strong chest. "It's five o'clock in the morning, my expensive Giorgio bubble bath is ruined, and I'm so much in love I can't think straight."

Tanner's hands gripped her shoulders and eased her away so he could look her in the eye. "What did you just say?"

Joanna hung her head as low as it would go, bracing her weight against Tanner's arms. "My Giorgio bubble bath is ruined." The words wobbled out of her mouth like a rubber ball tumbling down stairs.

"Not that. I want to hear the other part, about being so much in love."

Joanna sniffled. "What about it?"

"What about it? Good Lord, woman, I was here not more than eight hours ago wearing my heart on my sleeve like a schoolboy. You were so casual about everything, I thought you were going to open a discussion on stock options."

"*You* were the one who was so calm and collected about everything, as if what happened between us didn't really matter to you." She rubbed her hand under her nose and sniffled loudly. "Then you made everything sound like a foregone conclusion and—"

"I was nervous. Now, shall we give it another try? I want to marry you, Joanna Parsons. I want you to share my life, maybe have my babies. I want to love you until we're both old and gray. I've even had fantasies about us traveling around the country in a mobile home to visit our grand-children!"

"You want grandkids?" Timidly, she raised her eyes to his, almost afraid to believe what he was telling her.

"I'd prefer to take this one step at a time. The first thing I want to do is marry you. I couldn't have made that plainer than I did a few hours ago."

"But—"

"Stop right now, before we get sidetracked. First things first. Are you and Kristen going to marry me and Nicole?"

"I think we should," the eleven-year-old said excitedly from the hallway, looking smugly pleased with the way things were going. "I mean, it's been obvious to Nicole and me for ages that you two were meant to be together." Kristen sighed and slouched against the wall, crossing her arms over her chest with the sophistication that befitted someone of superior intelligence. "There's only one flaw in this plan."

"Flaw?" Joanna echoed.

"Yup," Kristen said, nodding with unquestionable confidence. "Nicole is going to be mad as hops when she finds out she missed this."

Tanner frowned, and then he chuckled. "Oh, boy. I think

Kristen could be right. We're going to have to stage a second proposal."

Feeling slightly piqued, Joanna straightened. "Listen, you two, I never said I was going to marry anybody—yet."

"Of course you're going to marry Mr. Lund," Kristen inserted smoothly. "Honestly, Mom, now isn't the time to play hard to get."

"W-what?" Stunned, Joanna stood there staring at her daughter. Her gaze flew from Kristen to Tanner and then back to Kristen.

"She's right, you know," said Tanner.

"I can't believe I'm hearing this." Joanna was standing in a sea of wet towels, while her daughter and the man she loved discussed her fate as though she was to play only a minor role in it.

"We've got to think of a way to include Nicole," Tanner said thoughtfully.

"I am going to change my clothes," Joanna murmured, eager to escape.

"Good idea," Tanner answered, without looking at her.

Joanna stomped off to her bedroom and slammed the door. She discarded her pajamas and, shivering, reached for a thick wool sweater and blue jeans.

Tanner and Kristen were still in the bathroom doorway, discussing details, when Joanna reappeared. She moved silently around them and into the kitchen, where she made a pot of coffee. Then she gathered up the wet towels, hauled them onto the back porch, threw them into the washer and started the machine. By the time she returned to the kitchen, Tanner had joined her there.

"Uh-oh. Trouble," he said, watching her abrupt angry movements. "Okay, tell me what's wrong now."

"I don't like the way you and my daughter are planning

my life," she told him point-blank. "Honestly, Tanner, I haven't even agreed to marry you, and already you and Kristen have got the next ten years all figured out."

He stuck his hands in his pants pockets. "It's not that bad."

"Maybe not, but it's bad enough. I'm letting you know right now that I'm not about to let you stage a second proposal just so Nicole can hear it. To be honest, I'm not exactly thrilled about Kristen being part of this one. A marriage proposal is supposed to be private. And romantic, with flowers and music, not...not in front of a busted pipe with bath bubbles popping around my head and my family standing around applauding."

"Okay, what do you suggest?"

"I don't know yet."

Tanner looked disgruntled. "If you want the romance, Joanna, that's fine. I'd be more than happy to give it to you."

"Every woman wants romance."

Tanner walked toward her then and took her in his arms, and until that moment Joanna had no idea how much she did, indeed, want it.

Her eyes were drawn to his. Everything about Tanner Lund fascinated her, and she raised her hand to lightly caress the proud strong line of his jaw. She really did love this man. His eyes, blue and intense, met hers, and a tiny shiver of awareness went through her. His arms circled her waist, and then he lifted her off the ground so that her gaze was level with his own.

Joanna gasped a little at the unexpectedness of his action. Smiling, she looped her arms around his neck.

Tanner kissed her then, with a hunger that left her weak and clinging in its aftermath.

"How's that?" he asked, his voice husky.

"Better. Much better."

"I thought so." Once more his warm mouth made contact with hers. Joanna was startled and thrilled at the intensity of his touch. He kissed her again and again, until she thought that if he released her, she'd fall to the floor and melt at his feet. Every part of her body was heated to fever pitch.

"Joanna—"

She planted warm moist kisses across his face, not satisfied, wanting him until her heart felt as if it might explode. Tanner had awoken the sensual part of her nature, buried all the years since her divorce, and now that it had been stirred back to life, she felt starved for a man's love—this man's love.

"Yes," she breathed into his mouth. "Yes, yes, yes."

"Yes what?" he asked in a breathless murmur.

Joanna paused and smiled gently. "Yes, I'll marry you. Right now. Okay? This minute. We can fly somewhere… find a church… Oh, Tanner," she pleaded, "I want you so much."

"Joanna, we can't." His words came out in a groan, forced from deep inside him.

She heard him, but it didn't seem to matter. She kissed him and he kissed her. Their kiss continued as he lowered her to the floor, her body sliding intimately down his.

Suddenly Joanna realized what she'd just said, what she'd suggested. "We mustn't. Kristen—"

Tanner shushed her with another kiss, then said, "I know, love. This isn't the time or place, but I sure wish…"

Joanna straightened, and broke away. Shakily, she said, "So do I…and, uh, I think we should wait a while for the wedding. At least until Nicole gets back."

"Right."

"How long will that be?"

"The end of the week."

Joanna nodded and closed her eyes. It sounded like an eternity.

"What about your job?"

"I don't want to work forever, and when we decide to start a family I'll probably quit. But I want that promotion first." Joanna wasn't sure exactly why that was so important to her, but it was. She'd worked years for this achievement, and she had no intention of walking away until she'd become the first female senior loan officer.

Tanner kissed her again. "If it makes you happy keep your job as long as you want."

At that moment, however, all Joanna could think about were babies, family vacations and homemade cookies.

"That's her plane now," Tanner said to Kristen, pointing toward the Boeing jet that was approaching the long narrow landing strip at Spokane International.

"I get to tell her, okay?"

"I think Tanner should do it, sweetheart," Joanna suggested gently.

"But Nicole and I are best friends. You can't expect me to keep something like this from her, something we planned since that night we all went to the Pink Palace. If it weren't for us, you two wouldn't even know each other."

Kristen's eyes were round and pleading as she stared up at Tanner and Joanna.

"You two would have been cast adrift in a sea of loneliness if it hadn't been for me and Nicole," she added melodramatically.

"All right, all right," Tanner said with a sigh. "You can tell her."

Poised at the railing by the window of the terminal, Kristen eagerly studied each passenger who stepped inside. The minute Nicole appeared, Kristen flew into her friend's arms as though it had been years since they'd last seen each other instead of a week.

Joanna watched the unfolding scene with a quiet sense of happiness. Nicole let out a squeal of delight and gripped her friend around the shoulders, and the two jumped frantically up and down.

"From her reaction, I'd guess that she's happy about our decision," Tanner said to Joanna.

"Dad, Dad!" Nicole raced up to her father, and hugged him with all her might. "It's so good to be home. I missed you. I missed everyone," she said, looking at Joanna.

Tanner returned the hug. "It's good to have you home, cupcake."

"But everything exciting happened while I was away," she said, pouting a little. "Gee, if I'd known you were finally going to get rolling with Mrs. Parsons, I'd never have left."

Joanna smiled blandly at the group of people standing around them.

"Don't be mad," Kristen said. "It was a now-or-never situation, with Mom standing there in her pajamas and everything."

Now it was Tanner's turn to notice the interested group of onlookers.

"Yes, well, you needn't feel left out. I saved the best part for you," Tanner said, taking a beautiful solitaire diamond ring out of his pocket. "I wanted you to be here for this." He reached for Joanna's hand, looking into her eyes, as he slowly, reverently, slipped it onto her finger. "I love you, Joanna, and I'll be the happiest man alive if you marry me."

"I love you, Tanner," she said in a soft voice filled with joy.

"Does this mean we're going to be sisters from now on?" Kristen shrieked, clutching her best friend's hand.

"Yup," Nicole answered. "It's what we always wanted."

With their arms wrapped around one another's shoulders, the girls headed toward the baggage-claim area.

"Yours and mine," Joanna said, watching their two daughters.

Tanner slid his arm around her waist and smiled into her eyes.

* * * * *

If you enjoyed this story, you will love *New York Times* bestselling author Brenda Novak's Silver Springs series, set in a picturesque small California town where even the hardest hearts learn to love again.

Turn the page for a taste of this wonderful series, with a short story featuring Mack Amos and Natasha Sharp, who first met in *Discovering You* (Whiskey Creek series) and whose story will continue in *When I Found You* (Silver Springs series). No need to read any of the books to understand the others— but if you have, you may find some fun Easter eggs (even if it is Christmas)!

Enjoy

Home for the Holidays

by

Brenda Novak

HOME FOR THE HOLIDAYS

Brenda Novak

One

To Natasha Sharp, nothing said Christmas like Victorian Days. She couldn't help smiling as she tasted the sweet yet salty kettle corn she and her mother had just purchased from a nearby vendor, something she hadn't had in years, and paused to admire the colored lights adorning the quaint shops and old-fashioned, Western-style boardwalk that ran the length of Main Street. The sight of the porch and yard of Little Mary's Bed & Breakfast, a historic building from the late-nineteenth century, jammed with noisy revelers wearing heavy jackets and scarves while drinking hot cider or eating homemade sugar cookies, reminded her of the type of idyllic scene you'd find in a snow globe. If only she could make white flakes swirl gently onto the people as well as into the valleys of the roof and along the banisters of the building before falling thickly to the ground, the picture would be perfect.

Real snow wasn't likely, though. Whiskey Creek rarely received more than a dusting.

"What are you doing? Why'd you stop?" her mother asked, turning back in surprise.

At forty-one, Anya Sharp was only sixteen years older than Natasha, but hard living was beginning to change the fact that they used to look more like sisters—hard living and substance abuse. Although Anya didn't seem to be high tonight—*thank goodness*—she had the voice of a longtime smoker and the stench of cigarettes clung to her hair and clothes, impinging on the pleasant aromas of gingerbread and roasted chestnuts.

"Just taking it all in," Natasha said.

Trying to keep her bleached-blond hair from whipping around her face, thanks to a stiff, cold wind, Anya gave her a funny look. "Taking *what* in? The festival?"

Apparently, Anya didn't feel the same nostalgia. Although she was now divorced, she still lived in Whiskey Creek, so it was easy to take the innocence of the small, California Gold Rush town, nestled in the foothills of the Sierra Nevada Mountains, for granted. Whiskey Creek hosted Victorian Days every year, usually the week before Christmas, but Natasha hadn't been back, not during the holidays, since leaving for college six years ago. She was trying to get through med school at UCLA, and she had a job at a nearby hospital working as an orderly. The demands of both were especially high in December, so she typically visited during the summer.

"Yes, the festival," she said. "The buildings. The people." Natasha had such fond memories of this place, which was ironic. When Anya had married for the third time and told her they'd be moving yet again, Natasha hadn't been happy about it. Barely a sophomore in high school, she'd already lived in so many cities and towns, and with so many "fathers"—both those who'd married her mother and those who hadn't—that she'd almost rebelled.

She would have, if she'd had anywhere else to go. But she didn't know who her biological father was. For that matter, neither did her mother. Given the type of encounters Natasha had witnessed as a child, she had little hope he'd be anyone she'd welcome into her life and had never tried to learn more about him. Dealing with Anya was difficult enough. She didn't need another deadbeat parent. But since Anya's behavior had alienated any extended family years ago, and Natasha had no father or anyone else to step in and help her, she'd had no choice except to move with her mother.

Anya had insisted that J. T. Amos, her new husband then, would take care of them as soon as he got out of prison, that this place would be better than all the others, and for once, she'd been right. Not that Anya or J.T. could assume any of the credit. It wasn't what *they* did that had changed Natasha's life. It was J.T.'s adult sons who'd made the difference. If Rod, Grady and Mack—the three brothers who'd still been living in the house where all five boys grew up— hadn't looked after her until she could graduate, this town would've been like all the others.

"Do you think you'll ever move back here?" her mother asked.

"Maybe. One day." She spoke as though it was merely a possibility, even though she'd always planned to come back to Whiskey Creek. When she closed her eyes at night, *this* was where she dreamed of setting up her pediatric practice.

But in those dreams, she was also married to Mack, the youngest of the Amos brothers—and he didn't seem to have the same dream.

"I think the Amoses, especially Mack, expect you to move back when you finish school," her mother said as they started walking again.

Natasha said nothing. If that was the case, no one had ever told *her*.

"Are you going to see any of J.T.'s sons while you're here?"

They passed a guy Natasha vaguely recognized from high school. She nodded to say hello before responding. "I've seen them already."

Her mother's head snapped up and her gaze sharpened. "When?"

Natasha had expected this reaction. She knew her mother wouldn't like that she hadn't been included. "Night before last."

"But... I thought you didn't get in until yesterday."

"Actually, it was the night before."

"Where'd you stay?"

She'd stayed at Mack and Grady's—Rod was now married and had moved out—in her old room, where she'd spent the happiest years of her life. It had been wonderful to be back, to feel that sense of home. And she'd been *so* excited to see Mack. Each time she came back to Whiskey Creek, she thought something might change between them. That he'd finally act on what she believed he felt. That he'd realize they were meant to be together. But he'd been as careful as ever to avoid saying or doing anything that could be construed as romantic.

Apparently, he didn't love her the way she loved him. Or he wouldn't let himself. He was hung up on the nine-year age difference between them and the fact that his brothers considered her a kid sister.

"Where do you think I stayed?" she asked. "In my old room."

"Why didn't you call me? Why'd you lead me to believe you didn't reach town until you came to my house?"

Natasha pretended to be too busy navigating the crowd to maintain eye contact. "I didn't lead you to believe anything."

"But... You had to know that's what I would assume."

"Does it matter? Now that Dylan, Aaron and Rod are married, they have so much extra room at the house. And I knew I'd be seeing you soon."

Anya scowled. "Oh, I get it. Well, I'm sorry I can't provide what they can."

Hearing her mother's injured tone, Natasha took her

hand. "Oh, stop. Your house might be a little cramped, but I don't mind sleeping in your bedroom." She didn't mention the many strangers who filled the living room almost every night, using the place as a flophouse. They made her uncomfortable, but her mother called them friends.

"I would've liked to go to the Amoses with you," she said. "Why didn't you invite me?"

They'd been polite enough to include Anya in the past, but Natasha knew in her heart that they'd rather not have her around. So she'd come to town before her mother was expecting her, and she'd gone to visit the Amos brothers alone. That way she wouldn't have to ask them—again—if she could bring Anya. And it had worked out so well. She'd really enjoyed not having to worry about what her mother might say or do. Anya embarrassed her too often. "I didn't think it would be a big deal to you. You live here. You must see them all the time."

"I run into them now and then, especially J.T. I can't seem to avoid *him*. But it's different since we divorced. I miss the boys, would like to spend more time with them." They paused to let another group cut through to reach a booth selling clam chowder. "What'd you do while you were there?"

"Just visited," she replied, but that wasn't strictly true. Mack had invited his brothers and their wives and children to come over and see her and have a big Christmas dinner. Everyone had brought a dish, and she'd exchanged gifts with them.

Some carolers, dressed in Dickens garb, were singing "God Rest Ye Merry Gentlemen." Natasha kept hold of her mother's hand as they navigated around the foursome.

"Was J.T. there?" her mother asked, raising her voice to be heard over the music.

"No." At least that was true.

"Where was he?"

"At his house, I suppose. I swung by, once I was on the way to your place, to drop off his Christmas present, but we didn't talk long. Looked like he'd just rolled out of bed."

Creases formed in her mother's forehead. "You gave J.T. a present? After how he's treated me?"

"The way you guys fought? I think you both treated each other pretty poorly. Besides, it was just a tin of candy." She'd brought some of her homemade fudge for her mother, too.

"Did he have a gift for you?"

Despite everything her mother had to say about J.T., Natasha could tell Anya still cared about him, or she wouldn't be so acutely interested in him and his sons. Natasha also suspected that Anya didn't find it entirely unpleasant to run into her ex. Maybe they were even still hooking up now and then. Regardless, they had to see each other quite often, since they traveled in the same circles and had so many mutual friends. "Of course not. But I wasn't expecting a gift."

"Since when has he ever had the money to give anything to anyone?" her mother asked bitterly.

Anya's mother had no room to talk. She hadn't made much of her life, either. But Natasha bit her tongue.

As they stopped to check out some jewelry and Natasha held a pair of silver hoops to her ears to see how they'd look against her honey-blond hair, she hoped Anya would forget about the Amoses. But her mother brought them up again as soon as she put the earrings back and they continued to meander down the row of vendors.

"I bet Mack and his brothers had a gift for you."

They'd gone in together to buy her a sweater and a new smartphone, since hers was ancient and the screen was shattered. She'd made the switch this morning. But she preferred that her mother not know about the more expensive part of their gift. It would only make Anya jealous. "They got me a sweater," she volunteered before her mother could ask for details.

"That's it? From five grown men? Three with wives? That surprises me. They have money. And you're their baby sister."

Natasha winced. She hated it when her mother or anyone else referred to her as part of the Amos family, because it meant that Mack would never view her in any other way. "No, I'm not. We didn't grow up together. And you and J.T. were only married for what…eight years? That hardly makes us related."

"You can say that after the way they took you in and looked out for you?"

Natasha gaped at her. "They took us *both* in because we had nowhere else to live. We'd just been kicked out of that crummy apartment in Los Banos when you married J.T. So you contacted Dylan and asked if we could meet him and his brothers at some steakhouse—that one in Sutter Creek, remember? Then, once we got there and you announced that we were their new family, you asked if we could move in until J.T. got out of prison."

"That was J.T.'s house," Anya said.

Natasha hugged the bag of kettle corn to her body so she could use her hands to pull her jacket tighter. "Not really. Not anymore. He would've lost it when he went to prison if not for Dylan." At only eighteen, the oldest Amos son had taken over his father's auto body shop and finished raising his four younger brothers. He hadn't done a perfect job as their guardian, but she didn't know a kid who could've done better at that age. He'd loved his brothers fiercely, and he'd worked hard to keep them out of foster care. Natasha had so much respect for Dylan.

"Well, they wouldn't have had it if J.T. hadn't bought it in the first place," Anya said.

"I think he owed them the house, don't you?" J.T. had gone to prison for knifing a guy in a bar, just for spouting off. Allowing his sons to take over payments on the house where they lived so they'd still have a roof over their heads was the least he could do.

"He wasn't himself when he did what he did, Natasha. His wife had just overdosed on depression meds."

Natasha was well aware of that. Mack was the one who'd found her. "I understand. But what about his responsibility to his children? Mack was only six when that happened."

"Not everyone can live their life as perfectly as you do," her mother grumbled.

Anya's defense of J.T. served as further proof that her mother was still in love with him. "I've never claimed to be perfect," Natasha said. "But I've never stabbed anyone, either."

A vendor selling wooden signs with various inscriptions came up. The Tanner Residence; Here Lies the Last Trespasser. May He RIP; No Trespoopers with a circle and a line through a dog taking a dump. Natasha chuckled at a few as her mother pulled out a cigarette. Anya was about to light up when Natasha nudged her.

"I don't think you can smoke here, Mom."

"Why not? I'm outside!"

"There're too many people."

Muttering a curse for all the "assholes" who tried to tell her what to do with her own body, she said, *"Fine!"* and put it away.

Setting her jaw so she wouldn't point out that it wasn't just her body at risk, Natasha stopped to admire some handmade ornaments.

Anya didn't pretend to have any interest. She rarely bothered with the holidays, usually didn't even put up a tree. Folding her arms, she cocked one hip while she waited, as though she was irritated or bored or both. It didn't take much to make her mother's mood deteriorate.

"So… How'd they treat you?" she asked once Natasha was ready to move on.

"Who?"

"The Amos brothers."

"You're talking about them again? *Why?*" They'd told Natasha they were planning to be here at the festival. She and her mother could bump into them at any moment, and she didn't want to be discussing them when it happened.

"Just answer the question. I'm curious. Was Mack excited to see you?"

Mack had been nice. But that was nothing unusual. He'd always taken a special interest in her. When she'd lived with him and Grady and Rod, he'd enrolled her in dance lessons, shown up for any events she was involved in at school, helped her with homework whenever he could, taught her how to play chess and tried to include her in whatever he did—if that was four-wheeling, seeing a movie or target shooting in the mountains—when the catty girls her age shut her out, which happened quite often. She knew he cared about her *a lot*. But he'd been careful not to let their relationship drift toward anything beyond kindness and support. "No more than Dylan and the others."

Her mother peered closely at her. "Are you upset about that?"

Shoving another handful of kettle corn in her mouth, Natasha averted her face. "Why would that upset me?"

Anya grabbed her arm. "Oh, come on. Quit pretending. I know how you feel about Mack. We all do. So does he."

Embarrassed, she looked around but didn't see anyone she recognized. Was Anya right? Had she been that transparent?

She supposed she had. She'd been so head over heels it'd

been difficult to hide her feelings. She was embarrassed about that now, especially when she remembered how she'd behaved the night before she left for college, when she'd slipped into Mack's room and offered him her virginity. She'd been nineteen at the time, old enough, but after she'd stripped off her clothes, he'd made her put them back on. His rejection had broken her heart, but the way he'd hauled her up against the wall and kissed her before shoving her out of his room suggested she hadn't been entirely wrong in assuming he'd want what she had to offer.

That certainly hadn't been a brotherly kiss.

It was, however, all she'd ever gotten.

"I'm over him," she lied. "I've been seeing this other guy named Ace."

"The *bartender* you told me about?"

"There's nothing wrong with being a bartender." That her mother, of all people, could say that in such a derogatory tone shocked Natasha. "Ace loves his job."

"Who wouldn't? He hardly has to work."

He'd mentioned the beneficial hours. Working part-time made it possible for him to surf and do plenty of other things he enjoyed. She suspected his wealthy parents helped him out; he couldn't go boating and jet skiing and do all the other things he talked about on his income alone. But he'd never specifically mentioned that. And who was she to judge? He seemed to have ambition, talked about owning his own bar someday.

"Do you think it'll get serious?"

She couldn't imagine it would. The only man she'd ever wanted was Mack. But she pretended otherwise. "Maybe. We've only been dating for a couple of months, so we're not exclusive, but we… We like each other."

Her mother eyed her shrewdly. "Mack's a fool to let anything stand in his way."

"Can we stop talking about Mack?" she asked in exasperation. "I'm sure he'll be happy enough without me. After all, he's never lacked for female attention." Although he'd rarely had a steady girlfriend, there were plenty of women who'd shown interest. She could vividly remember how heartbroken she'd felt whenever he brought one home.

"But you're the woman he wants."

She pictured the tall, muscular, rugged man she loved and remembered how badly she'd hoped he'd come to her room last night. "Even if that's true, people are complicated. And the way we met, my age at the time, your involvement with his father—I can understand why he's holding back."

"That's all bullshit," her mother insisted. "You could both be happy if only he'd quit fighting his feelings. I've watched him whenever you've been around. Last summer, when we went to the lake, you should've seen how his eyes followed you in that swimsuit when you weren't looking. I don't care what he says. He's in love with you."

Natasha wished she could believe that, but he'd never acted on those feelings, not in the way she wanted him to. "I'm fine," she said. "I still have two years of med school left and then my residency, which will take another three years."

Anya didn't respond. She'd recognized a friend and turned to greet her.

Relieved that her mother was currently distracted, and hoping that was all she'd have to hear about Mack or any of the other Amos men, Natasha was waiting for Anya when she heard someone call her name and looked up to see Dylan pointing at her from across the street. His wife, Cheyenne, his son, Kellan, who was seven, Grady and Mack were with him.

She'd known she'd run into one or more of the Amoses eventually and was glad to have found them. Even though it was more and more painful to be around Mack, at least she knew they hadn't been close enough to overhear anything her mother had said.

They smiled and waved, and she did the same. But the moment her gaze locked with Mack's, it felt as if they were the only two people on earth.

For her, it'd always been that way.

Then he said something to the others and started across the street toward her.

Two

As soon as Mack joined them, Anya nudged Natasha. "Like a bee to a flower," she muttered.

Natasha gave her mother a dirty look. Why did Anya have to embarrass her like that?

"What'd she say?" Mack asked.

"Nothing," Natasha replied. "My mom was just trying to be funny."

"I said it's cold tonight." Anya's grin made it clear she hadn't said that at all.

Mack glanced between them, but was wise enough not to press the issue.

"Where're Dylan and the others going?" Natasha asked, eager to take the conversation in a more stable direction.

"They're hungry and the Rotary Club's selling pulled pork sandwiches."

Anya slipped her arm through his as they joined the flow of people in the street. Sometimes she tried to act like Mack's stepmother, even though he was an adult when she'd married his father. Other times she tried to act like a sister or cousin or something, since she was actually between Aaron and Rod in age, much younger than J.T. And sometimes, especially if she was drunk or high, she flirted with them shamelessly, making it obvious that she'd be willing to become a lot more, which had to make them uncomfortable. It certainly humiliated Natasha. "You didn't want one?"

He didn't pull away from Anya, but Natasha couldn't help wondering if he wished he could. "I've already eaten."

So was it merely for practical reasons that he'd joined them? Because he didn't want to wait in a long line?

Natasha could never quite decide if she meant as much to him as it occasionally seemed. That was something she'd struggled with from the beginning.

Either way, they'd spent so much time together before she left for college that it would've been far more unusual if he'd ignored her. She was just glad he was willing to suffer her mother's company in order to be with her again, especially since she had to go back to LA tomorrow. The hospital where she worked was understaffed, and she lived on a shoestring budget, so she needed to earn as much as she could.

"Want some kettle corn?" She offered him the bag and he took it and scooped out a large handful.

"Have you seen the photo booth?" he asked as he popped a few kernels into his mouth.

"Not yet. Where is it?"

"Down by the Christmas tree in the park. They're doing those old-time photos again, like the one we took your sophomore year."

She'd kept that picture on her dresser until she'd moved out. It was still one of her favorites. In it, she was dressed as a barmaid and sat on a barrel, her hair twisted up and decorated with a long feather plume, while Mack stood behind her wearing a sheriff's star on a leather vest and a fake handlebar mustache that didn't quite match his dark hair. Grady and Rod had posed on either side of them dressed like regular cowboys drinking a bottle of whiskey. She laughed whenever she looked at the tough expression on Mack's face in that photograph. She knew there were people who had seen that expression when he wasn't joking. But he'd always been gentle with her, had gone above and beyond to keep her safe and happy.

He was even the one who'd tried to have "the talk" with her. She'd never forget the night she announced that she'd been invited to homecoming and would likely be out all night. After the others had gone to bed, he'd knocked on her door and hemmed and hawed about school and the auto body shop and anything else he could think of before he managed to work up to the topic he'd come to address.

"I want you to know that…that this boy you're going out with might try to… Well, boys your age are just beginning to feel…" At that point, he'd shifted uncomfortably and cleared his throat before starting over. "What I'm trying to say is that this boy might attempt to do something you may or may not want him to do."

"Like what?" She'd known exactly where he was going with this. A girl couldn't grow up with a mother like Anya without learning a fair bit about physical intimacy. She'd seen things that would shock most adults—not the best example for a child to have when it came to sexuality, which was obviously what he was trying to rectify.

She'd blinked at him, keeping her eyes wide and innocent while awaiting his answer, and that was when he'd caught on that she found the conversation—and his attempt to have it—funny. "You know exactly what I'm talking about," he'd grumbled with a scowl.

"Sex."

"Yes."

"You don't want me to sleep with Jason."

"I want you to think about it, be prepared, be smart."

"What's to think about?" she'd asked.

His eyebrows had shot up at this response. "What do you

mean? There's *a lot* to think about. You're only sixteen. It would be much better if you waited until you were older."

"Because *you* want to have sex with me."

His face had gone beet red. Instead of committing himself one way or the other, however, he'd said, "Because sex is much better when you're in love. And there are other things to consider—like venereal disease, pregnancy, your reputation."

"My *reputation*?"

"Yes. Gossip could make you a pariah at school."

She'd shrugged. "With a mom like mine, I'm already a pariah at school. I can't believe I even got asked to this stupid dance."

"I'm glad you did—and that you're going. I want you to enjoy it." He'd worried about her when the other kids were being unkind.

"Just don't have sex," she'd volunteered, summing it all up.

He'd sighed as he shoved a hand through his hair, which had been longer in those days than it was now. "Basically. But if you're not going to listen to me, you need to make sure he wears a condom, at least."

"Should I take one in my purse?" She'd known he'd *hate* the idea of her carrying around a condom, but she was always needling him, trying to figure out if he wanted her the same way she wanted him. He pretended he didn't, but she could feel the powerful attraction between them. Maybe she was young and naive, but she couldn't be wrong about that. Or…could she?

"Just…be careful, okay?" he'd said.

"Do you want to give me a condom?" she'd pressed.

He'd waved her off. "Forget I said anything," he'd replied in exasperation and went out and shut the door.

She still chuckled whenever she thought about that encounter. She hadn't had a mother who was paying any attention to her, and she'd never had a father, so he'd stepped in to fill whatever roles he could. He'd even taken her to the store to buy her a new dress for the dance so she wouldn't have to be so different, no less than anyone else, but finding one he considered modest enough hadn't been easy.

"Should we get another picture?" she asked as he returned the kettle corn.

"*I* think you should," Anya piped up. "Wait until Mack sees how well you fill out that waitress costume now."

"Mom!" Natasha gasped.

"What?" Her mother let go of Mack to be able to spread her hands in an innocent gesture. "Look at that curvy body of yours. You're gorgeous! I'm sure he's noticed."

A muscle moved in Mack's cheek. "I'd be happy to get another picture," he said as if that last exchange had never taken place, and they walked past the carolers again to reach the booth that said "McGee's Old-Time Photos."

Three

Mack knew he should've stayed with his brothers, Cheyenne and his nephew. Anya was difficult to take, and each time he saw Natasha, now so grown up and in command of her life, it only got more difficult not to imagine things he had no business imagining. Last night, knowing she was under the same roof made it impossible for him to sleep. He'd almost gone down the hall to her room half a dozen times.

Instead, he'd tossed and turned in frustration and indecision. He wanted her, and he was fairly certain she still wanted him. When she was younger, she'd done everything she could to get him into bed. She was far less obvious these days, but he sensed that, even now, she wondered where they stood, whether his feelings ever crossed into that territory.

So why couldn't he act on his desire? She was certainly old enough by now to give him informed consent.

He'd asked himself that over and over again while staring up at the ceiling, but the reasons were good ones. Their relationship had never been clearly defined. They weren't brother and sister. They weren't just friends. And they'd never been lovers. But she'd always meant a great deal to him, and he knew that once he let the relationship move in that direction, there'd be no going back.

What if they didn't make it? They'd lose the love and support they gave each other now. That would hurt him, without question, but at least he'd still have his brothers and the business to fall back on. He was afraid of what it might do to her. She'd already suffered far too many losses in her life. Would it really be smart to take that chance?

Besides, Mack understood what other people would think and say. They'd accuse him of having taken advantage of her from the beginning. After what he and his brothers had endured, thanks to his mother's suicide and the stabbing that sent his father to prison, he didn't want to give the people in Whiskey Creek any more reason to disrespect him or his family. He was part owner of a successful business in this small town, and that business supported them all—him, his brothers and their families and J.T., too.

He sent Anya a sly glance as they weaved through the crowd. If he and Natasha ever got together, it would also bring Anya back into his life and the lives of his brothers, and they were all relieved to be rid of her. Drug and alcohol issues aside, she had to be the most annoying person in the world. Mack would never be able to understand how J.T. had put up with her.

But J.T. was hard to put up with, too, so there was that.

He stopped to buy another beer before they reached the photo booth, and while they were there they happened to see Aaron, his wife, Presley, and their ten-year-old son and two younger daughters in the next line over, waiting to get some candied peanuts.

"Hey, what's going on?" Aaron asked.

"Not much." Mack offered to get him and Presley a beer, too, but they declined.

Natasha and Anya visited with Presley until Aaron was

able to get the kids their peanuts. Then Natasha asked someone to take a group photo of them all and, as they were saying their goodbyes, Presley told Anya about a great wine-tasting booth she and the family were planning to visit next and invited her to join them.

Anya was obviously shocked to be invited, but she readily agreed, and they started off in the opposite direction.

"Why do you think Presley invited my mother?" Natasha asked, once they were gone.

"I guess she thought your mother would enjoy it," he said, but he knew Presley hadn't done it for that reason. The secretive smile his sister-in-law had cast him just before she walked away suggested she was doing him a favor. Although he probably would've denied it had she asked him—he'd denied a lot of things where Natasha was concerned—Presley knew he'd love to spend some time alone with Natasha before she had to go home tomorrow.

But he wasn't entirely convinced that being alone with her put him in the best position. He was already experiencing the effects of what he'd had to drink so far tonight, felt his resolve and his restraint slipping, especially as they took the old-fashioned picture and the photographer suggested Natasha—wearing a boa with her barmaid costume—sit on his lap. As he held her, wearing cowboy attire but no fake mustache this time, it felt so natural to have her close that it was almost impossible not to continue touching her afterward.

Once they received their copies of the photo, they talked and laughed about a lot of different things as they made their way through the rest of the booths. Although Mack enjoyed the food and the festivities of Victorian Days, he had no real interest in the crafts and various trinkets. Natasha seemed to enjoy looking at all the objects people were selling, however, and he was happy just to be with her.

They returned to the park because she wanted another picture, this one a selfie of them in front of the big tree. After that, they meandered away from the festival, where there were no more lights or people. He'd always been impressed by how smart she was, but as he listened to her talk he was also impressed by how far she'd come, especially after the start she'd received in life. She was no longer the angry teen who'd gotten tattoos without her mother's permission, shaved her head one day on a whim, probably to let the kids at school know she didn't care about their rejection, and pierced her nipples—something he saw the night she came into his room and stripped off her clothes. He'd never been able to forget that sight—or how hard it had been to tell her to put her clothes back on—and it was something he couldn't quit thinking about right now. Were those piercings still there? She would always be nine years younger, but it was becoming very apparent that she was a woman now, no longer a girl. And the maturity of her mind matched the maturity of her body...

"What is it?" she said when he couldn't help grinning at her.

"I'm *so* proud of you," he told her. "I hope you know that."

She didn't respond. She just slipped her hand in his and the way she smiled made it impossible for him not to grasp on. There was no one to see them, so he didn't have to worry about that. Still, he knew he'd be stupid to get anything started while she was in school. Even if they could overcome all the other obstacles, they couldn't be together for another five or six *years*. She'd already explained how long it was going to take to become a pediatrician.

Right now, however, all that seemed to matter was this moment.

She continued to talk, but his heart had begun to pound

as soon as her fingers slipped through his, and he couldn't hear anything above it. He'd never stopped wanting her despite all the years he'd been so careful not to let her know it.

He knew he should probably stay away from her. But he also knew that was a fight he was going to lose—and he was going to lose it tonight.

The small building that housed the police station was on their right. Impulsively, he pulled her around the corner, just in case someone came looking for them, and kissed her like he'd always wanted to kiss her—with every bit of the desire he felt.

Finally.

Natasha hadn't lost her virginity until the end of her first year in college. She'd been twenty, at least three years behind most other girls she knew. Her roommates had been shocked when she told them she'd never been with a man, never even had a steady boyfriend. After watching how her mother handled relationships, Natasha had been—and still was—determined to do things differently.

She'd also been waiting for Mack. She'd fully believed they'd be together eventually. She couldn't imagine her life any other way. But when the contact they had remained as circumspect as ever, she'd begun to wonder if she'd misunderstood. Maybe he didn't feel anything. After all, he was the type who'd step up to take care of some poor girl who'd been overlooked and neglected just because it was the right thing to do—sort of like bringing home a stray puppy. He'd been good to her in so many ways. He didn't owe her his heart, too.

Once she'd realized she was taking too much for granted, she'd decided not to put her life on hold for him. She'd started dating more often and had been with three or four men over the years. Her first experience was pretty unremarkable, but her sex life had improved since. She'd slept with Ace, the guy she was dating now, for the first time two weeks ago, and she'd enjoyed it. She'd even told herself it was *amazing*.

But nothing could compare to this. Now she knew what real fulfillment and satisfaction felt like. It was Mack who was kissing her. Mack whose muscular body was pressed firmly against her own. Mack whose erection she could feel as they strained to get even closer.

When he lifted his head, she was afraid he'd pull away and it would all be over. She was tempted to cling to him, to try to crack through that warrior-like mentality to expose his true emotions. She was certain he felt *something*.

But she refused to be the grasping, desperate child she'd once been—far too eager for any kind of love, especially his. That smacked too much of her mother.

She tried to catch her breath while waiting to see what he'd do next. She expected an avalanche of disappointment, was already preparing herself.

But then he raised his hand, and one finger gently outlined her cheek. "Do you have any idea how beautiful you are? It makes me weak just to look at you."

"I don't care about that," she said, staring up into his dark eyes. "I don't care about anything except whether or not you want me."

His chest lifted with a deep breath, and he said, "Damn, Tash. You have no idea how much."

Those words sounded torn from him, as though he'd been reluctant to make that admission. But they meant the world to her. "Then what are you waiting for? Make love to me—at last."

"Do you really know what you're asking for?" he asked. "I'm nine years older—"

"The age difference is meaningless to me," she broke in. "It always has been."

"It's not that simple," he argued.

"Maybe not to you." Rising up on tiptoe, she caught his face in her hands and used her tongue to lightly outline his lips. "But it is to me. You're all I've ever wanted."

With a groan, he held the back of her head in his palm as he met her tongue, immediately taking the kiss to the same desperate, hungry place of moments before, and when he lifted his head again, she could tell he'd come to a decision. "Okay. Let's go."

Four

They were so eager to come together they almost fell inside the motel room the moment Mack managed to unlock the door, and they started kissing again immediately, before they could even get the door closed. Natasha had never felt such a rush of pleasure or such an upwelling of desire. This night had ramped up like a roller coaster, climbing slowly to the first big drop—and now she was about to come screaming down the other side.

"You taste better than I even imagined," she admitted, breathlessly.

"Let me see you," he said. "Take off your clothes, just like you did for me before."

She slanted him an injured glance. "You mean when you rejected me?"

"Believe me, that hurt me more than it did you. For weeks, even months afterward, I was tortured by the memory of what I'd missed. That night is still one of the things I think about all the time—and imagine handling differently."

"So you did want me in that way."

"How could you not know that?" he asked.

"You've done an admirable job of pretending otherwise."

"Everything I've ever done has proven how much you

mean to me. But we were living together under…odd circumstances. I couldn't allow myself to… I didn't want to feel as though I was taking advantage of you in some way."

"Even though I *asked* you to make love to me?"

"You know how complicated this is."

She did. But she was no longer too young, and she felt they could overcome anything, if they wanted to be together badly enough. "It doesn't *have* to be that complicated," she said, but she was scared to cross this line, too. Her love for Mack made her completely vulnerable, stripped away the defenses she'd spent most of her life building.

She almost told him she needed more reassurance. But she didn't want to ruin this night by bringing her emotional baggage into it. She was going to do the opposite—let go completely and just…trust.

Drawing a deep, calming breath, she lifted her sweater over her head and unsnapped her bra.

She heard him suck his breath in between his teeth as soon as he saw what she'd revealed.

"This would go faster if you helped me," she teased.

He grinned. "I like watching." His eyes were hungrier than she'd ever seen them. She'd barely started to unzip her jeans when he stepped forward as though he couldn't wait any longer. "They're gone," he said as his hands circled her bare waist. "I wondered."

"What're gone?"

"The piercings."

"Oh. Yeah. And some of the tattoos, too. The ones I could afford to have removed." He knew that, of course, because she'd focused on her arms first, but she was nervous and that made her talk just to talk. "I'll do more over time. I don't think the kind of tattoos I had would look very respectable on a doctor."

His hand gently cupped her right breast. "You're beautiful with or without them—the most beautiful woman I've ever seen."

As he began to kiss her breasts, she dropped her head back and closed her eyes. "This is beyond anything I could've imagined," she whispered. "Words can't even explain it."

"I agree." His hands were trembling by the time they'd stripped off the rest of their clothes. She could feel it when he cupped her face and looked down into her eyes. "Whatever this is, it's bigger than I am," he said and carried her to the bed.

Natasha woke up alone. Although Mack had spent the night with her, he'd had to get up early for work. Amos Auto Body was always slammed. But she was happier than she'd ever been—and even more in love with Mack. He'd offered to take the morning off until she had to leave, but she knew how difficult that would be to explain to his brothers. He'd be leaving them high and dry with work that needed to get done, and she had to spend some time with her mother, anyway. Anya would be hurt if she didn't.

She closed her eyes, allowing herself to remember what it'd been like to finally have Mack inside her. It certainly hadn't been a disappointment. She smiled dreamily as she relived his kisses, the care he'd taken to make sure she was satisfied, his thoughtfulness in letting her know their time together meant something to him, too. Since she had to leave today, they hadn't wanted to waste a second, so when they weren't making love, they talked or simply dozed in each other's arms. Natasha didn't think they'd slept for more than two hours all told, although she'd fallen back asleep after he left.

Her phone signaled a text. With a yawn, she gathered the energy to roll over so she could reach it on the nightstand.

It was Mack. She pushed the pillows against the head-board and pulled the sheet higher while she read.

Last night was…wow. I wish you didn't have to leave.

So do I. But I come back whenever I can. You know that.

This summer? That sounds like forever. Do you really have to live in LA for another five or six years?

She frowned. It sounded too long to her, too. But she couldn't give up on becoming a doctor. She was committed to it, knew that was what she wanted to be. And she'd put too much blood, sweat and tears into getting this far. The past six years didn't change anything. The next five or six won't, either.

He didn't comment on that. A few minutes went by before he sent her another message. Are you sure you don't want me to take you to lunch before you go?

No. I need to see my mom. How are you able to work? Aren't you exhausted?

Too pumped up to feel it yet. Every time I close my eyes, I see you, I feel you, I smell you. I could spend another week, at least, with you in that motel.

You'd have to buy a lot more condoms.

I'm willing to get as many as we need.

She laughed. He hadn't mentioned whether he was going to tell his brothers that they were now seeing each other. And she hadn't asked. She'd instinctively avoided topics that might pull them back to reality too soon or put a damper on their time together.

I'm glad I twisted your arm into sleeping with me.

Whatever happens, last night was worth it.

:)

Her mother called, interrupting their conversation. Mack seemed to be gone for the moment, anyway—probably had a new customer. "Hello?"

"Where are you?" Anya demanded.

Natasha hesitated. What'd happened with Mack was still so new. If they were getting together—as she hoped and believed they would—she wanted to be sure he had the chance to break it to his family first. She knew that wouldn't be easy, or the way they'd met wouldn't have been a problem in the first place. "I'm about to get some coffee at Black Gold. Would you like me to get you a cup?" she asked, dodging the question entirely.

"No, I'm fine. Why didn't you come home last night?"

"It was late. I didn't think you'd miss me."

"Did you stay at Mack and Grady's again?"

"There's an empty bedroom there for me," she said, still trying not to lie outright.

"Was it fun, being with Mack?"

"It was." That had to be the biggest understatement of her life. She'd never had a night quite like last night. But she hoped her response came across as normal, even casual.

"What'd you do after I left?"

She pulled Mack's pillow to her face and breathed deeply, trying to inhale the scent of him—to hold on to *some* aspect of what they'd enjoyed together now that it was over. "After we left the old-time photo booth, we just wandered around. What about you?"

"Went to the wine booth Presley wanted to show me."

"How was it?"

"Great. Presley even paid for my ticket."

Natasha couldn't help being embarrassed about that. Anya had never been good about paying her own way. But she didn't say anything.

"I tried calling you after Aaron, Presley and the kids went home," her mother continued. "But I couldn't reach you."

Once she was with Mack, she hadn't checked her phone. "It was so loud there, I probably didn't hear it ring. Or maybe I was already in bed." She winced, wishing she'd said "asleep" instead of "in bed."

Fortunately, her mother didn't pounce on that unintended but accurate double entendre. "What time do you have to leave?"

"About two."

"You're out of school for the holidays. Can't you stay longer?"

"No. I told you I have to be to work at four in the morning."

"Call in sick."

"I can't. There'd be no one to replace me. But if we hurry, we'll be able to have lunch together before I leave. I'm on my way to your place right now." She had to check out by eleven, and it was almost ten.

"Okay. See you here."

Natasha was about to press the end button when her mother spoke again. "Tash?"

"What?"

"How will you get here? Your car's at my place. I drove last night, remember?"

"Right. I guess you'll have to pick me up."

"At Black Gold Coffee?"

"Yes."

"Now?"

She calculated the time it would take to walk there. Fortunately, it was only a couple of blocks. "In like...fifteen?"

"Are you sure you wouldn't rather have me come to wherever you and Mack spent the night?" her mother asked, her "level with me" tone indicating that she hadn't been fooled at all.

Natasha gripped her phone tighter. "What're you talking about?"

"I went by the house last night, Tash. Grady was there, but you two weren't."

"We must've gotten in after."

"Except that Mack left his truck downtown all night. I saw it. After everyone was gone, it was the only one parked on the street, so it wasn't hard to miss. Does that mean something's finally happened between you two?"

Natasha hoped no one besides her mother had noticed Mack's vehicle. Fortunately, his brothers didn't keep track of him the way her mother kept track of her whenever she came home these days—something Natasha found ironic since Anya paid so little attention to her when she was a teenager. "Nothing happened, Mom."

"You expect me to believe that?" she asked. "With the way he was looking at you last night?"

"I'm telling you nothing happened!" She didn't care if that was a lie. No way did she want Anya to say anything to Mack or make a big deal about it to J.T.—or any of Mack's brothers, for that matter. It was important that Mack not feel any pressure. She'd been completely open and honest with him about her feelings. If they got together, she wanted it to be because he loved her in return, not because he felt obligated.

"You two must've gone somewhere alone last night," her mother insisted.

"So what if we did?" Natasha retorted.

This response was met with a long silence before her mother said, "I'm on your side, you know."

Natasha wanted to say, *"Since when?"* But that was resentment from the past welling up again—something she wrestled with on an ongoing basis.

Taking a deep breath, she assumed a more measured tone. "I appreciate that. I really do. But nothing's changed where Mack's concerned." Not yet, anyway. That would depend on the next few weeks. She understood that a sexual encounter was one thing and making a lifelong commitment was another. "So, can you pick me up at Black Gold Coffee?"

"Sure. Just let me get dressed."

Apparently, her mother was barely out of bed, too. But that came as no surprise. Anya didn't have a job; she lived on government assistance, stayed up late with her deadbeat friends and slept late, too.

After she disconnected, Natasha navigated to the pictures on her new phone. She didn't have many, since she had yet to download most of the data from her old mobile. But she had a few from last night.

She was tempted to make the selfie she'd taken of her and Mack in front of the Christmas tree her screensaver but decided against it and got out of bed.

As she started to dress, she noticed her reflection in the full-length mirror on the wall and paused to take a closer look. Her hair was a tangled mess, her mascara was smeared and she had a red mark on her neck that she wouldn't be able to hide without different clothes—or at least a little concealer. She knew Mack hadn't purposely left that mark, but last night had gotten crazy.

She couldn't show up at Black Gold Coffee, not like this.

It was too busy there. Someone would see her who might mention it to one of Mack's brothers.

She could have Mack come and get her. She knew he'd do it in a heartbeat. But making him leave work would be more obvious than any other option.

With a sigh, she grabbed her phone again and called Anya back. "Okay. Pick me up at Hotel Whiskey Creek."

Her mother didn't even skip a beat. "That's the old one above the Italian place?"

"Yes. Just down from the park. Call me when you get here, and I'll run out."

"I'll be right over."

Fortunately, when Natasha ducked into her mother's car, Anya didn't say anything about how bedraggled she looked or where she'd spent the night. Anya continued to let that stuff go while Natasha picked her way through those who were camped, once again, in her mother's living room. It wasn't until she'd showered and packed, and she and Anya were having lunch at Just Like Mom's—a café that served comfort food—before heading home that she said, "If, for some reason, Mack doesn't follow up on last night..."

Natasha looked up from her food.

"I hope... I hope you won't let it hurt you too badly," her mother finished.

Natasha set her fork down. "You're the one who always insists he loves me."

"I think he *does* love you. But like you said last night, people are complicated. The Amos brothers have been through a lot, so it's natural that they'd guard their hearts. I could see his defenses going up again if you're not around to keep breaking them down."

Natasha wanted to tell her that Mack wouldn't disappoint her. Everything he'd said and done last night—even the messages she'd received today—suggested he was finally getting serious about her. "We'll figure it out," she insisted.

"You will if you move home. He won't be able to resist you then."

Natasha gaped at her. Her mother didn't like her living so far away. Although Natasha didn't believe Anya's motivations were purely mercenary, it was true that she needed things she thought Natasha could help provide. Was this a ploy to get her back? "I can't move home. Not now."

"You could if you really wanted to."

"And give up on everything I've accomplished so far? Give up on becoming a doctor?"

Her mother shrugged. "That's what I'd do. You have a good head on your shoulders. There are a lot of other things you could do. Besides, Mack has money. You won't have to worry about how you're going to live if you marry him."

Natasha refused to expect anyone else to take care of her. That was Anya, not her. "I'm not going to give up my hopes and dreams for any man," she insisted.

Anya pursed her lips. "Okay, but… I hope you don't live to regret that."

Five

"What's wrong? You tired?"

Natasha blinked and straightened. After attending classes and studying all day, it could get difficult to remain as alert as she needed to be at the hospital, especially if it was slow. She knew she wasn't getting enough sleep. But that wasn't what was weighing her down tonight. "Not really," she lied.

Leanne Luttges, one of the nurses she liked best, touched her arm. "You look wiped out. You really need to take better care of yourself."

"You know what med school is like."

"It'll eat you alive if you let it."

Natasha managed a smile to cover the anguish she was feeling inside and headed down the hall. Fortunately, she was about to go on break. She could go outside and sit in her car, where she could eat alone and wouldn't have to worry about anyone remarking on the blank expression on her face or how quiet she'd become. She hadn't heard from Mack for several days. Right after she got home, he'd called her often, but now that it'd been six weeks, that was already changing. She could feel him slipping away from her again. The last time they talked, things seemed pretty much like they'd been before their night at Hotel Whiskey Creek.

They were returning to their old lives, lives that didn't intersect very often, and she didn't know what to do about it. Although he remained as polite, supportive and kind as ever, and she could tell they'd always mean something to each other, he was retreating, which indicated he wasn't going to tell his brothers about the time they'd spent together, wasn't going to pursue the relationship.

For once in her life, Anya had been right.

And it had to be about this...

As she sat in her rattletrap Honda, which was all she could afford, staring glumly at the people coming and going in the parking lot, she checked her phone again, hoping for a missed call from him or maybe a text. She wanted to believe she was wrong about what was happening. But she'd still received nothing, and even if she had, she knew in her heart that it was over—already. All she could do was try to throw up some kind of defense so the disappointment wouldn't crush her.

Her phone rang. She grabbed it, but it wasn't Mack. It was her mother.

Closing her eyes, she dropped the hand that held her phone in her lap while trying to swallow the lump in her throat. She couldn't talk to Anya right now. That would just make everything worse. Her mother was sure to ask about Mack, which would just bring it all up again.

Instead, she sent a text. Can't talk. At work. Everything okay?

Fine. Just missing you. Any word from Mack?

Damn it. That was the first thing Anya went to? Even in a text?

We talk every few days. She hoped her mother would leave it at that, but, of course, she didn't.

And? How's it going between you two?

Apparently, her answer wasn't obvious enough. Was she willing to openly admit it?

She may as well, she decided. She had to face the truth. What good did it do to pretend?

She'd been a fool to think one night in that motel would change anything. We're just friends. Like before.

You've always been more than friends, but I know what you're saying, and I'm sorry. For what it's worth, he's making a big mistake.

I'll be fine, she insisted. But she had no idea if that was true. She didn't think she could feel any more pain than she did. It seemed as though she was moving through a red haze, one in which she could scarcely breathe. But she'd given him all she had that night, offered her heart to him on a silver platter, and, apparently, he didn't want it badly enough.

Ace, the man she'd been dating before, had been asking her out, and she'd been putting him off, claiming she was too busy with school and work. Now, feeling like a fool for almost blowing up their relationship over Mack, she sent him a text. How's it going?

She chewed her peanut butter and jelly sandwich as she awaited his response, but she couldn't taste it. There was no enjoyment to be found in any aspect of life right now, even in her studies. Especially in her studies. It was so difficult to concentrate, she had to reread everything just to gather a small portion of its meaning. Work wasn't any easier. She could barely force herself to show up at the hospital, where her shifts suddenly seemed interminable.

She shoved her sandwich back into the sack only half-eaten. She didn't have the stomach for it, couldn't eat, couldn't sleep.

This is pathetic. She had to create some handholds—fast— or she wasn't going to make it out of the hole she'd fallen into.

Her phone dinged. Ace had responded.

I miss you. When can I see you?

She stared at those words. She had to go on living, couldn't allow Mack or anything else to destroy her. If she'd learned anything from her mother's example, it was that life wasn't for sissies.

I'm off tomorrow night, she wrote back.

Awesome. Let's build a bonfire on the beach.

She sent a smiley face and hoped she'd be able to gather the interest and the energy to go out with him tomorrow night.

She ended up canceling, but they got together the following week and the week after that. At least Ace made it clear that he wanted her. And he lived in the same area she did.

She needed to forget Mack once and for all. She was determined to patch up her stubborn heart and recover. Soldier on. After all, she was no stranger to pain and difficulty.

But then she realized that might not be so simple. Although she'd been too stressed and busy to notice, something important finally occurred to her—she'd missed her period at least twice.

* * * * *

Is it all over for Mack and Natasha? Is Natasha expecting a baby? If so, whose baby will it be?

Find out in When I Found You, *coming in June 2021!*

Copyright © 2020 Brenda Novak Inc.

Get 4 FREE REWARDS!

We'll send you 2 FREE Books plus 2 FREE Mystery Gifts.

FREE
Value Over
$20

Both the **Romance** and **Suspense** collections feature compelling novels written by many of today's bestselling authors.

YES! Please send me 2 FREE novels from the Essential Romance or Essential Suspense Collection and my 2 FREE gifts (gifts are worth about $10 retail). After receiving them, if I don't wish to receive any more books, I can return the shipping statement marked "cancel." If I don't cancel, I will receive 4 brand-new novels every month and be billed just $7.24 each in the U.S. or $7.49 each in Canada. That's a savings of up to 28% off the cover price. It's quite a bargain! Shipping and handling is just 50¢ per book in the U.S. and $1.25 per book in Canada.* I understand that accepting the 2 free books and gifts places me under no obligation to buy anything. I can always return a shipment and cancel at any time. The free books and gifts are mine to keep no matter what I decide.

Choose one: ☐ **Essential Romance**
(194/394 MDN GQ6M)

☐ **Essential Suspense**
(191/391 MDN GQ6M)

Name (please print)

Address   Apt. #

City   State/Province   Zip/Postal Code

Email: Please check this box ☐ if you would like to receive newsletters and promotional emails from Harlequin Enterprises ULC and its affiliates. You can unsubscribe anytime.

> Mail to the **Harlequin Reader Service:**
> **IN U.S.A.:** P.O. Box 1341, Buffalo, NY 14240-8531
> **IN CANADA:** P.O. Box 603, Fort Erie, Ontario L2A 5X3

Want to try 2 free books from another series? Call 1-800-873-8635 or visit www.ReaderService.com.

*Terms and prices subject to change without notice. Prices do not include sales taxes, which will be charged (if applicable) based on your state or country of residence. Canadian residents will be charged applicable taxes. Offer not valid in Quebec. This offer is limited to one order per household. Books received may not be as shown. Not valid for current subscribers to the Essential Romance or Essential Suspense Collection. All orders subject to approval. Credit or debit balances in a customer's account(s) may be offset by any other outstanding balance owed by or to the customer. Please allow 4 to 6 weeks for delivery. Offer available while quantities last.

Your Privacy—Your information is being collected by Harlequin Enterprises ULC, operating as Harlequin Reader Service. For a complete summary of the information we collect, how we use this information and to whom it is disclosed, please visit our privacy notice located at corporate.harlequin.com/privacy-notice. From time to time we may also exchange your personal information with reputable third parties. If you wish to opt out of this sharing of your personal information, please visit readerservice.com/consumerschoice or call 1-800-873-8635. **Notice to California Residents**—Under California law, you have specific rights to control and access your data. For more information on these rights and how to exercise them, visit corporate.harlequin.com/california-privacy.

STRS21MAXR